THE SILVER FOREST

BOOK ONE

OTHER BOOKS IN THE WANDERER SERIES

THE SILVER FOREST, BOOK TWO

THE QUASI-CRYSTAL
(2024)

THE GOLDEN TREE
(2025)

THE SILVER FOREST

BOOK ONE

J. D. RASCH

LAMINA PRESS
RYE BROOK, NEW YORK

THIS IS AN UNCORRECTED PROOF
AND IS NOT INTENDED FOR SALE.

PLEASE DO NOT QUOTE FOR PUBLICATION
WITHOUT CHECKING AGAINST THE FINISHED BOOK.

✦ AUTHOR'S NOTE ✦

I DIDN'T START OFF WANTING to write a novel. What I really wanted to write was an essay on ethics, so I got a piece of paper and stared at it. All that came to mind was "don't do stupid things," or "don't hurt others," or even "live and let live." I am the first to admit that those, while sound words to live by, don't make a very compelling essay. So, I decided to depart from my essay and to think about how and why we react to outside stimulus the way we do. I started thinking about dictators and despots. I can understand why they want to rule the world, but what was more difficult to understand is why we let them. If you are given an order, why obey? Sure, if you don't somebody might shoot you, fair enough. But that only begs the question, why do they do it? Or why do enough of "them" do it to change the world?

This is what I wanted to explore, but I decided that a scholarly treatise wasn't for me. Instead, I thought about creating a story, or a koan (sort of), to put my characters in situations that they have to react to. We are all controlled by the things around us: parents, teachers, politicians, religious figures. How can we strip away their influence to understand what we truly believe? That was the inspiration for *The Silver Forest*. It was basically a thought experiment where I would take my characters and put them in situations they had to respond to. All the characters in the book are good—in their own way—but have different methods to get to what they want.

It was important to me that, unlike in traditional epic fantasy, my wizards did not actually have powers that others didn't have or couldn't obtain. They were just more expert at manipulation so that everyone could obtain what they had. The key theme to the book is getting to know your own mind, getting rid of outside influences, and understanding what is true.

Granted, everyone has their own truths, but at least you should understand them and be true to them. I believe we fundamentally share the same ethics, like the ones I mentioned at the beginning, but somehow we get pulled away from them. We allow others to co-opt us and don't stay true to our ideals. *The Silver Forest* was my way of checking if I am true to the ideals I set. Hopefully you, as a reader, will take a similar journey.

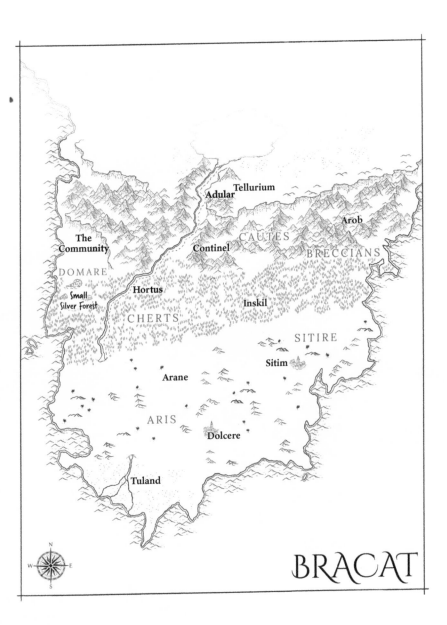

Tellurium
Adular
Arob
The
Community
CAUTES
Continel
BRECCIANS
DOMARE
Hortus
Small
Silver Forest
Inskil
CHERTS
SITIRE
Sitim
Arane
ARIS
Dolcere
Tuland

BRACAT

CHAPTER 1

SEVENTY YEARS. SEVENTY LONG YEARS wasted, searching for the golden pulcher tree, hoping to find it and tap its knowledge, to make things right. It was so long ago that he and the other eight wizards had left Insula to come to this backward land of Bracat. The Great Council in Insula, sensing the tree was here, had sent the holy number of nine wizards to this land, but when they arrived, they found nothing.

These thoughts echoed in Malzus's mind as he left the wedding hall. He had just been married. It was the only way to save the Nine now that Vetus was so sick. If Vetus died—Malzus shook his head—*when* Vetus died, there would only be eight wizards, and that was not enough to find the golden pulcher tree, the tree of knowledge, at least according to the Koan. The children of the other wizards, the children they had before they took their vows, were back in Insula. And the wizards were so old now that, even if they were given a waiver of their celibacy vow, as they had done for him, it was doubtful they could sire a child. So it was up to him, assuming he had a boy. If not... well, they'd have to deal with that later.

His wife waited for him; he was excited. He wondered what sex was like, but he was also scared. Celibacy focused his mind. If he gave that up, would he be strong enough to find the tree?

This shouldn't have been needed; he shouldn't have had to make the choice. It was his father's fault. The Great Wizard Preadus! His father had failed to bring peace and prosperity to Bracat, which is what the Koan said was needed before the golden pulcher tree would reveal itself. And even after this failure they still followed him, and he followed the teachings of the long-dead wizard Heil. But Heil's teachings were so passive, just like his father. They didn't allow the wizards to use their true powers, to control the minds of others, to bring prosperity to the land and have the tree reveal itself. As a result, the wizards had accomplished nothing in the seventy years since the Great Council of Insula sent them here. Not a sign of the golden pulcher tree. He felt there had to be another way to accomplish what the Koan demanded. Malzus had searched for years, studying the books they had brought with them from Insula and those in the dungeon library of Dolcere.

Then, two years ago, he found a book. It wasn't one of the local books; his father had brought it from Insula and hidden it among the dusty shelves of the cavernous Dolcere library. Malzus recognized the name, *The Book of Shammai*. Shammai was once as great a wizard as Heil, but his teachings were banned after the First Mind War that Shammai was said to have caused. As Malzus studied Shammai's teachings, he understood why the Nine had failed so far and what was needed. Unlike Heil, Shammai advocated using the full power of the wizards to take over minds of others and use their power to bend them to one's will. If he could take over the council and use the minds of the other wizards, he would have enough power to bring about the changes needed to have the tree reveal itself. He knew what he had to do, and the key was making sure his father didn't find out.

Go to your bride. His father's voice echoed in his mind. Malzus looked up at the Great Wizard standing in front of him, holding the staff of golden pulcher. That was the key; the golden staff would give him the power he needed to take over the Nine and draw on their power. Malzus shielded this thought from his father. *The council will meet later,* his father finished.

Malzus stood frozen, staring down the hall that led to his new bedchamber. He needed to concentrate on the council meeting; that's when he would act. Until then, he needed to pretend everything was normal. Malzus sighed. There was no more delaying, and he started toward his bride. His steps echoed in the emptiness.

Malzus paused at the entrance to the room that was to be his new home. Taking a deep breath, he pushed the door open.

"I was waiting for your arrival, my... my husband," said his bride, Asmeera. The words sounded awkward and hesitant as she spoke them for the first time. Malzus found the sound of her voice vaguely irritating. His new wife sat alone on the thin mattress of their wedding bed that occupied the far side of the room. The bed, Malzus noted, was larger than any he had ever slept in as a wizard. Asmeera had placed flowers beside it and had also chosen a collection of small orange and yellow lamp crystals to light the room with a warming, golden glow.

Asmeera rose. She wore a silvery gown that clung to her body, revealing the curves of her form in the soft light, the gown falling away carelessly to reveal her naked shoulders, her dark skin glowing in the golden light. He wanted to go to her, he wanted to hold her and possess her... but he stood on the other side of the room, holding himself back.

He walked forward hesitantly and sat down on the bed next to her.

"They don't understand." He wasn't sure why he said that, why he wanted to confess his plan, his years of frustration.

She placed her hand gently on his shoulder. "There is no need to explain. Here, with me, is where you can be at peace."

Her voice was soothing and her touch was electric. He realized in that instant how much he wanted to trust someone. To trust her.

He tried to resist, but desire overtook him. Grabbing her shoulders, he pushed her hard down onto the bed. She pushed back, instinctively.

"Not like that." Her words washed over him and he stopped, his hands shaking as he sat up, not sure of what to do. Asmeera smiled and took his hands, kissing them, then placing them gently on her breasts. Malzus felt her mind reach out to him, soothing and calming him.

How could that be? She wasn't a wizard. She wasn't trained. These thoughts drifted within him as Asmeera caressed him and gently lay him down on the bed.

Slowly she directed him, and Malzus felt her passion along with his own. He felt their connection, not just in body but in their minds. The golden pulcher ring he had given her at their wedding ceremony caught the light as she kissed him. That had to be what made her so strong and connected them; their wedding rings were linked, their minds were linked. He suddenly felt hope that he would not be alone anymore.

After they made love, Asmeera put her head on his shoulder and lay next to him, gently stroking his chest. In the quiet and stillness, his mind wandered. He was jolted out of his trance. What had he done? He had been distracted. He was being weak; he couldn't let himself be taken in by this woman.

"What's wrong?" Asmeera asked, putting a calming hand on his shoulder.

"Nothing," said Malzus hastily, getting up and brushing her hand away. Standing naked at the foot of the bed, he looked down at her. Part of him wanted to get back into bed with her—to make love to her again and forget all of the plans he had made. He shook his head, trying to clear everything from his thoughts, but couldn't. Was Asmeera somehow part of his father's plan to weaken him? Was she meant to make him more compliant and forget all of his hopes? Did his father know what he was about to do?

"Please, come back to bed, Malzus," Asmeera said, reaching a hand out toward him, the covers falling from her body.

Malzus stood, frozen. He thought he had felt a connection to her. He stared back at Asmeera. He should go back to bed with her; that's what he wanted. He came to her and wrapped his arms around her. He let himself bask in her warmth, her scent. But suddenly a piercing voice disrupted his thoughts: it was his father's summons, *Come to the council.*

How could they do this to him?! He wouldn't go. He wanted to stay with his bride. But he had to go. This was his opportunity to set things right, to take control of the council. Malzus grabbed the white crystal he had been given by his father as a wedding present and put its silver chain around his neck. Then he threw on the blue robe of the wizards and grabbed his silver pulcher staff. He rushed from the room, not looking back.

Malzus entered the council room, where he took his place among the Nine. *This is a joyous day for you,* Preadus proclaimed, reaching his mind out to Malzus and the others. Each wizard held their silver pulcher staffs as they turned to look at him. His father stood at the head of the council table, his silver hair tinged gold from the light of the golden pulcher staff he held. Malzus nodded, even though the day was anything but joyous to him. He kept this thought hidden from the others.

Let's begin by joining our minds in meditation, Preadus conveyed, beginning the meeting as all council meetings began. This was what Malzus was waiting for—the chance to enter the minds of the others unhindered, to be able to draw power from them and turn them. The Nine started to reach out to each other, sensing each other's frustrations and joys. Malzus felt all of them: Rogi's embarrassment at indulging in pastries on one of his fast days, Vetus's fear of his disease, and Dragorn's insecurity at being one of the weaker wizards. He even sensed Karal and Mentaire, who always held back, not wanting to share all of their thoughts with the others. Finally, the two strongest of the wizards, Thurmore and Wellum, opened their minds to the council, holding back even more than Karal and Mentaire. When his father joined, Malzus created the appearance of sharing his inner self, but he knew his father well enough to feel the secret barriers.

Now the others were waiting for him to join and open his mind.

That's when Malzus began his attack, reaching quickly for Vetus before the others realized what was happening. He twisted into Vetus's mind and dove deep into his thoughts, stealing the wizard's strength.

Malzus moved next to Dragorn, sending an icy touch into the wizard's mind that bored deeply into his thoughts and quickly drained him of strength. Vetus and Dragorn slumped over in their chairs.

With the power of the two wizards, Malzus moved swiftly on the others. Rogi fell quickly to his assault, but Karal and Mentaire held out against his onslaught. He had expected this, so rather than trying to overcome them, Malzus filled their minds with false visions of himself holding Preadus's golden staff, the symbol of leadership over the Nine.

My father has ceded control of the Nine to me, Malzus proclaimed, confusing Mentaire first, who then quickly fell under his control. This gave Malzus another surge of power, and he used it to quickly sweep away Karal's hesitation. Things were going exactly as he had planned. Only his father, Thurmore, and Wellum eluded him. He communicated to them all:

How we've searched for the golden tree will now change. The Koan decrees we must be worthy, but the tree is still hidden. We have been judged unworthy. I will find it. I will bring prosperity to this land. I will bring peace.

Malzus felt his father's horror. Power swept out from the Great Wizard, strengthened by the golden staff. Malzus resisted his father's onslaught, bringing his hand to the crystal at his neck. Locking eyes with his father, he grasped his silver staff tightly and drew more power from the wizards he controlled. His plan was working—power was surging into him. He focused this strength on Wellum and Thurmore.

We will follow the teachings of Shammai, Malzus continued, sending them visions of the land at peace and the golden tree glowing in the moonlight. *Open your minds to me so that we can be as one, and I promise the tree will be revealed!*

Rogi and Dragorn started to let down the final barriers that protected their innermost selves, the barriers that no wizard would let another cross, which were violated during the Mind Wars so many, many generations ago. As these barriers gave way, Malzus started to push their minds farther down, sapping more of their strength. Thurmore and Wellum still resisted, while Malzus blocked another powerful attack from his father. The room pulsed with energy.

Vetus's mind stirred and the old wizard found the strength to pull his mind away. *He should not be able to do this,* Malzus thought, and he shifted his attention back to Vetus and worked to calm him with another round of energy as their minds joined. Vetus's struggles faded as Malzus pulled him further and further down into the stronghold of his own mind.

Malzus had never felt such power. He went after Thurmore with renewed determination. Next to his father, Thurmore was the strongest wizard on the council. Malzus increased his effort and felt barrier after barrier give way.

Suddenly there was a flash of gold, followed instantly by a blinding, immobilizing light. A figure appeared in his mind, surrounded by a golden halo that blocked all his thoughts and sight. Emerging from the center of that halo was his father, his blue robes radiating a brilliant incandescence. He was holding the golden staff high over his head. Immediately behind him was Wellum, who joined his strength to the Great Wizard's. Malzus's hold on Dragorn and Rogi faltered, then crumbled away. Vetus pulled away as well.

"No! No! No!" Malzus screamed, feeling energy pour out of him, draining him of power. Then everything went completely dark.

When he regained consciousness, there was a profound silence. Malzus felt a gaping emptiness; everything was black. His sight was gone, the other wizards were gone, and he was utterly alone. His mind throbbed.

He lay groaning as the light trickled back and his vision slowly returned. His father towered over him, knuckles white as he grasped the golden staff, and he stared down at Malzus, his blue eyes like ice.

Malzus tried to reach out—to his father first, and then to the others—but his father had isolated his mind. He knew there was nothing he could do. His father had won, for now.

"You have found the book of Shammai!" His father's voice sounded so odd and cold, uttered out loud in the physical space of the chamber. "You tried to take away our minds so you could use our power to find the tree and leave us as mindless"—his father froze, the words stuck in his throat—"as Saeren."

"What have you done?" Dragorn groaned aloud, grasping his head, his face wretched with shock and anguish.

"How could you?!" bellowed Rogi, rising to join the others, who were surrounding Malzus.

Malzus stood up in defiance, but his father firmly reached into Malzus's mind and smashed Malzus into his seat. His father physically slapped him across the face with a force so hard it blurred his vision. Malzus's head didn't move. He stared at his father but was met by a crushing pressure coming from Thurmore. Malzus tried pushing back, but he was too drained and empty.

"YOU—you were willing to make us all your slaves!" Thurmore's words were slow and deliberate, his voice revealing the outrage and hate he felt for Malzus. "There is only one punishment fitting for you."

Malzus knew he meant death, but this wasn't going to happen. They couldn't kill him, not if they still wanted to find the tree. They needed him to complete the Nine. They had no one to replace him, unless they used a Bracion. No, Malzus reassured himself. Only those from Insula had the ability to become a wizard.

He needed to save himself, and he knew he had only one chance. If he could get the golden staff from his father, he would have the strength to escape. "Father." Malzus's voice was quiet.

"Please," he continued out loud, being blocked from the minds of the others, "I beg you to hear me. I am at your mercy." He paused, then went on, "You are right." Malzus walked cautiously toward his father.

"I didn't realize what I was doing." When Malzus was next to his father, he reached out and put his hand on the Great Wizard's shoulder. He felt his father relax. Now was the time.

With the hand that wore the golden ring, he grabbed the golden staff. The ring and staff melded together. Malzus saw the look of horror cross his father's face. The staff connected their minds. Now it was more even; now they both drew power from the staff. Malzus pressed down into his father's thoughts and tried to draw power from him, power he could use to subdue the others. But his father pushed back, joined by Thurmore and Wellum. Malzus needed more power. He attacked Vetus once again, but the old wizard was tired and weak from his illness. Malzus felt Vetus's strength waning. That couldn't happen; he needed to draw more power from the old wizard. Malzus pressed more. Vetus was slipping away; there was nothing Malzus could do. Malzus yelled and ripped away Vetus's memories, the thoughts of the other wizards that had come before him that were buried in a wizard's consciousness.

Malzus sank to one knee and held the staff tightly; his father looked over to Vetus and it distracted him, just for a moment. Malzus wrenched the golden staff from his father. Thurmore and Dragorn knelt by Vetus as Malzus pushed passed them. Rogi tried to block his way but Malzus raised the golden staff and struck him across the head. Rogi collapsed on the cold floor of the council room, alive but in no condition to pursue him.

Malzus ran out the door and onto the streets of Dolcere. The other wizards were slow but came after him. Malzus concentrated his mind. He felt the new strength the golden staff gave him. He reached out and clouded the thoughts of the others, creating a fog in their minds that protected him. He was free.

As he ran, he felt a mind reach out to him. It couldn't be a wizard—they were hidden in the fog he had created. He tried to concentrate. The mind called him again. It was Asmeera.

Where have you gone? Please come back to me.

Malzus clutched the golden staff tightly. He opened his mind to her.

You're hurt, she began, before adding quickly, *Malzus, what have you done?*

Malzus could feel her recoiling from him.

Come with me, Malzus pleaded, reaching out. *Together we can grow stronger, and together we can rule!*

No! came Asmeera's response. Her mind was floating away from him.

Malzus couldn't let her go. He tried forcing his way into her mind, but she pushed back, resisting his intrusion. He pushed in more forcefully. The more she resisted, the angrier he became. She had to come with him. He didn't want to be alone. He needed her; he must change her mind.

Malzus remembered the white wedding crystal around his neck and touched it, feeling the rush of power. He then gripped the golden staff tighter and an immense new rush of strength flowed into him.

He broke down the barrier she had created and was now inside Asmeera's mind. There was only silence; her resistance had stopped. At first Malzus thought he had finally reached her, that she had agreed to come with him. He spoke to her, but nothing was there. His hands started to sweat, and tears rolled down his face as he searched for her. He had gone too far. Her mind was now pushed so far back and down that she wasn't there.

He had destroyed her—the only one who had truly cared about him.

Malzus let out an anguished scream and then fled as fast as he could into the darkness.

CHAPTER 2

ASMAR OPENED THE DOOR TO the classroom, took a deep breath, and was greeted by the earthy aroma of wood. He didn't want to be there, but the scent of sawdust in the air calmed him.

All eyes followed Asmar as he made his way to his bench near the front. Dohler tapped his foot impatiently from behind his massive workbench. Asmar held his pack tightly to his chest as he weaved his way through the narrow aisle. One of his classmates stuck out a foot, tripping him. Several students snickered. Dohler cleared his throat but didn't utter a word, as Asmar shuffled to his bench. Taking a deep breath, he took out his tools and laid out the woodworking knives in front of him, in order of size and then shape.

"Today," Dohler began, "the upper classes will all work on the bronze pulcher. The younger ones will still work on the ordinary wood. Who can tell me the properties of the bronze pulcher?" A hand went up and Dohler nodded.

"The wood flows together, depending on how it's cut," one of the girls replied. "But it's difficult to know which way it will flow."

"And why is that?" Dohler asked.

"Because it's alive," Asmar blurted out.

Dohler sighed. This wasn't the first time Asmar had said this. "It does seem that way sometimes," Dohler replied under his breath. He gave Asmar an icy stare and then turned to the class. "The silver pulcher is even more difficult to shape."

"What about the gold pulcher?" asked the girl. "Have you ever seen it?"

"I'm afraid it's just a legend. Nobody has ever seen it," Dohler replied.

"My father did." Asmar knew this would upset Dohler, but Asmar knew it was true; his aunt had told him so. "And the golden pulcher is intelligent."

"Asmar!" Dohler cut him off. Then, in a calmer voice, he said to the class, "We're going to continue your work creating a bowl out of the bronze pulcher." Dohler's voice echoed in the classroom. "Remember, it's not about how perfect or skillful it is—at least not yet. What I want you to concentrate on is the nature of the wood. When you cut it, which way does it flow? How can you make the wood do what you want? I want to see your notes about how the pulcher flows when you cut into it." There was a rustle as the others reached into their packs and pulled out their bronze pulcher projects. Asmar stared at his hands.

Dohler glared down at Asmar. He reached into the pocket of his apron, pulling out a small bronze pulcher branch and placing it on Asmar's bench. It radiated a deep warmth into the air.

"I was told to train you to become a master carver and that's what I'm going to do, but for the life of me, I do not know why. They should've designated you a farmer." There was chuckling from the class as they pretended to concentrate on their projects. "At this rate, I don't know how you're going to get to the silver pulcher."

Dohler walked away and Asmar looked around. From the small branches they had each been given, the best of them had managed to work the wood into bowl forms about as large as a fist. The sides were so thin you could see through them. He picked up his own branch and rested it in his palm. It felt warm. Alive. Asmar would have to torture the wood to make it flow upward into a bowl. He would have to cut the flesh of the wood, forcing it into a shape that was unnatural to it.

Asmar closed his eyes and let his mind wander. He heard birds calling to each other outside the window and he wanted to be with them. He thought of his cousin, Remer, deep in his study at the library. Remer and his Aunt Lupa were the only family he knew. He rubbed the bronze wood between his hands. It calmed him, helped him turn his thoughts away from harming the wood.

Asmar didn't know why he had been chosen to be a master carver. Maybe because his father had been a great craftsman before he died. His aunt told him his father had been a great man, and yet nobody else in Tuland seemed to have known him. Even the stories his aunt told about his father were vague.

Asmar picked up his smallest knife, the one that would hurt the wood the least. His hand shook as he moved the blade closer to the branch. Asmar closed his eyes and allowed the warmth of the wood to envelop him. The blade slipped from his hand as the warmth went through his body.

"Asmar!" Dohler's booming voice broke through his inner fog. "What in the name of the golden pulcher are you doing?"

Asmar opened his eyes and looked down at his hands. The small bronze branch had wound itself around his middle finger. He even saw a tiny leaf that he swore hadn't been there before.

Dohler came over to Asmar and grabbed his arm. "How did you do that?" Dohler stared at the perfectly formed bronze ring and stuttered, "You *can* carve the wood. You've been lying to me!"

Asmar shook his head. "I didn't do it."

"You must have—I mean you *did*. You had to!" Dohler bellowed. "How else . . ." He trailed off.

"It did it on its own because"—Asmar paused—"it was happy."

The class went silent and Dohler just stared at Asmar. Finally he burst out, "Wood can't be happy. What did you do?"

"Nothing," Asmar answered.

"Don't you dare lie to me." Dohler's face grew dark with anger. "Get out!" he bellowed. Asmar stared up at Dohler, then stood slowly, his legs wobbling. It was happening again—he was being thrown out of class. Asmar made his way back through the aisles of desks. He didn't even bother to pack his tools.

Once outside, he looked around and inhaled deeply. He felt free. There was a tingling from his hand and Asmar looked down at the small pulcher twig around his finger. He smiled as he stroked the ring.

"You're safe now," he told the wood. Asmar crossed the broad lawn that lay at the center of Tuland's craft school and settled down on the warm grass. He closed his eyes and let his mind wander as he calmed himself. He thought of the wood and how it had formed into a ring without him having to use a knife. He knew he could never carve the pulcher, never cut into the flesh of the soft wood. Asmar knew more clearly than ever that he would never be a craftsman. He was meant for something else; he just didn't know what.

Having some unexpected time to himself, he spent the rest of the afternoon thinking. With the ring on his hand, his mind seemed to wander more freely, making the flowers smell sweeter, the bird songs more beautiful. In fact, everything seemed more alive, luminous, vibrant.

The one thing the ring's warmth couldn't ease or help with would be the reaction of his aunt to one more of Asmar's failures. He knew the classroom was not a place he was meant to be or would ever return to. Finally, the end-of-day bell rang and all of the other students flowed out to head home. Asmar picked himself up and made his way back to the elaborate bronze pulcher gates by the entrance to the school to await his cousin Remer, who he was sure would be late, as usual.

The school gates had been crafted generations ago, and no one seemed to know who had done the handiwork. They were flanked by six bronze pulcher trees, three on each side. Asmar touched his finger and felt the warmth of his new ring. He was sure it had come from one of those trees. Asmar examined the gates as if looking at them for the first time. There were no sharp edges in the wood... no evidence at all that the bronze pulcher had been cut or turned against its will.

"Asmar!" Turning at the sound of his name, Asmar saw his younger cousin, his face the warm brown of aged wood, with tangled hair falling across his face. It looked as though he'd run the entire way from the library, where he spent his days studying with his master, Vellum. "I know I'm late," Remer said, "but I have a good reason: it's a book!"

Asmar smiled, in spite of himself.

"Okay, it's usually a book," Remer added, still out of breath but unable to hold in what he wanted to say another moment. "But this is a *special* book, at least more special than any of the other books I've ever seen in the library. Vellum himself didn't remember ever seeing it."

Remer took a breath and looked at Asmar. "Something is wrong."

Asmar shook his head, but Remer persisted. "You might as well just tell. You know you can't keep secrets from me."

THE SILVER FOREST – Book One

Asmar looked around and up at the sky, and then breathed a long sigh. "I was let out early, that's all."

"Let out?" asked Remer.

"Sort of. I was kicked out."

"Asmar . . . really? Again?"

"Dohler didn't understand—I mean, he didn't like what I was doing."

"What were you doing?"

"I . . . I'm not sure." Asmar thought about the branch that nestled on his finger. "I made friends with the wood."

"You were refusing to carve it again, weren't you?"

Asmar was about to object, but dropped his head. "The wood doesn't *like* to be carved," he said.

"How do you know that?"

Asmar shrugged. "It's a feeling, that's all."

"What feeling is that? Nobody else seems to have that feeling," said Remer. "I bet your father didn't have that feeling."

Asmar cringed when Remer mentioned his father, and he could instantly see the regret in his cousin's eyes for having brought his father up. Both their fathers were gone. Remer's was killed by the Sitire fourteen years before, shortly after Remer was born. Asmar's had been gone even longer. Remer at least still had his mother, Lupa. Asmar didn't have that. His own mother died when he was born.

"I'm sorry, Asmar," said Remer. "I didn't mean to say that. It's just that Lupa's going to be really upset that you were kicked out of class again."

"I know, but I couldn't help myself. The wood's alive." Asmar raised his hand, showing Remer the bronze ring. "I know that sounds strange…" His voice trailed off.

"Did you make that?" Remer looked at the bronze ring with admiration.

"Sort of."

"What do you mean 'sort of'? A ring like that—so smooth and symmetrical—is one of the hardest things to make out of the pulcher. It always flows somewhere, ruining the perfect circle. How did you do that?"

"I didn't. The wood did it itself—because it was happy."

Remer laughed. "You didn't say that to Dohler, I hope."

Asmar chuckled. "Yeah, I did."

"What did he say?"

"He *wasn't* very happy."

Remer shook his head. "Lupa's going to be pretty mad."

Asmar nodded and sighed in resignation.

"Do you think the school will tell her?" Remer asked.

Asmar shrugged. "I hope not. Anyway, there's nothing I can do. I'm not my father, and I'll never be able to work the pulcher the way they want me to. I wish I could find something I was good at, like you did."

"You could be a pulcher carver if you wanted to be," said Remer, staring at the ring.

"I guess that's just it: I don't want to be." This was the first time Asmar admitted this to himself, and the first time he said it out loud to anyone. It brought him a huge sense of relief and peace. "I just wish Lupa wouldn't take it so hard."

"Well she does, and she will. I don't think we should tell her," said Remer. "And you need to get your mind off it too. Hey—we could go listen to Mendicus. He's back in town, telling his stories by the fountain."

"He's been away for a while now," said Asmar, curious. The two walked briskly and made their way through the winding streets of Tuland. The smooth facades of the baked mud buildings melded seamlessly together and seemed to ripple ahead of them. In the town square, they came upon a large crowd of students, many from the craft school, their attention drawn toward the center.

"Come on, come on!" Remer, who was nearly a full head shorter than Asmar, whispered urgently. "We'll never be able to hear from back here." Remer began to push his way to the front, with Asmar reluctantly following. Classmates could be heard muttering "Book Nose" at Remer and "Wooden Thumbs" at him, but he pretended not to hear. One student gave him a slight shove—but Asmar had long ago learned to ignore them.

Asmar and Remer were able to get through the crowd to a spot with a clear view. Mendicus was sitting in the center, speaking. The man was wearing a slightly frayed tunic that at one point had been white. His gray beard went down to his chest and his long, thinning hair was tied in a ponytail that reached to the middle of his back. Years in the streets and in the desert outside Tuland had taken their toll. His appearance was in sharp contrast to the large fountain where he sat, which was inlaid with alternating triangles of silver and bronze pulcher, sparkling in the golden glow of the afternoon sun. The fountain was dwarfed by a life-sized statue carved in bronze pulcher of Preadus, the Great Wizard, holding his staff high. The fountain was said to be a promise—by the wizards and Preadus himself—to protect the city and all its inhabitants.

Asmar stared at the statue of the Great Wizard. It seemed out of place next to the simplicity of the fountain, as if it was an afterthought.

In the center of the plaza, Mendicus paused his speaking to look at Asmar. Their eyes connected briefly, and then Mendicus turned away to continue.

The man was regaling the gathered students with the story of the Sitire Wars. He was nearly finished, but Asmar had heard it so many times he could almost recite the words by heart.

"The forces of the desert Aris were ready to defend their lands against the onslaught of the Sitire." Mendicus was saying. "The day was late, and evening was almost upon the world, bringing with it a darkness equaled only by the darkness of death.

"As the sun gently floated behind the world, leaving a bloody sunset as its trail, the battle began. The screaming Sitire came swiftly. They were led by a creature that looked like death, astride a horse as black as the midnight robes he wore. It carried no weapon; it was its presence that froze the Aris. The Sitire charged, slashing right and left with their swords made from the darkest metals and hardened to a razor's sharpness, barely visible in the falling night. The Aris stood, most of them unable to move, held in place by the will of the creature. Many, many were slaughtered, until a few managed to draw their crystal swords to charge the Sitire.

"The battle, if it could be called such at this point, would have ended in a complete massacre if it were not for Preadus, who stood with his silver staff, light flooding his face. The sight of him broke the paralysis of the Aris. The battle raged on through the night and into the morning. By midday, a calm had finally settled on the desert.

"The Aris had persevered and the Sitire withdrew... but they were not beaten and could rise again."

A hush fell upon the gathered crowd. This battle had occurred before Remer was born and Asmar was just a young boy. But on hearing its retelling, it seemed like only yesterday. There was always the fear, too, that "the Sitire would rise again."

"I always liked that story," Remer said. "Especially the part about Preadus appearing with a silver staff. I wonder what he could have done if he'd used the golden staff? Why do you think he didn't?"

"I don't know," Asmar responded—and then instinctively added, "Perhaps it's dangerous to use more power than you need."

"That might be," Remer said, pondering that thought. "Well, let's get home, quickly. I'm starving. Remind me later to tell you about the book I found in the library."

Asmar froze, realizing the unavoidable confrontation ahead.

Remer paused and looked at his cousin. "You're not going to tell her you got kicked out of school, are you?"

"I can't lie to her."

"Sure you can," said Remer. "It would be for her own good. Why do you need to be so honest?"

"Because it's the right thing to do."

"No it's not. In this case it's the absolute wrong thing to do. It'll upset her and for no reason. Please Asmar, for once, don't tell her."

Asmar didn't reply.

Remer sighed. "Alright, let's go. You know how Lupa hates it when we're late for dinner, especially if Mendicus has anything to do with it. And she'll be upset enough when you tell her about school."

"I'd rather be able to look around while I walk than rush around the streets just to get home a little sooner."

"You're just stalling because you don't want to see Lupa and have to tell her what happened. And we walk this street every single day. What is there to notice?"

Asmar shook his head. "For all you memorize, you really notice very little. Tell me, how would you describe this block?"

"It's like almost every other block in Tuland," said Remer, looking up and down the street and then closing his eyes. "Each house is made of wood, all one or two stories tall with tidy walkways of clay brick lining each street. On this block there are six houses on each side of the road, and each are separated by a yard, about half the width of the house, where there are herb and vegetable gardens."

"Very accurate," Asmar answered. "But you only described the aspects that are the same. Each street is actually very different. Tell me about the people who live in that house," said Asmar, pointing.

Remer, opening his eyes again, shrugged. "It looks just like everyone else's house."

"The people there have two small twin girls."

"How do you know that?" Remer asked.

"Their laundry is hung out to dry." Asmar pointed to their yard.

"But how do you know they're twins?"

Asmar shook his head. "There's two of each outfit hung on the line. People don't make two outfits exactly the same for the same child, which means there are children the same age living there."

"There's no way to know there are twins there."

As if on cue, the front door of the house opened and two little girls the same age, wearing identical outfits, burst into the yard and began chasing each other into the street, running straight into the cousins.

"Sorry!" the twins chirped in unison before they turned and ran off.

"Not bad," said Remer, glancing, impressed, at his cousin.

Asmar stopped walking. "You see facts, but not how those facts make you feel. What gives this street its character. What makes it different. There's a softness to the houses that comes from weathered wood aged by salty ocean breezes and storms as well as scorching sunshine."

He continued. "The people across the street have suffered a loss. The grandmother has passed away. They're remembering her and are sad, but happy, too. The people in the next house, they love flowers. They spend a lot of time cultivating their beds in the front yard. One likes purple and white flowers, so they planted those on the fringe, and the other—the wife—loves yellow and planted the tiny yellow ones in the center."

"You can't know that from just looking at their garden," Remer protested.

Asmar just shrugged. "But I do."

CHAPTER 3

AS THEY CONTINUED TO WALK, Remer tried to do what Asmar suggested: to see what was different on each street and to feel what was special. They rounded the corner and Remer saw a broken brick in one wall, a clay walk of a deeper red hue than the rest... a white fence with one plank missing on the side... the different sound the wind made as it gently brushed past the buildings and trees. The fourth house on the left, the one he and Asmar were now standing in front of, was the most unique of them all. This was home.

Lupa was waiting for them on the porch. Remer tried to look at his mother as if for the first time, just as Asmar had suggested. What made her unique, other than the obvious? She was forty, but seemed older, her back slightly hunched and her graying hair showing traces of the black it once was. Her arms were crossed in annoyance, but despite that, he could see the kindness in her eyes.

"Come on, hurry in before your dinner is completely cold," she called to them. Remer smiled, and the stern matriarch's grimace melted as she smiled back. "Next time, I'll let you cook for yourselves when you two finally decide to wander in—or better yet, you can both go without dinner for once."

Remer said simply, "We're sorry. We stopped to listen to the storyteller."

"He's back?" she said, looking down the street. Then she let out a sigh. "Never mind. Come in now and eat."

At this, Remer dashed up the walkway and kissed her on the cheek. He exclaimed to his mother how delicious everything smelled and he waited inside the front door. Lupa motioned to Asmar and said, in a soft voice, "Well, come on in, my child, and we'll eat."

"Thank you, Aunt," replied Asmar, ascending the stairs to the porch.

The aroma of the warm dark bread and rich vegetable soup made Remer suddenly realize he was ravenous. At the dining table, he and Asmar waited anxiously for their meal as Lupa set bowls and plates before them, while telling them about their neighbors. She enjoyed helping the family who had two small children, a boy of three and a newborn girl. Now that he and Asmar were older, Remer understood that this was giving his mother a sense of purpose, to feel needed each day.

When she was done, Remer talked about what he always talked about—the latest research Vellum had him doing.

"Vellum had me repair some of the oldest books in the library. The covers were cracked and they felt funny."

"What do you mean?" Asmar asked.

"I don't know," Remer replied. "They didn't feel like anything I ever touched before."

"If they were very old they could have been animal hides," Lupa said.

Remer shuddered. "That fits. Master Vellum thinks that these ancient texts were written in the days before Tuland became a city. Back then, Tulanders were nomadic, like the Aris. Everyone acts like Tuland has been around forever, but it hasn't. It was because of the bronze tree forests that used to be here that we settled in this particular region. And it wasn't until we almost completely destroyed the forests that we started to become better stewards of the land and took up craftwork and farming." Remer closed his eyes and tried to immerse himself in the thought of a bronze pulcher forest. He could see the trees gently swaying in the soft breeze of the ocean. The trees reached up high overhead and let in dappled sunlight. Everything smelled fresh and new; at least that's what he thought it would be like. What they actually had were a few scraggly bronze trees left by the craft-school gates, and another small grove in an oasis in the desert not far from Tuland. That's where all the new pulcher wood comes from. But most of what was used these days was recycled.

Lupa nodded automatically and started clearing the table.

Asmar was being quieter than usual, and Remer could see that Lupa sensed something was wrong. Finally, she turned to Asmar and shot him an inquiring look. Remer glared at his cousin and shook his head.

"I was asked to leave class," Asmar blurted out and then paused. "I just can't get used to working the pulcher."

To Remer's surprise, his mother's face was soft and calm. She didn't seem upset. "Asmar, dear," Lupa comforted, "the pulcher is difficult to work."

Remer was shocked at her composed response. "That's it?" he said. "You're not upset that Asmar got kicked out of school again?"

Asmar gave his cousin a betrayed glance.

"Sorry, I didn't mean to say that. But Asmar's been dragging his feet coming home, afraid you'd get mad, and even made us late for dinner—and you're not angry. I don't get it."

"I feel like I shouldn't be working the pulcher," Asmar explained, feeling the need to defend himself. "I'm out of place in that class. I don't fit in. It feels just... wrong. I should be doing something else. I just don't know what."

Lupa's next response was not what Remer expected. Looking out the window, her rough hands gently wrapped around a steaming cup of tea, she softly said, "Maybe you should find something else."

Remer sat at the table as if he was glued to his chair. What just happened? Lupa didn't seem to care if Asmar was kicked out of school or if he ever became a master craftsman. He wondered why she wasn't yelling at Asmar or crying over his failure. Did she not care about his future? If he had told his mother Vellum kicked him out of the library, she'd be upset. Wouldn't she? But this very thought was preposterous. He loved the library and all the books that seemed to hold worlds within worlds for him to discover. If anyone ever tried to kick him out, they'd have quite a fight on their hands.

The sound of dishes being collected from the table, chairs scraping the floor as Asmar and Lupa stood, returned Remer's attention to the scene that had been playing out at the dining table.

After they'd helped Lupa wash up and put all of the dishes away, Remer followed Asmar from the room. "I wanted to tell you about another book I found in the library," he told his cousin, as they sat together in the living area. "It's called *The Wanderer* and it tells about this person who lived back in the days when Tulanders still traveled through the countryside... before the wizards arrived. The Wanderer traveled from Tuland all the way north."

At this moment, Lupa walked in to join them in the living room, and Remer went silent. He knew she didn't approve of these tales of travel and adventure, whether told in a book or by Mendicus in the town square. The three sat in a companionable silence. Remer thought about the book, while occasionally stealing a glance at his mother. There was a new sadness to her that he felt but didn't understand. He was about to ask her what was wrong, when there was a knock on the door.

Remer jumped up and ran from the room to see who it was. After a momentary pause, Lupa called out, "Who is it, Remer?"

The stench of the street reached Remer's nostrils through the closed door, and he knew who it was even before opening it: it was Mendicus. Remer felt a chilling breeze as he opened the door to see the reeking old storyteller, his face darkened by dirt and years in the sun. Without any greeting, Mendicus pushed past Remer and moved through the now-open door without waiting for an invitation. Remer's heart raced as he followed Mendicus into the kitchen. Remer saw Asmar's shocked reaction as the man entered their house, but the look on Lupa's face seemed to be of sheer horror.

Mendicus stood staring at Asmar, and then at Lupa. The uncomfortable silence was broken by the sound of an old and deep voice saying, "Lupa, we must speak. Alone."

This demand from the storyteller struck Remer as incredible, but even more incredible was Lupa's response.

"Asmar, Remer," she said stoically, gesturing toward their bedroom, "please leave us to talk."

Once in their room, the cousins strained to overhear the discussion downstairs, but their efforts were fruitless. Lupa had insisted they shut their door, and then she had closed the door to the kitchen for good measure. The two sat on their beds in silence, craning to hear any random words that might float up from the kitchen, but it was to no avail.

"What do you think they're talking about?" Remer wondered aloud.

Asmar shrugged. "I know as much as you."

"Maybe it has to do with us being late all the time on account of Mendicus's stories," Remer speculated.

"Maybe," Asmar said, "but did you see how Lupa looked at Mendicus? It was almost as if she knew what he was here about."

"Maybe Mendicus has been sent by the great wizards of Dolcere to bring one of us to the city? That would explain why he was gone for so long."

"Why would they possibly want one of us?" Asmar asked.

"They do it all the time," Remer responded. "I have read about it in the books in the library. And wasn't there a boy in your class last year who was especially skilled with fashioning the silver pulcher and was called to Dolcere by the wizards?"

Asmar nodded. "Yes, but did Mendicus take him?"

"He could have." Remer shrugged.

Asmar paused. "If he has come for such a reason, I think he must have come for you. I've got no special talent, while you can memorize entire books."

"It could be you, too," responded Remer. "You are the one whose father was a master craftsman."

Asmar answered curtly, "But I am not."

"Maybe the wizards think you have potential and it isn't being properly cultivated in Tuland."

"I doubt that," Asmar said. But the expression on his face told Remer that, deep down, his cousin hoped it might be true. That he might have some skill, some talent. A greater calling.

If Mendicus had come for Asmar, that would mean he would lose him, maybe forever. Remer couldn't imagine what life would be like without his best friend. The idea of one of them leaving—of them being separated—was too much.

"Let's make a pact," Remer said, nervously. "If either one of us goes to Dolcere, the other will follow, even if he must wander through the desert for days on end without food or water."

Asmar laughed, but Remer insisted. "Promise."

Asmar replied, "I promise."

The conversation in the room ebbed and they grew quiet again, this time sitting in individual contemplation. Remer fantasized about what it would be like to be called to that magical city of wizards, Dolcere.

In the middle of his fantasy, he heard the solid wooden door to the cottage downstairs slam shut, followed by heavy footsteps coming up the stairway and toward their room. Soon Lupa was standing in the now-open doorway. She looked tired and drained, her eyes dark as if she had been fighting back tears. Remer ran to her, and said, "Mother, tell me what Mendicus said that has upset you and I'll take care of it right away."

Mother and son embraced. "No, my son," Lupa answered, choking back tears unsuccessfully, "there's nothing to be done. I knew this day couldn't be avoided. Both of you sit," she said, summoning composure. "I'll tell you what I can."

Remer's concern and curiosity were piqued in equal measure. Asmar and Remer quickly took seats together, facing her, and held their breaths.

"I guess its best just to say this outright." Lupa's voice quivered. "Asmar, you must go to Dolcere."

The silence was finally broken by a soft voice that Remer realized belonged to his cousin, uttering one small word: "Why?"

"Mendicus will tell you tomorrow at daybreak when he comes for you."

"Did you—did you know this was going to happen?" Asmar's voice seemed weak and lost.

Lupa nodded slowly. "Yes, I have always known this day would come. Why do you think I avoided Pr—Mendicus?"

"And what 'day' is that? What's happening?" Remer asked, wondering why his mother stumbled over Mendicus's name.

"I can't tell you any more than I have." She turned to Asmar. "Just remember how you were brought up, how I tried to keep the memory of your mother alive in you." Tears streamed down her face.

"But—" Asmar protested.

Lupa held up her hand, stopping him from finishing his question. "I can't say more. Believe me Asmar, I didn't want this to happen, but there's nothing I can do."

Remer looked over at his cousin. Asmar seemed like he wanted to ask more questions but knew he wouldn't get any answers.

"Please Asmar, Remer—go to sleep. Or at least try to rest. Asmar, everything will be ready for you in the morning. And there is nothing more I can do." Lupa walked quickly from the room, tears now rolling down her cheeks. "There is just nothing I can do."

For a time, both boys lay quietly in the ever-darkening light of their room, until Remer heard his cousin whisper, "Are you asleep?"

"No," responded Remer, in a hushed voice.

"What do they want from me? What will it be like in Dolcere?"

Remer felt adrift, wondering if any of the books he had read at the library could prepare Asmar for what was ahead. "I can't believe Lupa is letting you cross the desert with that old man." Remer paused before adding in a soft voice, "And without me."

"Tell me what you know of the desert."

"There are a few books that talk about it, and of course there are stories that some of the older people tell. But not a lot of details. You know my father used to travel in the desert?" Remer idolized his father, even though they had never met. Any story told about his father by any of the townspeople, Remer had committed to memory.

"Yes, I know."

"It's a dangerous place. You need to be careful of desert wolves that come out at night to hunt. And then there are the soft sands that can swallow you up." Remer paused. "They also say there's an animal that lives beneath the sand that can suck you down. That's all in addition to the intense daily heat and the bitter cold of the nights. Oh yeah—there are also ferocious winds and sandstorms every night at twilight."

Asmar was shocked. "It can't be that bad. People live in the desert. There are the Aris and the Sitire."

"Most live in protected oases, but you're right, they both travel throughout the desert. They have special clothes that protect them, like my father had."

"I've seen the clothes of his you keep."

"They're very good quality, almost as good as those of the Aris."

"Remer," Asmar said, continuing to voice the questions he was not yet able to ask of Mendicus. "Why me? What am I supposed to do?"

"Something important, I'm sure—no, don't argue with me," Remer interrupted his cousin's objection before it could be voiced. "There was always something different about you, you know that. That's why you never fit in. You seem to know things that you shouldn't. Like today when we passed by the house with the purple, white, and yellow flowers. You knew the wife liked the yellow ones. There was no way to know that, but you did. And you do that all the time; it's as if you can sense what other people are thinking."

"But what use is that to the wizards?"

Remer didn't have a ready answer. "I know the wizards are wise and they seem to have special powers, but if they could read other people's minds, or even control their minds, imagine what they could do. Wouldn't it be great to have that power?"

Asmar pondered this for a time. "No," he replied firmly. "You could cause a lot of damage doing that."

"Not if you used that power wisely—to help people."

"Perhaps," Asmar replied. He paused, and then his whisper took on an imploring tone. "Remer, can I make it?"

"Oh sure," Remer said confidently. "Dolcere is about twenty-one days' journey on foot into the Great Desert. My father used to travel into the desert pretty often." Remer fell quiet, remembering the story his mother had told him about his father's very last trip. Remer's father was going up north with a group of Tulanders in search of the silver pulcher trees. On their way back, they had been attacked by the Sitire. His father was wounded while fending off the attackers, giving his travel party the opportunity to escape. He made it back to Tuland but died of his injuries soon after. The father he had never known.

"Lupa wouldn't let you go with Mendicus if she didn't understand what he was doing."

"I'm sure you're right. I'll go if Lupa insists."

Remer uttered in a low, barely audible voice that drifted from his lips, "Remember our oath."

When Asmar fell asleep Remer began studying everything he could on survival in the brutal heat, intense cold, and harsh winds of the desert. He knew he could survive. His father had been able to, and so had that mysterious Wanderer. Page after page of books Remer had read long ago flashed through his mind. In a brief moment, he could read each page and absorb all the information, no matter how detailed. This was a simple matter for him because of the way his mind worked. He not only remembered everything he had read, but he also could recall items by topics or phrases. Sometimes even stray words were enough.

Remer didn't understand how this process in his mind worked—only how to use it. In this way, Remer began to prepare himself for his desert trip. Ancient books, forgotten and discarded by most Tulanders long ago, were permanently catalogued in Remer's mind. All night he reread passages about the Aris and how they survived in the desert: what clothes they wore, how to find food and water, and ways to avoid getting lost. He read about how the desert wolves attacked in packs around sunset, just after the winds abated.

Of all the books Remer read in his mind that night, he kept coming back to *The Wanderer*. Even though he had just happened upon it in the library recently, it seemed to have been written long ago.

In the text, the writer—the Wanderer—had become disillusioned with life and society and had decided to travel alone through the desert to the oasis of Dolcere, leaving everything behind. Remer was attracted to the story. He felt he understood the Wanderer, and that they shared the urge to travel, to shed the routine of everyday life. But for now, he needed to concentrate on surviving whatever lay in the path ahead. This first foray for him, out into the unknown, would be difficult and dangerous, unlike anything he had ever done. But he could do it; he knew he could. Just like his father had.

As dawn approached, he checked to make sure Asmar was still sleeping, and then silently readied his father's gear to take with him. It was well used but of high quality, and it was everything he would need. But for Remer it was much more. He always fancied himself a traveling spirit like his father, and now he was about to have his first real adventure, rather than just reading about them in books. He felt all his time in the library was leading him to this point, this adventure. He needed to be ready, so even though he had done this dozens of times before, he took an inventory of what was in his father's pack.

First, there was a green talize, a cloak woven from a plant that grew only in the oasis of the desert. It was soft to the touch and very light. The talize maintained the body's temperature and retained its moisture, so in the middle of the day in the Great Desert it would keep you cool, and in the cold nights it would keep you warm. He had wondered why a garment designed by desert tribes would be green. His mother explained that each tribe's talize was dyed a different color. Green belonged to none of the tribes, so unaffiliated travelers would use that color.

Remer continued to remove items from the pack, although he knew its contents by heart. There was the triple-wound rope, the finely woven tarp, and stakes for securing the tarp to make a shelter. In the dim pre-dawn light, he carefully checked that everything was accounted for: a small but well-honed knife Remer had made sure to keep in good repair, various cooking and eating utensils, and his father's travel sandals. His father's feet were larger than his, but it didn't matter. The sandals were of bronze pulcher and would conform to fit his feet. He put everything back in the pack, except for the talize and sandals. Slipping these on, he stood before the mirror in the room. It was dark and hard to see, but Remer knew the person in that mirror could survive in the desert.

He would go to Dolcere, not just because of the oath he had made, but because he knew Asmar would need him.

As the night was finally coming to a close and dawn about to break, Remer returned his pack to the corner where it always rested and he slipped back into bed, concealing his desert clothes beneath the covers. With the very first trickle of light, Lupa was there in the bedroom doorway to wake Asmar, who had already begun to stir.

"It's time," Lupa said. "Come eat your breakfast. Mendicus will be here soon."

Asmar raised himself to his feet. Even with his eyes shut tight, feigning sleep, Remer could feel the warm stare of his cousin, looking down upon him. He wanted to jump out of bed to embrace him and reassure him, tell his cousin everything would work out fine… but he needed Asmar to think he was asleep to gain the extra time needed for his plan to work. Remer was relieved when he heard the bedroom door shut, and he opened his eyes to find that Asmar really had gone.

Remer hurried to get ready, checking everything one last time. His pack was complete, except for food and water. He would see what he could steal from the kitchen once Asmar left. Quietly, he made his way downstairs, where Lupa had prepared a breakfast fit for a wizard— nine wizards, for that matter. Remer guessed Lupa had had a sleepless night too, as it was clear she had spent quite some time cooking. Remer hoped he would be able to steal some of that food later.

Carefully, he took up a vantage point where he could see his cousin but remain unseen. Asmar was just pushing food around on his plate, occasionally forcing a bite into his mouth. He looked worried but resigned.

Finally Asmar pushed his plate aside, looked at Lupa, and spoke. "I'm only going with Mendicus because you asked me to."

Lupa looked down and away from her nephew. "Yes, I know. I've known this was coming for many years and there was nothing I could do. I'm sorry. You must go with him." Lupa's voice seemed sad and far away. "But before Mendicus arrives," Lupa said, "I want to give you something. You must promise to keep it safe."

"I promise," Asmar said. Remer saw her reaching into her apron pocket and removing a small, simple box. "What is in here belonged to your mother. Your father fashioned it for their wedding day. When she lay dying after having given birth to you, she gave this to me to hold for you. No one knew what happened to it since her death. It's the only gift, other than your first breath, that your mother was able to give to you." Remer watched as Lupa held the tiny box in her hands and slowly, lovingly pushed it across the table toward Asmar.

Tears formed in Asmar's eyes. "My mother gave me this, and my only gift to her was to cause her death."

Lupa was standing behind him now, her hands resting reassuringly on his shoulders. "No, you mustn't think that. Your mother loved you. You were her reason for holding on as long as she did. She wanted to give you life. She believed in you from before you were born. You were the one who brought her out of her . . ." Lupa paused, and then dropped the subject and went on. "Your mother insisted you have this when this day came, as her link to you, and your link to her."

As Asmar gingerly lifted the cover, Remer could see a warm, sun-colored glow emanate from the box, which he instantly recognized from books he had read. Such a glow only came from one thing: the golden pulcher tree. Asmar's mouth was open in wonder as he pulled the glowing ring from the box. Remer inched a little closer and felt the warmth that emanated from the ring, filling the room, even as far away as the spot where he was hiding. Time seemed to stand still. His cousin slipped the ring on his finger, tears still in his eyes, and held it up. "How will I be able to hide it?" Asmar asked. Then they all watched as the bronze ring that Asmar had made in class morphed and slipped with fluid movements over the gold, fully covering it and causing it to disappear along with its special glow; hiding the golden pulcher ring and rendering it invisible to prying eyes.

"How…?" Asmar stared at the bronze ring. "I knew it was alive!"

Lupa looked away from the rings and towards the door Mendicus would pass through, "Please try to swallow a few more bites before Mendicus arrives."

Asmar attempted to force down a few more mouthfuls when, quite suddenly, the front door swung open and Mendicus appeared in the kitchen.

"Good," said Mendicus, "you're finished with your meal. I have supplies for the journey." Mendicus's voice was cold, and his meaning was clear; there would be no time for emotional sentiment.

But they weren't leaving just yet. Mendicus put a number of clumsily wrapped packages on the table. The loose coverings were weathered and stained.

Remer watched as Asmar reached for the largest, most bulky package and opened it with swift, efficient motions. Straining to catch a glimpse of what was inside, Remer could see that it was a pack like the one his father had used, only smaller. Asmar unwrapped the next, smaller bundle and unfurled a talize, holding it up and taking it in with a serious, wide-eyed gaze. This particular talize looked of unusual quality, so finely woven it seemed as if it were made of a single piece of cloth. Remer thought it was probably that of the first growth of the plant, when the fibers would be the softest. His talize, his father's green one, was of the second growth. Still of high quality, but not nearly as fine as the one Asmar was now holding.

The cloak was golden; it seemed to be the exact color of the desert sand. Asmar held the fine cloth in his hands for another moment before moving on to the last package.

Upon peeling back the layers of wrapping, Asmar now held up a fine-looking new pair of desert sandals. Remer saw his cousin pick them up and inspect them, turning them over carefully and feeling their material. "What are these made of?"

"Brare hide," Mendicus replied. Asmar dropped the sandals suddenly as if they burned his hands, and he stepped back. He looked up at Mendicus and said, "I don't understand."

You must wear them. Mendicus's words were now right inside Remer's head but Remer didn't remember the

Mendicus's lips moving. Remer knew the command was meant for Asmar.

Remer watched and silently found himself shaking his head, wishing he could intervene; he knew his cousin didn't want the sandals. Mendicus was forcing him to take them, somehow. He watched as Asmar bent down to put them on.

Remer's whole body tensed. He remembered the feel of the old books in the library, the feel of the dried, treated skin that had been ripped from the body of an animal. He tried to reach out to Asmar. *No!* he thought. Remer watched as Asmar suddenly jerked back up to stand defiantly, dropping the sandals again. Asmar turned to Mendicus. "I won't wear them." His voice was firm, although Remer could hear a slight quivering.

Mendicus looked back at Asmar. "As you wish," he said in a cool, calm voice. Remer detected a slight smile on the man's face as he fumbled through his large pack and produced a second pair of sandals, handing them to Asmar. These looked like the pair Remer had in his own pack; the tops were of bronze pulcher, so thin as to be soft and flexible to the touch. The bottoms were of an ordinary wood, less giving than the bronze pulcher when walking on a variety of terrain.

"These will have to do, then," Mendicus said. "Now put on the talize and we must be off." With those words, Mendicus left them to wait outside.

Asmar turned to Lupa, who was holding the sand-colored cloak. He slipped it over his head and put on his bronze sandals.

"Is there anything else I'll need?" he asked Lupa, trying to keep his voice steady. "This all feels so unreal."

"Only—to remember how you were raised. Remember all you have felt, and trust the knowledge that is within you. Mendicus has everything you will need for the journey." Lupa hugged Asmar deeply and said, "Go now, with all my love." With tears in her eyes, she turned away, so Asmar knew it was really time to leave, time to join Mendicus and begin the journey to Dolcere.

"Tell Remer... I will miss him. I know we'll see each other again." Asmar's voice cracked as he glanced up just once toward the stairs. And then he was gone.

In his hiding place just around the corner from the top of the stairs, Remer wanted to go, but he also wanted to stay, and he suddenly felt doubts about his plan. The thought of abandoning his mother, when she had already lost both her sister and husband, and now her sister's son whom she cared so much about, broke his heart, and inwardly, he started to panic. He didn't want to let down his cousin either. He was frozen, going back and forth between the two heartbreaking choices. But each second was time lost, and he knew if he didn't head off soon, he would lose his chance and deeply regret it.

"You can come out now," a voice from downstairs said, softly.

It took Remer a few seconds to realize it was his mother speaking to him.

"I know you've been hiding up there. Come down and have some breakfast. Before you leave."

He was trying to understand what Lupa had just said as he entered the kitchen.

His mother slowly walked over to him and embraced him. "You are just like your father. He couldn't turn away from adventure."

"I—I have to go," said Remer, looking up at her. He couldn't tell if his heart were breaking or coming to life for the first time. Or both.

Lupa nodded. "Asmar is going to need you more than he realizes."

"I'll take care of him."

"Remer, you're amazing and I love you more than you'll ever know. I knew I wouldn't be able to send Asmar off without you wanting to go with him." Remer hugged his mother and felt her wet cheeks against his. "Be careful." Lupa paused, "And come back to me."

The day was bright as Remer adjusted to the weight of the pack on his back and slowly, step by step, made his way out of Tuland. He found himself hearing Asmar's voice in his head as he looked one more time at each street and each building, remembering their walks to and from school and Asmar's instructions—to feel the uniqueness of each detail of this special place. As he reached the outer edge of the city, he read aloud to himself from a passage in *The Wanderer*.

"*I began my trip unsure of the way to go.*" Well, that was true enough, Remer thought. "*It was the youth of the day, a time when all possibilities abound. Unsure of which way to turn, I went ahead as the dim sun rose weakly to my left. I set my goals by tiny landmarks in the desert.*"

Remer felt certain: all he had to do was find the landmarks the Wanderer gave, and he would be in Dolcere, maybe even before Asmar. He could already see his cousin's face upon being reunited, and how proud he would feel to have stayed true to their oath.

CHAPTER 4

ASMAR FOLLOWED MENDICUS PAST THE familiar buildings of Tuland, past the house where the twin girls lived, past the house with the yellow and purple flowers . . . past everything that had ever been familiar to him. The streets were still and empty as the mismatched duo made their way past the last street of Tuland. He thought of Remer waking up to find him gone, of not being able to say goodbye to his cousin. Of all the things he was leaving behind, he would miss his cousin the most. At least he was free of Dohler's class and his insistence on torturing the pulcher.

Asmar followed Mendicus, struggling to keep up with his long strides. Asmar noticed some slight changes in Mendicus's appearance: he wore a golden talize, just like the one he had given Asmar. It was well worn, but clean and in good repair. Also, he seemed cleaner and smelled less, which Asmar noted with some relief.

Asmar adjusted his pack and worked to keep pace. The landscape became bleaker and more barren. The ground at first was quite rocky and then gave way to more and more sand, signifying the beginning of the desert, and it became more difficult to walk. The heels of his sandals churned as the sand gave way with each sliding step. But he also noticed the way the grains of sand sparkled in the sun as he walked. When he looked ahead at the vast expanse of desert, the dry sands stretched endlessly to the horizon. The sun beat down incessantly and even with his talize, Asmar found the heat oppressive.

The day wore on. By midday, Asmar felt hunger gnawing at him. But Mendicus didn't slow or offer any food or drink. The talize somehow managed to suppress the need for water, but it couldn't sate his hunger. And Asmar knew that he wouldn't be able to go on forever in a desert without water. He had so many questions, but Mendicus walked far enough ahead that Asmar couldn't ever catch up. They walked without a word passing between the two of them. It was late in the afternoon by the time they came to the Great Rock—the only thing Asmar recognized in the landscape, and the farthest he had previously trekked out into the desert. Up ahead, Mendicus finally began to slow, and Asmar found himself matching his pace.

His hunger, meanwhile, was growing more oppressive. But Asmar continually repressed the urge to ask for food. He was quite sure he was being tested. And greater than both his hunger or his thirst was Asmar's overwhelming curiosity. He wanted to ask... why was he chosen? Why was he on this journey, why did he have to leave his home? But those questions seemed stuck in his throat. With great effort, he forced himself to say something.

"Last year"—Asmar's throat cracked—"I came out here to spend the night."

"Why?" was Mendicus' curt reply.

"I don't know... a few of us just did. I guess it was to prove ourselves."

"To prove what, exactly?" Mendicus said, turning his icy gaze on Asmar. It made Asmar uncomfortable, but he looked straight into Mendicus's eyes.

"I'm not totally sure. I think it was to show we could survive on our own."

Mendicus shook his head. "That was a childish game." There was impatience in his voice. "The *real* desert is not like this. There are no blowing sands here."

"Yes there are," countered Asmar. The cooling of the day brought a breeze from off the desert, causing the sand to swirl in soft, curling eddies. Asmar gestured to these.

"Not like what is out there," Mendicus replied, pointing out into the heart of the Great Desert. "Out there, the sands will rip the flesh off bones, and the cold of the night can freeze you to the core. The wosakes can't venture this far south, as the sands are too tightly packed and the wolves are afraid to come so close to your city. This is not the desert, Asmar. You have learned nothing, risked nothing, by coming this far. But out there you will be tested—and you must be ready."

Asmar listened to Mendicus and wondered why he was following a man he hardly knew. He turned to Mendicus and tried to ask, but the question wouldn't come out. It was as though every time he tried to speak, something inside would stifle the words. Finally, Asmar concentrated and was able to blurt out, "Why me?!"

Mendicus then did something very unusual, and something Asmar never expected: he smiled. Asmar felt a palpable sense of relief. But then Mendicus abruptly stopped smiling and just responded, "You will understand more in good time."

Asmar wanted to know more now, but again he found the words wouldn't pass his lips. The questions were important and he couldn't understand his inability to ask them. A wave of anxiety gripped him, just as Mendicus started walking at an accelerated pace again. Asmar's questions would have to wait.

Gradually, the sky darkened. There would be no moon tonight. The horizon held the reddish glow of the setting sun, while high above, the first stars shone. After hours of walking in the burning heat, Asmar let the cooling evening breeze wash over him. He wondered if they were ever going to stop to drink or eat or rest. Asmar's mouth had become parched, and his throat began to swell. He refused, however, to give in to thirst.

In the fading light, Asmar saw a small copse of trees in the distance. As they grew closer, there was a bronze glow emanating from them. He remembered the stories from the master craftspeople about venturing out into the desert to harvest the bronze pulcher, and suddenly Asmar realized he was going to see them. He touched the bronze ring on his left hand, the one that hid the golden ring of his mother. The two rings sent a surge of longing through him, as if they wanted to be united with the living trees. They pulled him forward.

It was almost completely dark when they reached the tiny oasis. The trees cast a bronze light, warming the harshness of the desert. There were only three bronze pulchers, but they seemed to give life to all types of desert plants gathered at their bases. There were small succulents and even grasses that made the ground soft and pleasant to walk on. Asmar could see small animals scurrying around and through the grasses. The pulchers swayed gently in the winds caused by the dying heat of the desert. Asmar had almost forgotten about Mendicus when he heard a voice boom, "It is now time you rest." Asmar noticed the "you" in his statement, but he was glad of the opportunity. Mendicus remained standing, looking down on the prostrate Asmar. "I wouldn't lie in the grasses."

Asmar was about to ask why when he felt something scurry onto his leg. His instinct was to jump up and slap off the creature that was now making its way up his leg. The creature was about half the size of Asmar's hand and had two sharp claws coming from its head and a very long arched stinger protruding from its back.

"That is a desert scorpion." Mendicus explained. "And they do not like any sudden movement."

Asmar willed himself to stay as still as possible, though his heart was beating hard in his chest. "Are they dangerous?"

"Very."

"Okay. What—do—I—do?" Asmar whispered, half-stammering.

"Don't lie in the grass."

Asmar looked up. Mendicus made no move to assist him, so Asmar searched for something that might be helpful. Being careful not to make any movement that might upset the scorpion, Asmar reached out carefully and grabbed a leaf that had fallen from the pulcher tree. Slowly and as smoothly as possible, he moved the leaf toward the scorpion and, holding his breath, offered the leaf as a platform to the creature. The scorpion guardedly stepped forward onto the leaf, whereupon Asmar lifted the whole leaf off his leg and placed it—and the creature—gently into the grass. Once freed, Asmar jumped to his feet as fast as he could and brushed himself off, hoping no other oasis natives had found him attractive.

"Why didn't you help me?" he said, accusingly.

"I did," answered Mendicus. "I told you the scorpion was dangerous."

Asmar was about to argue, despite how scratchy and dry his throat was and how tired he was, but Mendicus had already turned his back, moving to where one of the pulchers loomed over a small pool. Asmar followed, and Mendicus offered Asmar water from their supplies but drank none himself.

Once the cool water reached his lips and began to forge a path down his dry throat, Asmar couldn't stop. He took one long, cool drink from the water bottle before replacing the stopper. Mendicus turned away while Asmar removed the stopper again and took another long drink. When Asmar handed the bottle back, he felt oddly humiliated and embarrassed.

"We can't camp here," said Mendicus, as he accepted the bottle and bent to refill it from the pool and started to leave. Asmar felt Mendicus draw him forward, but Asmar didn't want to go. Not yet. And more importantly, the rings didn't want to go.

The bronze pulcher called to him, and the compulsion to follow Mendicus broke. Asmar approached the largest bronze tree. Gently, he placed the palm of his hand against the bark. Rather than being the hard surface he expected, it was soft and velvety. He felt almost as if he was part of the tree. The pulcher rings felt warm against his skin. He started to notice that all the aches and stiffness of the day's travel melted away. He felt lighter, full of a warm energy— but there was something else.

He felt as if the tree was trying to speak to him. Asmar listened carefully, his hand on the bark and finally understood the tree in a way all his craft classes could never have taught him. He apologized to the tree for the torture caused by his fellow Tulanders; he was sorry the tree had endured so much.

Mendicus had been watching and, when Asmar was done, announced, "We have to go now."

"Why?" Asmar said, still looking at the tree. He wanted to rest next to it.

"It's not safe here. The scorpions swarm at night and are attracted to body heat." Asmar shuddered at the thought of more of those creatures on top of him. "And we need to make camp before the winds start," Mendicus concluded, and he set a fast pace away from the oasis. Asmar followed but now felt less compelled to silence, and his voice was freed from whatever had weighed it down before. There were things he wanted—no, *needed*—to understand. So as they hurried toward their place of rest for the night, he found himself firing questions at Mendicus.

"Have you been to Dolcere?" Asmar asked. Mendicus didn't answer. Asmar plodded on anyway. "What's it like? Is it as beautiful as they say?" Still no answer. "Did my father like it?"

Mendicus abruptly stopped. The winds were rising and the temperature falling. The answer came slowly and deliberately. "Yes, he liked Dolcere. He liked it too much." Asmar realized it would be pointless asking Mendicus what he meant by that.

They continued their journey. By now, Asmar had eaten nothing since breakfast—a full day of travel and no food. But despite how great the pangs were, he refused to mention his hunger. Mendicus hadn't even had the one drink Asmar did, yet he didn't stop. Asmar wanted to prove he wasn't a soft Tulander, if it was the last thing he did.

And then, like thunderclaps in the perfectly silent desert, Mendicus's voice rang out. "We will make camp here."

Asmar looked around. They were standing next to a rocky ledge, jutting up to about Asmar's height. It wouldn't provide much shelter, but there wasn't much choice. He took off his pack. Mendicus also layed down his pack, which was twice the size of Asmar's.

Their shelter for the night was a simple cloth lean-to. At first glance, it didn't look substantial, and Asmar thought he had overestimated Mendicus. But then he began to examine how it was put together. The flimsy-looking structure was secured against the protruding rock. The rope used to anchor it passed through a niche in the rock itself and wove around the cloth of the lean-to before extending diagonally out into the desert. It then wound back to the securing rock. Two flaps closed off the sides of the shelter and there was just enough room to stand at the highest end of the tent, but it sloped in such a way that it was more comfortable to remain seated. The strength of the makeshift lean-to surprised Asmar. Mendicus had used what was available to build strength and stability, rather than carrying many supports and ties with him.

Mendicus called out to Asmar from behind the lean-to. He had set up a small assortment of dried travel cakes. Asmar looked at the spread hungrily but waited for Mendicus to take the first cake. Mendicus hesitated for a moment, and then Asmar thought he detected the beginning of another smile. Mendicus took out a water bottle and slowly opened it and took one small sip. He then handed it to Asmar, who intended to take the same quantity but ended up swallowing another long drink from the bottle.

Mendicus indicated to Asmar that he should have one of the cakes.

Asmar hesitated. "What are they made of?" He waited, even though he was so hungry he wanted to cram a whole cake into his mouth. He knew he wouldn't be able to stomach anything made with animal flesh.

Mendicus looked up at him, then sighed. "Grains and some fruits and seeds."

Asmar nodded and took a small bite. They were nearly as dry as the desert. When he'd finished, Asmar needed to drink again. This time he managed to control himself and take only one small sip from the bottle.

Mendicus advised they shouldn't build a fire that evening as it would attract the wolves. The desert wind started to pick up and wail with real force. This was nothing like the cool breeze Asmar had experienced in the near desert with his friends. Asmar pulled his talize around him, trying to stay warm. It didn't work. Mendicus sat calmly at one corner of their shelter.

"How? How do you do it?" Asmar raised his voice to be heard over the pelting of the sand. "You go all day on almost no food or water and you hardly speak to me. It's not as if I wanted to come with you, you know." The emotion started to pour out of him. He was forced from his home, separated from his cousin and stuck with an old man who refused to explain anything. The questions gnawed at him: Who was this man? Why did he know so much about the desert? The biggest question was why his aunt let him go. Why had she abandoned him?

Mendicus looked at him with a weariness that made Asmar feel a little better. "You don't need the water or the food. Your talize prevents most water loss and, if I know Lupa, your breakfast should have given you enough energy to walk from Tuland to Dolcere without eating again." As

THE SILVER FOREST – Book One

Mendicus finished this sentence, Asmar heard a strange sound that he realized was a muffled laugh that had come from Mendicus. "It is only your *mind* that needs the food and water, not your body. You can and must get used to making do with less."

How much less could he possibly eat or drink? Asmar studied Mendicus more closely. While there was something about this man Asmar still didn't quite trust, his ability to survive in the desert, and probably anywhere else, was unquestionable. There was much more to know about this old man than he had previously understood.

The wind was gaining force, thrashing against the rock and their shelter. The temperature had dropped so dramatically, Asmar couldn't believe he had ever been hot. He felt a growing uneasiness about the desert and all its dangers and nothing but a small lean-to to protect him.

Mendicus sat calmly wrapped in his talize and was completely unaffected by the pelting of the sand or the drop in temperature. So Asmar hugged his talize around himself and repeated the words over and over, in a whisper, "It's my mind that's cold, not my body." After a little while he added, "But my body sure thinks it's cold." Amazingly, it seemed to work. First his mind calmed, and then his body followed. He was still cold, but it was becoming bearable. There was more to Asmar's discomfort than just the howling wind, the biting cold, and the gusting sand, however. The night had an eerie quality to it, as if someone were interfering with his thoughts. It might be from the long, drawn-out silences between him and Mendicus.

"If you ever venture out and are caught in a sandstorm, get as high up as you can. Find a dune or rock outcropping, and stand tall," said Mendicus with great deliberation. He spoke like a teacher giving his pupil instructions. "The wind moves the sand only a short distance, so it stays close to the ground. The individual grains of sand push each other to create the storm. The mass of sand is low to the ground and, by finding high ground and standing still and straight, you can rise above the storm."

"Rise above the storm" stuck in Asmar's weary mind as he was lulled to sleep by the rhythmic, incessant bombardment of the sand. He slept fitfully, and his head ached as he tossed and turned.

Asmar woke with a start to the sound of eerie laughter. He was in a cold sweat as he turned to look for Mendicus. But the old man wasn't there. Then he heard another eerie laugh. Asmar felt a shiver up his spine. Where was Mendicus? The wind had stopped. He ran blindly into the desert yelling, "Mendicus!" at the top of his lungs, but he didn't hear an answer, and panic gripped him. Asmar stumbled and heard the laugh again, but this time it was much louder and closer. He looked straight ahead. There were two eyes aglow in the dark, staring down at him.

Asmar could make out through the dim light that the eyes were connected to the body of a desert wolf. The wolf howled and Asmar heard the laugh coming from the creature's mouth. The wolf was calling the rest of his pack. Asmar froze, paralyzed by fear.

Suddenly there appeared a burst of light, followed by another, and another. In this unnatural light, Asmar could see at least ten desert wolves vanishing into the shadows.

A hand came down firmly on Asmar's shoulder. With a start, he turned to see a silhouetted figure illuminated. Asmar wanted to run, until he sensed something familiar. It was Mendicus.

He led Asmar back to their shelter, where Asmar fell to the ground exhausted and slept for what remained of the night.

When Asmar finally awoke, he was hot, thirsty, and unrested. He told himself, "It's only my mind that's hot," even though he didn't believe it.

The sole thing Mendicus said to Asmar that morning was, "Beware of the soft sands and the wosakes."

Asmar nodded to Mendicus, his belief in his own abilities shattered after coming face to face with the wolves. His cousin had told him about the dangers of the desert, but the reality was so different, so horrifying. Asmar realized, despite his distrust of the old man, he would have to follow close to Mendicus; his life depended on it.

They hadn't eaten that morning, and though he tried to put his hunger out of his mind, he was sure that it resided in his stomach, regardless of what Mendicus had said. Mendicus walked ahead, far enough that Asmar didn't think he would see him sneak a travel cake. He walked and ate it quickly and hungrily, letting the crumbs fall to the sand. Just as he was about to stuff the last morsel into his mouth, he sensed a presence, something nearby. It felt . . . hungry. He looked around, seeing nothing. But as he returned his attention to his meager breakfast, he felt a strong tug on his leg that made him drop the cake. He had the strange sense of another creature being nearby even before he saw a slimy tooth-filled mouth, as large as Asmar's fist, come up out of the sand and devour the cake. Asmar let out a panicked yelp just as a shiny brown tube wrapped itself around his leg.

"Help! Help me!" Asmar shrieked, as the creature began to violently pull him across the sands. Asmar looked for anything to grab onto as the sand became softer and softer. He sensed the desperation of this animal, the hunger it felt, as it wrapped itself tighter and tighter around his leg. Asmar did everything to pull himself free, but the tug only became stronger. The old man rushed to his side.

"Stop struggling," he commanded, but Asmar couldn't listen.

The sand was now up to his waist and he was being pulled down further. He looked up and the sky seemed to be slipping away.

Don't struggle, came a calm, clear, and strong voice from right inside Asmar's head. The voice compelled him to obey; it took over his will. His body went limp. He was still being pulled down by the creature, but at a slower pace. When the sand was up to his shoulders, he felt something wash over him and a coldness pass through his body. Then as suddenly as it had started, the pulling stopped. Asmar didn't know how or why, but he knew the creature was dead.

Asmar looked up at Mendicus. The old man had something to do with this. Two firm hands grasped his shoulders and slowly lifted him from his sandy encasement. He collapsed as his legs were spent from the effort to break free.

"What happened? What did you do?" Asmar asked.

The old man looked down at the young boy and said, "I did what needed to be done. That was a wosake." This time, Mendicus explained. "We eat at dusk to avoid them, since that's when they sleep. We travel by day to avoid the wolves." With that, Mendicus turned away to continue the trek. Asmar stood, shook off as much sand as he could, and followed.

CHAPTER 5

MALZUS SAT ON HIS THRONE, isolated in his castle at Tellurium near the northern town of Adular, the golden staff at his side. He had summoned the Sitire ruler, Zorin, to meet with him in person. Malzus's plan to destroy the Aris was too sensitive to communicate remotely through Saeren, and he also feared the wizards could intercept his message if he used his creatures.

Much had happened in the years since he escaped Dolcere. He was winning, for the most part. If only the other wizards had helped him rather than trying to stop him, it would have been much easier. Much less death, much less destruction. But Malzus was confident that he would triumph eventually. *His* mind was stronger, and the golden staff would assure his inevitable victory. Once he won, the other wizards would have to welcome him back and admit that his way was the right way to find the tree. But they kept fighting him, following the ways of Heil. It was his father's fault. He needed his father to understand what he was doing.

When he escaped Dolcere, he wanted to get as far from the other wizards as he could, and that meant going north. That was where the enemies of the Aris, Cautes, and Cherts lived. The Sitire were the first to fall to his influence. He had gently manipulated the minds of their leaders. It was easier than he had expected. They wanted power and influence, at least the ones whose minds were open to him, and he gave them that in exchange for their loyalty. And those who weren't loyal were easily replaced. There seemed to be a never-ending supply of Sitire who wanted power.

He led the Sitire to victories over the Aris. Small ones at first—capturing water sources and arable land. The wizards in Dolcere were slow to fight him, and that gave him the chance to achieve greater victories, but he needed more. He went further north to the Breccians and then the Domare, building alliances, giving them power and enhancing his own. At the end of a year he had accomplished much, but he was weary of all the effort it took to control so many. He needed a place to rest, to build his power, and Tellurium was that place.

Carved into a black stone mountain, the Tellurium castle shot up into the sky to twice the height of the wizards' tower in Dolcere, casting its long shadow as far as Adular. Like the wizards' tower, this castle had been abandoned long ago. Malzus had tried to find out the reason for the sudden departure of such an advanced people, but all his research had only turned up speculation. It was possible they were unable to grow enough food in the barren area as their population expanded, or it could have been an attack by their southern enemies. Neither of these seemed to be adequate explanations, though.

To protect himself, Malzus had all the floors of the tower removed except for the uppermost one. Here he kept two narrow pathways extending from the entrance of the room to the throne itself. One path ran along the wall, creating a narrow ledge that followed the curve of the circular room; the other made a straight line from the doorway to the throne. This was all that was left of the original floor. With every floor below having been removed, an abyss was created, with a sheer drop from the throne and its paths to the very base of the tower and the cold stones far below. It had taken years to complete the work, but he felt safe. Or at least safer.

Malzus had over five hundred soldiers in Tellurium, but he didn't trust them. The more generals that were near him, the more he needed to monitor their thoughts, and the greater the risk that one or more would turn on him. He needed to be more secure, so he sent the army away and confined himself to the tower with no floor. He maintained a few servants in residence to bring him his simple meals and attend to his basic needs. Any person or army trying to attack him would need to climb the twenty floors to the top of the tower to reach him, and that would be impossible to do unnoticed. This arrangement made him feel secure for a while, but he knew the other wizards

THE SILVER FOREST – Book One

might eventually send someone he couldn't detect, someone who could get close enough to harm him. To be completely safe and prevent this, he needed to be able to reach into their minds, like he had in Dolcere, and for that to be possible he needed more knowledge, more power.

He had searched for this knowledge by reaching into the past thoughts of the wizards that had inhabited Vetus's mind, the mind he had stripped when he left Dolcere. These were wizards who were much more ancient than the ones that he held in his own thoughts. There was Shammai, the wizard whose teachings his father had tried to hide from him. Shammai's thoughts were so far back that Malzus could barely hear him. But Shammai revealed techniques dating back to the First Mind War that had been hidden and buried in obscurity. Malzus learned from him how to draw power from the Saeren he created.

Malzus used this technique on the ruler of Adular, but the old man tried to fight him off and had turned into a useless, mindless lump as a result. Malzus destroyed him and then turned to the son. Lefi, who was younger and stronger, who became his first Saeren. It had taken far more energy and strength than Malzus had expected and left him weakened and dangerously vulnerable for days after. Slowly, he learned to draw power from the new Saeren he created, but the amount he could draw from these untrained minds was minimal compared to what he could siphon from that of a wizard. He needed to perfect the technique if he was going to use it on others with great power. Not only was the process exhausting to implement, but each time he did, the golden staff seemed to show signs of increasing resistance to his will. For now, he had created four Saeren, and the creatures added to his sense of safety. They were all connected to him, and what one saw, he saw; what one heard, he heard. They were of one mind—Malzus's.

But even the Saeren had their limits. He needed the Sitire to destroy the Aris, but he knew this couldn't be achieved from the outside, directly. He had a plan that was more subtle than anything he had tried before, and by working indirectly, it would bring an end to the Aris from within. With such a plan successfully implemented, he would sweep through the Aris cities and Dolcere would be completely isolated. Then, the wizards would have no choice but to recognize him as their Great Wizard.

Now the day of the meeting with the Sitire leader had arrived, and Zorin emerged at the top of the stairs. Zorin was out of breath and had to steady himself against the wall, as he looked down into the abyss beneath him.

Malzus could see and feel Zorin's fear like a fog filling the tower. He knew Zorin wanted desperately to turn and flee, but instead Malzus compelled him to bow down, shaking but trying to maintain his balance on one knee.

She must be stopped! Malzus's voice echoed inside Zorin's head. Malzus sensed Zorin's fear—the fear of being killed for displeasing him, but also the greater fear of being converted into one of the mindless Saeren. These were fears Malzus knew how to nurture.

"Yes, your holiness," Zorin replied. "But how? I lost half of my entire force in the last battle just trying to get anywhere near her. They protect Areana with their lives.

And even though we outnumber the Aris, they have all of Dolcere behind them—their weapons and their wizards."

Malzus felt the rage welling up inside of him. Zorin shouldn't have mentioned the Dolcere wizards. He breathed deeply and worked to hold back the anger rising in his mind.

"If one of their soldiers is worth five of yours, it's because of her, *not* the Dolcere wizards and their weapons. Her soldiers follow her because they love her—that is the only danger. Kill her and you kill their motivation."

Zorin looked away from Malzus and stared into the abyss as he pleaded, "How shall I kill her, your holiness?"

"You will take a Saeren," Malzus said. He then carefully communicated his plan and all of its details to Zorin before letting the Sitire leave, unharmed.

CHAPTER 6

AREANA STEPPED INTO THE COMMAND tent behind Adomas. She was nervous and impatient but knew that it was important that she reveal neither of these things. Her strengths were fighting and leading her soldiers into battle, not being a diplomat.

Her father—Olmar, leader of the Aris tribes—knew this, and it was the primary reason he had appointed her as the general of the combined Aris forces. But her father wasn't here, and that meant she would need to be diplomatic, whether she liked it or not. Her father, and the tribes of the Aris, were depending on her. She would not let them down.

Adomas crossed behind the table covered with papers and maps, and he embraced his father, Arkos, leader of the largest of the Aris tribes.

"It's been too long, my son," said Arkos. The silver that used to be confined to his temples now encompassed his whole head and framed his dark skin. He was growing too old for leading the largest Aris tribe in battles, and Areana knew he was anxious for his son to take over. But he also knew his son needed more experience. The older man turned to Areana.

"I've not seen my son often enough since he's begun serving as one of your father's generals."

"He has served well," Areana said. "We've been very fortunate to have him." She reminded herself to smile.

"I'd always heard that you were a skilled leader, but they hadn't warned me about what a diplomat you've become," said Arkos.

Areana looked down, trying to show she was humble. "From you, I take that as high praise," she said. "Your experience with diplomacy has helped hold our tribes together. Without your skills as a leader, I'm afraid we would all be Sitire by now."

The woman standing next to Arkos nodded. Somewhat older than Areana, she was tall and muscled and her dark hair was cut to shoulder length. Areana recognized Liance as one of Arkos's best commanders.

Arkos nodded. "Very flattering. Now, you must be tired from your journey. We've prepared food and drink for you and your soldiers. Once you've had a chance to rest, we should talk strategy."

"From what we've heard, there's little time to lose," said Adomas. "We can eat and strategize at the same time."

Arkos seemed pleased at his son's commitment. "Let's do that then," he said. He wrapped his arm warmly about his son's shoulders and led him off toward his private tent.

Before Areana followed, she glanced down at the documents spread out over the table.

Liance touched Areana's arm. "I hope they're right about you."

Areana looked at her. "What do you mean?"

"That you're a skilled commander." Liance paused. "Adomas has much to learn from you."

Areana looked closely at Liance. "It's good he has people like you by his side." Liance bowed her head in appreciation. Areana said, "Let's join the others."

The four settled into chairs facing each other in the smaller, private tent. Arkos looked at Areana and asked, "Tell me news of the capital. How goes it with your father?"

"The fighting appears to have shifted to here in the north. My father is anxious to chase the Sitire from our lands."

"It's been difficult," Arkos admitted. "With the number of troops your father has given us, we have been greatly limited. Your assistance now is much needed. The Sitire have been continually attacking in small groups and disrupting the farms. They attack and then flee with speed and precision. It's been quite difficult. But now that you and Adomas are here, things will change. Isn't that right, son?"

Adomas had been looking away distractedly, but being addressed startled him, and he had to reply, embarrassed, "What did you say, Father?"

"I said that—well, never mind what I said. You must be tired, Adomas. I should leave you to rest before you venture out to meet the Sitire."

"No, no—I'm fine, really. Not tired. It's just..." Adomas's voice trailed off.

"Just—what?" his father asked, with concern.

"I don't know... I'm sorry. Headaches, kind of. It has made it hard to... to concentrate."

"Why didn't you mention this before? Describe to me immediately what's going on," Areana directed. She would need to rely on Adomas for the upcoming battle.

"It's like there's something, or someone, in my head. It sometimes makes it difficult to concentrate. But it comes and goes."

"Can I rely on you against the Sitire?"

"Yes," said Adomas, straightening up and forcing his focus. "I can control it. I am sure I just need a bit of rest before we march. Please excuse me, everyone."

With that, Adomas left the room. Areana turned to Arkos and, rather than quizzing him about his son, immediately started on the strategy for the upcoming fight.

The next morning they rose early to march, Adomas and Areana together at the head of their contingent of two hundred soldiers. "We'll have to be clever to root out the Sitire," Adomas said. "They're all cowards and wouldn't dare attack a column of Aris. Once they know of our approach, they'll run."

Areana nodded, reflecting on this as she kept pace, and responded, "Perhaps, but I still intend to send out patrols daily to check up ahead as well as to both flanks. We're traveling light and rely on the supply lines from your father. If those are cut off, we could get into trouble."

"But the Sitire are only a small force," said Adomas. "They never have more than ten or twenty soldiers. They can't have more than fifty involved in these raids."

"That may be, but we can't chance it. I'll send out the patrols."

And that was the end of the debate. Most of their discussions of strategy were this brief, with Areana having the final word.

On the fourth night of their journey, Areana was awakened suddenly by the cry of a scout. They had set up camp at sunset, and the troops had bedded down following the nightly sandstorm passing over.

"Commander!" the scout yelled, from just outside her tent. "Commander, I am sorry to awaken you but—Adomas has marched against the Sitire raiders."

Areana snapped instantly to full consciousness. "Tell me quickly: how many Sitire, and when did he leave?" She was strapping on her crystal sword.

"Thirty-six were counted. He left just after moonrise," replied the scout.

"Thirty-six that we were allowed to see. There're more Sitire than that, I'm sure. We must hurry."

What possessed Adomas to go off on his own like that? *He is a better soldier than to act so hastily,* she thought to herself—but as soon as those thoughts went through her mind, small examples of Adomas's erratic behavior over the course of their march now came to her notice. He had been secretive, employing his own scouts rather than relying on the ones Areana sent out. It didn't matter, or so she had thought. But it was Adomas's scouts that had found the Sitire and not reported it to her. That was strange.

By this time, Areana was fully awake and ready. Her rescue plans—for she knew that was what was needed now—were already clear in her mind. "Was he mounted? How many men did he take?"

"His force numbered about sixty, all mounted."

Areana's fury rose as she sat astride her horse. If the orders had come from anyone other than Arkos's son, he would be fully stripped of rank! What bothered her most was not Adomas taking any initiative, but her keen sense that the attack was a trap. The Sitire were expert at hiding in the desert. If thirty-six had been seen, there could be one hundred and thirty-six hidden in the sands.

The troops were armed and ready to march in no time at all. Elaxa, a woman Areana had recently promoted, and Mar, one of her father's most trusted commanders, were at her sides. Their crystal swords, made from the sands of the desert, bent the cool moonlight into a ghostly spectrum. With weapons at the ready, the soldiers now hurried to the rescue.

After a brief ride, Areana, Elaxa, and Mar crested the top of a high dune and got their first view of the battle. Elaxa said. "It's unusual to see fighting in the moonlight. It's truly a wondrous sight." The three admired the gentle bending of the pale light by the crystal swords of the Aris, creating a pastel, moving spectrum against a black backdrop.

"It is," agreed Areana grimly, noting that from a distance, there was even beauty in battle. Areana fought the urge to attack right away before assessing the strength of the Sitire. Precious seconds passed as they scanned the horizon. The desert shone a silvery blue in the light of the moon, but then Areana spied the barely moving blot of darkness that sent a chill through her heart.

"See? Over there!" she said, pointing out the dark sands that seemed to come to life. "There are at least two hundred Sitire hidden among those dunes. Adomas has the advantage of being mounted and that will help, but he's extremely outnumbered."

Mar responded, hissing quietly with frustration. "We *knew* this was a trap. There are probably even more Sitire in reserve. We must attack them head on, and then move quickly to withdraw. We can't hope to defeat the Sitire under these circumstances. We just have to try to save as many of Adomas's soldiers as we can."

Elaxa objected. "We have them now," she said. "I say we can defeat them. This is an opportunity to rid ourselves of these raiders once and for all. If we cut across the flanks of those now moving into position, we can relieve Adomas before he's overrun."

It was a well-conceived plan, but Areana knew it wouldn't work.

Mar was opening his mouth to object, but Areana raised a hand to silence them both.

"Our attack must be quick and direct. We need to get Adomas out and then head due south. The Sitire reinforcements are probably to the east, blocking the way to

Arkos's camp." Areana's plan incorporated elements from both commanders and then added specifics of her own design.

"I'll go in and attack first and bolster Adomas's troops. Elaxa, you'll lead the second wave from the north to divert attention with a third of the troops. Mar, you'll follow up with the remaining force, attacking from the south—this will clear a path for our escape."

She sent her commanders back to their units to assemble for battle. She knew her plan was their only hope. Hers would be the first strike, and it must be strong and decisive if Adomas was to be rescued. Areana made her way back to her troops, and looking out over them, gave the signal to attack.

Not far off from the back of the group, she could hear Mar call out to his unit and the sound of their horses, snorting and moving. They rode off in the circling attack that would bring them toward the Sitire from the south. On the opposite side, Areana could see Elaxa and her contingent galloping off to reach their northern point for the battle.

As Areana spurred her horse forward, the battlefield came into view. She could see the Sitire swarming all over Adomas's forces. Areana paused as the rest of her soldiers caught up to her.

"This isn't going to be easy," said Rou, a short, muscular soldier whose face bore the scars of previous encounters with the Sitire.

"Nothing worthwhile ever is," replied Areana, riding next to him. "Now, everyone—stay close!"

She spurred her horse forward once again, straight toward where the battle was thickest. She drew her crystal sword and saw it bend the light of the moon, casting a pastel rainbow in her wake. As soon as it was raised, her soldiers raised their own weapons and gave a shrill battle cry. It was in this sea of pastel that they all drove forward to attack. As she and her soldiers worked their way deeper and deeper into the Sitire lines, Areana could tell they had not surprised the enemy, and a fresh contingent of Sitire fighters emerged from nowhere to take on the coming attack.

Areana smiled. This is what she had expected. Her plan would work and her forces would succeed. Her task was made more difficult by the new soldiers, but she could tell that the Sitire had expected her troops to attack at once, in one group. The three-pronged attack would be a surprise.

"Go for the center," Areana yelled. "That's where Adomas will be!"

She galloped closer, studying the Sitire. There was an odd blankness in the center of their ranks. It didn't make sense. Her mind fogged. She felt an emptiness, a coldness. Her heart raced. Areana concentrated in the cool moonlight on trying to clear her vision.

And then she saw it. Riding into view on a jet-black horse emerged a black-cloaked figure, barely visible in the dim light. She knew what this was from the stories the Great Wizard had told. She reached frantically for the name he had called it . . .

Saeren. The Great Wizard had called it Saeren.

Others saw the Saeren moving in and slowed.

"What do we do now?" Rou called out, eyes wide and sword poised in the air.

Areana felt the growing sense of doom begin to move like a wave through the ranks of her soldiers. Pulling hard on the reins, her mount slowed. Areana felt the Saeren reach into her thoughts—it was like a black cloud moving through the air, expanding. Instinctively, she closed her mind and spurred her horse onward, faster, toward the Sitire lines. She wasn't going to let this thing, this Saeren, stop her. Her soldiers mustn't see any fear, any indecision. She knew her strength was their only hope.

She held her sword high, letting the moonlight refract its colors.

"Everyone—follow me!" Areana cried out.

A resounding cheer rippled through the ranks and Areana turned and spurred her horse on. Quickly, she gave an order to Rou, galloping alongside, and pointed to the moving Sitire. "Cut them off!" she screamed over the noise of pounding hooves.

Her soldiers were with her once again. She looked for the Saeren, but it was gone. Areana hit the line of defending Sitire, swinging her crystal sword. Quickly, she cut her way through the moving human forest. She could now discern the trapped soldiers. They had begun with sixty, but it looked as if fewer than forty were still standing. Behind her, the clash of swords and screams of pain. At this point she didn't know who was screaming, who was winning or losing the battle. To turn around was to invite certain death. She had to keep going.

Adomas's soldiers were cutting their way toward her. They were ragged, but they were giving the battle everything they had.

There were so many Sitire, and they just kept coming.

Beside her, she saw Rou spur his horse forward, pushing with her further into the enemy lines. In spite of the Saeren, he and all the others had followed her steadfastly into battle. She stared at Rou. She had met his young daughter before they had ridden off to battle, and Areana wanted him to see her again. She shook her head. This was dangerous; if she let these thoughts dominate her, none of her soldiers would see their families ever again. She let out another battle scream through gritted teeth, purging the thoughts from her mind.

Areana could feel the energy of resistance was suddenly lessened. The attack from the north must have begun. She paused only long enough to take a brief survey of the situation.

Her soldiers had done well. Five of her troops were on the ground. They would ride the sands no more. But there were more than three times that number of Sitire lying dead.

Slashing furiously, Areana cut her way to where Adomas's troops had been surrounded. They were being led not by Adomas, but one of his commanders. It was Liance.

"Liance! Where is he?" Areana cried out.

"I don't know," she yelled back in response, a look of pure horror and exhaustion in her eyes. "We were ambushed. But they went right for Adomas. That's when we lost most of our force."

"Has he been killed, then?"

"No. Or—not last I saw," said Liance. "Those around him were killed, but he was captured. He just was gone, suddenly. We have been fighting, forcing them back, hoping to rescue him."

"It's my command, and I will help find him," said Areana firmly, ending any debate.

The northern group of Aris fighters had now broken into the center too, and the southern phase of the assault had just begun. Areana called out to Rou.

"Take this contingent and fight your way south to Elaxa."

"What about you?" beseeched Rou.

"I am going to find Adomas," she answered. "You must lead the others to safety."

"But Commander—we can—we must help."

Areana knew that would be a mistake for two reasons. First, she didn't want to risk her troops longer than necessary for no advantage. Second, she feared that if a large force closed in on Adomas, his captors would kill him. A small force was his only chance.

"Go!" she ordered, more firmly than she ever sounded in her life. "You are needed to lead the troops."

There was no more discussion.

Areana now turned to Liance, steadying her horse. "Gather eight of Adomas's remaining soldiers. The ten of us will rescue him."

A smile crossed Liance's face. By selecting Adomas' soldiers specifically, they had a chance to save their honor. Liance quickly called out to her soldiers, and the party of ten assembled. Liance had selected well. The soldiers she picked had suffered wounds in the battle; none of Adomas's troops were uninjured. Blood dripped from their arms, faces, and bodies. But despite their injuries, they were strong and ready to keep going.

Areana scanned the battlefield, searching the pale light and upward-moving clouds of dust from the swirl of moving horses and fighters. Where would they have taken Adomas? The Sitire were confused, but the majority had their attention focused on the three directions of the attack: north, south, and west. The only uncovered area was east, and her instincts told her that was where Adomas must be.

Rounding a dune, her small force came upon an encampment of Sitire. *This must be the commander's camp,* Areana thought—and then somehow she knew instinctively that inside the guarded tent at this site was where they would find Adomas.

With a quick movement of her wrist, Areana signaled to begin the attack.

Unmounted and caught by surprise, the encamped Sitire braced themselves for the onslaught. The Aris killed eight Sitire immediately, and now Areana had the upper hand. As her soldiers continued the fight, Areana dismounted and, wielding her sword with unfailing precision, cut her way right up to the entrance of the command tent. It took Areana little time to find what she was looking for: there was Adomas, lying in the far corner of the tent, semi-conscious. Areana took a step toward the fallen commander but then froze. Rising up from the shadows and looming over Adomas's prone body was the dark figure she had seen before. It was the Saeren.

The sight of the Saeren, its black robes and cowl creating a shadowy faceless void, made Areana want to turn and flee as fast as she could. With great effort, summoning all of her nerve, she planted her feet firmly and managed one step in the direction of Adomas.

"Stand aside," she heard herself say.

The response was only a mocking laugh that sounded as if it came from far, far away, making Areana's very bones cold.

"Stand aside!" she screamed almost in terror, her voice pushed to the brink, but her body and mind fixed firmly, fiercely, to her objective.

To Areana's complete shock, the shadowy figure quietly straightened and then stepped to the side. She rushed quickly to Adomas, passing dangerously close to the Saeren. Areana didn't understand why the Saeren moved aside. Something wasn't right—this was too easy. Areana knelt down to help Adomas, looking carefully for any sign of a trap. But she couldn't see any.

Keeping her blade between herself and the Saeren, Areana began to lift the bigger and heavier Adomas, draping his arm over her shoulder.

And still, the Saeren didn't move.

Summoning all her strength, she moved as quickly as possible with Adomas's weight leaning on her, and they fled the tent to rejoin the rescue team outside.

Hoisting Adomas onto her horse with help from one of his soldiers, Areana glanced around one last time, and saw an Aris lying dead. It was Liance. The casualties were fewer than she had expected, and she was relieved to note that. She signaled the remaining soldiers to break off their attacks and to follow her back to reunite with the other, surviving troops.

CHAPTER 7

WALKING BECAME DIFFICULT AND TIRING for Remer not long after he had left the firm roads of Tuland for the soft, seemingly endless sands of the desert. After just one day on the shifting, uneven terrain, his legs felt rubbery and weak. That night, he camped at what was still considered only the beginning of the desert, just beyond the warm, faint lights of the Tuland he left behind. There were no strong winds here and the wolves wouldn't come this close to civilization either, so it was a good place for him to rest and figure out his plans.

The easiest route would be to simply follow Asmar and Mendicus, but he couldn't risk being discovered and sent back. Remer took off his father's pack and realized he was on his own for the first time in his life. He felt at peace with this. Of course, his father had not gone out alone; he had been accompanied by trained Tulanders. And not to mention, his father was also older and more experienced—and his father had been killed.

Remer blocked the negative thoughts from his mind. He had all the books in his head that his father didn't. This would help him survive, he knew. But he needed to organize his thoughts. He wondered what lay ahead, until his mind grew tired and he eventually fell asleep.

He rose on the second day and looked back over the stretch of golden sands warmed by the sun. Lupa was back there. Safety was back there. He turned and looked ahead, to the north. Asmar was there. He packed his gear and headed toward his cousin. Asmar had been called to Dolcere, but Remer felt he was called too. Not to Dolcere but to something bigger, that he was to be there for Asmar, he was to be the one to remember all that happened.

The sun was rising on his right and would set on his left. If he didn't pay careful attention to the progress it made across the sky, he knew he risked walking in circles. How did others navigate this great sandy expanse? He flipped through pages in his mind and found the key in *The Wanderer*, who advised noting specific landmarks in the surroundings and walking toward them. The problem for him was there were so few landmarks in the open desert, and some of them could be illusions caused by the sun and heat.

All he could see were dunes. Nothing but dunes. And they all looked the same. He feared he would start in one direction and end up walking in another. There had to be something tangible about one dune that was different, and he squinted to see as far as he could. Finally, he saw one dune that stood out. In the soft beige of the sands, this one shone a deep crimson. That was his first marker. He relaxed; he was on his way.

As the sun moved overhead, the crimson dune seemed just as far away as it had in the morning. He felt hot as he moved sluggishly through the sand, even though his father's talize protected him.

Remer had known that wandering the desert wasn't going to be easy, but he hadn't known it meant your throat literally choking from dryness, being blinded by the intensity of the sun, and every muscle aching from unsure, sliding footing. He fingered the water pouch on his hip, resisting the overwhelming desire to drink. He shouldn't require much water, since his talize kept him hydrated—but thirst and the water called to him, with intensity. He forced his hand away.

As the sun sank further, he found himself touching the water sac again, the urge to drink becoming even more overwhelming. He couldn't go another step without it. Slowly, he undid the cord that attached the pouch and gently lifted it to his lips. He didn't have enough to make it all the way to Dolcere, so he would have to refill at some point, somewhere. Until then, he needed to conserve.

Just a small sip will be okay, he thought.

A few drops trickled from the container onto his tongue, but that only made him thirstier. A small swallow should have been enough, but it wasn't. A second swallow then ignited the need for a third. *Maybe a fourth would be alright.*

No! He knew better. He would be fine without water, no matter what his body was telling him.

Shielding his eyes from the intense sunlight, Remer walked with his head down, pressing forward, trying to ignore the pain in his legs. A cool, refreshing wind washed over him. The sun was setting, and it was turning the desert into a rainbow of glistening colors. He was struck by the immensity of the landscape, the openness. The freedom he felt. Tuland had been safe and isolated. The desert was the opposite: it was full of danger but contained vast beauty as well. It was what he wanted.

He breathed in the cooler evening air. It was getting dark. The crimson dune was still waiting for him on the horizon. The desert winds would begin soon, and he wasn't prepared. He tried to concentrate. What did the books say to do?

Page after page raced through his mind. He searched desperately until he finally found it. He had to dig down, make a hole in the sand, and cover himself with his tarp. That would also hide him from the wolves, after the desert winds subsided.

Remer dug with the same small collapsible shovel his father had used. For each shovelful he took out, almost an equal amount of sand fell back into the hole he was trying to dig. The wind quickened and the darkness grew. He chided himself for not having started earlier. It was really getting dark now and the hole he managed to dig could only fit half of his body, but that would have to be enough. He threw his pack in, jumped in beside it, and pulled the tarp overhead. In the dark he tried to secure the stakes, pushing them deep into the soft sand as best he could. Curling into a ball, exhausted, he prepared for the night.

The full energy of the winds began. The grains of sand bouncing off the protective tarp sounded rhythmic, almost musical. The pace of the sand increased as the wind quickened. Drawing his green talize closer around him, he wished for a warming fire, but that would attract the wolves and besides, he didn't have any fuel. He was cold and very hungry. He couldn't eat during the day when the wosakes were active, but now he gave in to the gnawing hunger. Reaching into his pack, he found a small berry-flavored travel cake Lupa had packed for him, and he felt the pangs of missing her and the safety of Tuland. He had taken too much for granted.

Biting into the cake, Remer closed his eyes and savored its sweetness and tartness. He had just settled in, his back against the cool sandy wall of his shelter, when a gust of wind found a gap over his head, blowing under the tarp and blasting sand into his face and eyes. He dropped the cake after only one precious bite and grabbed the corner of the tarp to re-secure it. Then another blast of cold air lifted the tarp, spraying him with sharp sand again. Remer again reached out desperately and grabbed the corner to secure it. The wind picked up more and wouldn't relent. After another strong gust lifted his overhead protection, all of the stakes flew up and away into the darkness. Remer held onto the tarp tightly with everything he had. The sand was everywhere—in his hair and nose and even his mouth. He shut his eyes tightly, trying to protect them.

What should he do? His instincts were to stay low and draw the tarp around him completely.

There must be a book that held the answer, he thought—and recalled quickly a passage:

"If caught out in the blowing sands, get as high as you can. The strength of the storm is closest to the ground, so always rise above it."

He struggled out of his hole and onto his feet, then pulled the tarp over his head. The force lessened on his upper body, but the sand cut painfully and relentlessly at his ankles. *I can hold out*, he said to himself. He was not going to let himself die on his first day out in the desert!

The wind and sand no longer filled his nose as he stood tall and straight in the sandstorm. When, after what seemed like an eternity, the wind started to abate, his legs were raw, blasted from the cutting, driving sands.

As the wind abated Remer felt hope and relief, until he remembered the wolves. He would need to dig back down into the sand to hide from them. He went back in his mind to *The Wanderer*. He pictured the page he had referred to so many times and reread the title at the top: "Surviving the Desert." After reading those words, he knew he could make it.

The wind was suddenly replaced by silence. The tarp dropped from Remer's shoulders and he wiped away the sand that was caked to his face. Prying his eyes open and squinting into the starlit desert, he saw that the sand was perfectly smooth, the storm having caused it to cover all traces of what had been his camp. The hole he had dug was nowhere to be seen and his pack—all of his supplies—were in that hole.

He fought back his growing panic. He had been standing right next to the hole; it had to be close. He needed to dig, but—his panic surged again—his shovel was buried. He fell to his knees and dug with his hands until his arms felt leaden. Then he heard the scream.

Remer froze, his arm half buried in the cool sand.

The scream came again, and he felt a shot of fear move through him instantly. The scream wasn't human.

Then there was a third scream, coming from what seemed like a different direction. More and more screams now, from different places. He was surrounded by these screams in the night. The desert was truly haunted; ghosts were coming to get him. He wanted to run for his life, but he knew he had to stay rooted. To run would be certain death. He had to find his buried food and water and all of his supplies.

Looking through the vastness of his inner library kept him rooted, despite his fear. But his relief was short-lived; the sound was from the wolves.

The pages were clear with their warning: the wolves always searched for food right after the winds died down. The books told him he needed to hide right away and to bury his scent.

He renewed his digging, his bare hands now aching beyond comprehension. When, a moment later, he felt something soft, he could've cried. Lifting it up to see it in the scant light, he recognized the travel cake he had dropped before the storm!

He dug deeper and deeper now, feeling the pure, thrilling energy of hope. His hands hit something—it was the shape and hardness of his pack, and he now moved at double the pace, finally dislodging it from the sand. He pulled out the shovel from the pack and dug down deep into the sand, making the hole waist high. Jumping inside, he covered himself with the precious tarp, hoping that this would prevent the wolves from seeing him.

As soon as he closed his eyes in his cramped, sandy encasement, everything he had gone through came raining down on him. His complete exhaustion from trudging through the desert and surviving the storm and relentless digging now made it impossible for him to stay awake. Remer heard the music of the pelting sand against the tarp. It was a melody that sounded familiar... perhaps one that Lupa used to sing to him? It was so reassuring and soothing that his body started to let go.

Now there was something new—a strange discordance in one part of the song that seemed to be coming closer. With all his remaining strength, Remer pushed at a corner of the tarp and managed to lift it enough to see out.

Two burning red eyes, fiery like embers, stared back at him. It was a massive black wolf, looking into his face. Remer stopped breathing.

What should I do? Move, or lie still? Panicked, he looked to his books. They were blank. His entire mind was completely blank!

All the books were gone. Everything he had relied upon since he was a child—erased. He had never experienced this before. What was happening? Was this wolf stealing his thoughts? Stealing his stories? His memories?

"You don't belong here," said the wolf.

A talking wolf—was this in his books? Remer searched and searched the emptiness. Nothing.

"Go home. Go to your mother. Go back and hide."

There was a scream, only now it was Remer himself, letting out a shriek. Thrashing about in terror and confusion, he awoke and realized he was completely tangled up in the tarp and his talize, kicking and struggling in the hole he had dug in the sand. In a panic, he worked to extricate himself from the twisted mess of tarp and cloak, and then looked around and saw nothing but sand, except where the sun just touched the horizon.

He felt like crying and collapsing in relief. It had been a dream. Everything since leaving Tuland seemed to be a dream. Remer looked into his mind for his books and found them all there; they were all back. Tears wet his cheeks. The winds and the sands and wolves couldn't beat him now. He had his books. Without them, he realized, he was completely lost.

Weary, but feeling emboldened for having survived the night, Remer prepared to start out. His stomach demanded food, but his mind knew the wosakes made it too risky. The wosakes were scavengers with an extremely keen sense of smell and would eat almost anything small enough to be swallowed whole. They couldn't swallow large prey, so instead they would work by dragging the prey under the sand, essentially suffocating them. When prey stopped struggling, the wosakes assumed they were dead and would leave them buried, only to come back and eat them later. If ever caught by a wosake, it was incredibly important not to fight back.

Remer remembered the travel cake and found it lying at his feet. He picked it up and threw it as far away as he could. The ground rumbled. Not much. Just a slight tremor. He crept forward slowly to where he had thrown the cake and peeked up just in time to see a sharp-toothed mouth, the size of two of his fists, close and sink away into the sands. The cake was nowhere to be seen. A wosake. While he felt fear, he also realized he wouldn't have any food until nightfall, and his stomach ached. If he couldn't have food, he would drink—and he didn't care how much. He broke out his pouch of water and drank ravenously. He would figure out where to get more later.

Having gathered up his small pack of gear, he set out. He pulled his talize close around him to keep the heat out, and he trudged forward. He looked up occasionally at what had now become his adversary—the crimson dune—with utter frustration. It was no closer.

The next time he looked up, he saw something that made his heart race. Close on the horizon, he could make out a sagu—a desert plant whose sword-like spines were sharpened by blowing sand to a fine edge, protecting it from the wolves and wosakes. More importantly, they had thick, tough skins to hold in precious water. A smile stretched across Remer's hot, parched face. Having emptied his water supply that morning, he desperately needed more, and this plant would be his savior.

Run! he thought to himself, picking up his pace. *Run to that plant.* He would get there and waste no time cutting the branches and sucking out the water. He might even be lucky and find water at its base, hopefully enough to refill his pouch. Everything was going to be alright.

Remer was now running as fast as he could. His pack bounced against his back, knocking against him as he tried to go faster and faster on the slipping sands. A moment later, his foot gave way as he stumbled.

With effort, he pulled himself upright, but something was wrong: he couldn't move his feet. He looked down and something was even more wrong: he couldn't see his feet. They were buried in the sand.

Wosakes! he thought, instinctively letting his body go limp. But... it just couldn't be. If it were wosakes, he would feel a sensation of being pulled down. This was like slowly being sucked into the mire.

As he searched the texts in his mind again, trying to figure out what to do, the sand had crept all the way up to his knees. Desperately Remer looked through hundreds of pages and finally found the text that could help him: he was stuck in the soft sands. He'd been walking a slow downgrade most of the morning, and that's why it had been easier. Now he was in a valley where water collected. Then there was the sagu, which grew near water. How could he have been so oblivious?

There was no time to waste, as the sand was continuing to suck him down. He had to find a way to escape, and quickly. His books said that the heavier the person, the faster they sank. To slow his descent into the sands, which was now up to his waist, the first thing he needed to do was get rid of the weight of his pack. He didn't want to let it go; it was his father's, and also he needed what was in it in order to survive.

The sand crept up, and there was no debating things any further. Reluctantly, he released the pack in the sand next to him and watched it slowly sink. His own descent slowed, but he was still sinking. He had only bought himself a little more time. Pages and pages flipped through Remer's mind, finally coming to a halt on a passage from *The Wanderer*:

"I discarded my old burdens to stop my progress toward certain doom, but that wasn't the answer. With the old burdens gone, I sank less quickly than before, yet I still sank."

This is painfully accurate, thought Remer, now up to his chest in soft, heavy sand. He began to wish the Wanderer would be just a tad more ... concise.

The passage continued.

"When I was certain my life was done, I still wouldn't give in. To go forward into the mire would be fatal. I knew I had to go where the sand was no longer soft. Suddenly, it occurred to me—I had just made one wrong step into the sands, so firmer ground should be right behind me! With great effort I turned, and my fingers felt for firmer ground, but they drifted slowly into the sands. I had one chance, and I took it. Trusting my intuition, I lunged with every bit of strength toward the solid desert floor. With the tips of my fingers I felt firmer land. I dug into the firm shore and pulled myself, little by little, to safety. As my body began to lose its strength, my mind took

over, telling my hand to pull. After what seemed like an eternity, I was back in the baking hot sun of the desert, safe at last."

Remer tried to follow the Wanderer's directions. Turning slowly, he picked landmarks. When the sand reached his shoulders he reached for the shore. It wasn't there. The only thing left was to dive to safety, but which way? Maybe he'd turned too much or not enough. He tried to shift to his right, then his left. It was too late; he couldn't turn anymore. The sand touched his chin . . . then crept up further and started to choke off his breathing. Then the sand found its way into his nose.

When the sand covered his mouth and filled his nose, something happened. He managed to breathe the air between the grains. A calmness washed over him. An acceptance. It was odd, but he noticed the smell all around him reminded him of fresh bread. Now he thought of Lupa—the way she would bake for them, humming in the kitchen in the safe, quiet city of Tuland.

Complete peace enveloped him. *It's a shame my travels have had to end so soon,* he thought, letting himself slip away.

This was the very last thought Remer had, and all sense of time passing was lost . . . when he felt something tighten around his shoulders. Something was pulling him. Maybe it was a wosake, but he seemed to be going upward, not being sucked down.

Suddenly, he was above the sand. Coughing and hacking to clear his mouth and throat, he inhaled the most wonderful, long breath. The soft sands were spitting him out. He was alive! He would see Asmar again. The force of the pull became gentler as he was dragged further and finally released onto firmer ground.

Dazed, disoriented, he worked to wipe the sand from his eyes. He tried to talk, but it came out as a low croak. He wanted to clear his vision, to see the beauty of the desert again; he wanted to see who had set him free.

He wasn't sure if he was dreaming, but he thought he heard muffled voices through his sand-clogged ears. Gently, a cool, damp cloth dabbed at his face, washing away more of the caked sands. He wanted to tell whoever was doing this how grateful he was. Remer could only make out the form of a hazy figure leaning over him. Slowly, his vision cleared and he could see others. Through the waning haze he suddenly was gazing into the clearest pale-blue eyes he had ever seen.

"Are you hurt?" The voice was clear and firm.

Remer shook his head. A steady hand on his back helped him to sit fully up, and he was handed a pouch of water. He drank uncontrollably until there was no more left, and then felt guilty for not leaving any for anyone else.

"Can you speak?"

"Yes, I think so," he rasped.

The figure rose and the cowl of the red talize fell back. It was a woman. Her hair was black and her skin, darkened by the sun, contrasted with the golden desert. She stood, arms crossed, her pale-blue eyes burning through him.

"Who in the name of the golden pulcher are you?" she asked.

"My name is Remer." He tried to rise to his feet, but it was too much of an effort.

"And what are you doing here?" She indicated the vastness of the desert.

"I've come from Tuland and am traveling to Dolcere."

The woman shook her head. "You're incredibly lucky we spotted you."

"How?" Remer coughed up more sand.

"We were up on that rise and saw you running toward the soft sands. We figured you were either a total idiot or you were trying to kill yourself."

Remer nodded. He knew how lucky he had been. "I assure you," he managed, as his throat started to clear, "I'm a total idiot."

The woman laughed, and it made Remer blush.

"Well Remer—it's your lucky day. We can take you part of the way to Dolcere and hopefully you'll be able to make it the rest. Where's your gear?"

Remer pointed to the soft sands.

"Ah. We can help with that also. Come, let's get you checked out and cleaned up." She reached down. Remer took her warm, calloused hand for support and pulled himself up. He held on to her hand a moment longer than maybe he should have, steadying himself and getting used to being back on his feet.

"Who can I thank for my rescue?" Remer said, getting more of his full voice back.

"I'm Areana."

Areana ... it was so familiar. In a moment, he remembered that name from Mendicus's stories—the Aris general! Embarrassed, he quickly grabbed his hand away.

"It's a real honor to meet you—I mean, be rescued by you!"

"And it is an honor to meet you, Remer of Tuland." She smiled as she bowed slightly.

"Elaxa!" she called, to a young soldier not too far off. Elaxa appeared next to them. Remer saw her red talize was cut and her leg was covered in a red-tinged bandage.

"Take Remer of Tuland to see the healers."

Remer's vision was improving and he could take in more of what was happening around him. There were many others—around two hundred Aris, all soldiers—and they were on massive horses. He'd never seen so many. As they walked through their encampment, he darted right and left to get out of the way of soldiers flowing past. The noise and smells overwhelmed him, after the two days of silence he had experienced alone in the desert. Remer was doing his best at moving through the crowd, but he soon realized his darting back and forth just kept putting him in the path of other riders. There were so many. He came to a standstill, fearing that if he kept moving, he would be trampled by the horses or the soldiers.

He heard someone shouting and turned to see a middle-aged woman instructing a woman who seemed to be about Remer's age. She was slight and was tugging at the reins of a huge, agitated gray and white-spotted horse in an effort to calm him. Her left hand held firmly to the reins; her right ... he looked for her right hand. It was gone. Just above the wrist was a bandage, stained red and covered with dark-yellow sand caked to it. Remer's stomach turned and he felt dizzy. This wasn't like a story told by Mendicus sitting at the fountain. He forced himself to look away, only to see another soldier on a dark-brown mare who had his leg bandaged below the knee, and nothing where the rest of his leg would've been.

Remer staggered when Elaxa tugged at his arm.

"I have things to do. I can't spend the day babysitting you." Remer tried to move, but he kept focusing on the carnage around him.

"Let's go!" Elaxa pulled him and Remer unfroze, as she guided him through the chaos of the encampment. Tents were set up and food was being prepared over large fires. Most of the soldiers wore red talizes, while others were in yellow. There were even a few in orange or pale purple. Everyone was in motion and busy. One soldier with a heavy bandage on one hand was feeding another who had both hands heavily wrapped. An orange-clad soldier brought a small fire to life and then put his companion's arm around his neck, bringing her closer to its warmth.

Remer wanted to help, so he looked at his books for information about healing. He reread the texts about what to do. But when he looked at the bloodshed around him, he realized this was different from the books; this was real. His hands shook when he thought about having to touch wounds and blood. He closed his eyes as he walked, trying to stop his body from trembling. But then his foot hit something, sending him tumbling to the sand, and a shout rang out. He looked up to see a yellow-cloaked figure—a man he had just tripped over—lying in the sand near him with a woman, also in yellow, working to wrap a bandage around the man's torso.

"Be careful!" the woman barked sternly.

Elaxa turned to the woman and barked back, "We should *all* be more careful."

There was sharp hostility in Elaxa's voice that Remer thought was strange to hear directed toward someone he assumed was an ally. There were others in yellow scattered about, and he noticed one soldier lying unmoving on a cart, with a large group leaning over him, speaking in hushed voices.

"Who's that?" he asked.

Elaxa looked at the commotion Remer pointed to. "Oh, that's Adomas," she said, with a dismissive wave. Remer recognized the name of another great Aris general.

"Is he badly hurt?"

Elaxa shrugged. "Don't really know. He hasn't woken since we rescued him." She paused and added almost imperceptibly under her breath, "The fool."

Remer wanted to ask why the great Aris general was a fool, but one look at her stern expression made him drop any further questions. It was only then, when he turned his gaze back to the scenes around him, that he finally noticed: the red- and yellow-talized soldiers weren't mixing. They were different tribes and there was some sort of conflict between them.

Remer and Elaxa arrived at an area with three tents, each with a golden pulcher painted on its side. This was the symbol of the healers. Elaxa strode up to one of the red-clad healers and pointed back at Remer. The healer nodded and Elaxa motioned for him to come over.

As he approached, the healer was given a bowl with water to rinse her bloodied hands. "What in the name of the golden pulcher happened to you?" the healer said, beginning to wipe the sand from Remer's face with her smooth, cool hands. He noticed there was still dried blood under her short nails.

"Soft sands," Remer answered, his voice still raspy. The healer's hands peeled open his eyelids and pulled at his ears. Next she rapped him on the back and asked him to breathe deeply.

"Nothing major wrong with you. We just need to get the sand out," she concluded. She had an assistant come over with a large sac of water and dump it over his head, and then put a metal stick in his ears to scrape out the sand. It hurt at first but he was feeling better after this cleansing.

Elaxa returned then and handed him a red talize and a new pack that had a rust-red slash on it. Remer presumed it marked the owner as a member of Areana's tribe. Elaxa moved to take his father's now tattered, sand-caked talize, but Remer wouldn't let it go.

"This belonged to my father," he said. "Like the pack."

"Your father's talize is ruined. It'll never function properly again, not in that condition. And we certainly can't spare a mender to try to fix it. Your father's pack and everything in it are at the bottom of the soft sands."

Remer nodded sullenly. He looked at the battered remnant of his father's talize and carefully folded it up. He put it away in the pack Elaxa had given him.

"I'm sorry your father's things are gone," she said, softening a little. "This pack belonged to Rou. I want you to know—he was a great friend." Remer noticed her use of past tense. "You're extremely lucky to be alive, Remer of Tuland."

Remer looked at the talize and the pack she had given him. The slash that he thought was a mark of the tribe, he now realized was dried blood. He swallowed hard and nodded at Elaxa.

Elaxa seemed to accept this and left to resume her duties, while Remer stayed and watched the healers. A steady stream of soldiers came to have their wounds cleaned and healing remedies administered. He watched the healers remove dirty blood-soaked bandages and replace them with clean ones. They inspected the wounds and then treated each soldier differently, although Remer wasn't entirely sure why.

Out of curiosity, he decided to consult his books. Several of them covered a range of medical practices, and one even had some illustrations. He moved through those pages devoted to caring for battle wounds and began to understand what the healers were doing. They were looking for redness and pus, the signs of infection. If there was an infection, a solution of sagu root and water was applied, but if not, just clean water was used. The master healer, a stern woman with short silver hair, tried to look over everything, but there were too many injured. A young healer treated one soldier after another and struggled to keep up with the steady flow. Remer watched him remove old red-soaked bandages from a soldier with a deep leg wound and wash it with clean water then re-bandage it. That wasn't right—the wound was infected and desperately needed the antiseptic treatment. He saw the soldier was being helped away by his comrades. Should he say something? Who was he to question the healer?

Instinctively Remer walked over to the soldier, trying to keep the healer from seeing or hearing him. "Please, can I take another look at the wound?"

"It's just been looked at," the soldier said, and started limping away again with his comrades.

"That was just the preliminary treatment. You need the next treatment as well."

"Are you a healer? I don't remember seeing you here before."

The soldier again turned to walk away.

Remer blurted out, "Your leg is infected and you need antiseptic treatment. All you got was water, and if you don't get it the treatment, you might die!" Remer stopped, realizing his voice was louder than he had intended. The commotion brought the older healer over.

"What is going on here?"

"This man needs antiseptic for his leg," said Remer, calmly.

"Rafe!" the healer called, and the other younger healer came over. "How did you treat this soldier?"

"I don't remember," said Rafe, uncertainly. "I think with antiseptic."

Remer was shaking his head. "No, it was water, and the leg's infected."

"How do you know that?" asked the master healer.

"It had all the signs."

"And what are they?"

Remer knew he was being tested. "There was swelling and redness around the affected area," he said, "and also red streaks and pus."

"Let's take a look." The master healer unwrapped the new bandage and examined the wound. "Rafe, get the antiseptic." The young healer did as he was told, and the soldier was quickly, efficiently treated and sent on his way.

"We'll discuss this later," the elder healer said to Rafe, and then she left to care for other patients.

When she was gone, Rafe and Remer looked at each other in awkward silence.

"Thank you," Rafe said, finally.

"You don't mind?"

"Of course I mind," said Rafe, gravely, but then his face grew softer. "I *mind* that I could have killed that soldier."

Relief washed over Remer.

"There've been too many to treat. I don't know what to do half the time. And it was even worse immediately after the battle."

"It must have been terrible," Remer said, trying to imagine how much worse things could've been.

"You have no idea," Rafe said, shuddering visibly. "Can I ask—who are you?"

"Remer. I'm a Tulander."

Rafe stared at him blankly. "What's a Tulander doing out in the desert?"

"That's a long story."

"I'd like to hear it." Rafe paused, and then asked, "Do you have anywhere to stay?"

Remer shook his head.

"C'mon, I'll look after you until they figure out where to put you," said Rafe. "I owe you that."

The sun was sinking, and the winds would begin soon. The Aris started preparations for the night, pitching tents with heavy stakes so they sloped away from the north, away from the direction of the wind. Doing this protected the front of the tent, so a fire could be lit against the cold. Remer tried to heed the words of his cousin—to observe. He watched the horses with their broad hooves crisscrossing the camp, carrying supplies and soldiers to different tents. He noticed the carts with their extra-wide wheels to prevent them from sinking into the sands, and he saw how the soldiers carried a liquid fuel to start their fires, unlike in Tuland where wood was more plentiful. Rafe told him that the fuel was a gift from the wizards who had the liquid mixed in Dolcere.

There was a constant flow of soldiers in their talizes colored in shades of red, yellow, orange, and purple. The soldiers were almost as diverse as their talizes. There were about an equal number of men and women, and they ranged in age from elders, like the healer, to approximately Remer's age.

As the sun set, the colors of the desert sprang to life. Rafe invited Remer to sit beside him outside his tent, and he began to recount the battle with the Sitire.

"I wasn't a healer when we started the march." Rafe laughed. "I'm not much of a healer now, either. How did you know that soldier had an infection?"

"He had all the symptoms, straight out of the book."

"I never read any books about it."

"What happened with the Sitire?" Remer asked. He didn't want to tell Rafe about the books in his head. He had learned from experience that others never understood, and pretty much avoided him once they found out, as if he was a freak—which, he guessed, he was.

"The Sitire were attacking our farms and we had to stop them. We chased them halfway around the desert until we caught them. But then they caught us." Rafe shook his head. "We raided a camp where we thought there were only thirty of them, but there were *three hundred*. They were hiding in the sand, the cowards. Fortunately, we were all on horseback and they were mostly on foot, otherwise every last one of us would be dead."

"Why couldn't you see them in the desert? There's nowhere to hide." Remer asked, gripping the hot cup of weak tea Rafe had given him.

"There are always places to hide if one knows how to do it."

"But..." Remer looked into the starlit black expanse that arched over them, and then thought: *The Sitire are out there, still.* The desert had almost killed him once. He didn't want to give it a second chance.

"Remer, it was a bloodbath. There were Sitire everywhere. Things really felt lost until Areana took charge." Rafe paused; his gaze seemed distant, as if he was seeing the battle again. "We tried to keep up with the commander. That's our rule, the commander is never alone. We always protect her." Remer nodded, understanding. "But there were too many of them. Aving—she was my direct commander—she got hit almost right away." Rafe paused again.

"Is she being looked after by the healers?" Remer prodded.

Rafe shook his head and looked down.

"What...?"

"Dead. A spear went through her. She was right in front of me. If she hadn't been hit, it would've been me." Rafe wiped away a tear as he looked up to the sky and out into the blackness.

Was this what happened to his father? Remer wondered. He had been ambushed as well. Remer touched Rafe's arm. "There was nothing you could do."

"I know that." Tears were now streaming down Rafe's face. "That's the problem." He took deep breaths to calm himself. "But that wasn't the worst of it. There was this— this creature with them. It sort of looked human, but not really. It seemed..." Rafe's voice trailed off.

"It seemed like what?" Remer asked, as he was frantically searching his mind to see what this creature could be. Nothing came up in any of his books. How could nothing come up?

"It seemed like death." A silence hung between them. "If only Adomas—" Rafe started, but then stopped and went into the tent.

Remer sat a little longer by the dying flames of their fire, but then he followed Rafe inside to where Rafe had made him a makeshift bed. He was more tired than he could ever remember. Every single inch of his body ached. He wanted to rest but when he did, he felt the sand sucking him downward. He searched his memory for the book that would explain it all to him, but the books weren't there. In the distance the wolves were calling. He sat up with a start, expecting to see the eyes of the wolf staring down at him. The only thing he saw was Rafe, tossing and turning under his thin blanket. Remer looked into his mind again, his panic subsiding when he saw that the books had returned once more. His heart stopped pounding. He was afraid that if he fell back asleep, his precious library would disappear again. After all that had happened, he realized his books couldn't save him. He knew nothing real, and the books only gave him a false sense of security.

Remer left the tent, clutching his red talize for warmth. The sky was covered with stars. In Tuland there were some nights like this, but mostly the moisture from the sea obscured a clear view of the stars. He always wondered about them—what they were, how many were there out there. He had searched for books that would tell him about the stars, but once again, they had let him down.

"Bad dreams?" a deep voice asked.

Remer turned. It was a tall man, his red talize looking nearly black in the moonless night.

"How did you know?" Remer asked.

"Everyone's getting them."

Remer nodded and introduced himself.

"I know who you are. I was there when the general saved you. I'm Mar, one of General Areana's lieutenants. I was looking for you to let you know the general would like you to ride with her when we break camp in the morning. I'll provide you with a horse."

"I—I can't ride." Remer felt inadequate among all these soldiers who knew how to do so many things that he didn't. In Tuland he had been the one to know more than anyone else—at least more than any other student. Here, knowledge from books seemed to mean nothing.

"You'll double with me, then. See you in the morning."

Remer somehow managed a dreamless night and felt less panicked when he awoke the next day. The morning air was clear, and waves of heat were already rippling off the desert. He looked out and wondered if the Sitire were out there, waiting for him. Soldiers were everywhere, milling about and making preparations. What had been so strange the night before was already accepted and familiar now. The horses no longer scared him and the soldiers with amputated limbs didn't make him recoil.

Remer was standing in front of Rafe's tent, just taking everything in, when Mar rode up on an immense horse with fierce eyes that seemed to bore into Remer, they were so intense. Mar offered a hand up into the saddle, but Remer backed away. Mar laughed. "She's actually quite tame and loves to have her neck rubbed." Mar stroked the horse's mane. "Go ahead."

Tentatively, Remer stepped toward the horse with his hand outstretched. He reached out and, holding his breath, lightly touched the horse's neck, and then quickly drew his hand away. She was soft; he hadn't expected that. He reached out again and laid his hand on the horse. This time he felt the warmth of the animal. She nodded, and her nods felt welcoming. Remer smiled. Mar was smiling broadly too, and he offered his hand down to Remer once again, who grabbed it and was pulled into the saddle. Rafe now appeared, smiling as he watched Remer get settled in the saddle awkwardly in front of Mar, and called up to him, assuring him there would always be space for him in his tent if he needed it. Remer thanked him gratefully, and then he, Mar, and the horse were on their way to join Areana.

The Aris camp packed up and started moving out quickly and efficiently as they rode up to Areana. The general briefly acknowledged Remer, but then turned her attention back to her soldiers.

Remer adjusted to life on the back of Mar's horse. He watched carefully how Mar controlled her, firmly yet gently. Remer started to access his library to learn how to do what he saw everyone else doing, but abandoned the idea in favor of learning from practice. He insisted Mar show him how to construct a tent against the fierce winds, how to light fires, how to break down and pack a tent, and even how to ride a horse.

Each morning they would join Areana at the head of the column, and each day she acknowledged them only briefly, but maintained that same far-away, searching gaze, focused out across the sands.

After the first few days, he finally asked Mar what the Aris general was searching for.

"A trap."

Remer made it a habit after that to take time to also look out into the desert and try to see something, but all he saw was the same thing he had seen since he first set foot on sand: the endless expanse of desert and a dune that was always far away in the distance.

After days of staring into the nothingness of the desert, Remer didn't see but rather felt a familiar presence. He turned to Mar, saying, "There is something out there."

"I don't see anything," Mar replied, staring out and squinting. "The sand can really play tricks on your eyes."

"There *is* something," Remer said, insistent. Mar stared again at him, and this time he took out a small spyglass and focused in the direction Remer pointed—and he saw.

He immediately guided his horse forward in the column to Areana. She nodded, altering the direction of the entire column toward the nearly unseen speck in the desert. The image gradually grew larger. Eventually, it was distinguishable as two figures.

By midday, Remer knew who they had found.

Areana pulled up her horse as the taller of the figures came forward to meet her. Remer ran past both of them toward the second figure, knocking him over with the full force of his hug.

"What in the name of the golden pulcher are you doing here?" Asmar said, as he got to his knees. He stared at Remer in disbelief, reaching out to embrace him. "I can't believe it!"

"I've been following since you left Tuland."

"And you brought an entire army with you!" cried Asmar, laughing incredulously and pointing to the massive column of Aris.

Remer looked over his shoulder. "I can explain that."

"Later—I'm just so, so glad you are here. What were you doing out in the desert anyway?"

Remer was caught off-guard by the question.

"Don't you remember?"

Asmar only looked confused.

"We took an oath," Remer said, slightly hurt. "If one of us were called to Dolcere, the other would follow."

"Yes, but..." said Asmar tentatively. "I didn't think you'd actually come." Remer looked down at the sand. "But I'm really glad you did." Asmar put a comforting hand on Remer's shoulder. "How did you end up with these Aris soldiers?"

"They actually found me—and thank the golden tree they did. I sort of got myself stuck in the soft sand. They had seen me from quite a distance away. Areana—she's the general—said she saw me walk right into the sands and couldn't believe anyone could be so idiotic. She half thought I was trying to kill myself." He laughed. "She came just in time to pull me out."

Asmar then told Remer his own experience with the wosakes.

"We're lucky to be alive," Remer told his cousin.

"Where are the Aris coming from, Remer?"

"Battle with the Sitire," Remer said. "They say that the Sitire have a soldier that's not human. They say he doesn't fight but paralyzes you with fear." Remer stopped.

Mendicus disappeared with Areana while camp was being set up again for the night. Meanwhile, Remer took Asmar around and introduced him to Rafe and Mar. Asmar and Remer walked among the wounded soldiers and talked to them. Remer couldn't hear what Asmar said, but each time he walked away, the soldier seemed calmer.

As the two cousins helped the healers, Mendicus appeared with Areana and Adomas, the man in the yellow talize that had been lying unconscious. Mendicus helped Adomas stay on his feet as he stumbled unsteadily forward.

"That's Adomas," Remer informed his cousin. The two watched as Adomas was walked around the camp. Those in yellow came up to him and would talk to him or touch his talize gently. Those in red walked away as he came near. Adomas didn't seem to notice either.

The soldiers all settled into a routine over the coming days. Mendicus spent most of his time with Areana and Adomas and left the two cousins to themselves. On the twenty-first day of the journey out of Tuland, Mendicus sought out the cousins for a rare visit and to prepare them.

"We're leaving the soldiers," he said. "From this point on, we travel our own road to Dolcere."

Remer felt disappointed at leaving the new friends he had made, and a bit afraid of venturing back into the desert without the Aris soldiers, especially with the Sitire still out there. But he had come all this way to be with Asmar, and Asmar was heading toward Dolcere, so he dutifully said his farewells to Areana and her lieutenants, Mar and Elaxa. Embracing Rafe, Remer encouraged him to become a full-time healer, so Rafe wouldn't ever have to be on a battlefield, but he knew that Rafe would likely be called to duty. It was the Aris way.

Remer watched the army retreat away from them into the desert, their forms rippling and blurring in the rising heat until they were no more than specks in a sandstorm on the horizon.

Finally, when the Aris column was fully out of sight, Mendicus turned to Remer and Asmar.

"We've arrived."

Remer and Asmar looked around, but they saw only desert. Remer was the first to blurt out, "There's nothing here!"

"No," came Mendicus's flat response, "you *see* nothing here."

"That's what I said," Remer retorted, defending himself. "I don't see a city anywhere near here."

Asmar said quietly, "The city is hidden, isn't it?"

"That's correct," replied Mendicus, "but in a way, it's not hidden. It just can't be found unless you know how to see it."

"I don't understand," said Remer.

"I think I do," said Asmar, suddenly.

Mendicus smiled, replying, "Follow me closely and I'll show you the way into Dolcere, but soon you must learn the way yourself, Asmar."

Remer couldn't help but note he was excluded from this.

"Grasp my hand," Mendicus said. A hand was only offered to Asmar, who took it and extended his free one to

Remer. Walking hand in hand, they went slowly forward. After three steps, there came a blinding light.

After three more steps, Asmar jostled Remer. "It's okay," Asmar assured him, "the light is gone."

Remer tentatively opened one eye and then the other. He gasped softly, in awe: a huge city spread out before him. It was an oasis—lush and green, a sharp contrast to the desert that surrounded it.

"It's beautiful!" he said, in delight and amazement. Asmar let out a laugh of relief.

Homes of dried white sand rose about him, flanked by tall trees that bristled with gently swaying fronds of green at their tops. Bustling lanes were bordered by gardens of native grasses and flowering sagu as the people went about their business. In the distance, a tower rose high above all the other structures.

"That must be the tower of the wizards," Remer said in a hushed voice.

Turning to look behind them, Remer could see the desert where they had just been. But no one could see the wizards' city of Dolcere from the desert.

Placed around the perimeter of the city stood an array of large, finely cut crystals. Each one, roughly the size of a person, was mounted vertically on spires that held them at eye-level. Their angles and multicolored facets reflected the light so expertly that the city was completely invisible from the outside. The crystals must have caused the blinding light they saw, Remer thought.

The trio walked briskly together down the city's hard-packed sand roads, past homes also made from the baked sands of the desert. The cousins followed closely behind the desert-worn Mendicus. Their disheveled and tattered appearance was a contrast to the tidy, well-tended homes that lined Dolcere's streets. Remer noticed the eyes of the townspeople following them as they passed, and those in the street would step aside with a slight deferential bow of their heads. Mendicus seemed to accept this tribute silently, as if he expected it.

"Remer," Asmar said, trying to get his cousin's attention.

"What?" Remer responded.

"Have you noticed how everyone is looking at us—and at Mendicus?" whispered Asmar.

"It's pretty hard to miss."

As they turned down a new street, the tower they had seen before rose into view.

"I have a feeling that's where we're going," said Remer. "I read about it in one of the books." The tower was massive. It clearly dwarfed all the other buildings in the city, rising ten times the height of any other, its body the color of sand. It reflected the sunlight, giving off a faint iridescent hue.

Remer consulted the books he knew that were written about Dolcere, and the tower in particular. Some of them were ancient.

Asmar looked at him with concern. "What's wrong, Remer?"

"What? Oh. Nothing. It's just that the book that tells of the tower was written before the wizards came to Dolcere."

"So?" his cousin asked.

"So, it means the wizards didn't build it."

"No, I suppose not," Asmar replied.

"So who did?" asked Remer. His books didn't divulge the identity of the builders, and neither he nor Asmar had the inclination to ask Mendicus.

Finally, they arrived at the foot of the great tower, the home of the wizards.

A massive solid gate stretching three times Remer's height and fashioned from the metals drawn from the Caute mines barred their way. Mendicus gently laid his hand on the gate and it smoothly moved on its hinges, opening to reveal a large entrance hall with floors inlaid with bronze and silver pulcher tiles. The three passed through the sacred doorway and the cousins stood in wonderment inside the hall where the work of craftspeople were displayed. There were bronze pulcher statues from the workshops of Tuland, delicate blown glass bowls made by the Aris, and intricately carved violet candleholders from the gems mined and crafted by the Cautes.

Everything was so exquisite that Remer was transfixed. He could spend a lifetime in this room alone and never tire of it.

A voice cut through Remer's trance and shook him. It was Mendicus, looking impatiently at Remer, but only uttering a terse, "Follow me."

The two followed Mendicus up a carved stairway of marbled stone and bronze pulcher to a doorway more remarkable for its lack of ornamentation in contrast to the hall where they had previously been. Mendicus opened the door, revealing a small, plain, sparsely furnished room, and said, "Wait in here." He closed the door behind him. Asmar and Remer heard it lock.

"Guest... or prisoner?" Remer asked Asmar, who shrugged his shoulders.

"I'm not sure we're either, cousin."

CHAPTER 8

THE COUSINS STARED AT THE gray walls of the small, cool room they found themselves locked in. The desert sand had permeated every pore of their bodies and the irritation and itchiness had Remer rubbing his back up against the course sandstone wall. He walked to the door and tried pushing, then pulling. It was locked.

"What do they want with you?" Remer asked, turning back to Asmar.

Asmar shrugged and sank to the floor. Remer came over and sat down next to him and the two waited for something to happen. Time passed, and Asmar started to wonder if they had been forgotten, when suddenly he heard a clanking and the heavy door swung open. Asmar expected to see Mendicus but instead, two young men, only a few years older than the cousins, stood in the doorway. He slowly rose to his feet, as did Remer, and tensed himself, preparing to sprint from the room—but then relaxed, realizing that he had no idea where to head, even if he succeeded.

One of the young men in the doorway spoke.

"We were told to give these to you."

The taller young man handed a soft white robe to Asmar and a gray one to Remer. The other, about Asmar's height, carried an empty bowl and a pitcher filled with water. Two small towels were draped over his arm. He looked around the empty room for somewhere to put them and, seeing no furnishings, placed them down in a corner of the floor.

"Why are we here?" Remer asked them. Asmar saw Remer also looking at the open door.

The taller one shrugged. "I assume to fashion the pulcher. That's what they expect of us Tulanders. We were just told to get you cleaned up." After a brief pause, they hastily retreated out the door. Asmar heard the lock click.

Remer went to the pitcher and poured some water into the bowl and splashed his face. "Well, at least it's warm."

Asmar turned to see his cousin stripped to his waist and pouring water over his head.

Soaking one of the towels, Asmar ran it down his cousin's sand-coated back before taking the clean one to his own face.

"I don't think I'll ever be free from the desert," Remer said, finishing up washing as best he could and reaching out for the gray robe. "But we made it. We're actually in Dolcere." Asmar handed him the gray robe and went over to the basin and poured the remaining water over himself. It was cool now but felt refreshing.

"It's more spectacular than I had imagined." Asmar replaced his own sand-colored talize with the white robe. He lightly touched the bronze ring on his finger, feeling the power of the golden one come through from underneath.

"Do you think he was right? That you're meant to work the pulcher?" asked Remer.

Asmar straightened his robe. "I couldn't even make a spoon out of the bronze. They certainly couldn't want me for my carving skills, so it has to be something else."

"I agree, but what else can you do?" Remer blushed. "I mean there's lots you can do, but..."

Asmar laughed and was about to say something when the lock rattled and again the door opened. This time, a tall man dressed in the shimmering blue robes of a wizard entered. He held a silver pulcher staff whose glow warmed the barren room. Asmar recognized him even with his beard shaved off and his hair cut short: it was Mendicus.

"You're a wizard!" Remer blurted out, eyes wide.

"Come with me," Mendicus responded, in a voice that was low and commanding—and directed at Asmar, who felt himself being pulled forward.

He resisted the impulse to move and forced himself to look Mendicus in the eyes.

"What about Remer?" he demanded.

Mendicus's firm gaze bore deeply into Asmar.

"He stays here."

Asmar nodded. He stopped fighting the force that was pulling at him. As he trudged forward, he thought of

Remer, and with an effort, he turned his head to look over at his cousin. Remer's eyes were glazing over. Something was wrong.

Asmar turned his body and forced himself to move back toward his cousin. It felt as if he was fighting through the strong winds he had battled in the desert. When he was facing his cousin, he slowly placed his hands on Remer's shoulders.

Asmar stared into Remer's eyes and didn't see him. It was as if his body were there but his mind had disappeared.

"Remer!" Suddenly, life came back into the body and Remer's eyes cleared. He smiled gently at Asmar.

"Go with him now, Asmar." Remer touched Asmar's hand still resting on his shoulder. "I'll be alright." As Asmar turned to leave, Remer whispered, "But we will stick together."

Asmar and Mendicus left the room, the door closing heavily behind them, but, Asmar noted, it remained unlocked.

They walked slowly down a long corridor of golden sandstone with floors and ceiling of the most intricately carved bronze and silver pulcher Asmar had ever seen. A warm, even light flooded the hall and made it seem like they were almost floating. Asmar searched for a light source but couldn't see one anywhere. Mendicus led Asmar to a large open foyer where the ceiling rose up over them, tripling in height. Two massive doors of silver pulcher carved with geometric figures stretched upward.

Asmar felt dizzy as his eyes followed the intricate designs all the way to the top. There was nothing like this in Tuland. The high vaulted ceiling and the magnificence surrounding him made him feel small and insignificant, but he was drawn to the marvels Dolcere offered. He knew he was meant to be here.

Mendicus's almost imperceptible touch caused the massive doors to silently glide open, revealing an enormous meeting hall. An oval table of translucent desert glass sat at its center. The room was bathed in a cool golden light which, in hitting the curve of the faceted table, bent into rainbows that danced upward, playing on the ceiling. Asmar again looked in vain for the light source. It was nowhere to be found.

Around the table, Asmar counted nine chairs, each of an opaque blue stone. He thought Remer might know the name of this stone from one of his books—and for a moment he again heard in his head his cousin's plea to stick together. The seats were filled by clean-shaven men with close-cropped hair, all wearing the same shimmering robes as Mendicus: the robes of the wizards. Four chairs were empty.

Asmar knew exactly where he was. This was the Council of Wizards, just as it was described in the stories Mendicus had told. His knees grew weak. Why had he been summoned here? He stopped shaking and made himself focus.

The seat at the head of the table was larger than the others and carved with the same geometric patterns that adorned the doors. The chairs at both the head and foot of the table were unoccupied. Each wizard held a glowing staff of pure silver pulcher just like Mendicus's. Asmar's eyes kept darting around the chamber, taking in all the details. With a slight nod from Mendicus, Asmar was directed to the foot of the table.

"Stand there," Mendicus instructed.

Asmar did as he was told; Mendicus circled the table and moved to the tall, throne-like chair at its head. There, the thin old man—the one that Asmar had known for most of his life as a storyteller, who had taken him from the only family he had ever known, and who had guided him through the desert—took his seat at the head of the table. Asmar remained standing.

"I am Preadus," he said, looking back at Asmar.

Asmar grasped the icy back of the blue stone chair to steady himself. Mendicus was not only a wizard, but the most powerful wizard of all. Mendicus had been hunched, with a long knotted white beard and gray scraggly hair. Preadus was old but majestic, clean-shaven, with close-cropped hair. He stood tall and straight, and strength along with quiet power emanated from him. It was Preadus's icy blue eyes that drew Asmar in—the eyes that looked through you; the eyes that seemed to know your every thought.

"We have nine seats at this table."

It took Asmar a moment to realize Preadus was speaking to him.

"According to the holy writings of the Koan, it is necessary to have a council of nine to fulfill the Promise of the Trees."

Asmar nodded even though he didn't understand. Why nine? What was the Promise of the Trees?

"Six seats are currently occupied. One wizard is guarding the tower room. One was murdered . . . by one of our own. The wizard who killed him has fled north. We now number eight." Preadus paused and Asmar absorbed the implication of his words. A wizard murdered, and the murderer was still a member of the council. The very idea was shocking. Asmar had always thought wizards, with all of their powers and abilities and knowledge, couldn't be killed.

Preadus cleared his throat. Asmar detected a hesitancy, a sadness.

"We need nine to be complete, and I—we have selected you, Asmar, for this role."

Asmar was lost in Preadus's blue eyes. He shook his head to make sure he understood. Words stuck in Asmar's throat.

"I'm . . . a *wizard*?" Asmar finally blurted out, loud enough to create an echo in the chamber.

Preadus tried to subdue his smile and he gently corrected.

"Not yet, son. You'll have to earn that honor."

Now Asmar's head was spinning. Had Preadus just called him *son*? Could such a thing be true? No, no, no—it had to just be an expression. Asmar steadied himself again and nodded humbly to the most powerful of all wizards.

"I don't understand. What do you need me to do?"

"All in good time. Lupa has taken care of you and helped in your training." Mendicus looked away and added quietly, "As unwilling as she was." Preadus looked back at Asmar. "We now come to the point where we need your consent and participation to complete your training. It is for that reason we brought you here."

There was a pause. Asmar suddenly realized he was expected to speak. He wanted to ask what Preadus knew about him, and more about Lupa's involvement. He tried to remember the stories Lupa had told him about his family, about his mother, the plans Lupa and his mother had made growing up, and what they did when they were children. But that's where her stories had always stopped.

As little as he knew about his mother, he knew even less about his father. Asmar tried to picture him but couldn't. Lupa had never told him what he looked like, except that he was tall. That was it—he had been tall, and he carved the golden pulcher. Preadus was tall and had a golden pulcher staff, or at least that's what the stories had said. He thought of the ring Lupa had given him—his mother's ring. Was Preadus the one who carved it? The ring was his only link to his identity and history, but it told him nothing.

Locking his eyes with Preadus's, Asmar asked, "Why do you need *me*?"

Preadus nodded. "You deserve to know the story. Great strife has befallen us. It was my son who disagreed with the council and was unwilling to abide by our ways and decisions. He committed two very serious crimes. He killed a fellow wizard—a good and kind man . . ." Preadus paused. "And then he stole and misused the greatest treasure of the council, one that gives him power beyond that of any other: he stole the staff of the golden pulcher, and then fled north. He's using his power, augmented by the staff, to attack us, and is causing great harm and misery."

Preadus paused and stared even more deeply into Asmar's eyes.

"You alone can reclaim the staff."

All of these words spun around in Asmar's head. He didn't understand why he alone could reclaim the staff. He realized he didn't even know who he was. Was Lupa even his aunt?

Asmar's voice seemed to come from far away inside himself. He managed to say out loud but in barely a whisper, "I don't think I can."

Preadus replied gently, "The seven of us united wield great power, but even we can't hold out for long against the golden pulcher staff. My son has corrupted the staff and uses it for evil purposes: to enter the minds of others in order to alter how they think. This is against the ways of the elders and the teachings of the Koan.

"If we can bring my son Malzus back to us and turn him back to the teachings of the Koan, many lives will be spared. If we don't get him back in line," Preadus concluded, his eyes downcast, "he will eventually be far too strong and beyond our ability to help. His destruction will go unchecked."

There was silence. Asmar was overwhelmed by everything he was told. Wizards killing other wizards, wizards destroying minds... how was this even possible? And what did the Great Wizard think he, Asmar, could do about such serious threats? As if reading his thoughts, Preadus continued.

"Asmar, we wish you to join this council as an initiate. Here in Dolcere you'll be trained and, in time, become a wizard. We'll also give you special training so that you will be unable to misuse the golden staff once it's in your possession. When your training is complete, your mission will commence: to retrieve the staff and bring it back to the council for purification." Preadus paused. "Will you accept your place at the council?"

Asmar looked at the wizards. They were all so impossibly old. Their tired, drawn faces seemed like they'd each been carved from the same cold blue stone as the chairs. How could they expect him—an outsider from Tuland and never particularly talented at anything—to fight a wizard that *they themselves* couldn't defeat, and to retake the golden staff? This all seemed fantastic and completely impossible.

"I can't do what you need of me," he said, looking at them gravely.

"Asmar, it's not a question of *if* you can do this. *You are the only one who can*," Preadus replied.

Asmar shook his head, refusing to believe Preadus. "And if I fail?"

"The deaths of many, many innocents, including your own Tulanders, will sadly be assured."

Asmar's mind ached, trying to take in all he was being told. He was sure the wizards had erred in some calculations somewhere. But, he thought, *they were wizards, how could they make a mistake?* And how could he do any of this alone? If he was going to do this, he would need help from someone he could trust. He remembered Remer's warning, *"Don't let them separate us."*

"I—I will try"—Asmar forced the words out—"but only if Remer stays with me."

Preadus shook his head. "Impossible. He'll be returned to Tuland and his mother, as soon as we can safely transport him."

"He stays," Asmar replied automatically—surprised by the firmness of his own words.

Preadus looked shocked.

"That's impossible. He is too young and inexperienced."

What Preadus said made sense; Remer was young. It wasn't safe for him to stay. Preadus was a wizard and had saved Asmar's life; Preadus must know what was best. Asmar started to nod in agreement, but somewhere deep within, Asmar knew he needed Remer—that they must stay together at all costs. He imagined himself alone in Dolcere, surrounded by these cold, stern men who didn't know him or care about him. Who wanted to send him on a mission he couldn't possibly complete or even survive. He realized in this moment how much he needed Remer; he needed his cousin's love. These thoughts rose within him and were, at the same time, being pushed out of his head, but he grabbed and held on to them as if they were an inseparable part of him.

"Remer stays!" Asmar shouted. The room echoed, and the wizards all stared in amazement. Asmar rose up from his chair stiffly, the yell having cleared his head. He stared defiantly back at Preadus.

Preadus was nodding.

"Very well," said the Great Wizard, with a new look of respect in his eyes. "Remer stays. So it is agreed. Welcome, Initiate Asmar, to the Council of Wizards."

Asmar now fully expected to be whisked away immediately for some unusual ritual. Instead, he was guided through hallways to a different part of the wizards' tower from where he and Remer had been detained. Gradually, he began to absorb the significance of what had happened, the full magnitude of what was going on, and the dreadful mission he had now been tasked with completing.

His escort led him to a small room on the ground floor. When the door was opened, Remer stood before him, waiting.

Asmar couldn't contain himself.

"I'm a wizard!" he blurted out, as soon as the two were left by themselves.

Remer stared back at his cousin and tried to correct him.

"You mean you were *with* the wizards, you spoke with them," he said.

"No—Remer, listen to me. I *am* a wizard. An actual wizard. Or, at least, I will be one when they train me. Can you believe it, I am going to train to be a wizard!"

"I ..." Remer let the thought hang in the air.

Asmar felt the impulse to run over to his cousin and hug him, but then he remembered what Preadus had said: Lupa knew who he was; she had deceived him. Asmar suddenly stopped himself from running to his cousin. Was Remer also in on the deception? Who could he actually trust?

He needed to know the truth.

"Are you really my cousin?" Asmar asked, hoping desperately that the answer was yes. If not, his whole life would be a lie.

"What?" Remer shook his head and seemed shocked by the question.

"They told me that Lupa knew all along. Were you a part of this, too?"

"Of course I was!" Remer crossed his arms indignantly. "Actually, right from the moment I was born, they gave me a list of things I needed to do to assist in your training. You remember when I was a baby and threw up on you—that was part of your training. I did a pretty great job, wouldn't you say?"

Asmar looked back at him. Of course Remer couldn't have been part of the plot.

"Are you really my cousin?"

Remer shrugged. "I actually don't know. But what difference does it make? We've always been more like brothers than cousins, anyway."

Asmar looked closely at Remer, seeking any sign of deception. There was none. Remer was his cousin and Lupa, his aunt—or if they weren't, it didn't matter; they loved him, and that was what was important. Asmar hugged Remer, and his cousin hugged him back. Then Asmar said, apologetically, "Cousin, never let me question you again."

"I'll always be here for you," Remer replied with a smile, wiping the wetness from his eyes.

Asmar sat on one of the hard beds in the small room. A silence fell between the cousins until Asmar broke it by asking the question that preyed on his mind. "What do you know about wizards, Remer? How does anyone 'become' one?"

Remer shook his head. "There isn't a single book that talks about it. Believe me, if there were, I would have found it ages ago. I'm afraid I can't help you."

Asmar put a hand on Remer's shoulder. "That's not true. Even if there are no books about it, you certainly can help me—I'm counting on it." Remer smiled, and Asmar went on to describe all that had happened since they had been separated. He told him about Malzus, Preadus, and the Council of Wizards. The chamber with blue stone chairs, and how he was seated at the great table of crystal that swept rainbow lights up to the ceiling. About the four empty chairs, and how he was seated opposite the great Preadus himself. He spoke of the mission they had put upon him.

"They want me to fight another wizard, Remer. How can I do that? I don't know anything about fighting, even with someone who isn't a wizard. I have never wanted to fight anyone, at all."

Remer shook his head in disbelief.

"Asmar, they must have a plan. I know this seems strange. Wait—no, it doesn't *seem* strange, it *is* strange. But I always felt there was something different about you. You knew things you shouldn't, like back in Tuland you knew about the flowers in the old couple's garden. And you think... differently. There may be something about you that we don't see, that only the wizards know."

Asmar was about to object, but then he thought... maybe Remer was right. Maybe there was a plan for him. He certainly wasn't meant to be a craftsman, that was for sure. But a wizard?

"If you stay with me, I'll try. Will you?"

"Of course," said Remer, coming forward to embrace his cousin. "Didn't I tell you to not let them separate us?"

"Good," Asmar nodded, relieved. "Because I sort of ordered them to not send you away."

"You ordered them?"

Asmar felt himself start to flush with embarrassment. "I didn't really know what I was doing."

After a pause, he continued. "Tell me, have you read anything about the wizard Malzus? I am hoping there is some mention of him in one of the books you have memorized."

* * *

"No, nothing in any book. And other than what Mendicus—I mean, Preadus—said in his stories, there's no mention of him anywhere. It's as if he doesn't exist."

When none of the wizards came for them, at the first sign of light the next morning, Asmar decided to venture out with Remer and explore Dolcere. The first thing Remer found was, of course, the library tucked into the lower levels of the wizards' tower. As if drawn to the musty smell of the ancient pages, Remer could always find where books were hiding, and the Dolcere library was filled with a vast array of books of different cultures.

The librarian, Shara, was surprisingly young, about the same age as the cousins. Her dark hair kept falling over her eyes and she was constantly brushing it back, only to have it fall again. The cousins noted instantly a very striking feature—her eyes, which were almost pure black. She had a tendency to blink quickly and then lock her gaze on you when you spoke. It made Asmar uncomfortable, but Remer didn't seem to notice. When she smiled, which was often, it made the cousins feel at home in the musty, dark dungeon air of the subterranean library.

Shara showed them where different books were housed. The volumes on the Cautes, the rugged miners of the mountains, were near the back of the library, while the ones on the desert Aris were right where you entered. There were sections on the Cherts, the horsemen of the hills. There were also books on the Sitire, Domare, and Breccians, as well as ones on more ancient peoples.

"We had a few books in Tuland that hinted about an older race, but those books were mostly destroyed," said Remer, moving his hand lightly over the bindings of the books.

"Most of the ones here are very technical," said Shara. "Some talk about building and others about rules governing behaviors and interactions. There are so many here, I think it would take too many years to go through them all."

Asmar looked at Remer and realized that this was entirely what his cousin intended to do.

"If you're interested," Shara said shyly, "there are two special books I can show you."

Shara led them back to a small, almost hidden nook in the very rear of the cavernous library.

"I've been trying to catalogue as many of the books as I can so that maybe, sometime in the future when people are more interested, they can rediscover their history. There are so many little alcoves down here that I'm always finding new books."

Shara guided them to a cramped niche tucked in behind the rows.

"I found these. If you look at the spine, these two books appear much, much older than the rest. And this one"— she indicated a large book bound in the same materials as the ones Remer had found in Tuland—"is very curious. I thought I had studied and read a lot, but this one is written in a language I've never seen before."

Remer gently took the book from the shelf, cradled it in one arm, and began leafing carefully through it.

"I'm pretty good at picking up new dialects and writing forms, but... I've also never seen anything quite like this. Most older writings I've seen are just variants of what we use now, but this—well, this is just very different."

"These are the books of the wizards," Shara told him, lowering her voice to a half-whisper. "They're written in the language of their people."

Remer pored over the two books, eyes wide as he gently turned the pages.

"How'd you come to be in charge of... all this?"

Shara blushed and looked away. "One of the wizards, Karal, needed assistance, so he took me in when I was very young," she said. "He taught me how to maintain the books so that he could have more time."

"Time for what?" Remer asked.

Shara shrugged.

Remer waited for more, but then went back to paging through the larger of the two books, intrigued.

"Have you been able to translate them at all?" Remer asked Shara.

"I did begin a translation," Shara responded. "But one day, when I had the books spread before me, one of the wizards came in. They don't come down here very often. It was Preadus himself."

"And—did he forbid you from translating them?" Remer asked.

Shara hesitated, as if unsure how to answer. "He—no— he didn't. Not that I recall. I don't think he said anything."

"Why'd you stop, then?" Asmar asked.

"I don't really know," she said. There was a flicker of confusion in her eyes. "In all the time that's passed... every time I see the books, I think I *should* start the translation again. But then I just kind of forget about it. When Preadus comes down, I hide the books from him. I'm not sure I'm allowed to translate them. And then when he leaves, I just forget about them. Until the two of you came down here, I hadn't thought of translating the books for a very long time—and I can't really say why."

"So, you've never done any work at all on the books?" Remer asked.

Shara looked around again as if to see if anyone else was lurking near, and then looked at them both very seriously.

"Before the Great Wizard came down here that day, I'd been compiling lists of words, in an attempt to assist in translating the books. The language—it seems similar to ours in terms of grammar. It's more a question of the vocabulary. I've kept the work I did hidden for a long time, and eventually I just forgot about it, but I think I remember where the list is."

Bashfully, Remer said, "If you don't mind, I'd like to help you. We could work much faster, since I don't have a need to write anything down." Then he added, a bit boastfully, "You see, I have total recall."

Shara looked up shyly. "I would be pleased if you would share my work, Remer."

From then on, Remer and Shara would spend much of their time together, going over the ancient books in the library. After their first day working, Remer reported to Asmar that Shara and he had been able to translate the books' titles. One was called *The Koan*, which meant "The Speaking" or "That Which has Been Said." The other was called *The Talum*, which meant "The Teaching" or "That Which we Teach." Asmar insisted that Remer keep working with Shara to try to find out as much as he could. But very quickly, it became clear to Asmar that as much as Remer was interested the books, he was even more interested in Shara.

On his own, and receiving no contact yet from the wizards, Asmar wandered the city of Dolcere. Compared to Tuland, it was very orderly. It was laid out in concentric circles radiating out from the wizards' tower, with streets cutting across its diameter. Tuland, by contrast, was more haphazard, less planned ... but Tuland was still home. He felt homesick but he forged ahead, exploring the streets of Dolcere. They were all paved in red and tan brick made from the desert sands packed and shaped into hard rectangles, as opposed to the simple tamped-earth streets of Tuland.

The houses of Dolcere were all built with the same hard-packed bricks that lined the roads, but each quadrant of Dolcere was home to a different people and held a different feeling and energy. In the neighborhood of the Cautes, the houses were formed of raw brick, and they gleamed as if golden in the sunshine. But on the side of town of the Aris, the brick walls were coated with a plaster of either cool gray or light brown. And in the streets of the Tulanders, the plaster walls had been whitewashed and glowed starkly, clean and bright.

The northern section of Dolcere was filled with all the smells, sights, and sounds of Tuland, and as Asmar walked there, he felt closer to home, and he found himself longing for what he had left behind—for the familiarity of Lupa, his bedroom there and the incredible aromas of Lupa's cooking. Thinking of Lupa, he wondered about her role in training him, and he fought back questions that arose in his mind. Right now, he preferred not to care about the answers. The most important question was this: had Lupa really loved him?

Asmar walked from workshop to workshop in the neighborhood of Tulanders, admiring the proud culture of his native city. At one stall, he watched the fashioning of lamps out of bronze pulcher.

"These are far superior to the ones the Cautes make from the metals they mine," the man forging the lamps boasted to Asmar, seeing him stop to watch. "The pulcher won't burn or get hot like metal." He tried to size up his spectator, recognizing a fellow Tulander.

"You're new here, aren't you?" he asked. Asmar nodded. "What's your specialty?"

"My specialty?" asked Asmar.

"Yeah, the reason they brought you here. What do you make? What material do you use, bronze or silver?"

"I'm not a craftsman."

"Not a craftsman?" The man looked puzzled. "You mean, you're working on the new crafts?"

"What new crafts?"

"Like the ones over there." The man pointed.

Asmar looked over at a woodsmith working, partially hidden by billowing puffs of gray smoke. The smith was raising his hammer and slamming it down. Each time he did, silver sparks cascaded off the bench. Dodging people and carts, Asmar hurried across the street toward the sparks for a closer look.

When he got nearer, Asmar could see the smith was working on a long, thin silver pulcher branch, banging it with a metal hammer. The smith's right arm—the one with the hammer—was larger than his left. Each time the hammer fell, a shower of silver sparks arced in the air and rained down on the bricks of the street, bouncing away in all directions. The man was too intent on his work to notice Asmar approach. He struck the branch with all his might, using the large, heavy hammer and then quickly switching to a small wooden mallet and giving gentler taps to the same branch, to direct the flow of the silver wood. What was he making? Asmar dared not interrupt.

More hard blows followed by slivers of light raining down. The wood was slowly taking shape. It was becoming longer and longer and the edges, thinner and thinner. Asmar could now make it out to be a sword. Asmar looked at the glowing sharp blade and felt a sudden icy cold wind cut through the heat of the forge.

The man finished his work and held it up to examine and admire it in the light.

"If the silver is worked right, it will never lose its sharp edge," he boasted, noticing Asmar there watching him. "The bronze is used for shields because it can absorb the impact of a blow."

He took a half-finished shield and brought it over to Asmar, all the while explaining.

"The shield must be fashioned in two layers. The thin outside shell to absorb the blow, and a thicker inner shell to protect the soldier."

Asmar walked over to see more of the stall. The work was the best he'd had ever seen. To get the different pieces to flow together as this pulcher artisan had done was incredibly difficult.

The sword was already cool to the touch, and beautiful. He reached out and gently touched the blade. He pricked his finger instantly on the sword's edge and jumped back, putting his hand up to his lips and sucking clean a small red bead of blood.

"How can you make something like this?"

The man replied, "Years of practice."

"But this is not for us. We don't do this," said Asmar, wanting to understand why a Tulander would make a weapon.

"No one asked us to fight with these tools," the craftsman said. Asmar noted he used the word "tools" instead of "weapons."

"But someone else could—and will," insisted Asmar, still trying to understand.

"That's quite different," the man began, but Asmar had already turned his back and was walking away. Did the wizards expect him to use weapons like these, made by the smith? Was this how he was expected to retrieve the golden staff? He couldn't do it, he was absolutely sure. He had made a promise to the wizards, and now he agonized that maybe, just maybe, he shouldn't have agreed so quickly.

He walked around to the stalls of other smiths, and suddenly, something clear emerged from the scenes all around him: they were all making tools of war. There was armor of bronze pulcher and collections of knives and short swords as well as devices that propelled arrows through the air. He felt fear rising up from deep inside. He was suddenly overcome with an urge to get away. Something was very wrong—these people were traitors, betraying everything Tulanders stood for.

He turned and ran toward the wizards' tower, making his way as fast as he could, knocking into people in the crowded streets. When he finally made it back to the tower, he felt cold and betrayed inside.

Under no conditions, he informed his cousin that evening as they drifted off to sleep, would he ever return to the Tuland part of Dolcere.

* * *

The next morning, with Remer heading back to the library—and to Shara—Asmar made the decision to set out to explore again, this time in a different direction. He went to the eastern part of Dolcere, where the Cautes worked on mountain stones. He watched as a stone carver chipped away at a pale-blue gem the size of his fist. It was the same color as the stone chairs in the council room. When the carver held the gem up to the light, he noticed Asmar standing there, watching.

"Hello, welcome to my workshop. I'm Meils."

Meils's face was lined, and, hunching over his bench, his back didn't seem to fully straighten. But his eyes—a pale translucent green—were sharp, clear, and alert.

"What are you carving?" Asmar asked.

"I—" He looked up at Asmar and seemed at a loss for words. Then he went on, "I'm carving light."

"What does that mean?"

Meils did not offer any words in response, but rose and beckoned Asmar to follow him into a small hut in back of the carving bench. When the door to the hut closed behind them, they were plunged into total darkness. But slowly, the room began to brighten.

Asmar turned his head from side to side, looking for the source. Just like in the wizards' tower, he couldn't find any.

"But where—?"

Meils spoke now, cutting Asmar off.

"The crystals I carve absorb the light, and when it's dark, they release it." His words were filled with pride.

"Can all the crystals do this?" asked Asmar, with more than a little awe.

Meils shook his head.

"Of course not. The blue stone is the best for absorbing light. The green stones, however, are best for bending it."

"Why would anyone need to bend light?" asked Asmar.

"To hide things, of course." Meils looked confused that anyone didn't know this. "You saw the crystals that guard Dolcere, didn't you?"

Asmar nodded.

"That's what they do. They bend the light, so it looks like the desert goes on forever. An entire city can be hidden from view and protected. It's all about the bending of light."

"And you carved those crystals too?" said Asmar, fascinated by what Meils said.

"No, not me," said Meils. "I've carved many crystals capable of bending the light, but not on that scale. I may be the best carver of the Cautes, but those crystals go way beyond my skill or that of any carver alive. No, those were carved long, long ago."

"By whom?"

"Good question."

Asmar waited, but no more of an explanation seemed to be forthcoming. Meils opened the door of the small glowing room and returned to his workbench, putting his head down to immediately focus back on the work of carving and polishing. Asmar made his way to the street and thanked him for his time.

Back on the street, there were stalls of carvers lining both sides of the alleyway, all working on gems of deep purples, reds, and yellows. There were also some there who were fashioning swords, different knives, and all types of arrowheads. Asmar again felt an inner sense of dread for what had to be preparations for war. Again he found himself returning quickly back to the tower, to the only place in this city so far where he felt any kind of peace.

Back in his chamber, Asmar didn't know what to do. He had agreed to the mission but he hadn't realized that what he was really agreeing to was going to war. It was all around him and it seemed like there was no escape.

The following morning, still being left to his own devices and receiving no instruction from the wizards, Asmar headed west into the Chert part of Dolcere. He was interested in the wild horses of the hills, which they trained. After a short time roaming the brick pathways, he found a street filled with smells he had learned at the Aris camp to associate with horses—mixed with scents of the spices, roots, and herbs that were a staple of the Cherts' cooking. It felt more exciting and different—and wild. In this part of the city, the houses were formed of bricks held together with mud and plaster. He remembered Remer showing him drawings of these buildings in books he brought home, but they looked so different in real life: warmer and more welcoming. Another thing Asmar noticed in this part of town was that half of the buildings used their ground floors as stables.

The Chert horses were smaller and stockier than those of the Aris, but still impressive. Their legs were muscled and their coats thick. Asmar thought they must be uncomfortable in the desert heat. He passed a stall where a young boy was removing a saddle from a horse with a dark-brown coat and varied white patches along the back. As Asmar walked over, the boy began to brush the horse.

"He likes being brushed," said the boy, smiling, and seeming happy at Asmar's interest.

Asmar nodded.

"You know about horses?"

"No. He's beautiful," Asmar said, looking at the horse's glossy, flowing black mane. It was clear that the horse was well cared for.

"I feel very lucky. I get to work with them every day. They're gentle animals. Why don't you give him some fruit? He likes that."

Asmar picked a red fruit slice from a bucket hanging on a nearby stall door and held it out, tentatively. The horse came over and sniffed, tickling Asmar's palm with his breath. Asmar laughed, delighted.

"I think he likes you," the boy said, smiling.

Asmar was about to ask how the boy knew what the horse liked or didn't like, but stopped short: the horse *did* like him. Somehow, he could feel it. Not only that, he also felt at peace—the first real peace he had felt since arriving in Dolcere—standing with this boy and his horse.

Asmar pulled himself away and continued onward to an open area at the intersection of one of the curved concentric-ring roads where a straight road crossed it. A corral was set up, and he reached the intersection in time to see two mounted Cherts, wooden swords held high as they spurred their horses forward. When they passed each other, they slapped the swords at the flanks of their opponent's horse, who each reared back in shock at the blow. The riders pulled forcefully on the reins.

Asmar moved forward, wanting to yell at the riders to stop the pain they were inflicting. He realized the urge wasn't from him but from the horses, who wanted the pain to stop. It was only the strength with which the riders controlled them that forced the horses to continue. Asmar wanted to cry out, to stop the riders. He moved toward the corral fence, but out of nowhere, a stocky Chert gently but firmly grabbed his arm.

"Where're you going?"

"They're hurting them."

"Of course they are. When they go into battle, these horses will face far worse. They need to be ready."

The horses turned their faces and looked at Asmar as if pleading for help, but he had none to give. He looked back at them, feeling useless.

"I need to help them," Asmar implored.

The Chert shook his head and tightened his grip. Asmar's anger swelled and he raised his arm, about to strike the Chert for letting the horses suffer. The Chert looked at him, surprised. Asmar stood frozen, then suddenly dropped his hand and fled back to the tower, ashamed at what he had almost done.

* * *

After that experience with the horses, Asmar cloistered himself in the room he shared with Remer. He told his cousin what he had seen and learned. Remer pretended to be sympathetic, but it was clear Remer only wanted to be back in the library every day. Asmar wasn't sure which reason was more important—the books or Shara. But Asmar knew he was on his own for now.

Asmar felt haunted by the pleading expressions in the horses' eyes, and for the next two days could not get himself to venture out. He mostly lingered in his room or in the halls of the tower, going over all he had seen and trying to determine what all the war preparations meant for him and his quest.

He knew he would not find the answers in his room or the hallways of the tower, so he decided to head out again—this time to the south, and to the Aris.

He prepared himself, because he knew he would see the signs of war from the Aris, just as he had seen in the other parts of Dolcere. He had already witnessed their wounded, and he felt the fear and anger and desire for retribution from the soldiers he had lived with in the desert.

Yet as he made his way into the Aris sector, he was struck by how ordinary it all seemed. Children played in the streets and parents yelled at them lovingly to be careful. Washed clothing swayed gently while drying in the breeze.

He then noticed one of the sand-colored houses he was passing had wash hanging out to dry but there was two of every outfit, clipped to the line. They were small and probably belonged to twin boys about four years old. For a brief moment he was back in Tuland and looked to his side for Remer, to share the moment. But no one was next to him. Remer was at the library with Shara. A cool breeze blew past Asmar back toward the center of the city, as he closed his eyes to stop a tear.

More and more children were now coming out of the houses around him. They all seemed to meet in the street, turn and walk together, headed in the same direction. A little girl of about seven, her hair braided down to the middle of her back, ran into him and almost knocked him over. Her cheeks brightened in embarrassment as she rubbed her forehead, which had just banged into his elbow.

"Where are you going in such a hurry?" he asked, absently rubbing his elbow.

"I'm so sorry, sir." She looked down but then smiled and looked excitedly at Asmar. "The soldiers are going to twirl their swords!" Then she scurried off to join the others.

Asmar felt pulled by his curiosity and followed the flow of the crowd to another gathering place where the curved and straight streets met. There, with onlookers lining both sides of the streets, two sword wielders stood opposite each other. The shorter of the two, who was approximately Asmar's height, wore a red talize. The other, a head taller, was in yellow. Both had their cowls up, hiding their features.

The red-cloaked figure unsheathed a crystal sword, and suddenly the air came alive with the colors of the rainbow. Violets, deep indigos, bright greens, and dark reds shot from the blade. As the curved crystal sword arched through the air, the colors connected back together, creating a rainbow circle. Then it was gone.

The crowd gasped as the yellow-robed figure, with small movements of his wrist and arm, made simple circular patterns of deep red and violet. With a slight twist, a burst of yellow was added to the delicate colored arches. Quick slashing movements created squares and rectangles that now incorporated all of the original colors, all swirling in shapes that expanded in the air.

Then it was all gone. The yellow-robed figure had placed the sword back in its sheath.

The red-clad one lifted a sword up high again and filled the empty gap in the air by slowly drawing a shimmering line that was all the shades and colors of a sunset. Then, moving deftly and slowly, the sword wielder touched points in the air and replaced the orange with indigo. Asmar suddenly caught himself holding his breath along with the others. Rainbows danced off the blade, at the same time shooting sparks of yellows and reds in the air, which were then followed by more sparks of blues and greens. With one grand flourish of the sword, the display ended with all of the colors collapsing gently into the original thin line of shimmering sunset gold and orange hues.

Now the two lifted their swords simultaneously and between them, a thin sheet of sky-blue light intersected a light-purple square. A moment later, a golden line cut through a yellow-green circle that emanated out from the center. The performance continued to build until, with two wide sweeps, the swords clashed together, creating an explosion of brilliant color: the greens and blues flying off the yellow sword wielder's blade and the crimson, purple, and golds radiating out from the red's. The crowd burst into frenzied applause as the lights radiated and faded out into the sky and the performance finished.

As the red sword wielder turned to the crowd to acknowledge the accolade, the yellow clad figure lifted their blade. Asmar felt something was wrong, but the crowd didn't seem to notice anything amiss.

Suddenly, the blade swung down toward the neck of the unsuspecting red clad figure. Asmar yelled. They looked up at the sound of a blade moving through the air and tried to leap aside, but it was too late. There was a sickening thud as the sword tore straight through the red talize. Blood gushed from a wound below the stricken sword wielder's heart. Asmar tried to move forward but was held back by the pack of spectators. The wounded figure parried the next blow, but the attacks kept coming.

Asmar needed to get to the wounded sword wielder. He pushed through the crowd and found himself in the middle of the circle with the two combatants. Another blow knocked the red sword wielder to the ground in front of Asmar, the sword now at the performer's side and clanging down on the bricks. The attacker's blade was raised for the final kill. Asmar rushed forward.

"Stop!" he shouted, mustering every last ounce of his will.

The attack slowed just enough to let its intended victim roll to the side.

Leaping in front of the injured Aris, Asmar stood eye to eye with the attacker. The sword was raised once again, and this time it was coming for him. He knew he should do something, but what?

He was frozen in place, waiting for the deadly blow.

A strong, sudden pull came from below as the blade descended, forcing Asmar off his feet and down into the dusty road, the blade ripping harmlessly through his robe.

Lying on his back, Asmar's head hurt and he felt dazed. Nearby crouched the injured Aris, who had just saved his life. A streak of blood marked where Asmar's robe had been torn. The red figure collapsed in a heap, blood oozing from the wound. Asmar struggled to his feet. What had just happened? Who was he fighting? He turned and faced the attacker, peering into the darkness of the yellow cowl. He saw a far-away, detached, and cold look in the man's eyes. The sword was raised once again. Asmar put his hands up, not knowing how to stop the blow, but knowing he had to do something. The bronze pulcher ring on his finger receded, exposing the golden pulcher ring—the gift from his mother.

The yellow-cloaked Aris's eyes instantly locked onto it.

Then a word slipped from Asmar's lips—one spoken so softly, so calmly, that it was shared only by Asmar and his assailant.

"No."

Suddenly, the man dropped the sword and collapsed to the ground. As his cowl fell back, Asmar could see the face, and the tears. He stared at him in shock. It was Adomas.

Asmar turned to the injured Aris, unconscious on the ground. Blood covered the entire right side of the robe and now moved outward in the seams of the street. He didn't know what to do. No one from the crowd moved or uttered a word.

Stop the bleeding, Asmar heard from a soft voice reaching out to him.

How? he thought.

Bind it. Use the belt, the voice insisted.

Quickly Asmar unfastened the sword belt and tore a strip from his own robe. When he was done, Preadus and two other wizards pushed through the crowd and seemed to be instantly at his side. Preadus bent down to examine the injured figure, his hands pushing back the cowl to reveal the face of Areana.

"You've done well," said Preadus to Asmar. "Now help us get her to the tower."

"What? What have I—wait, what about the other one?" Asmar asked.

"He will be taken care of," said Preadus.

The two other wizards lowered a wooden board for carrying the injured and they moved Areana onto it. Then one of them gently grabbed Adomas by the arm and those two left, moving through the crowd.

When they reached the tower, Preadus flung open its massive doors with a flick of his hand.

"To the right," came Preadus's roaring command, and the stretcher-bearers turned down the corridor. Preadus pushed aside another set of smaller doors, revealing a spotless room that seemed to be made entirely of white, milky glass. Even the walls and floors were opaque and had a glass-like gleam. In the center were positioned three clear-glass tables. Areana was set gently down on the one in the center. The wizards quickly walked to a corner basin and scrubbed their hands. Asmar was instructed to do the same.

Asmar washed the dried blood from his hands and arms thoroughly and changed into the white robe Preadus tossed to him. He realized he must have been quite a sight, with blood caked to his body, rushing through the city streets.

The wizards worked with efficiency. Asmar stood in the far corner, keeping out of the way. Preadus motioned to him.

"Come here, Asmar. You'll have to learn this if you're going to be a wizard."

He directed Asmar to come right to his side.

"You did well today," he said, while still looking at Areana. "We'll talk about it later."

Preadus pointed to Areana's prone form and explained to Asmar, "The first thing we must do is examine the damage done by the sword."

Preadus unfastened the sword belt and removed the blood-soaked bandage. The blood was now dry rather than the warm ooze it had once been.

Preadus moved deliberately and with precision. He wiped away the dried blood and produced a small piece of thread with a curved needle. Asmar's eyes looked down on her dark, soft skin. There, he could discern traces of long-healed scars. He blinked and worked to return his focus to Preadus's instruction. The wizard had now reached inside the wound and was sewing. Asmar could see an actual artery move as the needle entered and exited with amazing dexterity. Asmar cringed as Preadus joined together edges of loose flesh on the outside of the wound. It seemed like only a few more of the wizard's repeated, meticulous motions, and it was finally over—the wound was closed, and the bleeding completely stopped. All that was left was the now clean, raw line made by the thread and knitted flesh. Preadus covered Areana with a white blanket.

"We must keep her warm," he explained.

"Will she live?" asked Asmar.

"Yes, and you are a good part of the reason why."

"Why wouldn't anyone else help?"

"She's the daughter of the leader of the desert tribes. Adomas is the son of the leader of the largest tribe. The people here have loyalties to both, and if they took sides or even tried to help, there would have been a riot. This is why no one intervened. Only a wizard—and that's how they look at you—could have inserted themselves to help. This attack must've been motivated by the boy's father."

"You're wrong," said Asmar.

Preadus gave Asmar an icy stare. "You don't have an understanding of all the complexities here," he said, in a severe but controlled tone of voice.

"And *you* weren't in that circle staring into his eyes." Asmar then described to Preadus the far-away look in Adomas's eyes and how he had prevented him from striking.

"If he had truly wanted to kill Areana or me, he could have. She was unconscious and I was unarmed. Yet he let us both live. It was almost as if someone else was using him."

Preadus listened carefully. When Asmar was finished, Preadus took a moment to consider everything very deeply.

"If what you tell me is true, Asmar—and I don't doubt it anymore, after today—then you are our only hope."

He was looking down at Asmar with soft and serious eyes, and then turned to head toward his own chamber. Without looking back, he spoke again, this time directly into Asmar's mind.

"*Your training begins tomorrow.*"

CHAPTER 9

PREADUS KNOCKED ON THE DOOR to Asmar's cell with his silver staff, the loud thuds echoing down the empty corridor. He had separated the cousins. When Asmar was around Remer, Preadus noted, he became more independent. More obstinate. And that would interfere with Asmar's training.

There was a crashing sound on the other side of the door, and Preadus burst in to find Asmar sitting in a corner with the remains of the ceramic wash basin. Asmar, in his crumpled white robe, looked up quickly before covering his tear-stained face. After a moment, Asmar looked up again to the Great Wizard and cleared his throat.

"I've never seen so much blood."

His distress about the previous day's incident was not abating, and Preadus was impatient. Asmar needed to control his emotions if he was to be a wizard. Preadus nodded and placed a clean white robe on the small table, one of the few furnishings in the cold gray cell.

"You'll address the council today to explain what happened in the square, what you saw in Adomas's eyes," he instructed. He started to leave, but then stopped and turned back.

"Don't speak in the council until I tell you to. Only wizards are allowed that privilege."

Preadus sensed all of the questions racing through Asmar's mind as the young Tulander slipped on the clean white robe. He noticed with satisfaction how thin Asmar was becoming; he was shedding the excesses of his former life. Preadus still questioned the wisdom of having had Asmar grow up in Tuland. Its location made Tuland a safe city, far enough from Malzus and his prying—but Preadus had been afraid that growing up there would make Asmar too soft and undisciplined, like his cousin Remer most certainly was.

Preadus walked back along the sandstone hall to the crystal council chamber, leading Asmar. When they arrived, the other wizards were already seated on the cold blue stone chairs, silver staffs resting at their sides. Preadus took his place at the head of the council table and pointed to the seat at the far end.

Asmar, take your place, Preadus communicated with his mind.

Asmar hesitated. Preadus sensed Asmar's concern at hearing Preadus's voice inside his head. Preadus gave him a reassuring glance back, and Asmar tentatively made his way to the chair.

Preadus looked at the faces of the other wizards. He knew them all well and had already spent much time considering who he could count on for support of what was to come. Wellum was a friend and a scholar; he would be an important ally. Thurmore and Mentaire were the ones he needed to be wary of. They wanted the council to be whole again, as Preadus did, but they wanted to replace Malzus, and removal of a wizard meant one thing: Thurmore and Mentaire wanted to kill his son. This was something Preadus could not allow. Preadus knew the others would not go along with them, as there was no one else to bring onto the council other than Asmar, and he was needed to replace Vetus.

Besides, his son was too powerful to let that happen, as long as he held the golden staff.

But Preadus knew Thurmore also had a plan. He wanted to take the staff once it was seized from Malzus and keep it for himself, depose Preadus as the Great Wizard, and send back to Insula for a wizard to replace Malzus. This was dangerous, as traveling by ship was fraught with peril and there was no guarantee they could get to and from Insula safely. This meant not enough of the wizards would support Thurmore. But Preadus also knew Thurmore could never forgive him for what his son had done—the havoc and bloodshed and pain and loss unleashed on so many innocents.

Preadus looked at Thurmore calmly from his position at the head of the crystal table. He would not let Thurmore's plan succeed, but for now they shared the same goal of recapturing the golden staff.

Preadus scanned the faces at the table, continuing his assessments. Dragorn was in Thurmore's camp, but Rogi was not. Rogi had become used to the good life in Dolcere. He was even putting on weight—it was barely noticeable, but Rogi had acquired a fondness for pastries. His power of mind was weakened by his indulgences and gaps in his discipline, and Preadus could manage him when the time came for a confrontation.

Karal was a friend of Wellum's and could be counted on.

It was at times like these that Preadus missed Vetus the most. Vetus had not been the strongest of the wizards— in fact, his power had been diminishing as he aged, but he had the gift of great wisdom drawn from the ancient wizards that lived in his memories. The discussions with Vetus over the years had helped Preadus through many difficult times. The council respected Preadus's strength, but they had reverence for Vetus's wisdom. Together, Vetus and Preadus were able to keep the council unified through many challenging decisions. Without him, it was harder now to keep Thurmore and his followers committed to the same course of action.

Preadus began linking the minds of the wizards and began the council meeting.

We need to discuss the consequences of Adomas's attack on Areana.

Preadus's strategy was to bring Areana before the council and have Asmar testify as to what happened a day ago in the square. Preadus knew bringing Asmar to the council so soon was ill advised, but he didn't have any other choice. He needed Asmar not only to communicate what he had seen to the other wizards, but to make them feel as if they were in the square, looking into Adomas's eyes, something Preadus could not do by just telling Asmar's story.

Mentaire was the first to speak. He was thin and wiry, with skin the color and texture of the sands that surrounded Dolcere.

We must cut our ties to Arkos's tribe as a punishment for what Adomas did.

There were immediate and enthusiastic nods of agreement from all the others around the table, except for Preadus and Asmar. Preadus could feel Asmar's mind racing and his thoughts beginning to leak out, but it was too soon for him to speak. Preadus would need to invite him; otherwise, it would be a violation of council rules. Preadus felt Asmar's desire to speak rising and realized he should not have brought him to the chamber until later. He quickly tried to hold Asmar back, but it was too late.

You all should've seen Adomas's face—it was obvious he wasn't in control of his actions. He wasn't responsible.

The wizards all turned to look at Asmar, their mouths open in surprise. Even though the words were only thought by Asmar, the council heard him as though he had screamed at them. Preadus sighed heavily.

Mentaire shot back, his thoughts broadcast to all the wizards: *You were told to remain silent!*

Asmar looked around, bewildered. "You can hear what I'm thinking?" Fear and anger at this realization rippled out in waves from Asmar just as Preadus recovered and, belatedly, snapped a block upon Asmar's thoughts.

Only Preadus captured Asmar's next thought, uttered in complete wonderment:

When I'm a wizard, will I be able to do that too?

Preadus controlled his anger. It wasn't Asmar's fault; he didn't know. The Great Wizard nodded. The other wizards stared at Asmar, transfixed, wondering why an untrained, uncontrolled novice had been allowed to speak at the council table.

Preadus reached out and tightened the block muting Asmar's roiling thoughts. Turning to face the others, Preadus again addressed the council.

What Asmar says is true. I didn't plan for him to speak uninvited and so abruptly, however.

What proof do you have? asked Thurmore. His gray eyes seemed to pierce Preadus, who needed to recover his composure before he responded.

I have invited Areana to address the council in order to confirm what Asmar has brought to light. We all know of the battle between the Sitire and Aris, but there's additional information we need to consider. It is best coming directly from her.

Thurmore was about to object, but Preadus raised his hand.

I know this is highly unusual, but under the circumstances, it is best.

And just as Preadus was finishing, the doors swung open, interrupting any objections, and a dry wind swept through the chamber. All the wizards rose in their seats, surprised. Standing in the entry, supported by two attendants, stood a weak, pale Areana. Clearly in some pain from her recent surgery, she nevertheless had a fiercely determined look on her face.

"Areana," Preadus said out loud, addressing her, but apologetically. "Come in—although I regret that I can't offer you a seat at the table, as are the rules of the council."

"I understand," she said weakly.

Preadus was very much aware that the other wizards found the sound of spoken words in the council chamber jarring, and he would therefore keep Areana's participation as short as possible.

"Please begin," Preadus intoned.

Areana faced the wizards and recounted from the beginning the tale of Adomas's attack on the Sitire and the ambush. When she reached the rescue of Adomas, Areana's eyes grew more grave and she paused before stating, with complete conviction, "Adomas was guarded in the tent by a Saeren. I had never seen one before, but there was no mistaking."

"*How* do you know it was a Saeren?" Thurmore responded, with obvious skepticism—and then to the other wizards only, via their minds, *If it was a Saeren, she shouldn't be alive.* Preadus remained silent, observing the council, who were listening intently.

"It wore black robes and a cowl was drawn up over its head. I couldn't see its eyes, but I felt it looking through me. The entire tent was filled with an icy coldness." Areana shuddered. "Adomas was lying at its feet. I went to pick him up and the Saeren didn't do anything to stop us. I don't know why, but it let us leave."

"It could've been a soldier, disguised, afraid for his own life," Mentaire said.

"I can't imagine that creature being afraid of even a hundred soldiers. It *allowed* us to take Adomas. It was too easy. They saved him so he could kill me in the square. If it hadn't been for . . ."

Thurmore's hand gripped his silver staff and he didn't bother to hide his disbelief.

"You killed their guards and lost one of your own soldiers. I wouldn't describe any of that as being easy."

At that moment, Areana's knees buckled and the attendants quickly moved in to help her up. She waved them away with one arm and wrestled back to her feet.

"The Sitire forces outnumbered us by a significant amount. Yes, we had horses, that is true—but there's still no way we should've been able to make it behind their lines as easily as we did, much less escape right out from under them, carrying an unconscious wounded soldier."

Areana placed a hand against the massive doors to steady herself. "They wanted us to rescue Adomas. They wanted us to bring him back here." She tried to straighten up more but grabbed her side in pain at the effort.

Thurmore opened his mouth to continue questioning Areana, but Preadus had what he needed from her. Malzus had created a Saeren, and that meant there was no need to punish Adomas and Arkos; their actions were not their own. The alliance with the Aris could remain intact.

"She's not well," Preadus said, indicating to the servants to lead Areana from the room and back to the recovery chamber. After they left, Preadus returned his focus to Asmar.

What happened when you looked into Adomas's eyes? Carefully, Preadus released Asmar's thoughts to the other wizards.

Asmar began to describe it.

There was a presence within that overshadowed him. I could feel Adomas fighting back, but he was far too weak to push it out and away from himself.

The wizards felt Asmar shudder at the memory, unable to stop his emotions from flowing out to the others. After a moment, he collected himself and continued.

It was as Areana said. As though there was a coldness, or an emptiness, taking over his mind and his will. I tried to help him—

Preadus and the other wizards felt the emptiness as Asmar spoke. But Thurmore broke in abruptly, his impatience evident.

And are we to believe you managed to break the hold on his mind?

Asmar looked at him, understanding how preposterous what he had experienced might seem.

I'm—I'm not sure. The presence—whatever it was—seemed to be done with him and I felt it weakening.

He added, humbly: *I may have helped, but I'm not sure how much.*

This was enough, thought Preadus. He spoke into the thoughts of the group with impatience: *Clearly Adomas was under the influence of this Saeren in the Sitire camp.*

I don't believe Malzus could control Adomas's mind so completely from so far, countered Thurmore, *and no untrained novice could have defeated him.*

Thurmore's words had put doubt in the minds of the wizards. This wasn't going as Preadus had planned. Dragorn rose in his chair. He wanted to believe Thurmore—there were no Saeren, this didn't happen. Otherwise it was too horrifying.

Areana must be mistaken! We need proof that Malzus has the power to do this. The proof we need is to actually find the Saeren, if it exists. Only then can we be sure.

Dragorn sat back into the hard blue stone chair.

Preadus sat, drumming his fingers gently on the crystal table. He had thought what Asmar and Areana reported would be more than enough to convince the council. But the council didn't trust the unskilled, undisciplined initiate. And Areana, in their view, could easily have been fooled by the power of Malzus, and they felt that was far more likely.

Preadus tried to find other options. If he was to convince them, he needed to give them proof, but he feared looking for the Saeren. It would take him dangerously close to the mind of his son. Preadus remembered the other times they had tried. Each attempt failed, and Preadus was left with the pain of his son's rejection and rage. But... maybe this time, after all the time his son had spent in isolation, maybe he would want to connect, maybe he would want to see his father.

Very well, Preadus reluctantly agreed, and grasped his silver pulcher staff tightly.

The others looked around the room at each other and nodded, and then grasped their staffs as well. They would reach out to search for the Saeren.

One by one, Preadus linked their minds and directed their thoughts. Asmar tried to join, but Preadus stopped him with gentle force, still controlling his access to the other wizards. Asmar's mind was reckless and undisciplined and there was no telling what he might do if they encountered a problem. More importantly, thought Preadus, Malzus must not see Asmar. Not yet.

The wizards lifted out of their bodies, and their combined consciousness roamed north. They could feel the minds of the people below as they traveled. They could feel everyone in the land being torn apart and unity crumbling under their leadership. This was not what the wizards were supposed to do—they were meant to bring peace and prosperity to the people, not death and war. As their consciousnesses hovered over Baracat, they could experience the full scope of the pain and chaos and see how Malzus's actions were taking them further and further from the teachings of the Koan, and far away from the most important goal of all: to find the tree.

And then it started, just as it did every time they tried to reach out to his son: their vision grew cloudy. The further north they ventured, the thicker the fog became. It was no use, Preadus knew. He would not get to see his son.

He was about to give up when suddenly, there were holes in the fog, and it started to dissipate. This was the first time this had happened in sixteen years. Preadus's heart raced and he pushed further and further through the thinning fog. Up ahead appeared the outline of a black figure standing very straight and proud. It was Malzus.

Preadus had not seen him in so many years, that he was taken aback. Before him in the fog wasn't the hunched, dirty figure Preadus had feared and expected; there was nothing disheveled or decrepit about the figure looming ahead.

His son didn't seem to sense them, so Preadus began to reach out, but Thurmore stopped him. Preadus could hear Thurmore's thoughts being privately sent directly to him.

Our mission is to find the Saeren.

Preadus wanted to ignore Thurmore but knew he couldn't—not yet. But he knew that once they found the Saeren, Preadus would come back here. Preadus drew himself back to the present and focused the minds of the wizards with more precision, holding them together and feeling their collective strength.

There, in his son's domain, out of view but permeating the fog, Preadus could sense a peculiar coldness, a total absence of thought. It was like no other void he had experienced. Preadus led the wizards away from the image of Malzus and toward the coldness to show them what he was seeing and feeling. They all encountered a frigid blackness there, and they all knew what it meant: a Saeren.

That darkness had once been a man, but no longer—its mind was erased. Driven by the need to learn more, the wizards all continued to travel on to investigate, and within moments they sensed another pocket of emptiness, then another, and then another. In all, six minds were erased; six lives destroyed by Preadus's own son. Six.

Preadus continued, the others still joined with him. Carefully, he reached out into the minds of the Saeren, searching for clues. In one of them, he was able to sense the contact with Adomas, proving Asmar was right.

With these suspicions confirmed, Preadus was about to release the others and go back to the council chamber, but a quiet voice echoed in his mind.

Malzus can be saved.

Preadus was still. He didn't know where the voice had come from, but if there was even a chance... He pulled the others forward, dragging them toward Malzus. They tried to resist. They feared Malzus's power, but Preadus was not concerned for their feelings. This was his chance, maybe his only chance to confront his son, and to make him come home.

Preadus carefully isolated his thoughts from the others again. Now, it would be just father and son.

Their minds met, and Preadus sensed the anger, the hate coming from his son, but there was also something else—loneliness? As he was trying to figure out what that other feeling was, a searing pain shot through Preadus's mind. He felt himself losing control of his thoughts. His son's hatred of him was overpowering. Preadus gasped for breath and tried desperately to close his mind, but the pain intensified; it was unbearable.

Suddenly, everything went blank and they were all back in the council room, their minds reconnecting with their bodies, peeling their minds away from his thoughts one by one. He felt his suffering gradually lessen. Finally, when there was only his own mind left, Preadus was able to collect himself and focus.

As he looked up, everything in his mind and body clearing, his gaze was drawn to the other end of the crystal table. Tiny rainbows flickered across its surface, and there in his chair as before was Asmar, staring wide-eyed back at him. Preadus realized it was Asmar who had said Malzus could be saved. How did he know? And how had he been able to join them? That shouldn't have been possible; he had no staff, no training. Yet he had joined them—and not only that, but Preadus now knew that it was because of Asmar the fog had cleared.

The other wizards were recovering, completely shaken by the encounter with Malzus.

Thurmore, pushing aside the strands of pain from his mind, started to reach out to the others. Preadus tried to block his thoughts from reaching the other wizards, but couldn't.

He's too strong, Thurmore projected.

Preadus at first assumed Thurmore was referring to Malzus, but then wondered—was he referring to Asmar?

The thoughts of the other wizards flowed through their collective consciousness as they left the protective walls of Preadus's mind.

Malzus cannot be stopped . . .

. . . he has created the Saeren . . .

... so many of them—how could he...?

Gradually they all fell silent, and Preadus knew they were waiting for him to explain how they were to stop his son and how they could become whole. He didn't know what would convince the wizards his son could be recovered and redeemed.

Thurmore communicated gravely.

We've lost him. He's erased six minds, created six Saeren. There's only one choice left.

If we get the golden staff, he can be changed, Preadus shot back, with enough force of mind that even Thurmore fell silent. *When he returns, we can and must use his great strength to find the tree. Any other plan is impractical.*

Asmar's thoughts, meanwhile, were filtering through Preadus, as he slowly realized all that had just happened. Pulled along with the other wizards, the feeling of being released from his body and traveling with his mind had, at first, been exhilarating. But then, seeing the Saeren, Asmar had become filled with a sadness and dread, the depth of which gave him the overwhelming urge and sudden strength to pull back from Malzus and free the others.

Preadus realized everything Asmar had done was instinct; he *was* more powerful than any of the wizards realized. Nevertheless, Asmar was still a novice, untrained, and was unable to break through Preadus's control to address the council directly. So it was only Preadus that heard Asmar's thought: *He wants to come home. Don't give up hope.*

Preadus stared at Asmar. Was he right? Was there hope? The other wizards were waiting for him. He focused his mind. *Now is the time to come together. Are we agreed, Adomas is not responsible?*

All were in agreement, even, amazingly, Thurmore. Preadus rose; he spoke now to Asmar.

Please return to your cell. I will call on you later.

Asmar looked around the council chamber uncertainly, realizing that Preadus had not allowed his thought to be shared, and he was confused as to why—but he rose slowly and nodded to the Great Wizard. Pushing open the massive doors of the council chamber, he strode from the room.

As the doors gently closed, Preadus sank heavily back into his seat. He worried that the young Tulander would realize his power, and the council wouldn't be able to control him.

Dragorn spoke softly to the council.

Why didn't we know about the Saeren? It was bad enough when we had thought he had created one of them. But six?

He's grown even more powerful, Wellum added, green eyes flashing as he rubbed at the stubble along his jaw.

Asmar is powerful as well, Mentaire said, as he sat with his hands framing his head and elbows resting on the crystal table. He wanted his thoughts to be clear. *What he accomplished today shouldn't be possible for an untrained wizard. We need to be careful. We don't know what he's capable of.*

This made Preadus sit up straighter. *That's why we left him in Tuland with his aunt. The Tulanders are passive, not aggressive. That was passed down to Asmar. Also, we agreed* that he won't have the voices of the ancient wizards planted in his mind. He'll only know the skills we teach him.

Preadus shivered at that restriction. He couldn't imagine being a wizard without having access to the voices of the old ones. He thought of all the ancients he carried with him. Still, Preadus ached at not having Vetus in his mind to comfort and advise him.

He may be too passive, Dragorn said, looking at the other wizards with skepticism. We've all observed him roaming Dolcere over the last few days and how he recoiled at any signs of conflict. Could he really be a match for Malzus?

Wellum jumped in to respond quickly. He didn't seem so passive when he stood between Areana and Adomas!

It was Preadus who next spoke. Asmar risked his life to save Areana, and he managed to break Malzus's hold on Adomas's mind. All that with no formal training. It's a positive that he recoils at war and conflict. Once he has the golden staff in his possession, he needs to bring it back to us without falling prey to its power. Strength alone cannot and will not defeat Malzus. We have seen clearly that it's not enough. Asmar is the one. He is ... different.

Wellum shook his head and spoke. It should be one of us that goes against Malzus. You should go after Malzus. He's your son.

Preadus' back stiffened. Wellum was right: Malzus was his responsibility. But he also knew he wouldn't succeed. He made his case to the others.

We all know the only one who has a chance is Asmar. He's the only one Malzus would hesitate for even a moment to kill, and he wears the ring that Malzus himself forged from the

THE SILVER FOREST – Book One

golden staff. Malzus will understand what that means when he sees it. For now, we must shield our minds so that he doesn't find out our plan—that we're sending his son against him.

Preadus turned his eyes upward to the vaulted ceiling. He had lost his son and now he was sending his grandson to do what he should do. He risked losing both of them. Slowly, he returned his gaze to his fellow wizards.

We must continue Asmar's training. I'll remain in Dolcere with Wellum. We'll teach Asmar the Talum and Koan. Dragorn will also stay and help guard the holy relics. The rest of you will return to your duties with the Aris, Cautes, and Cherts. We must conclude this conflict with Malzus and return all our energy to our search for the tree.

Preadus sighed. He knew he was asking them to take a risk with Asmar. Even though they had agreed not to give him access to the minds of the ancient wizards, or to teach him how to control the minds of others, Preadus understood that Asmar's power was such that he would learn anyway. With that knowledge, Asmar would become as powerful as Malzus, and all of the wizards would be at his mercy.

There is another issue that we need to discuss. We need to defuse the tensions between Olmar and Arkos caused by Adomas's attack on Areana. Rogi, that's your territory. Visit both leaders and inform them the problems between them were caused by Malzus. They must be made to understand that. It is critical to our plans.

Rogi rose. His skin was tanned and his eyes the same blue as Preadus.

How much influence am I to bring to bear on the two?

Use as much as necessary to undo the damage and bring things back to the way they were.

The wizards all rose and bowed slightly to Preadus as they filed out. Thurmore linked his mind to Preadus as he bowed, and communicated: *I'm with you, even if you don't believe that.*

You want to take my son from me, Preadus replied, and cut off Thurmore's intrusion.

Thurmore followed the others out of the chamber. Only Wellum stayed behind.

Preadus—do you really think you're the best choice to teach Asmar?

He's my grandson.

That's why I ask. Can you truly ignore that when you train him?

It'll make me try even harder, Preadus shot back.

Wellum stood and put a kind, warm hand on Preadus's shoulder.

I'll be here, no matter what, to help.

Preadus nodded wearily.

After a moment of peace in the quiet, empty chamber, Preadus left and walked slowly down the corridor. Everything the wizards had done since Asmar's birth revolved around stopping the destruction Malzus was causing, rather than finding the golden pulcher tree.

Preadus made his way up the narrow spiral stairs to his cell, with only his plank bed and a small wooden table. His one luxury was a blue crystal he had carved himself. Preadus gently touched the stone, and light spread through the room. His thoughts turned to Vetus.

THE SILVER FOREST – Book One

It was so long ago that his great friend and mentor had been killed. He regretted not having Vetus's memories and wisdom inside to guide him. But what Preadus feared most, and was now sure had happened, was Malzus discovering that he now held the thoughts of the wizard Shammai in his mind. Shammai was the one who had started the First Mind War and created the first Saeren. The wizards had thought the consciousness of Shammai had been lost after the Mind Wars, but Vetus had discovered him buried deep in his own thoughts. Nobody other than Preadus knew Vetus carried this memory, and now it was with Malzus.

Preadus looked back on all of the decisions he had made when Asmar was born and agonized over whether they had been the right ones. Asmar's mother had been so young and vulnerable.

Preadus remembered sitting by her side after his grandson was born, holding her hand as she slipped away. He saw his chance of finding the tree, of realizing his life's goal, dissolve. So when Lupa's husband wanted to tell Asmar about his lineage, Preadus had had to stop him. If Asmar had learned then who his father was, their plan to bring Malzus back would be destroyed.

The memories were flooding back. When Lupa's husband went north to harvest the silver pulcher, the wizards had arranged for the Sitire to ambush him. He had been gravely wounded, and Preadus made sure he didn't recover. Preadus regretted what had happened, but he'd had no choice.

He was sure Lupa knew, or at least suspected, but she never questioned him again.

Preadus closed his eyes, his heart heavy from what he'd had to do in the past. He took out his worn copy of the Koan and started reading. *Asmar would learn the beauty of the book,* Preadus thought, as he drifted off to sleep.

* * *

The next day, Preadus called Asmar to the wizards' study, halfway up the tower. Preadus came to this particular room often to enjoy the luxury of the oversized chairs with padded seats and the double height ceilings that gave a spaciousness his cell lacked. It was smaller than his study in the old country, where the walls had been lined with shelves of books containing the wisdom of the ancient wizards. Here he had only two shelves, a paltry sample.

The door creaked open and Asmar stood there in the white robes he had been given. He entered and faced Preadus, unsure of whether to remain standing or sit on the blue padded seat opposite Preadus's own. Preadus nodded to indicate the chair and Asmar sat, hands folded in his lap. Preadus felt Asmar's mind reeling with questions about what had happened at the council meeting. Preadus touched his mind to let him know it was okay to ask.

"Where—" Asmar started to ask, speaking aloud in the quiet study.

Preadus interrupted, *Think your questions.*

Where did we go? asked Asmar, this time using only his mind.

Into Malzus's domain.

He—Malzus—is your son.

Yes.

And . . . he hates you?

Yes, he does. This was difficult for Preadus to admit, particularly to his grandson.

How do you know he can be saved? Preadus asked.

Asmar shrugged. *I just felt that in his mind. He is very lonely and wants to come back to the council, but not until he accomplishes what he set out to do.*

*When you meet—him—*Preadus had almost thought "your father" but caught himself—*you can save him?* It was spoken as half question.

Asmar looked up, and his cool gaze rested on the old wizard.

I don't know if I'll ever be ready to face so much hate.

Preadus blocked his mind from his grandson. This is not what he wanted to discuss.

How did you manage to come with us? Preadus asked, shifting the conversation.

Asmar tried to hide his smile by looking at his folded hands. *It was like a wind dragged me along, and I just followed. There was something at the other end calling me. It was so exciting.*

You'll be trained so that you can be part of that again.

And how do I do that? Asmar asked.

First, we need to teach you to block your thoughts. Wizards can read the minds of those who don't protect themselves.

You've been doing that for me, haven't you? Asmar asked.

Yes, but you need to be able to do it yourself.

I can, Asmar said simply.

Preadus was about to argue when he reached out and found nothing there. His way was blocked. He was sure he could push through the block, but he was impressed that Asmar could even do that much.

How—

I felt what you did when you entered my mind. How you shut down the pathway. I know I'm not very good at it yet, but I understand the basics.

Excellent. Preadus was proud of his grandson, but also a bit fearful. Asmar was capable of so much, becoming so powerful, so quickly.

Next you need to learn the stories of the Koan and the interpretations in the Talum.

What are they? Asmar asked.

They are the holy books of the wizards. The Koan is the word of God handed down for generations to the wizards. It teaches us how to obtain our enlightenment, how to find the golden pulcher tree.

How does it do that?

Through stories that have been interpreted by the leading wizards of their time. That's what is contained in the Talum.

And how does one obtain enlightenment?

Preadus sighed. What could he tell Asmar? This is what had caused the rift between the council and Malzus. *The Koan teaches us to honor and help one another. To lift up others and make their lives better.*

That's what the stories are about?

Yes. They present different situations and show how the wizards have responded. By studying their responses, we can understand what our God wants of us.

And that's what's in the Talum?

Yes.

And what about interpreting the stories on one's own?

If you mean ignoring the interpretations in the Talum, that can be very dangerous.

Why?

That's what Malzus has done. Preadus looked sternly at Asmar, hoping he had quashed his curiosity, at least partially. To Preadus's relief, Asmar just nodded.

The books are in the language of the ancient wizards, Preadus went on, *but I can transfer my understanding of the books to you. Later, when there's more time, you can read over the lessons and you will understand them, even in the old tongue.*

Why are you doing this? asked Asmar.

This caused Preadus to sit up. Was his own grandson questioning him?

Asmar further explained his question. *I mean, you're the Great Wizard. I would have thought you'd be busy doing more important things.*

Preadus relaxed.

There's nothing more important than teaching you, Asmar, but Dragorn and Wellum will help as well.

With that, Preadus leaned over and rested a hand on Asmar's shoulder.

Are you ready to begin?

Preadus felt Asmar's hesitance at not knowing what would be involved in the transfer, or how much of his mind would be opened. Preadus also needed to be careful not to allow Asmar to see too deeply into his own thoughts, to protect what was there about his history.

Preadus leaned back in the cushioned seat and held his staff. His eyes closed as he reached out to Asmar. The minds of grandfather and grandson met. It was very different from connecting with his son. Here, there was no hate. He felt a gentleness which relaxed and warmed him. But this gentleness could not be encouraged too much, or Asmar wouldn't have the temperament to defeat his father. For just this time, this moment, Preadus enjoyed the warmth.

As he prepared to share the contents of the sacred texts with Asmar, Preadus again thought of the stories his mentor, Vetus, had imparted to him. In their lessons together, Vetus would encourage Preadus to focus on the stories in the Koan, when all Preadus wanted to know more about were the lives of the ancients, related in the Talum. The Koan was the foundational text upon which all the commentaries of the Talum were based. The Koan would come first. So Preadus focused and retrieved its first book from his memories. He would act as Vetus once had for him.

Clearing his consciousness of extraneous thoughts, Preadus carefully placed the first section of the Koan into his memory and reached out to Asmar.

Asmar's mind was blank. For just an instant, fear gripped Preadus as he faced the emptiness he found there. But then Preadus felt a calming presence reach out to him. Asmar had instinctively closed down his mind, allowing access so that Preadus could give him the knowledge he needed—but not read his thoughts. Asmar was showing an understanding that shouldn't have been possible without training.

Preadus started the transfer with the words of the book "The Beginning," the passage he had spoken when Malzus and Asmeera wed.

"In the beginning, the world was unformed. Then there was darkness over the land, and a mighty wind swept over the desert."

It took only a day for Preadus to finish imparting the Koan, and then another five days to relate the entirety of the Talum. Usually the process would take twice that long, and many before this had struggled after having the full weight of the teachings in their minds so quickly.

Even though Asmar had been able to integrate the teachings into his memory relatively quickly, there would still be years of work for him to understand what it all meant. For now, though, he had undergone the first ritual of acceptance. There were other tests to come that he would need to pass before he would actually be considered a true wizard.

CHAPTER 10

ASMAR SAT ALONE IN HIS cell, trying to understand all that Preadus had put into his head. The Koan held the stories of the wizards, of their relationship to their god, and their relationships to each other. Asmar tried to understand them, but they were just a jumble in his mind. If he concentrated, he was barely able to isolate individual stories, but mostly they blended together and confused him. And most were so fantastic, they couldn't be true.

One story he had isolated was that of Utan, who lived in a land where the people were only interested in wealth. Utan spent his days thinking of the relationships of people to each other and to the land, and as a result, he was poor. The shallowness of the society disturbed their god, and before the god sent a flood to wipe out the evil from the world, the god gave Utan advance warning of torrential rains he was bringing. He instructed Utan to build a boat for himself and his family. The flooding water destroyed all that was in its path, except for Utan and his family, whose boat was lifted up onto the waters for one hundred fifty days. When the rains stopped, Utan found himself stranded on land where there were no others, and the waters were rough, making it impossible for him to go back to where he had come from. The new land became Insula, the home of the wizards.

Asmar searched for the meaning of this story in the Talum. But there were so many interpretations. Asmar wanted to discuss these stories with the Great Wizard, but Preadus kept putting him off, so instead, he looked for his cousin.

He found Remer sequestered in a far corner of the library, something that by now was his daily routine. Shara was tucked away in another corner, poring over the wizards' books. Remer looked up as Asmar approached, and he ran to his cousin and almost knocked him over.

"Where have you been?"

Everything Asmar had been keeping inside suddenly welled up and came pouring out: he told Remer about the council meeting, Areana, and the feeling he had from the cold, empty creatures Malzus created. Remer was spellbound.

"I don't know how to describe the Saeren. It was like their souls had been ripped from them, like they weren't even there. Except... they weren't *totally* cold..." He shivered at the thought of the Saeren. Remer looked back at him, expectantly. "There seemed to be some small spark left in them. Like there was still something there of the men they had once been."

"You can let your mind travel—without your body?" Remer said in awe, not really comprehending the tale of the Saeren.

"The others can. I don't know how to do that without their help. At least not yet. It was like they created a great wind and all I had to do was lift my feet to be carried along. Preadus was helping me control my thoughts, and everything he saw or felt, I did as well.

"When we met Malzus, I felt hate from him and love from Preadus. Malzus attacked his own father. He was so strong."

Asmar felt a sense of relief, letting all this out, and he realized how much he missed his cousin.

"How do they expect you to stop Malzus?" Remer asked.

"I don't know. They must have a plan, though."

Asmar thought of the hate and the power of Malzus, and it scared him. He knew he couldn't defeat Malzus; it seemed utterly impossible, yet that's what he would have to do.

"There has to be more to all of this," he said.

"Are you sure the wizards are telling you everything?" Remer asked, eyes narrowing.

Asmar shook his head. "Oh, I'm sure they *aren't*. There are things I need to learn and understand, levels of knowledge I have to attain before I can even attempt to do what they want."

THE SILVER FOREST – Book One

Remer crossed his arms. "When it comes time to confront Malzus, I'm going to be with you."

Asmar opened his mouth to object, but immediately silenced himself when he was hit with the realization that he didn't want to face Malzus alone.

"I'll have to ask the wizards if they'll allow that," he said, but immediately regretted saying anything. Why should it be up to the wizards? He could make up his own mind.

Remer put a hand on Asmar's shoulder and stared at him. "I don't care. I'm going with you."

Asmar nodded. He was relieved that Remer was coming. "They're getting me ready to go against Malzus, as soon as possible," Asmar said. "At least I think that is their plan, seeing how they crammed my head full of all of their holy books at once."

"The Koan?" Remer said, excitedly. "If you can just tell me a little—share with me something, anything you can— then I can probably learn enough to translate the rest."

"It's not like that, unfortunately. Preadus put them in my mind directly, but I don't understand them, yet. I can see them, I can look through them, but I don't know what most of it means."

Remer laughed. "That's perfect—now you know what happens in *my* head." He grinned. "I can see all the books I read. They're all just floating around.

"Get the wizards to actually explain the stories. Even if it's just a little bit of information, I can do a lot with just a few words. And Shara is amazing." Remer looked over to where Shara sat. "She's an intuitive translator. If we get the basic idea of the story, we can translate it. I don't know why Shara hasn't done even more translation. Did I say how great she is?"

Asmar smiled. "Well, I do know some stories," he said. "Like the story of the first wizard, Utan. That comes from the first book, which is called 'The Beginning.' It's all about how the world was formed from three golden pulcher trees."

"The three golden pulchers? I thought they were a myth," Remer said, looking at Asmar's hand that had the bronze ring. Asmar caught Remer's glance and wondered—did he know about the ring hidden underneath?

"Malzus has a staff made from one of them," Asmar replied.

"And if Malzus has such a staff, then we're in big trouble."

"You're right indeed, cousin."

Talking with Remer helped Asmar see things more clearly. All that mattered was that Malzus had the golden staff and he needed to be stopped. Asmar realized he needed training more than ever. He turned to his cousin suddenly.

"I'm sorry—I need to return to Preadus, now."

"I'll walk you there," said Remer.

They stopped at the top of the stairs.

"We'll get through this together," Remer said, and then turned to head back down into the depths, to the library and Shara. Asmar stood there until the echoes of Remer's steps faded into silence.

"I know you're there," Asmar called out into the emptiness of the passageway. Preadus stepped from the shadows.

There's no need to use words, Preadus thought, directly to Asmar.

"I don't want to let you into my thoughts," Asmar said—aloud.

"Speaking will not stop me from doing that," Preadus replied out loud. "But if you insist on communicating like this, I will oblige you. Your training must continue."

"If I am being trained, why can't I understand the books you put into my head?" Asmar asked.

"They take years of study to understand. You can't do it on your own. You need someone to guide you."

"And that someone is you?" Asmar asked.

"Together we will explore the Koan, and the Talum which explains it. In time you will learn everything."

Asmar didn't know what to do with his frustration. He wanted to know the words of the Koan unadulterated by the voices of older generations. His thoughts were so confused every time he was with the wizards, and all of their voices in his head, that he kept wondering if his mind was his own anymore.

Preadus spoke, encouragingly. "What you're feeling we all have gone through during our training. Try to be patient. Your first step toward greater understanding begins today. Come with me."

Asmar didn't feel the tug of Preadus's words pulling him forward, so he knew he wasn't being influenced or compelled against his will. After a momentary hesitation, he chose to follow. Preadus led him down steps that led farther and farther down the tower, even below the library, where he pictured Remer and Shara deep in study. No outside light reached this deep inner corridor. Preadus's silver staff glowed, and he held it aloft to light their way through the grayness.

"Where are we going?" Asmar asked, trying not to show his nervousness.

Preadus remained silent, leading the way down, and Asmar became resigned to follow in silence as well. Finally, they stopped in front of an unadorned door that shone with a warm glow as if lit from within. It was made completely of bronze pulcher.

Preadus barely touched the wood surface with his staff and it swung open. Beyond the door seemed to lie nothing but darkness. Asmar peered into the room but couldn't make out anything. There was something wrong in there, but he couldn't understand what it was. Preadus motioned to Asmar to enter. The darkness enfolded him as he heard the door start to close. Looking back, he saw the last glimmer of light fade as the door swung shut behind him.

Alone, Asmar now realized what had bothered him: on this side of the door, the bronze pulcher didn't glow. Reaching out his hands in the dark, he felt for something solid; a wall, a chair, anything. There was nothing. He thought of yelling for help, but calmed his thoughts and focused on figuring out what the wizards wanted him to do. He was positive this was some kind of test, and after he had figured out what he needed to do, surely he would be let out.

Asmar decided to walk farther into the strange darkness. The room wasn't warm or cold, neither airy nor stifling. It simply was a silent space. Sensing nothing else other than the floor, Asmar decided to sit down on the ground and wait.

Once seated, Asmar listened carefully. There were no sounds except his rhythmic breathing. It reminded him of the times he and Lupa would sit together and she would tell him to still himself and listen intently to the sounds around him. He did that now, with all of his concentration, and in the silence, and with sight deprived, his breathing seemed suddenly deafening. He found himself losing his sense of time, and all he had was his body as a reference: he was hungry, and his legs had begun to ache from sitting. Time stretched on and nothing happened, nothing changed. His panic rose, but he worked to control his fear by convincing himself someone would soon come for him to let him out. When nobody did, he began wondering if he had been forgotten. He knew he was being tested, but what was the test? The wizards were not going to come for him—he was being abandoned. A cold jolt flashed through him. Was he being left to die?

A wave of panic propelled Asmar to stand up for the first time in he didn't know how long. His legs were stiff and sore. The pain felt oddly good, though. It was the only sensation he could latch onto. He would find a way out of this room. This prison. He started to walk again, not sure of direction. He carefully counted his steps, trying to determine the dimensions of his prison, but he started to realize there was no wall, no end, no frame of reference. How could that be? How was there a space with no boundaries? He was trapped in some kind of void.

He felt a painful thirst and hunger. Asmar felt weak, and he abandoned his search for escape, sinking back down to the floor. He craved food and water—but then Preadus's words from the desert came back to him, floating invisibly in his mind.

"You only think you are hungry."

But compared to his current thirst and hunger, what he had felt in the desert seemed like nothing.

Asmar buried his head in his hands. He needed to take his mind away from his needs, and he fought off his rising despair. He thought of Lupa and what she might be doing. He pictured her two-story house, the room he shared with Remer, and the smells of her cooking. This only made his hunger worse, so he tried to block his thoughts of the freshly baked breads and the pastries she made, with the warm filling of dried fruits inside.

He shifted his mind to Remer. How had he ever doubted his cousin? They were best friends, connected over so many years and experiences. He thought of Remer and Shara, and their connection. Through the pain of his hunger, this made him smile. He wasn't sure if Remer realized he was falling for her, but he knew Shara was falling for his cousin, and he thought of them both warmly and with happiness. Remer, he knew, would come looking for him, but he was likely so focused on Shara and her books that he might not realize until it was too late that Asmar was gone.

Time was passing. Asmar knew it was, even though he couldn't feel it or see anything. Hunger and thirst were his consistent companions, and he fought back feelings of weakness as best he could. His mind wandered everywhere, and now was back to that terrifying day in the square. He could see Areana and the fear in her eyes as she faced almost-certain death. He knew she had accepted her fate even as she struggled against it. The faces of the crowd came back to him. There was fear in their eyes as everyone stood frozen, watching the spectacle unfold. The wizards feared Malzus, but even more they feared failure, of living a life without finding the golden pulcher trees. It drove them and determined all that they thought and did. They were desperate to succeed in their mission, and failure could not be entertained.

Asmar thought of his connection with Malzus. Felt again the strong hatred Malzus had for his own father, and for everyone. But Asmar also felt a severe loneliness. Malzus hid this, but Asmar had detected it when their minds joined. He wondered if Malzus had sensed him as well. The world seemed paralyzed and ruled by fear. But he pulled his thoughts back to Remer and Shara: they weren't afraid. They had found each other and had a shared sense of purpose and wonder.

Asmar wanted the warmth that Remer and Shara shared. He wanted Remer to come and rescue him from his loneliness. Asmar tried to reach out to his cousin with his mind, to tell Remer where he was, and to ask for his help. He concentrated and summoned all his energy, but it was no use. Without the other wizards, he was trapped in his own mind. At first this paralyzed him, and he sat, head in hands again, trying to push the feelings of abandonment and loss from his thoughts.

He focused on his breath. In and out, in and out. The rhythm of his inhales and exhales now pushed all thought away. His hunger and thirst disappeared, as he focused on his breath.

A cool breeze washed over him even though nothing stirred, and he continued to focus on his breathing. Without comprehending how, he began to feel the warmth of sunlight in the blackened room. Asmar didn't understand what was happening, but he *could* feel, and that was all that mattered, and it didn't matter *why*. He looked up and saw himself sitting with his head in his hands. His mind had floated into the room, no longer tied to the constraint of his body.

He was conscious of this, but he focused on his breathing. He was calm. He was at peace.

He concentrated only on his breath. In and out. More slowly now.

His mind took off, freed from his body, freed from hunger, freed from pain, freed from everything that had held him. Joy flooded his consciousness. Small things made Asmar feel the purest happiness: the smell of Lupa's cooking, the sun shining on his face, Remer's laugh. His mind tried to float free of the room, but something held him.

Asmar's disembodied consciousness now searched the books Preadus had put in Asmar's mind. Asmar had fought to understand the Koan. He now sorted through it again, starting with The Beginning. But there were other books that were part of the Koan: The Book of Wisdom, The Book of Responsibility and The Book of Leaving. The Book of Wisdom encouraged learning and understanding.

The Book of Responsibility described how that knowledge was to be used—and The Book of Leaving encouraged the sharing of the knowledge. Nowhere in the Koan were wizards mentioned, or the controlling of minds.

As he read, emotions flowed into him, as did questions. At first he felt compelled to answer the questions by using the knowledge contained in the Talum. But he soon realized that there were other questions—ones that couldn't be put into words. Feelings such as these could not be put into language. The beauty and simplicity of the Koan overwhelmed him. He now understood what drove the wizards; he understood their desperation to find the tree, the source of wisdom. But he knew the Koan was incomplete. The wizards had created the Talum in their efforts to make it complete, but neither the Talum nor the Koan in its current form could answer everything the wizards searched for. There was more to be discovered, and there were more answers to find. This would always be the case. His euphoria slowly faded and he felt his consciousness being poured back into his body. He felt he had been awakened in some way.

His euphoria was gone, but the quest for answers and understanding remained. The quest had begun in this room—this strange void—but the answers were to be found somewhere else.

Asmar tried to rise to his feet, but the stiffness was overwhelming. At first he could only crawl on hands and knees. Slowly, eventually, he struggled to his feet and he started to walk. As he shook off the aches of his body feeling frozen in one place for so long, his strides became bolder and more fluid.

Having regained this precious ability to walk, the next question was *walk—to where?*

As soon as the question formed in his mind, Asmar suddenly knew exactly where the doorway was. Asmar touched the wall lightly and the door swung open. It had never been locked. Of course; the wizards didn't work that way. Their power lay beyond merely "locked" doors. Their power lay in perceptions.

As long as Asmar believed escape impossible, it was. He had not been forgotten by the wizards at all—just taught a lesson he would never forget.

CHAPTER 11

REMER WAS FRANTIC. HE KNEW Asmar was busy with training, but Remer hadn't seen his cousin since their discussion in the library—*a full twenty days ago*. He was afraid for his cousin and needed someone to talk to about what to do. But he also realized the only one he could rely on was Shara, so he went to find her in the library.

When he pushed open the heavy doors, she was where she always was: at the small study table buried near the back of the cavernous room, with the Koan open in front of her. She was working away on her translation, papers spread about, and deep in concentration.

When he finally turned, a big smile appeared on her face, but then disappeared once she saw his expression.

"There's something wrong," she said. Remer told her his fears.

"They wouldn't harm him," she said, when he was finished. "After all, they need him."

He knew, of course, that Shara was right, but still, this didn't bring him any comfort. He didn't say this to Shara, but he didn't totally trust the wizards—particularly Preadus. He wasn't quite sure what it was. All Remer knew was that he needed to see his cousin now, to make sure he was safe. He sat down next to Shara and tried to go back to the work of translating, but he found it impossible to concentrate.

Shara closed the book. "We're not going to get anything done when your mind keeps wandering. I think you need to go and get answers."

"And how do I do that?" Remer said.

"You need to ask one of the wizards directly."

Remer laughed. "You think they'll tell me?"

Shara reached out and placed her warm, soft hand on Remer's cheek. He wanted to reach up and take a gentle hold of it . . . but he was afraid she'd pull away. He sat still until she returned her hand to the pages on the wooden table and his cheek became cold.

"You need to ask. They need to know someone still cares, even if they don't tell you anything."

Remer sighed deeply. "You're right." Remer had promised to always be there for his cousin, and he wouldn't let him down.

Shara stood and tucked the Koan under her arm. "We can pick up on this later, when you're ready. With the help you got from Asmar, I'll be able to start work on the translation while you look for your cousin."

Remer stared at the book. "We always seem to be starting from the beginning. Every time we make progress, the next day it seems like we are back at the beginning."

"It's a difficult book to translate," she said, with a shrug.

Remer was about to nod in agreement, but something just didn't seem right. He knew how his own mind worked. Even if he didn't understand something, he always remembered it. Ever since arriving in Dolcere, he felt like there were parts of his mind that had been shut down, that had become inaccessible to him.

"It's more than that, Shara. We keep forgetting things. Things I feel sure we have done already."

"You have a lot on your mind. You need to locate your cousin. When you do that, I'm sure your thoughts will come back."

Shara reached out her hand again toward Remer. Remer looked at it, not knowing if he should take it. He hesitated and was about to take her hand in his when she let it fall back to her side.

Remer watched as Shara's hand fell. He wanted her to touch his cheek again, to feel the warmth of her hand on his face. Instead, he rose from the table and started to help organize the papers. "I really need to find Asmar. I'm sorry—about not working more on the translation."

He looked up and was captivated by Shara's jet-black eyes. In his mind, he saw himself embracing her—and kissing her. He was overwhelmed by his feelings, but he had never kissed a girl before, and he didn't know what to do. If he tried to kiss her and she rejected him, he would be so embarrassed that he might never come back to the library. He didn't want to risk both losing her and losing access to all of the books. He cleared his throat.

"I'll let you know what I find out."

"Yes, you do that," Shara said, sitting down and turning away.

Was she upset with him? He hadn't done anything to upset her that he could think of.

"Well, okay, yes ... I'll be off, then."

Shara had reopened the Koan and didn't respond, and Remer left the library, silence hanging in the air.

He headed straight up the wizards' tower, hoping to find someone, anyone, to answer his questions about Asmar. The halls were empty. Remer wondered why it had taken him so long to search for his cousin. Every time he had resolved to go out and find Asmar, something had happened to distract him, and he would find himself forgetting about the search for days. This wasn't like him, and it added to his growing sense of anxiety. Not being able to remember the passages he and Shara had already worked on was not like him, and putting off the search for his cousin was not like him.

It must be Shara who is distracting me, he thought. He had never felt the way he felt about her. Part of him longed to tell her, but he just couldn't. It wasn't that he was afraid she didn't feel the same way; it was almost worse if she did. He had already decided he was going with Asmar to find Malzus. He would have to leave Shara and he might not come back to Dolcere—and he might very likely die. What could he offer Shara? Nothing. It was best she didn't know how he felt.

As Remer searched the empty tower, looking for a wizard, any wizard, he had become uncertain whether it was a good idea for him to go with his cousin. How could he help Asmar with his mission? If anything, he would probably slow him down. Possibly even get him killed.

He turned to go back to his room, wondering why he was wandering the empty halls of the wizards' tower. There was something he was forgetting... again. Something he was trying to remember. It was about his cousin. Something Shara had told him. "What am I meant to do?" he asked his shadow.

All the confusion dissolved away in that moment. He was supposed to be looking for his cousin. He was supposed to find a wizard to tell him where Asmar was. Looking away from his shadow, Remer was determined: he was going to find a wizard—*now*—and demand to know where Asmar was. Remer strode down the hall with a new determination, to find a wizard, somewhere. Anywhere. He turned a sharp corner quickly and almost knocked over a man who had been standing there. Remer looked up and saw the pale-blue robes and silver staff. A wizard. Remer looked at the wizard's face and realized he knew his name, even though he had never seen him before. It was Dragorn.

Before taking any time to think, Remer blurted out to the wizard, "Where is my cousin?"

Dragorn didn't answer.

"I want to see Preadus," Remer demanded, crossing his arms.

"Of course you do," Dragorn replied calmly. "And I am here to take you to him. Follow me."

The wizard turned and started down another hall, leading the way as if Remer's visit was the most expected thing in the world. Too stunned to follow at first, Remer quickly recovered himself and ran after Dragorn, following until he was led to a small, windowless room that was empty, save for two chairs at its center. Dragorn pointed to one. Remer dutifully sat, and Dragorn left the room.

He waited. And waited. No one came. He thought of what he was going to say to Preadus, and then his thoughts wandered back to Shara. Maybe he should just tell her how he felt. After all, they had spent almost every day together since they had first met. The translation was serious work, but when he was with her, he didn't feel serious. She made him laugh. He needed to tell her how much he loved her laugh and how happy he was during the hours they spent together. He wanted to run back to the library and hold her hand and share his feelings with her, be honest with her—maybe even to give her a kiss, if she would let him.

Suddenly, the door burst open and Preadus the Great Wizard strode in. He stood in the center of the room, his robes shimmering and flaring slightly. Remer had wanted to tell him how angry he was for being made to wait all this time, but the thought had already faded from his mind.

"Your cousin will be leaving Dolcere when his training is over," said Preadus. His commanding voice froze Remer in place.

Asmar was going to be leaving Dolcere, which meant he had to be alive. Remer felt relieved to have it confirmed. Preadus continued.

"And you will be accompanying him."

Remer nearly choked, stumbling over any hope of a reply. He was going to go with his cousin.

"*Your* training begins tomorrow morning. I will send someone for you."

With that, Preadus turned and left Remer alone and dazed.

He could barely contain his excitement—he was going with Asmar. The euphoria faded when Remer remembered what happened the last time he went out into the desert. He'd almost died. But he knew more now, and would study more, and the wizards would be training him. This time would be different.

He couldn't wait to tell Asmar what had happened, but then realized he'd never asked Preadus where Asmar was; it had just slipped his mind. These gaps in his once-perfect memory scared him. He shook his head and ran to the door.

He needed to talk to someone, and once again, the only one he could count on to listen was Shara. He headed toward the library, wondering if she would still be there. If she wasn't, he had no clue as to where she would be; he had no idea where she actually lived. She might live with her parents, Remer thought, but she never mentioned any family. All they ever talked about were books. She knew about Asmar, of course, but he had never told her about his own mother or his father, either. Despite all this, he still felt he knew her better than he knew anyone else in the world, except for Asmar. He continued quickly toward the library, wanting to know more about Shara, wanting to tell her about himself.

Remer ran down the echoing corridor. He pushed open the library doors, and rushed to the place where she usually studied. But she was not there.

So, Asmar was gone, and Shara was gone. He stood alone in the center of the library, the stacks rising about him on all sides.

Of course she is gone, he thought to himself. *It's late. She probably has gone home to bed.* He felt his heart sink a little. But he would see her in the morning, like he usually did.

With a heavy sigh, Remer made his way back to his small room and tried to sleep. The meeting with Preadus played over and over in his head as he tried to fill in the missing pieces. Gradually, they started to fall back into place. He knew he could translate the Koan—and had no idea why he'd had so much trouble with it before. He felt better, and as he drifted off to sleep, his thoughts turned back to Shara.

Remer was awakened the next morning by pounding on his door. Startled, he jumped out of bed and scrambled to the door, throwing it open. He hoped to see Asmar standing there, grinning and ready to tell him where he had been.

Instead, a small, dark man with close-cropped white hair greeted him. He was at least a head shorter than Remer. The man was dressed in the dark-blue clothes favored by the Cautes of the mountains, including the sleeveless shirt that revealed well-muscled arms, and loose-fitting pants.

"I'm Geiz," said the man.

The name meant nothing to Remer.

"I was told to train you." The man crossed his arms, waiting for Remer's response.

The discussion with Preadus again came back to him. The Great Wizard had said that he would be going with Asmar and that he was to begin his training. Remer needed to find his cousin and talk again with Shara.

"Come back later," Remer said, starting to close the door. "We can start this afternoon. I have some things that I must do this morning."

But Geiz moved quickly. The door shot open and Remer found himself on his back with the small man on top of him, his knee pressing into Remer's throat, making it hard to breathe.

"I don't think you understand," said Geiz. "Your training begins now, when I say. If you're in a fight with the Breccians or Sitire, you can't tell them, 'Sorry, can we have this battle this afternoon?' You have to be ready at all times. Do you understand?" He was leaning right over Remer's face.

Remer tried to speak but couldn't do anything but nod. Geiz stood, and the pressure eased off Remer's throat.

"You didn't have to do that!" Remer rasped, struggling back to his feet.

Remer followed the Caute behind the wizards' tower to a small field that was hidden, walled off from prying eyes. Geiz made his way to a large covered wooden box. Remer watched closely. When Geiz opened the box, there were at least a dozen metal swords of different lengths and styles. Geiz looked at them, considering his options, before deciding upon two that looked to Remer as though they were the shortest in the box.

"This one's for you," he said, as he handed Remer a rusty blade about the length of Remer's arm. Geiz took another for himself that was slightly longer and in better condition, and he turned to Remer.

"What do you know about handling a sword?" he asked.

Remer looked down at the sword he held in his hand, and let it drop like it was burning him.

"Nothing. And I don't want to learn."

Geiz smiled. "You're a Tulander, aren't you?"

"That's right." Remer was defensive about his people. "We don't fight."

"But you die, don't ya?" Geiz countered, looking at him with disdain.

"Of course we do—everyone does. We just don't go to war."

"Well that's so very nice of you. Except the Sitire and Breccians and the others don't share your views."

"I know," Remer answered. "That doesn't change anything."

"Maybe not. But now you're not in Tuland, and you're going north to protect your cousin. And when a big, fat Sitire soldier comes up to you, sword in hand, what are you going to do? Say 'I'm from Tuland, and we don't fight'? He will lop your head right off." Geiz spat on the ground. "And then he lops your cousin's head off as well. Mission over, and Malzus comes and kills all the rest of us."

Geiz kept standing, legs apart and arms crossed, his sword resting against his leg. He waited for Remer to reply.

Remer stared at the rusty sword at his feet but made no move to pick it up. Geiz walked slowly toward him, and Remer backed away. Geiz's pace picked up, and Remer turned to run. He needed to get away. He just couldn't pick up the sword. But even as he thought this, he suddenly felt unsure. Geiz, he knew, had a point. Remer had come all this way to defend and protect his cousin. If they were attacked, what *would* he actually do? What skills, besides his memory, were going to help him save Asmar?

Remer sprinted a few more paces, and for a fleeting moment thought he'd actually gotten a safe distance from Geiz, when a sharp, intense pain shot up his leg, throwing him face-first into the sandy soil. He tried to raise his head but then felt a solid weight upon his back. Every time he tried to look up, his attacker shoved his face back into the sand, filling his mouth. He tried not to panic, and summoning every ounce of strength he had, he instinctively kicked out his leg, putting all his energy into that one kick, and sent Geiz rolling off.

Remer struggled to his feet and frantically wiped the sand from his face and the corners of his eyes so he could see. Geiz was already back up and coming straight at him again. Remer knew he couldn't run—Geiz would just catch him again. So he crouched down low, hoping it would make him a harder target. Geiz got closer to him, straightened up, and then threw something at Remer's feet—the rusty sword.

Should he give Geiz the satisfaction of picking it up? He didn't want to. And now it was too late; he'd thought about it for a second too long and Geiz had already leapt forward, shoving Remer down to the ground.

Remer struggled back up to his feet only to be pushed down to the sand once more. As he fell, his hand touched the sword on the ground, his fingers moving instinctively to close in on the hilt.

This is only for defense, he thought to himself; he only knew he had to stop Geiz from hurting him. He pushed himself back up to his feet and held the sword out with both hands.

"Stop!" Remer yelled.

"Good." Geiz smiled. Remer looked at him—the Caute hadn't even broken a sweat. "We've gotten over the first hurdle. Now I'll teach you how to use that thing."

Remer looked down; his ankles were bloodied. Geiz had actually cut him. Not deep, but the pain made him shake. He felt beaten up. Remer realized that he had no protection whatsoever from people like Geiz, from the fighters and soldiers he and Asmar would be encountering.

The lesson was painfully learned: he really needed Geiz's help. He would learn how to use the sword. He told himself he would still be free *not* to use it, if he chose. But he needed to learn.

His first lesson went on all day, and by the end, Remer was exhausted. He wanted to go to the library and find Shara, but it was late and he knew she'd be gone. For now, all he could think of doing was crawling back to his room and falling asleep.

Remer was awakened the next morning by the gruff voice of Geiz. Remer now knew better than to say no to his torturer, and he hastily dressed and followed the old man back out to the hidden practice field.

"It's not even light out," Remer muttered, his entire aching body wanting to crawl back to his bed. He was still recovering from the cuts and bruises he had received the day before.

"You didn't expect to sleep the whole day away, did you?" said Geiz, as he pulled out the swords they had used the previous day. The rust was gone, Remer noted immediately, and they glinted like new in the pale morning light.

Geiz noticed, and smiled proudly. "It bothers me to see good weapons languish, so I cleaned and polished them up."

Remer touched the blade of the sword Geiz passed to him, and let out a sigh of relief—it was dull. Nobody would be getting hurt. But then in the next moment he realized that he only knew for sure that *his* blade was dull. He gave Geiz a worried, mistrusting look.

Geiz let out a laugh. "Don't worry, Tulander. The wizards would be very upset with me if I cut you into pieces. My blade is dulled as well."

Remer allowed himself to relax. A little.

"Our lesson today is on how to hold a sword."

Remer repositioned the sword in his hands. He pictured the images he had seen in books and tried to copy what he remembered. Remer was much, much younger than Geiz, and now that he had set his mind to the idea of self-defense, he felt some confidence that he should be able to stop the old man.

Geiz walked over and looked nonchalantly at Remer. In an instant, Geiz lashed out, and Remer's hands shook as the older man effortlessly knocked the sword from his grip. It landed in the sand at his feet.

"Pick it up," Geiz instructed.

Hesitantly, Remer crouched to pick up the sword, keeping an eye on Geiz, who didn't move. But the moment he had the weapon in his hand, Geiz swung at him again, knocking the blade back to the ground. Remer's hands stung.

"Pick it up," Geiz instructed, again.

"I *will*, if you just give me the chance!" Remer said, exasperated.

"Are you going to ask the Sitire that as well? Do you think they will just let you retrieve your sword if you ask nicely, in a battle?"

"I actually think the Sitire will be nicer to me than you are," Remer replied. To his surprise, Geiz laughed heartily.

"I will show you how to properly hold it, so you won't drop it so easily."

Remer bent down again and picked up the sword, still not completely trusting the smiling Geiz. To his huge relief, Geiz kept his word. When he came over to Remer this time, he did so only to adjust Remer's grip on the sword hilt, very subtly. The difference though, was profound: the sword immediately felt more secure in Remer's hands.

"Now, let's try it once again," Geiz said, as he raised his own sword.

The first strike stung Remer's hands, but he held onto the blade. Remer felt proud; he was getting better. But then a second blow came swiftly after, and once again the heavy sword was on the ground with a thud.

Geiz glanced over at his student. "That's just so you don't get too full of yourself."

The rest of the day, Geiz instructed him, and Remer was constantly in motion, on the defensive, learning. By the end of the session, he was more tired than he had ever thought possible. He had added a few more large bruises to his arms and legs, but he had gained a little confidence, and was getting a little better. He once again dragged himself back to his chamber at the end of the day and had no energy left for anything but to get into bed.

After three more days of training, Geiz had moved from focusing solely on sword instruction, to teaching Remer how to read maps and find his way over unfamiliar terrain. They settled into a routine of swordplay first thing in the mornings, and map, navigation and survival skills after a brief lunch. Remer learned all about the great forest that was north of the desert, and of the paths that went through the mountains, from the maps Geiz showed him. Remer's memory and studious nature helped him excel at this part of the training. He was kept so busy each day and was so incredibly tired by the time evening fell, that it was always too late to go see Shara. His whole life became about the mission he was being prepared for.

Remer's body ached even as he slept and gave him nightmares of wandering the wizards' tower searching aimlessly for Asmar. One night, when he was having the same nightmare, he heard the door creak open...

Remer shot up suddenly in his bed, terrified and awake.

"Who's there?" he yelled into the dark room, unsure whether the sound he'd heard had been in his dreams or in his actual room.

Remer's thin blanket drifted to the floor. He was still in his gray robe, not having had the strength to take it off. His heart was pounding. Remer rubbed his eyes, trying to make out shapes in the darkness. Working to calm himself, he took long, deep, controlled breaths.

Inhaling, he detected a familiar, flowery scent in the air. His heart sped up and he held his breath.

"Shara?" Remer said, incredulously.

"Yes," came her voice out of the darkness. She was very close to him.

"How—how did you know where I was?" Remer said, wondering if he was in a dream. He had broken out into a nervous sweat and was drenched. He hoped Shara couldn't detect this in the shadows of the dark, small room.

"Where else would you be?" she replied, her voice sounding even closer now. Remer could feel her warm presence as she sat down near him on his bed.

"I never told you where I lived," Remer said, amazed. "I've been wanting to get back to the library to see you, but it was always so late, and I knew you would have already left for the evening. How'd you find me?"

Shara let out a soft laugh. "I asked. Everyone knows you."

Remer could just make out her outline.

"I—missed you," Remer let out, before he could think.

"You've got a funny way of showing it. I waited for you in the library every day, but you never came back. I thought you'd given up on me."

"How could you ever think that?" Remer replied.

"Well, you abandoned me," she said, gently. Remer couldn't make out Shara's features in the unlit room, and he didn't dare move to turn on any illumination.

"I didn't!" he exclaimed. "I wanted to see you, but it was always so late."

"You could have come to my home."

"I didn't know where that was."

"You could have asked, like I did."

Remer was thankful he had not turned on any light, because he felt his cheeks practically burn from his blushing. Of course he could have found her, but he just hadn't thought to ask anyone. He was too exhausted to think.

"I am glad you decided to come to me," Remer confessed. He reached out into the dark and touched her arm. It was draped with a soft, thin fabric that tickled his fingertips. Shara pulled back and Remer quickly pulled his hand back in response.

"I'm so sorry," he said, worried he had done something wrong.

"No, don't be. It's just that I couldn't see you." Shara put her hand on Remer's cheek like she had done in the library. This time, he reached up and touched her hand. Shara leaned closer. Remer felt the warmth of her breath. His heart beat even faster. Her lips gently touched his own. The pain from his bruises seemed to melt away. Remer pulled Shara closer and held her. Everything seemed to stand still. He felt her heartbeat, and her breath was short. He realized she was crying.

"What's wrong?" Remer said, hoping he hadn't done anything to upset her.

"Nothing . . . I just had told myself you didn't care."

"I care," Remer said, pulling her in even more tightly, wanting to reassure her. "I care more than you can imagine."

Remer's voice faded as they were suspended in an embrace. Shara gently put Remer's head on her shoulder. It felt calming and made him feel safe and protected. He listened to the soft beating of her heart. He couldn't hold back his exhaustion any longer. He closed his eyes, secure and safe in Shara's arms.

The next thing he knew, there was an infernal banging on his door.

Remer awoke with a start and looked around frantically for Shara, confused and wondering if it had all been a dream. The banging continued.

"In the name of the golden pulcher tree, get your sorry self out of bed! If I was a Sitire soldier, I'd have lopped off your head in your sleep." This was Geiz's way of gently waking him.

"I'm up! I'm up already. Stop banging."

"Meet me on the practice field, quickly."

Remer looked around the room, disappointed, trying to find some evidence of Shara. There had to be something.

He went to the basin and splashed tepid water on his face. As the water dripped down his cheeks he looked down and saw it: tucked between the bottom of the basin and the nightstand was a small piece of paper.

His heart raced and his hands shook slightly as he unfolded the small piece of paper and read the message: *Meet me in the library tonight. I'll wait for you.*

So it wasn't a dream? he thought, his mind racing.

Remer slid the note back under the basin and ran outside, heading to the now-familiar training field to meet Geiz.

Remer had been hard at work and practicing for fifteen long days. He had advanced in his training to the point where it took Geiz at least three tries to knock the sword from his hands. He made the mistake of pointing this out to Geiz, who promptly decided to show Remer how much more he had to learn by peppering him with a series of blows that had Remer back on the ground, feeling the tip of Geiz's sword pressed against his neck. It was then Remer wondered if he would ever be good enough to help his cousin.

When he once again managed to pull himself back to his feet, the sword drooped in his hand. He was exhausted from his lack of sleep and he couldn't concentrate. His mind kept returning to the meeting with Shara. When Geiz knocked him down one more time, Remer barely noticed. Even Geiz's threats to "lop his head off" didn't upset him. He just felt like he had nothing in him.

"It's pointless to go on," Geiz said. "Go rest. Tomorrow, we'll have to go at this twice as hard."

Exhausted, Remer left the practice field and headed for the library. There was a warm light down the hallway that felt like it was showing him the way... to Shara.

He thought about the dream-like encounter of the previous night and wasn't sure how to react when he saw her. Should he kiss her like she had done when they had been alone?

Shara immediately spared him from his indecision by running over and embracing him. She felt warm and comforting, and he felt instantly relieved. With a shy awkwardness, she then proceeded to give him a soft, quick kiss—and then she stood back, releasing him, and looking at him nervously.

Remer couldn't help but smile at her, and he could see Shara was relieved too.

"You fell asleep last night," she said. "I wasn't sure what that meant."

"All it 'meant' was that Geiz is making me practice so hard that I can barely keep my eyes open," he said, his tiredness barely concealed. "Shara, I'm really sorry for not coming to see you before tonight. I've wanted to; I've missed you. But the wizards have assigned me a—a weapons trainer." He shook his head, incredulous at the very idea. Saying it out loud made him feel even worse. "These past days have been exhausting."

She nodded and stroked his cheek.

"And tonight?"

"The same," Remer replied, eyes downcast.

"But... you came here anyway?"

"Yes."

"I'm really glad you did," Shara said, smiling.

The two stood awkwardly until Shara reached out her hand, and Remer took it.

"I want to show you something," she said, leading him back amid the stacks of books.

"What do you want to show me?" Remer said, squeezing Shara's hand.

Shara paused, turned, and pressed herself against him, kissing him quickly and decisively.

"A book," she said, and then resumed guiding him further along the stacks of books. They stopped in a remote corner of the library he had never seen.

"Most of the books here are very old," she told Remer. "So I have to take care that they don't disintegrate."

"Yes, I know. You do a wonderful job, too."

"Thank you, but that was not the point I am making."

Remer nodded. "Please, go on."

"A few days ago I was here, caring for the books in this section, as I have always done. I took them down to dust, oil, and check the bindings and pages for mildew."

"Did you find any damage?"

"Of course not. I must have cleaned these books a hundred times; they're all spotless." She crinkled up her nose, looked at him pointedly, and added: "That's what's so very strange."

"I'm not sure I follow you. What is strange about not finding mildew?"

"No. I found a book—one that I've never seen before."

"So?"

"I just told you—I've taken care of all the books in the library. I may not have your memory, but after caring for the books this long, I've basically memorized their titles. This one I've never seen. And no one has added a book to this library since I've been here. And even more extraordinary: it's written in an old language. Similar to the modern one, but different."

Remer knew what Shara meant. Many of the books in Tuland were written in the old tongue. He had learned to read it quite well.

"Let me see it," he offered. "I know the language."

Shara reached over and pulled the book from a nearby shelf and handed it to Remer. As Remer took in the title embossed on the cover, his eyes opened wide and his jaw dropped.

Shara saw his shock and grew concerned.

"What is it?"

"*The Wanderer...*" This was all Remer could utter.

"Have you read this book before?" Shara asked in disbelief.

"No—I mean, yes. I mean—sort of." Remer raised his eyes from scanning the pages. "I read a book found by the old librarian in Tuland. The book had the same title, but this text is different."

Remer raised up the book close to his face and continued to read the pages feverishly, excited by this find.

He sat down, Shara standing beside his chair and placing her hands on his neck and shoulders to massage them gently. Remer distantly felt her warmth but remained focused on the text. He felt obsessed with the book and its mystery. Despite the deep fatigue from his training, he stayed in the library all night, poring over the book. Shara had curled up by his side and remained with him, sleeping while he read.

This version of the Wanderer was much longer than the one he had read in Tuland, which had mostly talked about the Wanderer's journey to Dolcere. This version included that story but also contained travels onward from Dolcere, going through the desert and into the forest. It had been difficult at first, but then the Wanderer began to relish the freedom and openness of the desert and the cool, protective comfort of the forest. The Wanderer related how to survive in these places: which plants were nourishing, which ones to use when ill, and which ones made you sick. All of this would be incredibly useful when Remer and Asmar left Dolcere.

Remer had been so engrossed in reading that he finished the book as morning arrived; he knew it was morning as the brilliant light from outside managed to trickle in, slowly brightening the dusty grayness of the library. And suddenly, pulling his eyes up from the last page, his exhaustion came flooding back. He looked over at Shara, who was fast asleep on two chairs that had been pulled together.

Remer, still filled with wonder at all he had read, started to realize what lay ahead for the day. Geiz was probably already at the door to his room, threatening him to get up and out for practice. What would happen when Geiz realized Remer was not there?

"You think the Sitire will tell you it's okay to take a day off? They'll lop your head off." The predictability of this actually made Remer smile. He heard Shara stir at his side, slowly waking. Looking up at him sleepily, she smiled.

"Good morning," she said, with a yawn and a stretch. "Did you finish?"

Remer nodded, and sighed heavily. "Yes . . . and now I need to go to training. Geiz will be looking for me. I wish I didn't have to leave."

It was Shara's turn to nod, with more than a hint of disappointment.

"I hope you'll come to me whenever you can." She got to her feet, and they stood, smiling at each other.

"I still don't know where you live," Remer said.

Shara handed Remer another slip of paper. Her address was written upon it in small, careful handwriting.

"This is where you can find me if I'm not in the library." She gently kissed the top of his head, adding, "I'll be waiting for you."

Remer squinted as he left the half-darkness of the library, rubbing his eyes, trying to wake himself, and making his way up to the light of the world outside. He knew exactly what Geiz would have in store for him today, like other days, and he already started feeling the pain of the impending blows. Today would be a particularly difficult day.

As he walked around to the back of the building, he thought of Shara—how she had stayed with him while he worked. Thinking of her would have to get him through his day.

Geiz sat on the edge of the practice field, his eyes closed. He looked to Remer as if he had fallen asleep. Remer's sword was by Geiz's side. He thought to try to retrieve it and be ready for Geiz once he woke. He slowed as he neared Geiz and crept forward, softly. Could he get his sword without waking the old man?

"Don't be silly," said Geiz, opening his eyes and rising to his feet, his sword at the ready. "You're making enough noise to wake an army."

Remer knew he had to accept the inevitable. Even though the training swords had blunted edges, they still left painful bruises. There was no avoiding things; he would take his usual beating from his instructor, and get on with his training.

Remer held the sword at the ready to continue with his training, although given how tired he was, he knew he wouldn't be able to mount much of a defense. If this had been a battle, the Sitire *would* have lopped his head off. He steeled himself for the expected blows that would accompany his missteps.

But Geiz was distracted by something behind his young trainee. Remer turned to look. There was a white-clad figure at the edge of the practice field. Remer took only a moment to realize who it was.

"Asmar!" Remer yelled, running to his cousin, sword in hand. At the sound of his name, Asmar looked up. Remer flung the sword to the ground as he reached Asmar and threw his arms around his cousin. "Where have you been? I've looked for you everywhere!"

"I know you have. I could feel it," Asmar replied. Asmar's voice sounded familiar but strange; it was as if he hadn't used it for a long time.

"Where were you?" Remer implored again.

"Lost." Asmar's voice was soft, but strong.

"I don't know what that means, cousin," Remer said.

"I know. How could you understand?" Asmar looked down at the sword and pointed at it lying on the ground. "What are you doing here... with this?" Asmar's voice was grave.

"Preadus said that I can accompany you when you leave Dolcere."

Asmar nodded.

"I needed to be ready, so I've been in training."

"With that?" Asmar asked.

"I'm just learning the skill as a precaution. I don't have to use the sword."

Asmar stared at Remer, their eyes locked together. Finally, Asmar spoke, his voice more severe than Remer had ever heard it sound.

"I don't want you to pick up the sword again."

"But—" Remer started to object.

"*Never pick up a sword*," said Asmar, again. "I want you to give me your word."

Now it was Remer's turn to hold his cousin's gaze in silence. It was clear: there was something very different about him.

Geiz had quietly come closer and was near enough to overhear Asmar's demand.

"Remer is being trained to protect you—" Geiz began. Asmar instantly switched his gaze to Geiz, who saw Asmar's face and immediately fell silent. Nodding his head in deference to Asmar, Geiz just backed away.

It came to Remer, right then in that moment, what was different about his cousin: he seemed like a wizard.

CHAPTER 12

BRADOC FELT THE RHYTHMIC MOTION of his tan mare as her breath misted into the early morning air. His hand rested on the white metal hilt of his late father's combat sword, a gift from Lord Montan, the Cautes' ruler, whose life his father had saved years ago. The long blade was cut from a single red translucent stone and polished to a point that never dulled. It was an honor for a Chert to receive such a valuable possession from a Caute, especially as they were said to give nothing away. Bradoc grasped the hilt tighter.

He looked down from the hill at the Breccian force they were about to attack. His muscles tensed as he calculated how long it would take to reach them and how many of his soldiers would die. His mission was to stop their constant raids on the Chert farms, but he also had a personal mission he had carried for far too long—he was going to teach them a lesson for killing his father.

His three hundred soldiers outnumbered theirs two to one, and he knew his were better trained. Still, he couldn't take anything for granted. It could be a trap, and the Breccians had had ample time to dig into their positions and fortify themselves. The terrain below was rocky, which would make it harder for his horses, and it did leave the Breccians exposed, to some degree. Bradoc's eyes scanned the terrain. The woods dotting the landscape could also be hiding more Breccian soldiers. Although his scouts had gone in advance to check and had reassured him of the numbers they were facing, it was always possible they could be mistaken.

The sky glowed a deep crimson red as dawn broke. The air smelled fresh … everything peaceful and serene. Behind him, the sound of horses neighing restlessly at being held back, and the air filled by the sounds of soldiers sharpening swords that were already honed, one final time. Closing his eyes, Bradoc could feel the anticipation of his troops waiting for his command.

Bradoc nodded to Sagit, his second in command who would lead the archers, and signaled him and the other lieutenants to convene once more. They would go over the strategy again, to leave nothing to chance, but Bradoc hoped the wizard Rogi, who had come into their camp three days earlier, would stay away from this meeting. It was difficult to command when the wizard was there. His lieutenants would continually look toward the wizard for confirmation of Bradoc's strategies and directives. But the wizard was useful. It was the wizard who had told him where to locate the Breccian camps, and the wizard who had suggested the attack. Despite this, Bradoc was relieved when Rogi didn't join them.

His commanders gathered around him. There was Sagit, with his bow slung over his shoulder, and the two brothers, Clivus and Collis, mounted on identical black-and-white stallions. Bradoc remembered the special promise he had made to their mother to keep them both safe. Finally, there was Ager, who had been his father's close friend and advisor. Ever since his father's death, Ager had become Bradoc's surrogate father.

"We attack in three waves," Ager was saying, going over the plan with the others. "Clivus will drive at their center to break their lines. They will continue forward to draw fire from the archers. That should confuse the Breccians."

"I'll command the second wave," Bradoc interrupted.

The second force moving in would be one of the most dangerous phases of the attack, exposing the fighters to the bulk of the Breccian force, but it was also the most crucial part of the campaign. Clivus and his men would be extremely vulnerable in the moments before the second wave struck; there could be no hesitation, and no mistakes.

Ager looked at him, ready to argue, but then stopped himself, sighed and simply nodded. "Collis, you will follow Bradoc, and Sagit you and your archers handle any who escape."

Bradoc looked at his lieutenants; they were good and loyal soldiers. As with any battle about to begin, he tried not to wonder if any of them would die today, and whether or not he himself would die, or if his death was still in the future. All emotions, and fear especially, had to be checked when it came to battle.

"We have the chance to teach the Breccians a lesson today," he said. "Let them die well in battle."

Ager saluted. The others followed his lead and all headed back to their command positions. Bradoc knew Ager was concerned for him and had a right to be, but Bradoc had never and would never be the kind of commander who led from behind. It was bad enough that he had allowed Clivus to lead the first wave.

Mounted, and once again alone, Bradoc felt the euphoria of the oncoming battle. He unsheathed his sword, getting ready to signal the attack. The blood-red blade matched the color of the fiery dawn sky. He stared at the sword held ready in front of him and thought of his father.

An unwelcome voice broke into his thoughts.

Bradoc—

Bradoc didn't hear the words, so much as *feel* them inside his mind.

He turned to face the wizard Rogi, who was standing next to Bradoc's horse, leaning on his silver staff.

"Bradoc, you need to prepare for the Saeren," Rogi said.

Bradoc fought the urge to tell the wizard to go away. When the wizards were present, they always became the ones in command. Rogi had told him about the Saeren when he first arrived, about the creatures that could control your mind . . . but Bradoc didn't believe such creatures could truly exist.

"My troops are ready for anything," he said, trying to sound confident.

"The Saeren will seep into the minds of your soldiers," Rogi warned. "It will attack their courage and sap their strength. Very few have the will needed to overcome the power a Saeren wields." The wizard summoned the image of a ghostly figure, placing it into Bradoc's mind, and Bradoc, taking one glimpse of it, felt a chill run straight up his back. An understanding of what the Saeren could do crept through his mind, and it unnerved him.

"Wizard, I need you to get on a horse and into formation to counter this Saeren." Bradoc had wanted this to be a command, but it came out as a plea.

Rogi shook his head and replied, "I must hold back and wait for the right moment."

"You need to be—" Bradoc wanted to continue with, "*on your horse*," but the final words stuck in his throat. Bradoc stared helplessly as Rogi walked slowly into the crowd of soldiers, disappearing into their midst. Bradoc knew he would not see the wizard again until the wizard wanted him to. There was nothing left but to carry out the plan.

Bradoc signaled Sagit to begin. His archers fired salvo after salvo down the hill straight into the Breccian positions. Bradoc heard the soft muffled thump of bowstrings releasing, and the swoosh of arrows flying sharply through air—and then silence as the arrows fell.

The Breccians carried light shields to protect themselves from the arrows, and they raised them in defense, but the hail of arrows struck them wherever limbs were exposed or faces peered out, or in the backs of those who turned to flee the piercing storm. Bradoc was eager to be in the thick of the battle with his sword, facing death—but he restrained himself and knew he had to be patient. The Breccian archers attempted their own salvos but had the disadvantage of firing uphill, so most of their arrows didn't reach Bradoc's men.

Sagit's archers had done all they could. Now that the Breccians were clumped together as was expected, it was time for the second phase.

Bradoc raised his sword again and Clivus nodded and spurred his horse forward, with his troop of eighty soldiers following close behind. As they came within range of the Breccian archers, Clivus and his soldiers held their shields in front of themselves to form a unified barrier, as powerful arrows embedded into the wood. Two horses and riders went down from either side as Clivus moved ahead, closing in on the Breccians. He and his troops continued to surge forward, shields raised, protected by one more hail of arrows from the Chert archers. The Breccian archers loosed more arrows at his troops, but Clivus didn't slow the charge.

Bradoc clenched his teeth as he watched several more soldiers and horses fall, proud of their courage, and proud to be their commander. Soon it would be his turn. He steadied his mare as Clivus's soldiers rammed into the Breccians' lines, leaving enormous gaps.

Bradoc raised his red sword once again; now it was his turn. Behind him, one hundred fifty soldiers would follow. Rogi's warning of the Saeren still, irritatingly, entered his thoughts, but the ghostly figure was nowhere to be seen, and Clivus and his men were depending on him. His confidence returned. Battle was something he knew, and the confusion among the Breccian formations called out to him like a welcome invitation. His blade came down, and his mare started at a full gallop. He was alone in front, smelling the sweat of his horse and the dirt she kicked up as she ran. The pounding of her hooves merged like white noise with the cries of his troops to create an eerie pocket of silence.

His heart beat faster and faster. He thought of his soldiers—the friends who would be killed in this battle today. He thought of the Breccians, who would die as well. He could stop all this death simply by pulling up his horse. The thought was always there in his mind, in any battle, but Bradoc had no time to give to such an idea, and no time to hesitate for even a second. He spurred his mare forward as she slowed on the rocky hill. The terrain required that he and his horse be careful, picking surefooted steps all the way down, which gave the Breccians more time to prepare.

Ager's white stallion drew up beside him. Bradoc didn't want to let Ager be the first to engage the enemy, so he spurred his mare, pushing her to go faster. Now it was both men leading the charge, the horses kicking up dust instead of dirt as they hit the rocky gully, making it difficult for the scattered Breccian archers to fire at them with any accuracy.

As Bradoc and his fighters advanced on the Breccian lines, everything slowed. The dust dispersed, and he could suddenly see more clearly. The arrows had stopped; it was all hand to hand and sword to sword now. Bradoc's soldiers screamed, letting loose tension and fear. He screamed with them.

He was a fierce and experienced fighter, fully at home in battle—slashing to his right and his left. His sword only slowed as it passed through flesh and bone. At times he managed just for a brief moment to look back. There were flashes of metal, horses falling. The dust made it hard to see clearly. Metal clashed against metal. One of Bradoc's fighters fell, his throat cleaved open; it was Frazin. Bradoc recognized him from his gray leathers and family crest. Bradoc had warned him to keep his sword up.

Bradoc continued relentlessly forward, slashing powerfully with his sword and catching a Breccian in the face, the red blade slicing through the man's head. In front of him, Ager was pulled from his horse by a short, sturdy Breccian soldier. Bradoc rushed to his side, dismounting in one fluid motion and engaging the soldier as Ager was swallowed up by the turmoil and chaos of the battle.

The two circled each other: Bradoc stood a head taller than the Breccian and was far more agile, but the Breccian was broad and muscular. Bradoc lunged skillfully at his opponent. He was slow but precise and strong. The Breccian attacked and Bradoc lunged back at him, only to have the Breccian retreat a few steps, just out of reach. This pattern kept repeating—the Breccian continually moving in, stabbing and retreating, trying to exhaust Bradoc, and it was working.

Bradoc knew he needed to end the fight as soon as possible. He led the Breccian closer, purposefully allowing himself to be beaten back. Bradoc parried the Breccian's sword and deliberately left his side exposed. If the Breccian attacked, then doing so would leave the soldier's chest unprotected, and be Bradoc's much-needed opportunity. One single swing would decide which of them would survive.

The Breccian swung, and Bradoc thrust at the heart of the powerful Breccian and twisted, his sword passing cleanly through his opponent's chest as the Breccian's blade simultaneously ripped into Bradoc's exposed side. A wave of pain rushed through Bradoc as he dropped down to one knee. His breathing became rapid. He took two controlled gulps of air to force himself to regain calm and control. Blood flowed from his side; he could feel the wet moving down his leg. Wrenching his sword from the Breccian's lifeless body, the world tilted and the battle around him began to fade as he struggled to remain conscious. Taking another deep inhalation, Bradoc steeled himself to examine the wound. Another wave of pain shot up his spine as he used one hand to probe the injury to his side. It was bad, but wouldn't be fatal if he could get help quickly.

He looked around and saw Ager rushing to his aid. Ager ripped open Bradoc's shirt fully to get a look and his face twisted in horror.

"It's not that bad," Bradoc said to his friend, with a voice that insisted upon calm and control. "Use the crystals Rogi gave us. I want the men to see me."

Ager's fingers trembled as he ripped open a pouch of fine, powdered yellow crystals. Bradoc placed his hand over Ager's. The crystals floated into his wound and the pain immediately lessened as the bleeding began to slow and the dizziness fade. It was only a temporary fix, but it would do for now.

Many of his soldiers had gathered around them in a defensive position as Bradoc struggled back to his feet. He looked down at the dead Breccian. "Too bad he wasn't on our side. He was a capable soldier."

Ager nodded. "Can you ride?"

"Yes. I've had more serious injuries than this." Bradoc winced slightly as he scanned the battlefield. Collis was directing the attack. Bradoc counted at least twenty horses down and about that many of his soldiers lying on the field, but the Breccians had fared much worse, with about twice as many soldiers killed and their position degrading as Collis drove them back toward the forest.

Bradoc pulled himself slowly into the saddle. His vision clouded, and the bleeding from the wound worsened. He shook his head to try to clear his thoughts. It wouldn't be long now. He knew the Breccians would have to surrender or scatter into the woods, but either way, it would be another Chert victory.

Clivus's men had already circled back, cutting off the Breccians' one possible route of escape. The enemy was completely trapped now and would have to surrender; either that, or Bradoc and his men would have to kill every last one. Once his victory was no longer in doubt, Bradoc disliked any further killing.

Collis rallied Bradoc's troops for the final assault. The sun was golden as it approached midday. Bradoc felt proud of his soldiers and what they had achieved.

Bradoc followed behind Collis into the Breccian lines, his side aching with each stride of the mare. He struggled to stay in the saddle, and his sword became heavy. Maybe, he considered, his injury was worse than he had previously assessed. His eyes clouded as he looked around at his soldiers. There was blood everywhere, death everywhere. He suddenly felt an unfamiliar feeling creeping over him... a feeling of fear. He now wanted to run, to save himself. He turned his horse away from the battle, ready to spur her to safety. Suddenly Bradoc didn't care, even when he saw Collis being cut down by a Breccian. He thought of the promise he had made to Collis's mother, a promise now broken. Collis had barely raised his arm to stop the attack. Something was very wrong.

Bradoc used all of his will and forced himself to pull on the reins and turn back toward the fighting. A Breccian advanced on Ager, but his friend stood frozen, not even raising his sword. A scream leapt from him, prompting Ager to jump aside just in time to avoid the attack, receiving only a glancing blow. Bradoc spurred his horse toward Ager, his legs leaden and his arms heavy. Lifting his sword, he could not remember a time when it had ever been so heavy. He swung at the Breccian in a slow, arcing blow that he just barely managed to land, allowing Ager to escape. The Breccian turned to defend himself from Bradoc, but now Ager seemed to have awoken from his stupor, and he joined in as well. Together, the two attacked and Bradoc ran his sword cleanly through the soldier's back.

Bradoc looked into the middle of the Breccian forces and froze. A black-cloaked figure riding a jet-black horse

was silhouetted in the bright sunshine. The figure was death. It was gaunt, like a skeletal shadow. Bradoc felt his heart sink into darkness: this had to be the Saeren that Rogi had warned him about. It seemed to move through the crowd of warriors, reinvigorating the Breccians, as it sapped his own men of all strength. The Breccians were now slashing their way through Bradoc's soldiers, who were helplessly frozen in place. It was a slaughter. With great effort, Bradoc raised his sword and struck out at a Breccian that was closing on him. He didn't think he would be able to lift an arm to raise his sword again.

Rogi had warned him, but Bradoc hadn't listened, hadn't believed him.

Where was the wizard? They needed him now, but he was nowhere to be seen. In his fear and pain, he let out a shrieking battle cry that pierced the air and seemed to at least partially propel him through the hopelessness he had been feeling. A few nearby soldiers heard him and rallied to his call, but most remained paralyzed, immobilized targets for the enemy.

His own paralysis broken, Bradoc fought on furiously with the small group of soldiers beside him. But they fought as a lone, isolated force—and Bradoc knew now that he was going to die, but he had done all he could. At least he would go like a soldier.

It was then that an explosion racked the battlefield. Bradoc raised his eyes and saw the wizard Rogi up over the crowded field, standing on what had been their original lookout hill. The old wizard held his silver staff high over his head as fire and colored lights streamed forth. Bradoc instantly felt a wave of irrepressible joy and relief; a huge weight lifted from his mind, and his pain and fatigue were replaced by hope and newfound determination. Around him, he could see the same effect on his soldiers; they were infused with energy and coming back to life. The Saeren's spell, broken. A victory cry rose up through the survivors as they renewed the fight, and Bradoc was buoyed by the momentum. He wouldn't die after all . . . at least, not today.

But just as Clivus began to reposition his men, the battlefield clouded with a dense, fast-moving mist. The Breccians disengaged from their opponents and retreated into the gathering fog. Soon, everyone was enveloped by the thick cloudy air. His soldiers were out there, and so was the enemy, but he couldn't fight what couldn't be seen. He gritted his teeth and, desperately frustrated, kept his horse in one place.

After a short time, a cool, fresh wind came down from the hill where Rogi stood. It blew across Bradoc and his mare, and through the fog across the field. When the mist finally cleared, the Saeren and the Breccians were gone.

CHAPTER 13

LASUM PACED BACK AND FORTH at the bottom of the tower. Being summoned to Tellurium, Malzus's stronghold, was never good. It had to be because of the losses from the recent battle with the Cherts. He knew he was going to die, or be converted into one of those horrific creatures, but it wasn't fair; it wasn't his fault! He hadn't even thought the battle was a good idea to begin with. He knew his people were outnumbered and had an inferior tactical position. Yet the high commander, Taror, had ordered them to fight. Lasum had been shocked by that. Taror had always been an extremely levelheaded and smart commander, never putting his people at risk unnecessarily.

The only advantage the Breccian army had was that horrible, skeletal creature. His own soldiers were just as afraid of it as the Cherts were. He tried to push the violent scenes from the battle out of his thoughts but couldn't. The way the Cherts came down the hill and decimated every one of their positions had been brutal. Taror was killed almost immediately. As second in command, Lasum had tried to hold his soldiers together. They fought bravely, but the Cherts on their horses slashed right through them.

Then the light over the entire battleground shifted, and he remembered how everything suddenly changed. That horrible creature, the Saeren, was in their midst, and cast some type of spell over the Cherts; every one of them ceased fighting. Everything turned in his soldiers' favor. Hate and rage surged through his soldiers and gave them an otherworldly strength. He had seen many battles, and experienced many strange things as a fighter, but there was something even stranger about how he felt in this battle. He had been angry, but he wasn't sure who he was angry at; it felt directionless. He had been overcome with the thought that he had been wronged and needed revenge, but the feeling seemed to come from outside of himself, like he was being controlled.

The feeling gave him strength until suddenly, from up above them on the hilltop, the cascading flood of bright lights had appeared. At first he couldn't make out what it was, but as the light dispersed, he could see the blue robes of a wizard from behind the Cherts forces, holding his staff high—and just as suddenly as the strange feelings of rage and anger had appeared, they disappeared, leaving him feeling weak and afraid. Then the Cherts, coming back to life, resumed their attack, and the battlefield filled with mist. He had just stood, transfixed, until he knew he was supposed to flee into the mist.

The next thing he remembered was suddenly, somehow, just being back in his village, alive, unsure of how he got there. Two days later, he was summoned north by Malzus.

He was there now, knowing that many who were summoned to the tower never were seen again. When a sharp pain entered his head, he knew what it meant: it was time to climb the narrow stairs to the topmost room of the tower where Malzus would be waiting. There was nowhere to hide and no avoiding this call, so he steadied himself and began the long ascent to what he thought was a sure death—or worse.

Lasum counted the steps as he made his way higher and higher into the dark tower: one hundred fifty steps . . . two hundred . . . two hundred and twenty-five . . .

At two hundred and eighty steps he paused, breathing heavily. Only one more very short flight of stairs separated him from his destiny. He wished he could turn and flee all the way back down the two hundred and eighty steps he had just climbed. Why *had* he followed the order to come here? He didn't want to die. But making Malzus wait could get him killed just as easily. *The only way is up,* he knew. And so he forced himself to climb on, ascending the final steps until his foot landed on the very last step. His eyes stayed aimed at the floor. He didn't want to look up; he didn't want to see the figure that had commanded him to this tower. But his head lifted despite his efforts to keep his eyes downcast, and there, sitting on the other side of the chamber across from him, was a figure robed in black, seated on a golden throne.

Lasum took a moment to collect himself. This wasn't what he expected... it was just a man. Lasum had thought he would be coming face to face with one of the wraithlike creatures with rotting flesh and hollow eyes. But he was looking into Malzus's face, and the eyes looking back at him held no malice. Lasum breathed a sigh of relief and felt himself relax.

Don't fear. Malzus's voice filled the tower, seeming to come from everywhere at once. *I've seen the battle through my Saeren. It was as I expected.* The voice next came from the seated Malzus. "Come to me."

Lasum stared at him across the ribbon of stone that floated through nothingness and connected the two sides of the circular room of the tower. He took a shallow breath and tentatively put one foot on this bridge of stone and felt his knees buckle. As he swayed, he steadied his breathing, forcing strength back into his legs. He focused on Malzus, calm and sitting on his golden throne, a beautiful golden staff clutched in his left hand, and Lasum moved forward. He made it across to the landing and prostrated himself in front of Malzus's throne.

"It's time you made yourself useful to me," said Malzus. Lasum raised his head and felt caught in the power of the wizard's eyes. Words came into his head, but Malzus's lips didn't move. *I'm making you the commander of all the Breccian troops, second only to your king, Ramez.* Lasum smiled gratefully as he looked into the dark eyes of the wizard. He had not expected this. Instead of receiving a death sentence, he was now being made the commander of the king's forces. He would be respected and listened to—Malzus would make sure of that.

You'll attack the Cautes in the mountains. I want you to find their mines and take any gems and metals you discover. Lasum bowed deeply. He felt such great relief that things were turning out well, that he was being spared.

All I require is that not one of your enemies is left alive.

This request was presented simply enough—stated not unlike the way Lasum's wife would ask him to stop by the baker's on his way home. Lasum's muscles tensed. Malzus felt his hesitation.

"You will do this for me?" Malzus smiled sweetly as he rose, clasping the golden staff.

Lasum nodded weakly.

"Good. Then maybe we can have some peace in this land and finally find that tree."

Lasum didn't know who the wizard was speaking to. Malzus's voice trailed off before his focus returned to Lasum.

"A Saeren will accompany you. I have battle plans already prepared." Malzus turned and disappeared behind the golden throne. Lasum knew he had been dismissed. He stood for a moment, letting it all sink in. He was now the commander of the Breccians, but only if he traveled with that deathly creature. While trudging down the seemingly endless stairway, he contemplated the real magnitude of the task he had just been given. It seemed simple enough at first, but just finding the Cautes' mines alone was not going to be easy. His people had actually been

searching for the elusive mines for years but had not succeeded. Only three had been located in all the years they
had searched. Judging by all the gems and metals they had
recovered from their raids on the Cautes, there had to be
at least a hundred mines hidden all throughout those hills.

The Cautes were expert miners and gem cutters. That's
what made it so difficult to find their mines. They cut
stones that twisted and bent the light, hiding the entrances.
Lasum's forces had only been able to find those three mines
by following miners themselves back to their locations.

Reaching the bottom landing and stepping off the final
step, Lasum let out a deep sigh. He looked up from where
he had just descended and his legs shook again, this time
with exhaustion and relief. He hoped never to have to
climb those stairs again. A hundred soldiers had come
north with him, and it was time to head back south and
take on their new mission.

As Lasum stepped from the tower, the two lieutenants
he had stationed below stepped into formation beside him,
one at either side. Botley, scarred and deformed by many
battles, was his right hand. Tiox, tall and broad shouldered, was at his left. Lasum remembered when Botley's
face suffered the cut that sliced downward from his right
ear, across his cheek, and ended at his chin. Two years
later, it still looked raw and unhealed. His limp came from
a previous battle where a Chert ran his sword through
Botley's left leg.

"Get the horses; we're heading south," Lasum
commanded.

Lasum wished he had had the horses in the last battle with the Cherts; it could have made all the difference. These horses were a recent gift from Malzus.

Botley nodded and turned to obey, but stopped suddenly. Right in front of them was a skeletal creature. They all stood frozen. Lasum had a feeling of dread as a cold shiver ran up his back: the Saeren. Lasum swallowed hard, trying not to let his fear grab hold of him—but Botley took off running, panicked. He didn't get very far. The Saeren turned its hollow eye slightly in the direction of the fleeing figure, and Botley fell forward, hard. Lasum watched as Botley's body convulsed on the ground, kicking up dirt. The creature walked up to Botley and stood over him. Tiox took a step toward the Saeren, wanting to help his friend, but Lasum put an arm out to stop him.

When the Saeren moved away, Botley lay still, his breath slow and labored. Tiox now ran to his side, lifted him up, and carried him to a healer. Lasum stared horrified at the Saeren, afraid of what it could do. He turned back to the rest of his soldiers and shouted to them to mount their horses. Beside him, Tiox had returned and was silent, but Lasum sensed the lieutenant's disapproval of the Saeren.

They left Malzus's stronghold at Tellurium with some relief, the Saeren trailing behind the men. Each night they made camp and pitched their tents. The Saeren remained out in the open and never seemed to sleep. Instead, it sat cross-legged, usually with a tree or boulder at its back, and not even by a fire. No one ever saw it eat or drink and it always sat apart. It had to be alive, yet it seemed more dead. None of Lasum's soldiers would go anywhere near the Saeren, and after a few days, Lasum noticed they started avoiding him, as well; they undoubtedly blamed him for the frightening and uneasy presence of the creature, and also for what it had done to Botley. With the Saeren remaining right in the camp with them, drinking became more open and frequent as anxieties rose. There were mutterings among the soldiers and trust among them felt like it was eroding. Lasum himself had nobody to confide in, and nobody to ask for advice.

He looked over at Tiox, who seemed to keep himself apart from the group gatherings and didn't join in the drinking and commiserating. For the first time in his career, Lasum felt afraid of his soldiers. He started pitching his tent closer to the Saeren, despite his own unease about the creature, now feeling forced to rely upon it for protection.

Botley recovered after a few days and no longer needed to be strapped to his horse. Once they were settled in a camp, Lasum gathered the soldiers and explained their new mission, and told them about the gems Malzus promised them were to be found in the caves of the Cautes. The soldiers seemed to revive in spirits, learning of the potential riches that lay ahead.

The problem was Lasum still had no idea where exactly the mines were, or even where to start looking. Now they were encamped deep within the Cautes' borders and lands. Knowing they should, in principle, be near a mine, Lasum started sending out scouting parties to see if they could pick up the trail of the Cautes, but day after day, these scouting missions returned, having found nothing.

Time wore on; days turned into weeks, and Lasum could see his soldiers' increasing discontent both with coming up emptyhanded and also with having the disconcerting figure of the Saeren seemingly watching over them from right within their midst. Botley seemed to be stirring up the discontent. Lasum saw soldiers entering Botley's tent in the evening, and Lasum couldn't help but notice hushed conversations during the day that would silence quickly when he came by. Lasum knew he needed to confront Botley and round up the disloyal soldiers and make an example out of them for their attempts at mutiny. The problem was Lasum wasn't sure who was loyal to him at this point, or if any soldiers would stand by him. He realized he really only had the Saeren to rely upon, and that scared him.

In the morning, Lasum stepped out of his tent into the sun. But on this particular morning, Botley and a group of soldiers stood shoulder to shoulder in a semicircle around the tent's entrance. Beyond this ring, the rest of his men seemed content to sit back and just watch to see how things would play out. Lasum squinted in the morning light but noted Tiox standing out beyond the semicircle with the spectators.

"Where is this mine we were promised?" demanded Botley, looking a bit shaky but doing his best to be a confident, imposing leader. Another one of the soldiers, Dragar, stepped forward, hand on the hilt of his sword, attempting to appear menacing. Lasum felt stupid relying so heavily on only the protection of the Saeren. He should have somehow cultivated a few guards loyal to him who would protect him and been on guard outside of his tent. It was too late now.

"I wish I knew. You will need to ask 'it,'" said Lasum—his voice stronger and more confident than he felt. He pointed to where the Saeren sat in a deep trance, knowing he couldn't show any signs of weakness.

"Dragar," Botley ordered, "rouse the Saeren!"

Dragar looked terrified at Botley then at the Saeren. Lasum felt sorry for the soldier. But Dragar had chosen his side and now was trapped.

As Dragar approached the skeletal creature sitting absolutely still and alone, his steps slowed. When Dragar was finally standing right next to the unmoving figure, he reached out a hand ever so tentatively. As Dragar's index finger barely touched the shoulder of the creature, a skeletal hand whipped out so fast as to be almost invisible and grabbed his wrist. All the soldiers watched as Dragar screamed and lurched, falling to his knees in agony. The Saeren then reached around with its other skeletal hand and slowly, efficiently crushed Dragar's throat. With a horrible gurgling sound, Dragar's body slumped and fell to the ground.

Botley had gone silent watching this, and he now stood frozen in fear. Lasum approached him. With the back of his hand, Lasum slapped Botley full force in the face. Botley's head was whipped to the side, but he remained standing. Lasum walked away from Botley and moved toward the Saeren, approaching it but being careful to stay out of its reach.

"I need you to tell us: where is the mine you promised?" Lasum spoke with a calmness he didn't feel. A sharp pain shot through his head and he fell to his knees, grasping his temples. Through the pain, he heard Malzus's voice.

The entrance is near. It's protected by a strong force. You'll know where it is when I'm ready. Do not disturb the Saeren again, or you will suffer the fate of Dragar.

Lasum stumbled to his feet, shot one last look at Dragar's crumpled, pathetic body, and gave the order to his soldiers—now, all willing to follow his commands—to bury him. Tiox was the first to respond to the order and lifted Dragar, carrying him off. The look Tiox gave Lasum, before he turned to pick up the lifeless corpse, was sympathetic. Almost.

Days of waiting followed, days that tested everyone's patience and nerves. The weather was raw and they were all exposed, the wind ripping through their camp as darkness fell. His soldiers were cold and morale was low, and they became increasingly disquieted. Lasum saw their icy stares when he passed them. They were angry, and they were afraid. Their enemy was also their ally and this relationship only confused them. Dragar had been well-liked by the others; his horrible, needless death made the soldiers furious, and it made Lasum furious. He needed every soldier he could get if they were going to attack the Cherts. It was the only reason he had let Botley live. Lasum sensed all of the growing frustration, but there was nothing he could do about it.

Despite his own fears, Lasum moved his tent even closer to the Saeren. He didn't feel any safer doing this, but he had no other choice: it was the only way to even remotely protect himself against Botley and the others. He knew they were only becoming more and more angry and frustrated with him. And, as he had feared, on the fourth night after Dragar's death, Botley orchestrated another insurrection. Leading nine soldiers loyal to him, Botley marched on Lasum's tent, pushing in at dawn to try to catch him by surprise.

Lasum had been warned by the Saeren and was completely ready for Botley and his crew. When Botley entered, Lasum was alone. Botley moved quickly to take down his commander, sword raised and ready to kill. Lasum sat, eyes downcast and seated in place. In the same instant that Botley's sword went up, Lasum felt an icy wave pass over and through him, as if death had just walked into the tent. When Lasum looked up a moment later, he saw Botley and his soldiers, all ten, lying on the ground with their eyes forever frozen open wide in terror and shock. They were all dead.

Malzus had saved him. He swallowed, stood up, and gathered his sword and cloak, stepping gingerly around the bodies and out of his tent to see all the others standing around. They were all nervously shuffling, awaiting word of what had happened. Lasum looked at them and then gestured to Tiox, now his second in command.

"Get these bodies out of my sight," he said, and then turned and went back into his tent, dousing the small light. He didn't want his soldiers to see him as he cowered in the corner, unsure of what was to come and what to do next. Unsure if he would survive this mission.

As he sat in the darkened tent, hugging his knees to his chest, the flaps parted to reveal the black cloaked figure, its form silhouetted by the campfire outside. Lasum tried to make himself smaller, pushing himself further into the corner as if to shrink away from the skeletal figure in the tent opening.

I have discovered the mine.

The voice, again, was Malzus. When the Saeren turned a moment later to exit the tent, Lasum understood exactly where he had to go.

CHAPTER 14

SOMETHING FELT WRONG. KARAL SCANNED the mountains that spread out before him and all around him, searching. With his silver staff grasped tightly in his hand, he peered intently into the dense fog enveloping the mountain. He sensed shadowy images lurking. Inhaling deeply, he decided to have the new crystals put in place right away, just in case. He turned and walked back into the mine. The extreme dampness mixing with the crisp air of the mountain sent a chill right through him.

"You look worried. What's out there?" asked Prince Wetell, the oldest son of the Cautes' ruler, Lord Montan. He was also looking up at the mountain ridges. The prince had grown in the years Karal had known him. He was tall and dark, his silver hair striking for a man only in his twenty-fifth year. He wore the clothes of a miner:

simple rough-woven fabric, turned gray with a coating of mine dust. Still, you could tell he was a prince just by the straightness of his back and the command in his voice.

Karal had spent much time with him over the years as he taught the Cautes new techniques in mining stones and gem cutting. The prince had matured from an awkward, shy teenage boy to a thoughtful, stubborn man. Karal had grown to like him, as frustrating as the young prince could be. There was a gentleness about him that was unexpected from someone being groomed to be a future ruler. Karal thought Wetell's younger brother, Rubea, had more of the ruthlessness needed to be a decisive ruler, but it was Wetell who would one day take over for their father. Karal looked into the prince's eyes and felt the weariness behind them.

"The Breccians," Karal replied, distracted by his own uneasiness.

"The Breccians are always out there."

"Yes, they are." Focusing on the prince, he said, "We need to put the new crystals in place immediately."

"Are they that close?" Wetell asked.

Karal wasn't sure. He didn't sense an imminent danger. It was just a vague feeling. "I want to make sure they work."

"We know they work," Wetell shot back. "Can't it wait? The miners are just bringing a new load of ore to the surface and it will have to be sorted."

Karal turned quickly to face the prince. He wasn't used to being second-guessed, and Wetell's defiance angered him. The prince stood staring back at the wizard. It was a look Karal knew too well. He was tired of this, and he reached into Wetell's mind. The combative look disappeared and the two turned and walked further into the mine, past where the gem cutters sorted crystals, deciding which to facet and which to use for other purposes, such as being ground into medicines.

This particular mine had been a disappointment in the overall quality of the gems that were being harvested. When this place had first been discovered, all the wizards had felt the power coming from it and had been so hopeful. The gems and their power were critical to being able to defeat Malzus, but most of the crystals they had found in the mine so far were small and uninteresting. However, the sheer abundance of metals being mined made this place an important resource.

Karal had been given responsibility for this mine because he had worked in mines on the wizards' home island of Insula. He had enjoyed the work and the solitude and coolness of the caves, and he had valued the connection it gave him to the earth—the same earth that nourished the golden trees. He had set up the same excavation process the Cautes used, but it was his own skills that made them highly efficient. The faceting and refining techniques he had taught them had given the Cautes an easier life than the Breccians, whom Malzus had primarily taught only the minimum needed for survival: how to fashion weapons with their extremely limited resources. Now, Karal wondered privately if the Cautes had become too soft. If the wizards had trained them to be better soldiers, maybe Malzus wouldn't have been able to reverse the sixty years of movement toward peace and prosperity that the wizards had gently nurtured.

The prince disappeared down a shaft and returned with three miners who brought the new crystals covered in rough gray cloth. Even through the cloth, Karal felt the power of the gems. He had helped facet them—something he hadn't done for many years—and it had felt good to do this type of work again. The two crystals, each about half the size of the prince, were heavy and difficult to maneuver over the uneven floor of the mine, even on their small, wheeled platforms. The prince enlisted four other miners to help lift them off their bases and edge them just inside the entrance.

When Wetell ordered the cloths removed, light streamed from the crystals, momentarily blinding everyone near them. Eventually, the deep blue of the stones came back into focus for Karal, and he was momentarily lost in their translucence. The air vibrated as the entrance blurred. But the placement wasn't precise enough, and a gap in the coverage made the image fuzzy. Karal had the miners reposition them, making tiny adjustments until the entrance was completely blotted out with an image of the rockface that would have fooled even a close-up observer.

When they were sure the placement was right, the prince ordered the stones covered, and the entrance sprang back into view.

"Should we call all the miners in?" Wetell asked, breathing hard from the exertion of moving the crystals.

"Not just yet," Karal said, but added, "Just be ready."

"We've been through this before. The Breccians have never been able to pierce our defense."

Karal nodded. "That was before."

"Is there something else? What aren't you telling me?"

Before Karal could answer, Jamica, the chief mining engineer, rushed in and blurted out, "We've found a gem pocket!"

This was what they were hoping for when they first felt the power of this mine. The gems might be powerful enough to help fight Malzus.

Karal looked at Jamica. She was a head shorter than the prince, with darker skin and shoulder-length curly brown hair. Karal could feel the connection between the two. They were lovers, and he didn't need to use any of his skill as a wizard to figure that out.

He cleared his throat. "I would like to inspect the find." He controlled the enthusiasm that made him want to rush past the two Cautes and run through the passages to immediately get to the gem pocket.

"Yes," Wetell agreed. "Take us to see what you found. How big is it? What type of crystals are there?"

Jamica reached for Wetell's hand. "We don't know yet. They were just removing the last of the rock at the entrance. I realized you'd want to be there when it was opened." Jamica looked over at the wizard. "And of course, I knew you would want to see it as well."

As they walked at a brisk pace, Wetell turned to Karal to say, "You know what this means—finding the gem pocket?"

"It means more crystals," replied Karal, controlling his excitement. The prince couldn't possibly understand the power the crystals gave the wizards. Winning the war against Malzus was a big enough goal, but these crystals could mean so much more. They could help them find the golden pulcher tree.

Jamica laughed.

"It also means more marriages. Don't you know it's good luck to be married in a crystal chamber?" she said.

Jamica continued leading them down the mine shaft, turning at one point where it branched off, and led them deeper under the mountain through what seemed like an unending maze of tunnels. Each path glowed dimly from the warm, flickering light of torches hung at intervals all the way down. Crystals would have provided a cleaner, steadier light, but they were being saved for more important tasks. Jamica knew each curve and bend intimately. Karal felt secure in her presence, and her confidence and skill impressed him.

He had met her about two years after he'd been introduced to the prince, and she was the very opposite of Wetell. Where he was shy, she was outgoing, and where he was thoughtful, she was impulsive. Karal looked at the two of them, unconsciously holding hands as they walked in front of him. She was a good influence on the prince.

The entrance to the gem pocket was twice Karal's height. As the miners finished clearing the last rock and pushed it aside, a rush of musty, ancient-smelling air burst out, along with an incredible arc of colored light. Jamica and Wetell looked at each other and entered together. Karal hesitated—he could feel the power of the crystals, even standing outside the chamber.

Entering, he closed his eyes and let the full power of the surrounding crystals flow through him. His anxiety faded, and he felt a sense of pure elation. When he opened his eyes, light bounced from one side of the chamber to the next. A prism of colors danced around him. Pale blues mixed with deep golds and rich purples. The chamber, left undisturbed for so long, had become a perfect ground for nurturing the growth of gems of every size, shape and color. Giant crystals grew up from the floor, down from the ceiling, and out of the walls. They illuminated their surroundings, creating mysterious shadows and sparkling surfaces. The light emanating from the crystals was of a clarity that was remarkable, and Karal moved closer to various crystals and peered deeply into them to admire their inner structure—a mix of overlapping flat planes and triangles. He wanted to stay there, drinking in the power of the raw crystals and taking in the beauty that surrounded him, but after spending some time absorbing it all, he stepped outside the chamber to reach out to Preadus and inform the Great Wizard of the important find. After doing so, he went back inside, taking more of the energy and euphoria in.

"I want to stay in here forever," came Jamica's soft words.

An uncomfortable feeling nagged at Karal. At first it was barely noticeable, but as the crystals' power went deeper into his bones, the feeling grew more unsettling. Karal reached out into the space before him and beyond that, the gems allowing him to pierce the haze of colored light that had blocked his view, and there it was: he discerned the unmistakable icy coldness of the Saeren.

Controlling his panic, Karal immediately sought out the Great Wizard's mind again, and joined with him. The crystals enhancing both of their power, through Karal the two traveled out from the mine, out into the mountains, out over the immediate area, and froze—the Breccians were there, and with them, a Saeren.

Karal returned to his body and looked around to see Wetell and Jamica. He looked at the other Cautes he had grown to know and love. He knew the new crystals at the entrance would not be enough; the Saeren would eventually see past the illusions. And once the Saeren found the mine, the Breccians would slaughter the Cautes. Even worse, they would seize the newly found gems for Malzus, who would harness their power to further his dominance. If they could tap into the newly discovered gems before Malzus did, they might have a chance.

"The Breccians," Karal gasped under his breath.

Only Wetell heard him, and he looked at the wizard anxiously.

Karal's fear grew. He had never felt this much power coming from Malzus, who must have sensed the gem pocket and been able to use its power. Preadus, from far-away Dolcere, tried to calm Karal, to steady him and get him to focus on what could be done, but Karal also detected the Great Wizard's fear. He looked around at Jamica and the miners that were there, all celebrating the incredible find. Many were holding hands, lost in the rapturous beauty that surrounded them.

"How many? How far are they?" Wetell said with concern, his eyes darting around the mine. Karal knew the prince was strategizing on how best to protect his people.

"Hundreds—and they're almost here. There is no time."

Wetell stood, looking to Karal for any details or instructions or ideas, but the wizard stood there, frozen, with nothing to offer. Going to Jamica and putting a hand on her shoulder, Wetell signaled her and the others to follow him out of the gem pocket, and he started giving orders.

"Have everyone in the area come into the mine. When that's done, uncover the crystals at the cave entrance. Have a runner take this information to my father—tell him to send help immediately!"

With everything and everyone set in motion, Wetell turned to Karal. "We'll be okay. We've faced this before."

"This time is different—" but Karal stopped. He didn't want to say more. What good would it do? Wetell glared at him. Karal took a deep breath.

"The Breccians have a creature with them—a very powerful and very destructive being—who will be able to see through the crystals. It will be able to locate this mine and see the entrance. There is no hiding. Our best hope is to put your people in every crack and crevice." He repeated, with a grave look, "There is no time."

Wetell stood motionless, fists clenched, trying to control his anger.

"What is this fearsome creature?" he shouted. "Why didn't you or anyone prepare me for this, or even tell me about its existence, before now?"

"There was no need before this," Karal replied, trying to sound calm. Wetell's anger was rising. "I can explain later, but now we cannot waste time."

Wetell just stared back at him; his eyes seemed to blaze with defiance.

"I'm not going to hide in the shadows, cowering! We'll fight the Breccians. We'll fight this creature."

He tried to turn to Jamica but stood frozen; Karal had entered Wetell's mind and taken control, stopping him from moving. The wizard understood Wetell's urge to fight, even respected him for it, but this could not be allowed. Though the miners lived with death on an almost-daily basis just from the dangers of their work—potential explosions, cave-ins, and deadly gases—Karal couldn't allow them to risk their lives in a senseless and impossible-to-win battle. Wetell had no idea how danger-ous the Saeren were; the Caute miners were not good sol-diers, and Karal and Preadus had already reached out to their fellow wizard, Thurmore, to rally the Caute army he was with, led by the younger prince Rubea. They were too far away and wouldn't be able to get to the mine in time to prevent the attack, but if the Cautes could hide, maybe some of them would be alive when Rubea arrived.

Karal had erased Wetell's desire to fight. He released the prince, who blinked several times as he came back into awareness of the chamber where they all stood, and turned to Jamica.

"I want you to take charge," he directed. "We must hide everyone in the mine. We need to protect as many as we can."

Jamica gave the prince a worried look.

"Some places are safer than others. How do I know? How do I decide?"

"Our first obligation is to protect this mine and not let it fall into other hands. As for the people—you must decide, based on how essential each one is to the mine's protection and operation."

Jamica grew silent and nodded.

"As you will, my prince," she said calmly, her expression grave as she took hold of his hand and held it tightly for a moment, and then hurriedly disappeared into the gray caverns, calling to others to follow.

Wetell turned his attention back to Karal.

"I need your help. It's imperative—the Breccians must not find the entrance to this mine. You wizards—aren't you good at this sort of thing?"

"I can help, and I can make it more difficult for them, but they will still find the entrance."

"That's not good enough. Why can't you do what you did with the Hilltop mine? There were many times more Breccians to hold back then."

"As I said, it is very different this time. They have that creature—the Saeren. They are . . . very powerful." Karal didn't tell Wetell that Malzus had already tapped into the power of the crystal pocket and was drawing strength from there. If they couldn't sever that link, they would be overrun.

"Look," Wetell replied, his voice rising in anger, "we work to supply you with gems and metals. You're supposed to protect us in return. That's the deal my father made with the wizards."

Karal felt his blood rising. He was a wizard and he shouldn't let a Caute trouble him. But Wetell's passion for some reason stirred Karal's own emotions. And this was rare for him. It felt good, like a release, to let his emotions come to a boil. To allow himself to feel his own anger and frustration. He was about to lash back out at the prince, but the familiar, calming touch of Preadus stopped him. The Great Wizard reminded Karal to stay in control. Karal repressed the words he had been about to say and regained his composure. He then reached into Wetell's mind and redirected his anger.

"If you keep your people well-hidden, some will survive. Now I must leave you."

"Wait—aren't you going to help defend us?" Wetell's face darkened.

"I'll stay by the entrance of the mine. There's nothing more I can do here."

Karal took his leave of the prince and made his way back up to the entrance. Once there, he settled into the shadows near the crystals and, in the eerie quiet, turned his concentration to listening to the voices and thoughts of the miners. Normally he would block them out, but now he wanted to listen to everyone—to capture their thoughts, record their last words and feelings, knowing that soon, many would be dead. These people were his responsibility; he needed to help them. They were his connection to the real world, the world outside of council meetings and Koan readings. He felt so useless, knowing he couldn't control whether they lived or died. How could Malzus be doing all this? Thurmore was right: they needed to do away with the threat. They needed to destroy Malzus.

Karal's senses signaled him, as he detected the Breccians closing in. He felt the Saeren with icy tendrils of energy reaching like smoke into every crevice of the mountains and surfaces around him, probing for the concealed opening. Karal closed his eyes and reached out to the other wizards. He found them all there, ready to help.

He now was fully engaged in the struggle to keep the entrance hidden, fighting with Malzus for the power of the crystals. It was helping, at least for the time being, but Malzus, through the Saeren, kept reaching, searching, and prying.

Karal and Preadus began to draw in the others, except for Asmar. Dragorn was in Dolcere with Preadus. Next, they reached out to the wizards who had traveled out from Dolcere. There was Mentaire and Wellum who were with the Cherts. Next came Thurmore, who was helping the Cautes, and Rogi who was with the Aris. They were not as strong when they were not together, particularly when they left Dolcere where they kept the treasures from Insula. Preadus took control of all of their minds and drew them together as one. Now, as a unified force, they all pushed back against the Saeren, preventing it from piercing the illusion to see the entrance.

But the Saeren was pushing forward with its own power, and the wizards felt Malzus's control over the gem pocket strengthen. As he tapped into its power, the other wizards felt their power being drained away. Karal opened his eyes, and the others, through his eyes, saw the exposed entrance to the mine, the illusionary block of the entrance crumbling. The dust of the mine swirled in the air and was touched by the bright sunlight outside, creating a glittering veil the Breccian troops now swarmed through—hundreds of them—swords drawn and battle cries rising.

They poured in, passing so closely to Karal he could have reached out and touched them as they flooded by. The wizards pushed back against the Saeren's intrusion, to keep Karal concealed. With the remainder of their strength, they sealed off the hiding places of each of the Cautes, hoping at least some would be spared. The Saeren stood in the center of the entryway to the mine, coming to a complete stop, with the Breccian soldiers passing around it, none breaking the invisible barrier that surrounded the skeletal creature.

"Where are they all?" the Breccian leader cried out. Having stopped, he held up a hand to quiet his soldiers, and stood, looking all around him. An eerie silence fell upon the mine. Still hidden, all Karal could hear was the leader's voice and the more distant panting and scattering footsteps of the soldiers as they ran through the shafts, searching for Cautes and any treasure.

"And where are the metals and gems?" the leader continued. "There's nothing here—this mine looks abandoned.

"Tiox, have the men spread out," barked the leader. "I want every inch of this mine turned inside out. The treasures must be here somewhere, hidden."

Karal's head began to throb, and he felt the wizards straining to maintain their connection and power. Karal felt the Saeren tearing at their thoughts, shredding apart the powerful interwoven unity of the wizards. The barriers that the wizards had so skillfully constructed were starting to collapse. With a concentrated effort, the Saeren ripped through the last of the wizards' connection to the gem pocket, and all Cautes in hiding became exposed, with only the natural barrier of the rocks to protect them. Without hesitation, the wizards quickly connected their minds and shifted all their remaining power to protect the chamber of gems at all costs. Karal watched with sadness as the Caute miners tumbled out of their now-visible hiding places and fled deeper and deeper into the mine. The Cautes fought valiantly with everything they had, trying to defend themselves with any crude mining tools—picks, shovels and axes—but it was useless.

It was taking the wizards every last bit of their strength to keep the gem pocket hidden from the Breccians. They could not let Malzus have the crystals. If the crystals were removed and brought to him, all would be lost. In focusing all their energies there, they couldn't protect the metals and gems stored at the mouth of the cave. The two crystals at the mine entrance came into view. The two Cautes on guard ran from their hiding place and were immediately killed by Breccian soldiers.

"We found the gems," Karal heard a Breccian breathlessly reporting to their commander. "They were being protected by two Cautes."

"Bring them to me immediately for questioning," the leader instructed.

"That's impossible," one soldier responded. "They've been killed. We were told to kill anyone we find."

"You fool!" the commander said, spinning around to address one of his other soldiers, a tall, silent Breccian with broad shoulders and dark shoulder-length hair.

"Tiox, if you can't keep the soldiers from doing idiotic things like killing prisoners who might have important information we need, you're useless. There's something going on here, and we need to know what that is. I need to question a Caute. Find one—alive! Bring them to me at once."

The tall Breccian said nothing, only nodded once to his commander and signaled to the others to go.

Karal could hear the continuing sounds of battle coming from the mine shaft. He had to withdraw his mind from the Cautes. He didn't want to feel their pain, the agony of their deaths. Instead, he found and entered the minds of the ones who remained hidden, calming them. They each wanted to break out; to fight and defend their comrades, but the wizards had managed to hold some of them safe in the shadows.

Finally, Karal watched as a Breccian soldier returned, and an old Caute miner was dragged in front of the leader and shoved forward. Karal knew him; he himself had taught this man faceting techniques, many years back. He remembered how pleased the miner was to learn something new and how proud Karal felt to be guiding this student. He reached out to the mind of the Breccian commander to stop him from what he was about to do, but had to pull away quickly. His head throbbed and he felt cold. He felt the unmistakable touch of the Saeren.

"We're not armed," the old miner said, in a weak voice. "Please, just take the gems and leave us in peace." The miner's face was bloodied, one eye swollen closed, and a deep gash oozed on his right arm.

"Silence, old man," ordered the commander. "Where are the rest of the gems and metals? Tell me, and you'll be allowed to live."

The miner straightened in defiance, his voice a little stronger. "Will you also spare the others?" he asked, looking the leader straight in the eye.

"Worry about your own life, right now."

"Then"—the miner seemed calm—"I don't know where they are." Karal, watching this all happen, desperately reached out again. He pushed as hard as he could, but it didn't work; the Saeren's barrier was impenetrable. A Breccian soldier stepped forward and in one deadly move, buried his sword in the Caute's back, and withdrew it. The old man crumpled to the ground, as a pool formed around him. Karal stifled a gasp.

"He'll not be so impudent again," the soldier said.

The wizards' contact with the gem pocket continued to weaken. Soon the council's power just wouldn't be enough to hold up the last layer of protections, and the chamber of gems would be unprotected. Karal watched as one after the other, captured Caute miners were dragged forward before the leader, briefly questioned and then callously murdered; their bodies thrown out of the mine, and the miner's choosing to die in silence

Karal sat, cloaked and invisible, feeling his anger surge, but he felt something else surge with it: a renewed power. This power was completely alien to him. It was wild, and incredibly strong. Karal attempted to control it, to use it to supplement the wizards' unified force. His efforts were somehow thrown aside.

The power surged through him, tapping into the strength of the crystals first at the entrance to the mine, and then pulling from the newly discovered chamber of gems. The forces kept building and kept expanding, finally ripping through the tenacious hold of Malzus on the gem chamber, and—to Karal's astonishment—finally breaking Malzus's connection and sapping his power.

The wizards now had control of the gem pocket, and their power surged. The barriers protecting the Cautes were reestablished. Walls changed and shifted, and seemed to flow.

The Breccians looked around, confused, trying to understand what was happening. Panic started to spread among the soldiers. They looked to their leader, who seemed lost and dazed.

And then it began: an explosion and then a low, steady rumbling. The rocks began to shake, crack, and crumble all around them. Karal heard the Breccian leader, sounding shrill and terrified, scream, "They set off explosives, the mine is collapsing—get out!" as soldiers rushed quickly, gathering what treasures they could, and rushing for their lives toward the exit of the mine, unable to even take with them the heavy, impressive crystals guarding the entrance. As the last Breccian soldier escaped, a rain of rock showered down with thunderous noise. The entrance was fully sealed.

Karal stood shakily, his knees weakened from crouching for so long in his hiding place. He stretched his aching legs and watched through the barricaded entrance, amazed, as the Breccian troops fled farther and farther away.

He sniffed, then deeply inhaled, fresh air. There was no collapse; the air was from outside and was clear. The power Karal had felt only moments ago was gone. Preadus spoke as he struggled to hold the wizards' minds together.

"What was that?" Preadus asked the others, sounding shocked.

"Was it—could it have been—Asmar?" Rogi asked, sounding shocked as well.

"No, I don't think so," Preadus replied. "It can't be. He's far too inexperienced."

With those words, the effort of holding them all together became too great, and the link faded.

Karal was alone.

With the Breccians now fleeing somewhere into the distance, the remaining Cautes slowly ventured out from their hiding spaces. The prince and chief engineer, both alive, looked at the wizard upon rejoining him and nearly wept with a mix of despair and relief.

"You saved us, Karal," said Jamica, her voice tired and soft.

Wetell was on the other side of the entrance, bent over the bodies of the dead miners, thrown upon each other in a pile. Fifteen had been killed. Fifteen lives taken, in that short battle. Karal watched as Jamica went to the prince and lightly touched his shoulder.

"This old man," the prince began, his voice cracking, "he was my first instructor in gem cutting. He also taught me how to make fine rolling stones. I used to win at stones often because of him. Now he's gone. He wasn't even a soldier."

The prince took a deep breath, then called out, "Ferman." A small, stocky miner came forward at his command. "Take three miners and bury the dead."

"Yes, sire."

"Where is the master cutter?" Wetell continued, further collecting himself and clearing his throat. A slight man with thin, long fingers, who looked like he hadn't seen the sun in many years, approached.

"Meils," instructed the prince, "find out what's been taken." Meils nodded and was off.

With those things being seen to, Wetell came over to join Karal and Jamica.

"Wizard, we are deeply in your debt. You saved our lives."

Karal bowed his head slightly, and could only respond, under his breath, "I wish I knew how."

"Your brother will be here shortly with his soldiers," Karal quickly went on, changing the subject. "That will stop the Breccians from returning. The wizard Thurmore is accompanying him. I reached out to him to come. They will arrive before dark."

As the sun set, Rubea arrived riding a pure-white horse, her mane braided with blue and red gems. He was trailed by two hundred mounted soldiers. Rubea was an impressive sight, wearing the finely woven gray cloth of nobility with a family crest featuring a faceted blue gem at its center. He was in deep contrast with the outfits of all the miners in their work uniforms cut from the coarsest, roughest cloth.

Karal rose to greet them, joining Wetell in welcoming the new arrivals. His fellow wizard dismounted and approached them with Wetell's younger brother. Thurmore was clearly as exhausted as Karal. The two wizards' minds met.

"What's the damage?" Rubea asked as he strode over to his older brother.

"Fifteen killed, brother, and twenty more injured," Wetell replied.

"Death in a war is to be expected," Rubea began, his hand resting on the jeweled hilt of the sword at his side. "What of the stones? What's been taken?"

"You'll have to speak with my gem cutter, he's taken the inventory. I have to look after my people."

Rubea's face darkened. "They're my people as well," he corrected.

Karal didn't need his wizard abilities to sense Rubea's impatience with his brother.

"Yes, of course they are," Wetell responded, quickly. He put a hand on his brother's shoulder and called his gem cutter over. Then he returned to helping with the injured.

Rubea joined Karal and Thurmore. "It is lucky that Thurmore warned us in time. If we'd waited for the messenger, the Breccians would've been long gone."

"Unfortunately," Thurmore began, "we were too late to stop the attack."

"We must now go after the Breccians," Rubea declared. "They need to be punished."

"The Breccians have a half-day's lead," Karal replied. He didn't want to go after the Breccians, not with a Saeren at their side.

Thurmore was still linked with Karal.

We must go after the Breccians, if only to show the Cautes we are with them. In a few days, we'll break off the pursuit.

"First," Rubea said, "I need to see if my brother wishes to join us."

Wetell stood over a pile of freshly dug dirt, Jamica at his side and fifty miners intently listening to his words. He was leading a ceremony to honor the lost.

"I knew and loved these men and women," Wetell told those gathered for the burial. "They were a part of all of us. Their deaths were unjust. It's up to the living to put an end to these tragedies. We must rise above those that committed these acts and—"

"Brother," interrupted Rubea. "We must be off now, to make good time and bring justice to the Breccians. You will be riding with us?"

Wetell turned and gave his brother an icy stare, but when he spoke, his voice was calm. "No, my brother. I leave the revenge to you."

CHAPTER 15

ASMAR SAT IN THE DIM light of his cell, beads of sweat rolling down his forehead.

Something had happened, but it was all blurry. He knew, somehow, that there had been a battle. He felt a struggle—the wizards using all of their energy trying to protect Caute miners. He had tried to help but didn't know how. He'd felt powerless, alone.

He sat on the floor, trying to shake away the images of killing and fear and death, when the door to his cell was flung open, startling him. Preadus was in the entrance, blocking the light and towering over him. There was anger in his voice although it was steady.

"You've become powerful, Asmar. Now, you must learn to control yourself."

Asmar looked up at him, surprised. There was something Asmar was supposed to understand and admit to, but he had no idea what it was. He remained seated and didn't—couldn't—respond. He was exhausted. This seemed to annoy Preadus. The Great Wizard moved from the doorway toward him, until he was standing just an arm's length away. Neither spoke.

Finally, Preadus broke the silence.

"Was it you?" he demanded.

Asmar stared at him, not comprehending what was going on. But then he realized: the power that he had seen in his mind, saving the lives of miners—it wasn't from the Council of Wizards at all. They didn't know where it came from. Preadus thought it was coming from ... him.

Preadus waited for any glimmer of recognition or understanding from Asmar. There was none. Anger drained from the old wizard's face and was replaced by an expression of confusion.

"It wasn't you." This was not a question.

"No," Asmar said simply. But the implication shocked him. If there was a power that was so strong it was able to push back Malzus, then there had to be wizards the council didn't know about, powerful wizards who remained hidden. Preadus turned abruptly and left.

Asmar fell back onto the hard bench he used as his bed and put his head in his hands. The images and feelings coming from the mine—of death and agonizing loss—surged back into his head, making him dizzy. Maybe, whatever this new power was, whoever it was, was the answer, and Asmar wouldn't be needed to fight Malzus. He felt deeply relieved by this thought, but also a little disappointed. He had been getting used to his training, his new skills, his growing responsibility, and had begun thinking of himself as a powerful wizard, even though he was still an initiate. Although he sometimes secretly questioned whether he could actually defeat Malzus, he wanted to believe he could.

These thoughts nagged at him as he struggled once more to his feet. He had to get moving; he was still in training, and the wizard Dragorn was waiting for him. Today, Dragorn was going to teach from the Talum, the book that explained the Koan.

Asmar's studies had opened up a new world to him, one he didn't understand quite yet, but he wanted to learn now more than ever. He thought he could maybe become the savior the council wanted if he worked hard enough and learned enough.

As he got ready, he wondered what today's lessons would be about. He didn't see how the study of the Talum was going to be helpful. The words of the Koan had been jammed into his mind by Preadus. They were complex, but at the same time beautiful and poetic. Asmar was still trying to understand them, unraveling them bit by bit, line by line, and layer by layer. He hoped he could talk about the Koan with Dragorn or Preadus, but they only actively taught the Talum. The beauty of the Koan was getting lost and buried under so many explanations contained in the Talum, and that made it difficult to get to the true meaning of the Koan.

Asmar trudged up the winding stairs of the tower that overlooked Dolcere. He paused halfway up and looked out a window to admire the lines and arcs that made up the city's beautiful grid. Out there, embedded in that orderly pattern, was the street-level disorder of the city. He closed his eyes and felt the warmth of the morning light wash over him. He lost himself in that light and tried to float away, to reach out into the desert, searching for any new wizards. He wanted to meet them, to speak to them. Mostly he wanted them to tell him what to do, and how he could help. He picked up nothing from scanning the desert, and his hopes faded. He stood gazing out, taking in the silence, until he felt the terse unmistakable call of Dragorn. Asmar ran the rest of the way up the stairs.

Once Asmar entered the wizards' study, Dragorn motioned for him to sit.

We'll continue with the Talum. Dragorn's voice was like a weak signal reaching into Asmar's mind, his tiredness very evident. Asmar seated himself on a hard wooden chair across from the wizard, who had taken the softer, upholstered chair for himself.

Where are the other wizards? Asmar asked.

What do you mean? said Dragorn. *Thurmore and Karal are with the Cautes . . .*

No, said Asmar. *The other wizards. The ones that didn't come from beyond the sea.*

There are no other wizards in these lands, Dragorn said, flatly.

But I felt them. They were in the mine. They saved the miners.

We don't know what that was, Dragorn snapped impatiently, *but it certainly wasn't a wizard.*

How do you know?

Because wizards study the Koan and the Talum.

How do you know the other wizards don't?

There are no other wizards. Asmar felt anger rising more in Dragorn. *Only the council studies the Koan,* he said, working to sound calm. *It's our book and ours alone.*

They locked eyes. The implication to Asmar was very clear: there was someone who had the power of a wizard without having studied the wizards' holy books.

Why can't we study the stories directly from the Koan rather than using this book? Asmar pointed to the Talum.

Dragorn rubbed his eyes, clearly tired and wanting to go on with the lesson, but Asmar sat in stubborn silence. Dragorn sighed.

This book, he explained, *just happens to be the Talum. It was written by the wisest, most powerful wizards that ever lived. Ever since the Koan existed, these wizards have studied and examined it and distilled its very essence into the Talum. You have been studying for only forty days. Be satisfied with the wisdom of the ages. Now, let's get back to the story of the creation.*

He opened the massive book that was laid out on the table between them and he thumbed to the right passage. Placing his index finger on the page, Dragorn recited.

The Koan says, "The land was formed in seven days and on the seventh day, three golden trees were planted whose roots meet and intertwine at the center of the world. The three together bind the world. And three times did the Lord enjoin the man and woman to care for them." Now tell me: *what does this passage mean?*

Asmar looked down at the table and muttered, *I don't know.*

Of course you do, Dragorn insisted. *We've gone over this before—how does the Talum interpret this story?*

That's a different question, Asmar responded.

Dragorn's face reddened. Asmar relented and answered.

The Talum says the three trees are needed to rule the earth, to keep it from falling into rubble, and that the number three is thus a symbol of perfection, a sacred number. This is further supported by the command of the Lord to care for the trees appearing three times.

Asmar hesitated, but Dragorn gave him an insistent look, so he continued.

Further, in the beginning, there was the Lord, the man, and the woman: three beings. Three trees, three commands, three beings. Three sets of three, the formation of the sacred nine. From this comes the number of wizards on the council.

Correct. The Council of Wizards must be in harmony with things as they were in the Beginning. Only then will we find the three trees which were lost. Dragorn let out a sigh of exasperation. *Now you know why it's so important for you to be a wizard: you bring our complement back up to nine.*

You could use the other wizards; you don't need me, replied Asmar.

There are no "other" wizards, Dragorn said, with finality.

Asmar realized it didn't matter. It was the trees—roots intertwined at the center of the world, joining together for strength—that the story was really about. He felt the number three wasn't important. He continued to sit, quietly thinking. Something suddenly occurred to Asmar.

Yours was not the first council to seek the golden pulcher, was it? he asked.

The older wizard's eyebrows raised. *Why do you ask?*

The golden staff came from one of the trees, so there must have been a time when the wizards found it.

Dragorn nodded. *That was both a great and troubling time for the wizards.*

Troubling because when you found the staff, you lost the tree?

Yes . . . Dragorn said, and let his voice trail off. He didn't go on, but Asmar could tell he wanted to.

Is the story in the Koan or Talum?

Dragorn shook his head.

It happened many generations after the Koan was finished, he said. *It involved two of the greatest wizards of all time, Heil and Shammai.* Dragorn paused and Asmar stared at him until, reluctantly, the wizard went on.

Dragorn sighed. *It was the time before the Great Council. Heil felt a strong power coming from a cold, frozen land in the far north. He asked his closest friend Shammai to search with him for the tree. They brought provisions as well as some seedlings on their travel over the half-frozen land and seas. When they arrived, they spent most of their time either in deep, contemplative meditation, or doing the hard work of clearing the frozen land to nurture the seedlings. Years passed, and the two became close friends, their minds fully linked and their power increased by their connection.*

On a cold, clear day three years after their arrival, Heil and Shammai finished their meditation and walked out onto the flat, ice-strewn plain. Despite the harsh environment, their garden was flourishing and their bond had grown incredibly strong. As the sun rose, they saw a silhouette far in the distance that hadn't been there before. Starting out early and walking toward it, growing closer, they were able to discern the shapes: it was the silver pulchers.

Their minds raced and their hearts beat fast in unison, as they stepped into the glowing oasis and realized . . . they had found the Silver Forest. Both were certain it was the bond of their minds, united together, that had made the forest reveal itself.

They wandered in silent awe through the stand of silver trees until, at the center, they discovered a golden light. Nothing could prepare them for the sight. It was the beautiful golden pulcher tree. Heil stepped forward and gently laid his hands on the golden tree. When he did, he immediately felt the interconnectedness of the world. He then sat next to the tree in deep meditation.

It was Shammai's turn, and now he stepped forward to touch the beautiful tree. When he did, he grew cold, feeling only hollow emptiness. There was nothing there. He realized this was because his knowledge was incomplete. He would be denied the chance to connect to the oneness of all things, and this deeply angered him.

Dragorn pressed his lips together for a moment. The look on his face was grave.

Shammai, outwardly, pretended to share Heil's enlightenment, but he'd closed his mind to Heil. He was enraged that he didn't receive the same knowledge that had gone to his friend. Shammai wanted the understanding that he felt he deserved, that had been denied him. If the tree wouldn't open to him, accept him, he would take part of the tree—and with it, a part of its power—with him.

One day, while Heil was deep in meditation, Shammai took a knife and cut a large branch from the golden tree, and then he carved a staff from the stolen limb. The distressed tree shook and there was a rumbling through its roots deep in the ground. Heil was jolted from his deep meditations. But there was nothing to be done. By the time Heil ran to the tree to discern what had happened, Shammai had vanished.

As word spread that Shammai had a part of the tree in the form of a golden staff, Shammai found a following that were willing to join their minds to his. Those that did, voluntarily subjugated themselves to Shammai's will, giving him their strength. For those who didn't submit voluntarily, Shammai used his own power and the power he was gaining through the staff to increase his control of others—to enter their minds without invitation, taking their will, their minds, and their strength, leaving behind only a shell. These were the first Saeren.

Dragorn stopped and shivered. He took a deep breath and went on.

Shammai fed on the strength and energy taken from the Saeren, becoming even more powerful, but this accumulated power only made him desire more and more. Thus began the First Mind War.

What happened to Heil? Asmar asked.

Heil reached out to the most powerful wizards in Insula and they formed the first Great Council. Together, they erected a barrier around their minds to protect themselves from Shammai. These wizards shared their power with Heil, giving him the strength to resist Shammai's assaults. Shammai fought back, trying to strip Heil's mind and turn him into a Saeren, but Heil fought back with the combined force of the council.

For forty days, neither moved, their minds locked in silent battle. Their struggle cast waves that rippled outward and were felt by all the wizards, each giving their strength to one or the other. Over time, the minds of the two greatest wizards began to ebb, their powers lessened, and finally the battle ceased when both Shammai's and Heil's minds were drained out of existence. They were there and they were "alive," but they were no better than the Saeren. All that was left was their shells. The war was over.

The wizards who survived were able to take the golden staff, and they went on a pilgrimage to the Silver Forest, hoping to reunite the staff with the golden tree. To their great dismay, the forest was gone, no trace of it to be found. All they had was the golden staff as a reminder of what had been, and what could have been possible, if they ever found the golden tree again.

Asmar sat quietly, absorbed in the story and this new information. The golden staff didn't belong to the wizards—or anyone—as he had thought. It was stolen. It belonged to only one entity: to the tree.

After his day with Dragorn, Asmar returned to his cell to practice meditation as Preadus had taught him, and as he had done every day since. He sat on the floor and focused on his breathing, following his thoughts and allowing his mind to guide him. He tried to recapture the feeling he'd had when he was alone in the darkened cell without direction or sensation. In his own chamber, it was more difficult to clear his mind. He kept thinking about the story of Heil and Shammai, wondering if there were other wizards who had also found the golden tree.

As his thoughts continued on their path, he felt something, or someone, reaching out to him. He tried to move toward it, but it was too weak, too far away. When he found he just couldn't concentrate any longer, he got up and abandoned his meditation, leaving his chamber to wander the empty, echoing halls of the tower, and soon found himself at the library where Remer was working with Shara.

Asmar found the two of them sitting with the Koan open between them on a table. He entered quietly and sat so he could hear their soft voices. Shara was gently turning the dry, fragile pages. They were seated very close to each other, and Asmar thought he detected something different in the way they spoke: a tenderness, where before there had been more of a tentativeness. They were just finishing a story in the Koan.

"And the governor imposed another tax on the people," Remer read aloud. "'We can't pay another tax,' the people cried to Gamal, their leader. 'Already our children go hungry, and we do not have enough grain to feed our animals. We need you to lead us against the governor.' Gamal linked his mind to his people and told them they must pay the tax. Many followed him to the governor's palace and laid down their tax on the steps to the treasury. But thousands of other followers of Gamal refused to pay, and the governor ordered his soldiers to attack them. Hundreds were killed. When the fighting was done, the leaders of the revolt came to Gamal and said, 'We should have listened to you.'

"'You fought the tax because you wanted what the governor wanted,' Gamal replied. 'There is no way to win a battle like that.'"

Remer turned to Shara.

"It seems a strange place to end the story," he remarked.

"Not really." Asmar's response caused Remer and Shara to jerk upright at the sound of his voice echoing in the empty room.

"Cousin!" Remer exclaimed, jumping up with a smile that made Asmar smile as well. They embraced. Shara smiled and nodded shyly. Asmar could tell she was unsure whether to treat him as Remer's cousin or as a wizard.

"Please, sit with us," Shara said, standing and motioning to an empty chair at their rough wooden table. After Asmar took a seat, she quietly asked, "What do *you* think?"

Asmar paused before answering. He wanted to talk about the stories, what he learned and was thinking. But mostly, he found himself yearning to just sit with his cousin and Shara. He craved the warmth of friendship and camaraderie.

"The last sentence," he began, "'*You wanted what the governor wanted. There is no way to win a battle like that.*' That's extremely important."

"Why?" Remer asked. "What does it mean?"

"It seems that Gamal thought the tax wasn't important," he said.

"Why not?" Shara asked.

Asmar thought of what he had learned, about Heil's battle with Shammai. Both wanted the power of the tree, and the result was the First Mind War.

"That really is the question, isn't it?" Asmar replied absentmindedly. Remer and Shara waited for him to go on, but he just sat there, trying to decipher the story in his own mind. Finally Shara and Remer went back to their book, leaving him alone once again. He got up from the table and left them in the library, returning to his cell in the tower.

The next afternoon, when Asmar was about to leave for his lesson with Dragorn, he was surprised to find Preadus again in the doorway to his cell.

There's no need for your lesson today, Preadus's voice boomed inside Asmar's head. *The next phase of your training will begin instead.*

Asmar then saw that the old wizard held his silver staff in one hand, but was holding a bronze staff out toward him in his other.

When you become a wizard, you will be given a silver staff. Until then, you will use this.

Asmar took the staff from Preadus, feeling its warm energy immediately. He was relieved not to have to sit with Dragorn and his Talum any more, but he was also curious.

What will I be doing?

You'll now be trained to develop your coordination and stamina and the ability to defend yourself.

What's involved in that? Asmar said, with a bit of apprehension, remembering his cousin relating his own training and how Remer's instructor had taught him how to use a sword.

You'll learn to be a wizard, to be superior to the commoners . To protect yourself by use of your wits, reflexes, and, if necessary, the staff or sword. Now, come with me.

These last four words were said as a command, and with them, Preadus exited the doorway. Asmar tried to resist, but instead was soon following Preadus out of the tower to a secluded area for this next phase of training. They were met by his new instructor, who was cloaked in the red talize of one of the desert Aris, the cowl hiding his trainer's face.

As they approached, Preadus began introductions. "Asmar, this is your trainer: daughter of Olmar, leader of the Aris." Hands reached up and the hood was flung back—and Asmar found himself staring into the blue eyes of the woman whose life he had saved. It was Areana.

Over the previous months of training, Asmar had learned to control his outward emotions, but at the sight of Areana, discipline fell away and he couldn't help but smile broadly. He felt a connection to her from the one time they had met, even though they had not seen each other since. As he looked at Areana, though, his smile faded—the look on the face of his new teacher was not one of joy.

"Your training begins immediately," she stated, in a voice devoid of all pleasantries.

Asmar turned to Preadus, but the Great Wizard was gone, disappeared without so much as a word. Asmar was alone with Areana.

Asmar turned to her. He was confused by her indifference.

"Why are you displeased to be my instructor?"

"If you must know," she began, clearly irritated, "I shouldn't have to be here. My place is with my people, leading my father's army."

"Then why aren't you there?"

"Politics," she replied, disgusted. "The disagreement that you witnessed between me and Adomas had to be downplayed so his father wouldn't lose face. The wizards felt I should remain safely in Dolcere until things cooled off."

"You mean—until *you* cooled off?" said Asmar, taking this all in.

"Yes. I was humiliated in front of the city by Adomas, yet he walks away free. I know he was under the influence of Malzus—but that's only one more reason why he shouldn't be trusted."

"Yet you didn't kill him when you had the chance, when he attacked you."

"I was wounded, if you recall."

"Yes, I recall. I also recall that even with the wound, you could've killed him, but instead you only defended yourself until your strength gave out."

"I was trying to hold out until someone intervened," Areana said, looking at Asmar. "I—I don't believe I ever thanked you, officially."

Her tone softened, and Asmar felt his face flush. "Do you know what would've happened if I'd killed Adomas? War among the Aris."

"Even though it would have been obviously self-defense?" asked Asmar.

"There were members of both of our tribes in Dolcere, and both witnessed what happened. Each would have reported what they wanted to see. Indeed, both have already reported what they wanted to see." She shrugged and looked skyward. "The truth doesn't seem to matter."

"But how can the truth not matter?"

"You are very naïve," Areana replied, and then turned her back on him and started to walk toward a corner of the practice field, where Asmar could see an odd-looking machine.

"Let's begin now," instructed Areana.

Asmar walked to where she was waiting for him and eyed the mysterious machine. It had a round central core of some kind that seemed to be made of a light wood, which towered over Asmar at twice his height. In the center of the column he could see a red gem about the size of his fist. The machine had many flat planks extending outward from it horizontally, each about two arm's lengths. The planks were all moving—spinning—in the same direction, but at different speeds and different heights.

"What is this thing?" Asmar asked, trying to figure out how this related to his training.

"Its official name is the Warrior Wheel. But most of us just refer to it as the Headbuster." Areana tried to suppress a laugh, as she motioned him to come forward.

"Jump in and avoid the wooden planks," Areana instructed.

Asmar laid down his bronze staff and tentatively approached the rotating arms as they swung. He glanced back at Areana to see if he was at least beginning to follow her instructions correctly, when the next thing he knew, he felt a terrific blow to his head and found himself flat on the ground, a shooting pain through his whole head and body, and his vision blurry.

Areana laughed. From his vantage point of agony on the ground, he couldn't help but notice how alive she looked at that moment.

Asmar struggled to his feet and steadied himself.

"Well, I guess I did that wrong."

"I guess you did," said Areana, with a twinkle in her eye. "Pay attention. You were too tentative. You must approach with authority and respect. You must understand the Headbuster, but even more, you must also understand yourself."

Asmar dusted himself off and tried to look more confident—in part to save his pride—as he jumped back into the flailing, spinning arms of the training machine. He concentrated. One arm approached his knees; he jumped right over it. Another came at his head; he ducked underneath with dexterity. Two more bars then came at him, one aimed at his head and the other at his shins. He didn't know what to do—it wasn't possible to go over and under the arms simultaneously. There was nothing he could do in that moment, and he let his body go limp as both arms struck him full force. Once again he was on his back on the ground, holding his head in anguish.

Areana smiled and stood over him.

"You didn't listen to what I said. You can't know yourself or the machine if you don't even look at it before jumping in, can you? Try again, when you're ready."

Nodding in the direction of her voice, he sat up on the dusty ground and gently shook his head, trying to clear his vision. Areana waited for a while, but then, seemingly impatient, left him to himself.

Asmar sat watching as the planks passed, first high, then low, then high, and so on, never stopping or resting.

How could he compete against this never-tiring device? The day was waning, but he vowed not to attempt to challenge the machine again until he had an understanding of what he was meant to achieve, and how he could avoid getting hurt.

Asmar sat and watched, intently. The arms' movement was random, unconnected, relentless. It seemed impossible to continually avoid his head being pounded, as high planks would consistently pass at the same time as low ones; eventually, anyone sparring with the wooden arms would find their head meeting a plank, painfully. Asmar winced and continued to study the movement of the many arms—twenty-one in all, he had counted—and the changing patterns of highs and lows.

Then suddenly he realized: he had been approaching it all wrong.

It was starting to get dark as Asmar again rose to his feet and cautiously approached the swirl of pummeling arms, bowed down low to the Headbuster, and then jumped into its swirling limbs. There was little time to think. Asmar ducked as an arm passed over his head, and then jumped quickly to avoid the next. When two planks approached and he knew he couldn't possibly avoid them, this time he didn't give up but quickly stepped outside of the wheel, and then jumped back in.

It wasn't the machine that he needed to defeat; it was his own preconceptions. He didn't need to figure out the machine's patterns; he had to modify his own. After watching for hours, Asmar had figured it out.

He was exhilarated, and now he couldn't stop. He moved deftly in and out of the machine's arms like it was a game, continuing until dawn: jumping, ducking, retreating, returning—never once so much as being grazed in the head or leg. As the sun rose, Asmar felt peace come over him. He abruptly stepped back from this dance with the machine and made his way back to his cell, where he fell into a heavy, satisfying sleep.

Over the next several weeks, Asmar met Areana every morning. They never revisited the Headbuster, but she kept him continually busy learning other skills. As he gradually began to master them, she seemed to warm to him. On one of these occasions, she was showing him how to scale a sheer rock face that was embedded in the side of the wizards' tower, using only his hands and no ropes. Distracted by her touch when she repositioned his hand, he lost his grip and fell flat on his back. When he regained his senses and looked back up at her, Areana's face was stern, but he caught a hint of her smile. Asmar worked to control his feelings and wondered if learning this control was part of the training; if so, it was the hardest part. He knew he couldn't let his mind be distracted from the goal of defeating Malzus, but he was intrigued by Areana, and he couldn't stop himself from trying to understand her.

Whenever Areana was in the markets, other Aris would stop her and touch the fringe of her talize out of awe or deference, or both. Despite the constant attention, she always had a kind word for anyone that approached. And yet, Asmar also knew she was a fierce soldier. He knew she had been ruthless in battle after battle and had slain many opposing soldiers without blinking. He found it hard to reconcile that side of her with the side of her that seemed so gentle.

After training together day in and day out for nearly sixty days, Areana met him on the practice field one morning with two long crystal blades.

"Today we'll learn how to use the swords," she announced, holding one of the clear, crystalline weapons out to him. He hesitated a moment before taking it, and when he pulled it from its sheath, the light danced along its sharpened edge. Looking deep into and below the translucent surface of the blade, he could see all the many facets that had been etched into the crystal to make it strong.

He stared at the blade for a long time and wondered if this weapon had ever been used to kill. Areana's voice suddenly seemed very far away. He lifted the blade, one hand on the hilt, the other on the sharp edge. Areana was yelling something at him, but all he felt was the crystalline blade slice into his palm as he grasped it. Blood trickled down his arm as he raised the sword and snapped it into two pieces over his knee. He opened his hand and saw blood on his palm. He was able to block out the pain. Areana froze, a look of horror on her face. Her voice came back into focus.

"Why'd you do that?"

Asmar just turned, silent, and walked away.

Back in his cell alone, Asmar sat on the floor, letting the blood drip from his hand onto the stone beneath him. The cut was inconsequential and would heal. He felt calm, almost empty, listening to the quiet of the room. Seeing the blood drip down on the floor, he thought: *if I were seriously hurt, who would I call?* Except for Lupa and Remer, he knew nobody cared about him. To the wizards, he was only a tool to defeat Malzus. And to Areana, he was just an unwelcome assignment.

He glanced at the bronze staff leaning against the wall in the corner and walked over and grasped it tightly. He slid back to the floor and let his eyes fall closed and his mind wander. It was easier this time—the pain in his hand seemed to help him focus. He wanted to reach out into the world, but all he sensed were vague, shifting feelings. He felt pain, but not the physical pain of his body. There was also joy and love along with the pain. He tried to concentrate on those positive feelings, to amplify them, but the fear and mistrust that came from the north, from Malzus, was drowning them out. He tried to push back the fear, but it was powerful. He let go of the bronze staff and looked down again at the gash in his hand. The blood had dried and the bleeding stopped. The severed skin had started to slowly re-connect and mesh back together. The wound was almost gone. The fear he felt began to ebb.

Asmar stood up. His joints and legs were incredibly stiff, as if he had been sitting in place for days. He took a drink of water from the pitcher in his room and ate some bread he had wrapped protectively in cloth. It was made from a bean that grew in a small garden planted behind the wizards' tower. The bread tasted slightly sweet, and his whole body seemed to feel relief as he chewed.

Asmar remembered the miners and all the fear he kept trying to sweep away. He couldn't help but connect the fighting of the Cautes and the Breccians—how they both wanted the gems and metals so badly, they were willing to kill or be killed—with the ancient story in the Koan, where the citizens rose up against the governor.

Asmar knew he needed to continue his training, but he vowed to himself that he would not fight with swords. He wanted to help, but he would not kill.

Arriving that morning to the practice field, he saw Areana waiting for him.

"You've been absent for three days, but Preadus told me you'd come today," she said. In her hand, she held a sword, but there was only one. Nothing for him.

She quickly drew her sword and raised it high, yelling, "Defend yourself!"

Asmar just stood still.

"You need to defend yourself," Areana repeated, irritated and impatient.

"From exactly *what?*" Asmar yelled back at her, standing motionless, refusing to engage.

She stood, paralyzed, looking back at him. It was the first time he had raised his voice at her. At anyone.

"If you're attacked, you'll need to fight back," Areana said, her voice calmer now.

"You mean, I will need to kill?" Asmar spat back.

"Yes, if needed."

"I can't—" Asmar crossed his arms and corrected himself. "I *won't* do that."

Areana slowly approached Asmar and with one swift move, lifted her sword, putting the tip to Asmar's throat.

"Not under any circumstances?" she said, looking straight down the expanse of the blade into his eyes. Asmar stood motionless, feeling the pressure of the dulled point against his neck.

She held the sword there for several long, tense moments, but then just as swiftly, she withdrew the blade and returned it to her side.

"You cannot know what you'll do, or need to do, going forward. You lived a protected life in Tuland. Now the wizards are protecting you. How do you know what you'll do if a Sitire soldier comes at you with his sword raised and death in his eyes? You've never faced the desert wolves, half-crazed with hunger and only thinking of you as their next meal. But when you do, you'd better be able to defend yourself."

Asmar felt the bruise left on his neck where the sword had been pressing.

"Is there no other way?" he said, his voice now soft.

"None that I have found."

"And ... you've stopped looking?" he said, his voice challenging, but gentle.

"Understand—this is the way things are. You, as a wizard, need to know that."

Asmar stood looking at her quietly, not responding. After a few moments, he turned and started to walk away.

When he was just a few steps away, Areana suddenly bolted toward him, her sword raised high, and she let loose a warrior cry from her throat. Asmar sensed Areana's thoughts and stepped casually to the side just as she was about to make impact with him. She fell forward and rolled on the ground, then got back on her feet in one fluid motion—a look of intense determination on her face.

She launched at him again, this time thrusting the sword powerfully with her arm outstretched. Asmar kept stepping aside, and perfectly, effortlessly evading her attacks. She went at him again and again, assailing him with all her might; each time he was able to outmaneuver her and not even suffer so much as a nick from her sword.

"When I come at you," Areana said, winded and struggling to catch her breath, her anger rising, "don't just step aside. Try to immobilize me. If you don't, I'll keep coming after you, and I will kill you."

Asmar stood, shocked. This wasn't the calm, disciplined teacher he had seen in all the previous weeks of training. This was Areana: soldier and killer, and she was coming at him again, now with a wooden practice knife she had pulled from her sleeve. Asmar stepped aside again, this time leaving one leg out, sending her sprawling face-first into the dirt. Areana sprang quickly to her feet for another attack, flinging herself at Asmar.

Again, down she went sprawling to the ground, earning a mouthful of dust—but she sprang quickly back to her feet once again and circled Asmar as if she was stalking prey. Asmar kept his mind focused on Areana. He had learned to move in new ways these past months. But he also sensed Areana's moods and could anticipate her thoughts and movements.

Areana held the wooden knife low, poised and ready to strike. When she saw an opening, she lunged swiftly. But as she did, the young wizard evaded her again and, once again, Areana ended up face down in the dirt.

"Enough!" she called out as she rolled onto her back. Her sweat had mixed with the reddish dirt, and her face was completely caked and stained.

Asmar leaned over and offered a hand to help her up. In that moment, the anger completely drained from Areana, and all she could do was smile. She accepted his extended hand, and he pulled her to her feet; their hands clasped and he stared, smiling, into her eyes.

In an instant, Asmar was down on his knees, the wooden knife pushed into his throat. Areana's warm breath could be felt on his ear.

"You are too trusting."

She had him pinned to the ground with her body. While he could have easily pushed her off—he had more than enough strength—he didn't. An awkward hush now fell between the two of them; everything stopped, until Areana broke the silence.

"There's nothing more I can teach you, Asmar. At least, nothing you're willing to learn."

"Yes, I know," Asmar responded.

As he brushed himself off, he kept looking downward, unable to meet her gaze. He had known for some time that he had already mastered all that Areana could teach, but he had purposely held back. He liked learning from her, and he liked being near her—but her violence was not something he wanted to learn. He looked into her eyes and wondered what, if anything, she saw in him: was he a boy, a man, or a wizard? And did she now think him weak for not wanting to fight? Her eyes stayed locked with his and didn't waver.

"Asmar! Areana!" Preadus called, striding out onto the practice field. "You're needed at once. Come with me."

Areana turned quickly and followed. Asmar tried to reach out to Preadus, but the Great Wizard's mind was closed. Preadus was leading them toward the Aris section of Dolcere, but even before they arrived, Asmar knew what he would find. He sensed pain, a lot of it. When the shouts and cries became audible, Areana ran ahead and disappeared around the corner. Asmar looked at Preadus, who maintained his steady pace. When the wizards turned the corner, Asmar gasped. Preadus put a hand on his shoulder and made it clear he was to remain calm. On the ground were about a hundred Aris soldiers, wounded and bleeding.

You're a wizard—show them what to do, Preadus communicated to Asmar.

Areana was immediately down among the wounded. She was hunched next to a bleeding soldier, trying to stanch her wound, when Asmar found her.

What happened?" Asmar asked Preadus.

A battle with the Sitire, Preadus said simply.

Why didn't we know about this?

There were no wizards with them, Preadus said, as he moved on.

Asmar turned back to the wounded and looked for those with the most serious injuries. As he walked among the injured, he sensed who needed help the most and who could hold on. He sat next to a soldier who was maybe a few years older than he was. The bandages on her side couldn't stop the bleeding. Asmar reached out and touched her mind. The woman knew she was dying and was trying to control her fear. Images of a young girl flashed in her mind. She struggled to hold onto life for her daughter, but with each passing moment as her life ebbed, her fear and sadness grew. She wanted her child to know what she felt, and to know that she loved her.

Asmar closed his eyes and reached out his mind across Dolcere, the image of the girl burned in his memory. His mind flew over the houses and tents that lined the Aris part of the city until he found her—the girl was asleep, unaware her mother's life was slipping away. Asmar pulled the little girl's mind to him and joined it with her mother's, the love flowing from one to the other. The connection was cut as the soldier's life drifted away. Tears rolled down Asmar's face. The pain and the loss of death made it impossible for him to move. He sat in the sand until Preadus entered his mind. *You need to be strong. Others need your help.*

Asmar forced himself to rise, and he slowly reached out to the injured to relieve their pain. He avoided touching the minds of the dying.

Asmar found Areana crouched next to a young soldier, binding his wounds. "Orien, tell me what happened."

"We had reports of Sitire raiders harassing our people just south of Arane," Orien began. "Your father ordered a column of soldiers to deal with the Sitire. Since you left, Adomas has been leading the armies. We sent out two hundred soldiers, then we came on the trail of the Sitire. There seemed to be thirty or forty at the most, judging from the tracks. They were headed toward the dunes."

"That's treacherous terrain. Perfect for an ambush," said Areana.

"So I told Adomas, but he wouldn't listen. He led us between two great sand pillars." Orien continued, "I had some of your father's soldiers hold back. They don't like taking orders from Adomas, especially after what he did to you."

"Go on," she said gently, though her lips pressed into a hard, straight line.

"As soon as the last of Adomas's troops were between the pillars, the Sitire attacked. Not thirty or forty, but hundreds. There was no hope of winning, but we had to rescue our comrades. I ordered an attack. I knew it was hopeless, but what else could I do? The Sitire weren't expecting it, and we made some headway. We reached Adomas's force and cleared an escape route. But he ordered us to stand

and fight! Why did he do that? I disobeyed his orders. I had the soldiers retreat."

"You made the right choice, Orien," Areana said to him. Her voice was no longer soft, but firm.

"Thank you, commander. Adomas's soldiers stood by him. Almost all were killed, but I think they managed to get him to safety before that."

Areana stood and turned to face Asmar.

"All of these injured must be cared for and properly tended to. Then, I'm leaving."

CHAPTER 16

MALZUS WALKED AIMLESSLY THROUGH HIS stronghold in Tellurium. He had done this so many times that he knew every detail of the fortress. In particular, he was impressed at how the ancient builders had carved the castle right into the side of the mountain. There were no seams in their work, and the stone was smooth as if polished. The skills of the builders had been so advanced and refined, it was shocking to Malzus that they had been lost to time. He had become obsessed with these ancients and wanted to understand why they had just vanished without a trace.

He practiced the skills by cutting new rooms deep into the mountain—at first crudely, but then getting better and better. It still wasn't as fine as the work of the lost people. His walls were not as smooth and his corners not as square, but his work was still impressive. He would often work through the night, trying to perfect his carving skills and increase the power each crystal gave off, but these crystals that the Breccians had given him were not of high quality. They were inferior and weak, and no amount of carving skills was going to bring more out of them.

In another room, Malzus painted the most intricate, detailed patterns on the walls. He also meticulously ground plants and stones to produce the various pigments he needed. The repetitiveness of the painting and the hours of intense concentration it required helped him open his mind and reach out farther.

Often, as he roamed the rooms, taking in his own handiwork and skills, he would imagine how impressed the other wizards would be, how impressed his father would be, if they could only see what he was creating. *One day,* he thought, *I will show my work to all of them, and to my father. Then they will finally understand how powerful and brilliant I am.*

The room he took the most pride in was where he meditated. It had thick walls to keep out any outside sound, the temperature was kept constant and perfectly controlled, and there was a single blue crystal in the corner. This was where Malzus spent most of his time.

Today, before his meditation, he was going to prepare the special powder that helped him go deeper into his trances and reach out further.

The powder was made from the poisonous olera plant and used the small bright-green larvae on the underside of each leaf. These were from the edenda bugs that ate and lived off this particular poisonous plant. They laid their eggs and died. Malzus methodically scraped the green larva off the bottoms of the leaves into a shallow bowl and then slowly, methodically, ground them into a powder.

When that was done, Malzus stood and slowly stretched out his cramped legs. The repetitiveness of the task had calmed him, and the powder he made was concentrated, much stronger than what he usually prepared. He needed the stronger mixture for what he planned to do next, which was to delve deeper than he had ever done before into the memories that had been a part of Vetus. It had been an unexpected surprise when Malzus recently discovered that Vetus's memories contained the thoughts and teachings of the ancient wizard Shammai. Like all the wizards, Malzus had been taught that Shammai's mind, like that of Shammai's rival Heil, had been destroyed in the Mind Wars—yet it was still here; Vetus had kept it buried all this time. The old wizard had never talked about this when he was alive. Malzus now wondered if Heil's mind was also alive somewhere, residing but hidden and protected with one of the great wizards.

Malzus reflected on the story of these ancients. In their time, Heil and Shammai had joined their minds, but Heil had insisted that joining had to always be voluntary and as such, it was forbidden for the wizards to take control of the minds of others. If they did, the "peace" created would be false, manipulated and therefore meaningless, and because of this violation of true choice, the tree's location would never, ever become known. All of the wizards since that time followed the teachings of Heil and were rooted in the principle of respect for the individual mind.

And yet Shammai had also found the tree, but he felt that having each individual choose the right path based on their own free will was an utter fantasy, simply impossible. To obtain enlightenment and find the tree, he espoused, they needed to be directed; they had to be led. So not only was it encouraged to take control of others' minds, but enlightenment couldn't be accomplished without it. A little influence was considered "necessary" for the greater good and spiritual advancement of all.

These contradictions concerned Malzus. He needed to know why the two Great Wizards disagreed—after all, they *both* had found the tree. The current Council of Wizards had followed Heil for generations, and yet they hadn't found the tree. Malzus wondered if Shammai was really the one who was right. But he needed to learn more.

Malzus had been able to tap only the strongest thoughts of Shammai. It was from those thoughts that Malzus had learned how to create the Saeren, but there was much of Shammai that was still hidden. In particular, there was something that had happened when he had found the tree, but this continued to elude Malzus. Today, he was going to meditate and go deeper into Vetus's mind in the hopes of finding the answers.

He sat back on the stone floor by the red mat in the center of the room, stirred the dried remains of the larva, and then gently tapped them into a special crystal pipe. Lighting this, he drew the thick warm smoke deep into his lungs and quickly felt its power course through his body.

His mind released and he began to travel, going deeper and deeper within his own consciousness.

He pushed past the surface of Vetus's memories and fell further into Vetus's thoughts, flowing past the first generation of wizards; their understanding, so limited. Malzus kept working his way into the depths of Vetus's mind, traveling past older generations and fainter voices. There were the memories of wizards from the Second Mind War, where the teachings of Shammai had been renewed. These were all echoes of what he needed; the mind of Shammai was further down. He drew in another lungful of acrid smoke and touched the white crystal that hung around his neck—the one he had worn during his wedding. Touching the crystal shocked him. He saw an image of his bride and started losing control—slipping—but then regained his focus, banishing her memories and presence completely.

Malzus reached further into the abyss of Vetus's thoughts and sensed a presence reaching up to him, floating to the surface, wanting to connect. Shammai's thoughts were at first so faint that Malzus could barely sense them. But when their minds touched, Malzus was sucked down into Shammai's earliest thoughts and awareness. There was the memory of Heil arguing with him on the interpretation of the Koan. Malzus could feel the two ancients at the time of their minds' connection in deep meditation, looking for the tree. Next Malzus experienced the rush of joy when Heil and Shammai's minds met in peace and they felt the serene, powerful presence of the golden pulcher tree. It was incredible, almost overwhelming.

This was as far as Malzus had previously penetrated into Vetus's mind, to retrieve Shammai's memories. The immensely powerful wave of feeling of knowing the tree was near was only provoking more frustration for Malzus; he wanted to experience the same ecstasy, the same wonder, that Shammai had felt upon seeing the tree for the very first time.

Malzus drew in another lungful of the dried edenda and pushed further.

Then suddenly he heard a new voice. It startled Malzus from within his meditation, as if he were hearing the voice of someone entering his chamber.

But just as quickly, he realized the new voice came from inside his head. This wasn't supposed to happen. The other wizards were just memories; they weren't really there—just thoughts and ideas floating in his mind. And why was Shammai able to talk to him? Was Shammai more powerful than any other wizard? Or, even more troubling, could Malzus be losing his mind?

Why have you come to me? The voice was difficult to hear, but it was, unmistakably, Shammai.

I want to know how you found the tree, Malzus replied.

Silence followed. For a moment, Malzus feared he had lost Shammai. Finally, the voice came back.

I didn't find it.

Malzus felt ripples of his own shock and confusion through the haze of the conversation. *I don't understand. The stories tell of you and Heil finding the tree and of the disagreement between the two of you,* he insisted.

The thoughts of Shammai became agitated, sending out vibrations of discontent. *Is that what you have been told?*

Malzus suddenly realized Shammai didn't know the stories of the First Mind War. All Shammai knew was what happened in his own life, the events he experienced.

Shammai was quiet as Malzus conveyed everything he knew. When Malzus was done there was a deep silence, and Shammai responded in the faintest voice.

Heil and I went north, as your story says. We combined our minds and found peace and understanding in each other's thoughts. There was a purity . . .

The thought trailed off, but Malzus felt a warmth and closeness that he had never experienced before.

The Silver Forest was revealed to us and we excitedly rushed in—but there was no golden tree to be found.

Malzus clutched the staff in his lap tighter. *But the golden staff . . . it is from the tree you found.*

There was no tree, Shammai insisted, cutting off Malzus. *We searched the forest for forty days. It wasn't there. We never found it.*

I don't understand, Malzus said. He was deeply confused. This had to be a mistake. *How could there be a staff if there was no tree?* Malzus thought to Shammai.

Again a brief silence followed, the length of a timeless exhale.

A wizard came to us, named Yoezer. He carried the golden staff with him. He told us that we were not ready to find the tree.

Malzus tried to take this information in. His head spun, he had so many new questions. *What more did you have to do to be worthy of finding it?* he asked Shammai.

Shammai became silent again, and then proceeded slowly. Carefully. He seemed reluctant to go on. *That was the question Heil and I considered.*

Malzus drew again on his pipe and listened intently.

Yoezer would not tell us anything. Heil grew wary and decided to leave the forest and return home to continue his studies, but I stayed behind with Yoezer. I wanted to find the tree. Yoezer kept on spouting ridiculous platitudes about obtaining peace within oneself.

But then he gave you the golden staff—to help you in your meditations? interjected Malzus, trying to understand.

Shammai again paused, and Malzus drew more smoke from his pipe, letting renewed power flow to the ancient wizard whose voice again wafted to the surface.

He was never going to give me the staff. He said that it could never be removed from the Silver Forest.

Then—how did you get it?

Shammai's voice seemed to be getting farther away, as he answered the question put to him. *While Yoezer slept, I took the staff from him. Then I immediately started into the forest, or at least, that was my intention. If I could harness the power of the staff, I thought it would lead me to the tree.*

But Yoezer woke before I had gotten very far and he tried to get the staff back from me. I wouldn't let him have it. He entered my mind and tried to compel me to give it back to him, but, as I had the golden staff in my hands, I was much stronger than he. I prevailed.

Malzus thought of his battle with the wizards. Shammai sensed these thoughts, and Malzus felt him smile.

Yes—I did the same as you. I destroyed Yoezer when he tried to steal the staff back from me. That's when I knew the right way: that I could bring peace by eliminating those that opposed me. I knew the tree would be revealed to me. I took the staff and I fled the forest.

Heil, from back in Insula, soon sensed what I had done and tried to stop me. He connected with the other wizards, and he created staffs of the silver pulcher for each of them. He wasn't strong enough to defeat me, but . . . Shammai's voice trailed off.

How did you know your way was the right way? Malzus asked, wanting to know that what he had devoted the last eighteen years of his life to building was moving on the correct path.

I could have found the tree . . . said Shammai, his voice trailing off.

Malzus took another lungful of the edenda and was not going to release Shammai until he got the information he needed. He pushed for more, but there was nothing. Shammai had escaped his hold and was now truly gone. Malzus collapsed.

As he slowly recovered his strength and his consciousness returned, a great emptiness filled him. He had believed in Shammai's teachings all these years, but he hadn't found the tree, Heil hadn't found the tree, and he believed now that his own father Preadus knew this all along. His father had lied to him and to all the other wizards. The lie had been passed down knowingly by the great wizards for generations. Of this, he was sure.

Why had they lied? Why had they insisted on following the ways of Heil? His head ached even more now, when suddenly it came to him: the ancient great wizards knew Shammai was right. They knew that if they told the others, then every wizard would want all of the power—and that's what led to the Mind Wars. The great wizards kept the information for themselves, and meanwhile taught others to follow the teachings of Heil.

It was even more clear to him now than ever before, that if he wanted to find the tree, he would have to take even more control, and to do that he needed even more power. The thought scared him; no wizard had ever tried what he needed to do, or at least none had done it successfully. He started to make his plan. The first thing he would need were the powerful crystals the Breccians had promised him—the ones that came from deep in the Caute mines. The gems that Lasum had lost.

Malzus picked up the golden staff, contemplating its smooth surface as he had so many times since it became his. It reminded him of when he was younger and things were so different—training back in Insula. His father had helped him fashion a silver staff when he first became a wizard. Malzus couldn't have been more than sixteen. That was the last time Malzus remembered his father being proud of him, and he remembered feeling like a son. After that, Preadus treated him like the others. No matter what he achieved, no matter how strong he became with work and study, it was Wellum and Vetus who attracted his father's attention.

Malzus reached out to Lasum and told him to come north to meet with him. It would be many days before Lasum arrived, and Malzus needed to stop thinking, to release himself from all the confusion his search into Vetus's mind had caused. So he reached out into the desert, but not to his Saeren.

Instead, he joined a pack of desert wolves that were roaming freely. It was a pack he had joined with before; they were the dominant pack, larger and fiercer than any others. He joined minds with the leader, and they ran in the night, howling and searching for food. He roamed with them deep into the desert, leading them in their hunts and kills, feeling the closeness and bond of the animals as they crowded together during the day and slept. As dawn approached on the tenth day, he drew himself back to his body. Back to Tellurium. There was much to attend to, since Lasum had just arrived.

As Malzus emerged from the secret rooms by way of a door hidden behind the throne, Lasum was there waiting, one knee touching the stone floor, his head bowed.

"Lord Malzus," Lasum's voice trembled. "It's been done—as you commanded."

The general had laid out a selection of the gems he recovered from the Caute mine. It was paltry compared to what Malzus knew had been left behind.

"You haven't done what I asked. The best gems are gone and the Cautes still live." Malzus scowled, causing Lasum to shiver.

"But—the cave-in, sir. Nobody inside could possibly have survived."

Lasum's earnest words echoed in the vast canyon of the tower. Malzus spoke deliberately and slowly.

"There was no cave-in, you fool. You were outwitted by a cheap illusion created by the wizards."

Malzus entered Lasum's mind and effortlessly suppressed the soldier's urge to flee. Malzus needed Lasum for other reasons.

Lasum was completely frozen in place. Malzus stifled a laugh when he discovered that Lasum was planning to kill him with a dagger hidden under his cloak. Instead, he sighed. Just once, he wished he could be surprised.

"Come closer," Malzus said out loud.

Lasum began to approach, and as he did, his hand went for the dagger, his grip tightening around the handle. Malzus pretended not to notice—he would give the Breccian a shred of hope, just for one moment. Lasum lunged quickly, thrusting the dagger upward. And that's when Malzus suddenly tightened his grip on Lasum's mind, squeezing him and freezing his arm in mid-air. Lasum was caught, and he collapsed inwardly, knowing there would be no escape.

The process was always the same: Malzus's mind bore down upon his victim, sending them into spasms of agony. Lasum, like others before him, tried to scream, but no sound would emerge from his tightening throat. Malzus was now in Lasum's mind; he could feel the Breccian's shock and horror as all of Lasum's memories became Malzus's.

Malzus sifted through them carefully to find the right one, the one that would allow him to trap Lasum in a small part of Lasum's own mind.

It was a memory of a ten-year-old Lasum and a younger sister. His sister insisted on playing on the ice and—it broke. The ice collapsed and she fell into the frigid water. Lasum watched as his sister disappeared under the surface, and he didn't move. He did nothing.

Malzus made Lasum relive his sister's death over and over, making him feel trapped in a vortex of helplessness and failure. Lasum kept backing away from the onslaught, and gradually his consciousness was pushed into a smaller and smaller space, until finally he was trapped—imprisoned in a tomb constructed of his own despair.

Malzus collapsed on his throne at the effort and saw himself from the eyes of his new Saeren, and for a very brief moment, he felt afraid—of himself. He had experienced something like this each time he created a Saeren. He knew it was just the residual fear Lasum felt, but it still made him feel untethered and uneasy.

Whenever he took control of a Saeren, Malzus felt alone, isolated. Lasum was now in an empty body. One that had no feeling, no hate, no love. It drained Malzus to create him.

This Saeren would go to the Sitire and serve as Malzus's eyes and ears. As it went out into the world it would bring more strength to him—not nearly as much as he would have from a wizard, but enough to slowly increase his own strength, compensating for what he lost in converting the Saeren.

He also needed to find a new general for the Breccians.

Malzus drew a name from the memory of the Saeren: Tiox. This Breccian lieutenant had actually accompanied his general to the tower and was waiting down at the base.

Lasum is no more, Malzus said, reaching into Tiox's mind. *You are the new general of the Breccians.*

Tiox's surprise and his fear rose quickly, but the Breccian was able to suppress it. Tiox's mind was stronger than Lasum's had been, and Malzus wondered if this was a good thing or not. He was too drained to probe further.

He managed to pull himself off his throne and make his way down the stairs and back to his cell, the golden staff still tightly clutched in his hand, the new Saeren following mutely behind. Once there, Malzus took a black robe from where it was hanging and threw it at the Saeren's feet.

Malzus himself couldn't bear the presence of the Saeren and sent it away before he collapsed on the hard plank of his bed, his mind finally able to rest.

CHAPTER 17

ASMAR FELT HE DIDN'T BELONG. He wasn't a real wizard. Not yet. He couldn't reach into others' minds and didn't possess the vast knowledge they all had and took for granted. What about this new power, new energy—who was it? It had to be a wizard. Should he step away from the mission and his training and let this new power take over? Asmar wondered if he would ever be strong enough to defeat Malzus, and then he wondered: if he himself was that strong, would he end up becoming just like Malzus?

These thoughts played over and over in his mind as he navigated through the tower maze on his way to the crystal chamber for the winter council meeting. When he finally reached the chamber and he pulled back the heavy chair and was about to sit down, he noticed all the others were still standing. He pushed the chair back and his hand rubbed against the smooth stone channels cut into intricate patterns in its back. At Preadus's silent command, the wizards sat down as one. Only Preadus remained standing, his hand holding tightly to his silver staff.

Where did this power come from, Preadus started abruptly, *and why didn't we know about it before?*

His thought resounded through the minds of the gathered council. Thurmore was the first to respond:

It seems to coincide with Asmar joining us.

Then Thurmore glanced Asmar's way, as did the others. Asmar slid down in his stone seat, worried.

Could it be a wizard from Insula who was sent here to see why we haven't returned? Dragorn asked. Asmar sat up. They turned their focus back to Preadus.

It's not a wizard sent from Insula, Preadus replied impatiently, taking his seat. *If that were the case, we would have felt him arrive. This is different. This is a new power who's been hiding from us.*

But how? demanded Mentaire, *And why is he revealing himself only now?*

I can't answer those questions, Preadus replied.

We don't know anything about him. He could be dangerous, Wellum said.

Thurmore replied, *This wizard has only helped us so far.*

That isn't true, spoke Karal. *It was through me his power was directed, and it felt to me as though he had a purpose all his own. I don't think he intended to help us.*

You mean it was an accident? Thurmore asked.

No, not an accident. I mean only that our goals appeared to coincide at that time.

Wellum looked at Preadus. *What happens if he uses his power against us? If Karal is right, could he destroy the council?*

No. Preadus shook his head. *He used our strength to hide the mine rather than being able to do it on his own. For now, we're safe, but we must find out where he came from and if he can be controlled.*

This wizard could be very important to the council. We need nine wizards working together to find the tree. Thurmore stopped and looked at the others. His glance temporarily rested on Asmar.

This is it, Asmar thought. *They are going to replace me.*

Thurmore went on. *If we can't control Malzus,* he said slowly, *then this wizard could complete the council instead.*

A silence descended on the council.

Are you suggesting we eliminate Malzus? Preadus's thoughts were controlled and cold.

Thurmore replied defensively, *I've suggested nothing and say only that we find this wizard.*

The other wizards shifted uncomfortably. Thurmore continued.

I'll look for him.

Preadus pushed back his chair, and it slid noiselessly from the table. Asmar tensed for a confrontation, but instead, the Great Wizard sank back into his seat and nodded slowly at his rival, his face weary as he begrudgingly accepted Thurmore's proposal.

Thurmore, you will take Rogi with you to search for the renegade.

Thurmore hesitated, looking at Rogi, then the other wizards, and finally nodded.

We move—Preadus straightened, but Asmar could tell it was an effort—*to our next issue.* Preadus seemed less focused. Distracted.

Olmar's daughter has asked permission to leave Dolcere and rejoin the Aris army. She has asked to address the council.

Before any objection could be given, the great doors of the council room opened. For the second time, Areana appeared before the wizards.

"I wish to be allowed to return to my people." Her voice was quiet yet firm. "They need me to lead them against the Sitire."

"You have an obligation to fulfill here," Wellum objected. "You need to complete Asmar's training."

She looked over at Asmar and then turned to Preadus and said stiffly, "I have no more to teach the wizard Asmar."

"We'll be the judge of that," came Mentaire's quick response.

Areana stood frozen in place until Preadus said, "You are dismissed from the council."

Almost by reflex, Areana turned, and the great doors opened before her. But then, with some effort, she was able to pause before stepping from the chamber.

"Please," she said sternly, "let me go where I'm needed."

As the last words were uttered, she walked briskly out into the hall, and the council doors closed behind her. The wizards were alone once more.

She's strong willed, observed Wellum.

Yes, agreed Rogi, *but what are we to do with her?*

Let her go, Asmar said.

Are you sure? How do you know she has taught you all that she can? asked Mentaire.

I'm sure, Asmar replied. *Besides, if she wants to leave, what right have we to stop her?*

What right? exclaimed Wellum. *We are the council! We decide what's in the best interest of the Aris or anyone else. You should understand that by now.*

If it can be established that she's taught me all that she can, Asmar offered, *would Areana then be allowed to go back to her people?*

Preadus looked at Asmar, surprised.

If you are trained sufficiently, she might be allowed to leave, he responded.

Test me then. See if I'm trained, Asmar insisted.

Very well, agreed Preadus. *Follow me.*

Asmar rose from the table and dutifully followed Preadus out of the council chamber and through the winding halls of the tower, out into the warm air. They stopped at the practice field where Areana had taught him. It was late in the afternoon and the sun would be setting soon. Already, Asmar felt a cool breeze coming off the desert. He watched the horizon and knew if he passed the test, Areana could go. As much as Asmar wanted her to stay, he wouldn't be a part of keeping her in Dolcere against her will. He had to pass the test—for her. He felt the golden ring that hugged his finger beneath the bronze, and thought of Lupa and Tuland. He had been so happy then. Now he was a wizard, and happiness no longer seemed important.

As they entered the field, Preadus turned to him suddenly.

You claim to be trained, Preadus began.

No, Asmar corrected, *I claimed to have learned all I could from Areana.*

Preadus raised his staff, ready to attack, and Asmar raised his bronze staff in defense. Despite its size, the staff felt feather light. Asmar remembered the statue that stood atop the fountain in Tuland, the wizard with his staff held high, vanquishing his enemy. That same wizard was now about to attack him.

Before Asmar could move, Preadus was on him. The old wizard was every bit as agile as Areana, and even quicker. Asmar was knocked to the ground by the first painful blow to his shins.

He knew better than to expect time to recover, and he deftly executed the roll Areana had taught him, performing it better than his teacher could have done. He was on his feet as he brought his staff up to defend himself, but Preadus's next blow still landed in Asmar's stomach. The young wizard was on his back again, his body aching. Asmar fought through the pain and clambered to his feet, just as Preadus's next blow was descending.

This time Asmar was able to dodge the strike. Preadus attacked again, aiming at Asmar's head. Asmar parried the blow, but it was followed by one aimed at his knees. This too was fended off. The next strike, however, found its mark in Asmar's chest. Asmar fell hard to the ground but managed to scramble back up and regain his footing before the next attack.

THE SILVER FOREST – Book One

Asmar suddenly became painfully aware of the difference between fighting a soldier and fighting a wizard: Preadus seemed to know what Asmar was going to do even before Asmar did, but he also knew how to conceal his own emotions and thoughts from Asmar. This is what facing Malzus would be like. Asmar could not rely on his ability to read his opponent, as he had with Areana. He needed to rely purely on the instincts he had developed over the months of physical training and meditation.

When the next attack came, Asmar didn't think, but reacted instinctively, parrying the blow as he had before. But now as Preadus initiated more attacks, Asmar reacted automatically to the incoming blows. The older wizard's onslaught was errorless, but now Asmar's defense also was perfect. Then Asmar saw it—the old wizard's first mistake, leaving himself open for Asmar to attack. It was his opportunity, but just as Asmar was about to strike, he stopped; he had nothing to gain from injuring Preadus.

Instead, Asmar threw his bronze staff down at Preadus's feet.

Enough, he said.

You won't seize your advantage? Preadus asked.

The fight is done, Asmar said, knowing now that the vulnerable opening had been deliberate.

Preadus nodded at the young wizard. *As you wish. We have concluded your first test.*

What was the point of it? Asmar said, feeling confused and upset.

That, you must answer for yourself. You're expected back in the council chamber. Clean up and make yourself presentable.

Asmar brushed himself off, picked up his staff, and went back to his cell. He had just enough time to splash water on his face and shake the worst of the training field dust out of his robe before the council ordered him back.

Asmar walked to his place as Preadus began to speak.

You've passed the first test of your skill. Are you ready for your next and final one?

Asmar looked around at the assembled wizards, still aching from his combat with Preadus. As he observed the wizards, he felt their anxiety. They needed him, but they didn't yet trust him.

Asmar projected his thoughts outward to the group with as much confidence as he could. *I am ready.*

Preadus informed him and the others that the final test would be the following morning. Asmar was to meet the Great Wizard at the edge of Dolcere with only his white initiate robe and his bronze staff. That was it. Asmar returned to his cell and tried to reflect on the challenge to come.

* * *

The next morning, Asmar arrived just as the sun was beginning to warm the sand. Preadus stood in front of the carved crystals that cloaked and protected the city. Seeing Asmar, the Great Wizard nodded, a signal for Asmar to follow him, and the two walked past the massive, powerful crystals and out into the exposed desert. Preadus paused as the two went beyond the city limit, turning to Asmar and pointing out into the vast desert, to direct the young wizard-in-training's gaze.

Do you see where that dune rises?

THE SILVER FOREST – Book One

Asmar looked out in the direction he was pointing and nodded.

You are to go there and return, Preadus instructed succinctly.

That *is the test?* said Asmar.

That is the test, the old wizard responded.

How long do I have to make it back here?

As long as it takes, said Preadus calmly. *Now, begin.*

With that, Preadus turned and walked back through the crystals that formed the doorway to Dolcere, back into the oasis and the safety of the city, and Asmar found himself once again completely alone.

No one was there. No one was watching to see if he would actually walk to the dune or simply return right away to Dolcere. Asmar thought this was likely part of the test. Could they be testing his loyalty? His truthfulness? If he didn't go to the dune, would he fail? Or were they testing his free will, in which case he would fail if he did go all the way to the dune? Could he even survive going to the dune, with no supplies, no support, no protection and no water?

He figured he would just start toward the dune and try to sort out what the wizards wanted on the way. He pulled up the cowl of his robe so that it shielded him from the worst of the intense desert heat. He walked on and on as the sun rose higher, passing midday.

He was grateful that his training had taught him to postpone such trivial needs as food or water. Asmar continued to walk through the heat into the glare of the early afternoon. His eyes ached from the sun reflecting off the sands. His feet throbbed from the unforgiving pace he set across the shifting surface underneath him. Occasionally he looked up, but the distant dune never seemed any closer.

Finally, he paused and attempted to gauge the distance he had already traveled, looking back in the direction he had come from, toward Dolcere. When Asmar did turn and look back, Dolcere was completely gone—the city had vanished. Now he understood: he was to return to Dolcere, *if* he could find it. The wizards had hidden the city from him, and if he returned alive, he would pass; if not, he would die out here in the desert, alone. Asmar turned to look forward again, and before him was a completely empty horizon. The dune no longer existed, or rather, had never existed. Asmar realized now why the Great Wizard asked if he could see the dune. The wizards had deliberately affected his thoughts and obscured his vision—just as they were doing now to hide Dolcere from his eyes.

Asmar's only hope of survival was to find Dolcere, but that would not happen today. The sun was setting, and the evening sandstorms would soon begin. Then, the desert wolves would appear. Asmar's first priority was to find shelter for the night and, hopefully, water.

The evening breeze was a welcome relief from the day's blistering heat, and after a short search, Asmar was able to find an outcropping of rocks that would provide a small but serviceable shelter for the night. He still had time to find water. He had been told to bring only his staff and robe, and had nothing else to help him survive. Areana had told him there was water in the desert if you knew where to look. He scanned the horizon for the desert sagu, but there were none to be seen. The other place to look in the desert was under the sand. Asmar scanned the area for the best place to dig. He looked for signs of runoff, no matter how faint, but couldn't find any. There were no desert plants, no slight depressions, and no faded runoff trails. Rather than giving in, Asmar started to dig near the rock outcropping. If there was water, the rocks would trap the moisture and prevent evaporation.

Asmar dug continuously until the sun dipped below the horizon but encountered no moisture. Finding no water, his concern shifted to sheltering. The ditch he'd dug, while not yielding any water, was deep enough to provide some protection from the wind and the wolves. Asmar removed his robe, leaving him bare-chested in only the light pants he wore underneath. Using his staff as a support, he draped his robe over the top of the hole. Then he secured its corners into the sand with smaller rocks. From under this flimsy roof, Asmar surveyed his handiwork. Considering he had no tools or rope, his shelter was as secure as could be. Asmar leaned his naked back against the cooling sand. Now all he had to do was wait out the night and find Dolcere the next morning.

Asmar listened as the wind lifted the grains of sand. They made a ping that reminded him of music as they hit the outcropping. As the wind grew stronger, the music transformed into random noise.

The rocks protected Asmar from most of the flying sands, and the robe provided some insulation from the falling temperatures, but Asmar still felt the sharp contrast from the morning's blistering heat. He tried to meditate and prepare for his journey the next morning, but his growing thirst and the pounding sand wouldn't let him.

When the blowing sand finally stopped, the howling of the wolves began. "If the wolves can survive in the desert," he considered, "then so can I." But the food they found in the desert came from the flesh of other animals, and the water from their blood.

The night dragged on, and the howls came closer and closer. Asmar gripped his staff as a wolf's howl seemed to come from right outside his shelter.

Suddenly, a needle-like snout pushed aside a flap of the robe that was his makeshift roof and snapped teeth-filled jaws at him. Asmar's heart surged with fear as he narrowly avoided that fearsome mouth. All in the same instant, Asmar grabbed his staff and snatched the white robe and wrapped it around his arm. He leapt effortlessly from the hole and landed on his feet, to find himself standing face to face not with one wolf, but with a pack of ten hungry animals. He took a deep breath and tightened his grip on the staff.

The wolves circled, preparing to attack. Then, suddenly, they came, one after the other. Asmar reacted instinctively, automatically—avoiding one wolf, then another, then the next, using only the outcropping and bronze staff to shield himself. As he fought off the wolves, his early training of jumping over and ducking under wooden boards came back to him. Just like the rotating wooden arms, now it was the wolves who kept coming at him, one at a time— never in a concentrated attack, but in individual advances.

The animals, he noticed, were very thin, and while their hunger fueled their ferocity, Asmar hoped it would also cause them to tire more quickly.

As one wolf came at him, the others snarled and clawed at the ground while slowly advancing and then backing away, as if well-rehearsed, to maximize the fear of their victims. Asmar found he could sense which wolf would take the lead next, and as each advanced, Asmar swung his staff menacingly in front of him and the wolf would back away. At first he was encouraged, seeing that he could defend himself and keep them at bay, but to his alarm, the wolves weren't tiring as he had hoped. Asmar's arms burned from the exertion and his reactions slowed as he felt exhaustion setting in. His heart beat hard as he swung at another wolf, who danced back out of his reach.

Asmar needed rest, even if just for a minute. His legs were weak from standing on the uneven rocks. The wolves paced and kept up their threatening advances as Asmar sunk to one knee, letting his arms fall and resting the tip of the staff on the rocks. He felt the blood rushing back into his arms, and he breathed deeply to try to get energy back into his wobbly legs. He looked down just for a moment to try to steady himself and catch his breath, but his eyes instantly shifted back up to see the largest wolf with piercing dark eyes leap at him, snarling and with jaws open wide, ready to make the kill.

Asmar stumbled backward, trying desperately to rise to his feet, but the wolf's teeth grabbed him and tore into his left shoulder. The pain was staggering in its intensity. Asmar tumbled to the ground, feeling the full weight of the wolf upon him, paws shoving him down, and the knife-like teeth digging in deeper. From the corner of his eye, Asmar could see the other wolves edging in closer. The warm flow of sweat and blood could be felt dripping down Asmar's back.

Gripping his bronze staff tightly in his right hand, Asmar used all of his strength to jab hard into the wolf. He swung frantically, not being able to raise himself fully up to see, but after making the effort, he heard a piercing yelp and the sound of a sickening crunch as the staff landed, causing his heart to leap and his stomach to turn. Instantly, the jaws of the wolf sprang free as the beast fell away from him. Asmar forced himself to concentrate and leapt quickly to his feet, swinging furiously at the pack. They backed away warily, but didn't fully retreat; he could sense their anticipation at the scent of wounded prey. He kept fighting off the exhaustion and pain and saw the wolf he had struck lying motionless on the ground beside him. From deep within, Asmar let out a bone-chilling scream and swung his staff wildly, staring coldly and defiantly into the vacant, half-starved eyes of the circling wolves. The pain was so excruciating it felt like the teeth were still embedded in his shoulder.

The desert around him was becoming hazy, and Asmar's consciousness was fading; he knew he couldn't hold on much longer. His instincts said he should run, but his legs wouldn't move, and he knew that he could not outrun the wolves. A wave of nausea hit him and he began to sink down to his knees again. The pack cautiously moved closer as Asmar managed to push up enough to weakly swing his staff.

Just as his strength threatened to completely give out and tears rolled down his cheeks from the sheer effort of protecting himself, he heard a distinct, distant howl. The pack heard it as well, and they all froze in place. Their ears stood up and all their necks craned forward, pointing in the direction of the sound as it pierced the sky again. This time, the pack answered. At the sound of a third howling cry, the pack charged off into the night, leaving Asmar and the body of the one injured wolf.

Asmar collapsed flat onto the rocks, his staff dropping to his side with a soft thud. He shivered in the still-freezing night air, becoming suddenly aware of the cold now that he was able to stop moving. He tried reaching over with his hand to check his damaged shoulder in the dim moonlight, but the unbearable pain stopped him. The unconscious wolf lay completely still on the ground, barely an arm's length away. Through the darkness, Asmar sensed the wolf's labored breathing, and he felt another surge of panic. He knew he should kill the wolf; that's what the other wizards would do. But the very sound of his staff making contact with the wolf's body had sickened Asmar.

I can't kill this creature, he thought, as he lost consciousness.

Asmar woke the next morning to the growing warmth of the slowly rising sun, and a burning sensation coming from his inflamed, infected shoulder. He knew he would need the wizards' salves to prevent an infection from worsening, so he tried reaching out to the council—any one of them—but he could find no one to connect with.

A low whine came from nearby and Asmar looked over to see the wolf, still lying there, now partly conscious. He crawled weakly over to the injured creature to examine her wound. His blow had struck the wolf squarely in the ribs and there was a deep gash where blood still oozed. Asmar gently wiped as much of the sand from the injured area as he could, before tearing his robe to make a bandage. Carefully, gingerly, he examined the injury; one of the ribs seemed broken. Without thinking, Asmar set the rib gently as he was taught, then managed to crawl back into the shelter of the rocks.

His hand shook as he used his robe to wipe the blood away from his own wound. His shoulder throbbed and searing pain shot down his back. There were at least three puncture wounds in the front of his shoulder. He knew there were more on his back, and he tried to feel for them. The ones he could see were red and swollen, not a good sign. His exhaustion was overpowering and he fell back into a feverish sleep.

When Asmar next pried open his eyes, the sun was high and directly overhead. The full warmth of its rays felt soothing on his aching body, in contrast to the freezing night he had just endured. Asmar rolled over to see that the injured wolf was still there, having barely moved all night. Asmar felt stronger from the rest and warmth, and pangs of hunger and thirst set in. He needed water, and he thought surely the wizards would come and help him.

He tried reaching out once again to his fellow wizards, but there was nothing.

He crawled back to his hole and began digging with his one working hand. The heat became more intense with the physical labor, but he continued working until he felt dampness. Finally, the hole began to fill with a trickle of muddy water. Asmar, feverish but relieved, used his robe to soak up every drop. His left arm was unusable, so he had only his right to pull and drag himself out of the pit. He put the damp cloth to his lips and felt its coolness. On his hands and knees, he made his way to his injured companion. The wolf was awake now, and Asmar approached cautiously, afraid that the desperate beast might have enough strength still left to attack him again.

Their gazes met, and Asmar could feel the thoughts of the wolf. He knew she had no will left to fight. She slumped back, too weak to resist, and allowed the young wizard to open her jaws and insert the moistened cloth on her tongue. Asmar felt the relief coming from her as she sucked moisture from the garment.

When the wolf was finished, Asmar crawled back to the pit and dug more, soaking the cloth again and placing it in his own mouth. A trickle of water ran down his throat, giving him strength. He repeated this process, giving the wolf more to drink, then himself, and over and over again until the meager vein of gritty water ran dry.

With these life-saving drops, Asmar now had the energy he needed to turn back to finding Dolcere, to get the medicine he needed to survive. He looked over at the still-weak and injured wolf and knew he couldn't leave her. From what remained of his shredded robe, Asmar fashioned a sling and tried to slip it under the wounded wolf. He looked under the bandage at the bloodstained fur and gently pushed it back to reveal an ugly blue-black scar. The wolf let out a faint whimper. Instinctively, Asmar stroked her head.

He secured the fabric as best he could and got to his knees and tried, with only one good arm, to lift the wolf in the sling. With this load now on his back, he started making his way slowly out into the desert.

As he trudged along, he stared at the horizon. There was nothing ahead but a vast, flat, sandy expanse. Asmar decided upon a direction and walked, his bronze staff sinking into the sand as he pulled himself forward. The sun burned his exposed back and the sling cut into his shoulder, pressing into the swollen flesh. He fought exhaustion and thirst, but just shut his eyes and plodded forward.

The wolf would gain consciousness occasionally and shift in the rudimentary hammock, the slightest movement causing the sling to cut deeper into Asmar's shoulder. Tears and dust mixed on his dirty cheeks and he craved rest and water, but he knew to stop in that desert would mean stopping forever.

Asmar's shadow shrank as the sun rose, and then it started to stretch and grow again as the day began to wane. He tried to stay positive—he was alive and the wolf was alive—but he doubted he was going the right way. The heat was intolerable; his skin burned and he couldn't support himself and the wolf any longer. Asmar stopped and dropped the wolf on the sand. The wolf howled in pain as Asmar fell down next to her and reached out to stroke her head. The wolf looked up at him and then, unexpectedly, she nuzzled her nose under Asmar's arm while he sat, continuing to stroke her bristly head. As he started to let his eyes drift closed, through his half-closed lids he saw the injured wolf struggle to her feet and hobble away. Asmar sat up and watched her limp into the desert. After a few painful strides, the wolf turned back and looked at him.

Asmar pushed himself to rise and walk, struggling to stay upright, his legs feeling numb as he urged himself forward. All he wanted to do was fall back down onto the warm sand and sleep, let go. But as he hesitated, the wolf would limp over with a sense of urgency and nip at his legs. She was gentle, but it was clear she wouldn't let him rest. Fighting off his delirium, Asmar forced himself to focus on the wolf and follow her. But he was too weak, and he sank into the sand. The wolf, again, nudged and nipped at him, but Asmar looked up at her, almost apologetically. He knew now that it was over. He didn't have the strength for one more step. This was it. He reached up weakly to pet her head one last time.

As he did, with the wolf continuing her insistent nips and nudges, he saw something just over her shoulder, sharp, pointed, gray or green against the sky. It was the spiky fronds of a desert tree.

That can't be real, he thought, as he felt himself melt into the hot desert sand.

Then came a voice and blurry, insubstantial moving shapes. *I believe I am dying*, Asmar thought, feeling his mind separating from his weak and depleted body, desperately searching for a last connection. His mind traveled to the wizards' tower in Dolcere. He tried to reach out to them for help, but they had closed their minds to him. He searched down in the bottom of the tower and then out into the streets, and found Remer wandering Dolcere looking for him.

"*Help me!*" he called out silently to his cousin, but then almost as quickly as he saw Remer, he was suddenly pulled back into his body.

Asmar once again opened his eyes to see two warm, brown eyes staring down at him—the eyes of the wolf. Asmar bolted upright quickly and was met by the searing, sharp pain of his shoulder injury, forcing him to collapse back onto soft, clean bedding. The wolf began licking his face. Asmar was confused and tried to sit up again, but a gentle hand restrained him.

"Do you want to undo all the work I've done?" came a raspy voice.

Rays of sun trickled into his eyes. As everything came into focus, Asmar saw a woman with pure-white hair and browned, creased skin standing over him. Her face looked old, but her eyes danced with youth. For a moment, he thought of Remer, searching for him, and now Asmar realized he had no idea where he was. He tried to understand what had happened, what was happening. He thought back to his last moments: he had been dying in the desert. There was a mirage, maybe some trees ... the wolf ...

"Relax. You are weak and your injury was very bad. Your stitches need to heal. One more thing: you are being nourished through this tube, and we can't have you ripping it out."

Asmar looked down at his arm and saw a thin metal needle protruding from it. Asmar stared back at the woman. *Could she be the wizard they were looking for?*

"Who..." Asmar tried to speak but it was too much effort. He reached his right hand to touch his throbbing shoulder. It was now heavily bandaged and he felt a dull ache where a tube went into his arm.

"Where am I?" he managed to say, his voice seeming, even to himself, to come from far away.

"You're safe now. Just sleep."

His mind grew heavy and he was pulled back into his fog. All he could sense was light and darkness following each other. He could see bits of the oasis around him, and the woman looking over him even though he wasn't awake. He heard muffled sounds and tried opening his eyes, but the lids stayed locked shut until he felt a cool cloth gently move across his face, soothing his skin.

"Swallow this broth, now. You'll feel better," the woman said, gently lifting Asmar's head to put a wooden cup to his lips.

"What's this..." Asmar tried to form words again, but still failed.

The mysterious woman, nevertheless, seemed to understand. "You've nothing to fear from my broth. It's very nutritious, made of plants and herbs."

Asmar relaxed into acceptance and gratefully sipped the warm fluid. A great hunger overcame him as the broth touched his lips and then flowed in. He eagerly drank the rest and looked up at her for more.

"I'm afraid that's all for now. Too much at once will make you sick." The woman looked at the suspended bottle of liquid. "You won't be needing this anymore," she said, and gently pulled the sharp needle from Asmar's arm. Back he drifted again, this time to a real, deep sleep.

When he next awoke, the woman was nowhere to be seen, but the wolf rested at his side. Asmar, his energy returning, looked around. The oasis hadn't been a mirage! He was resting on a bed that was under a shade tree near a pool. Tall grasses arched lazily about the edges of the water, and the scent of desert flowers tickled his nose. Asmar sat up gingerly, inching away from the wolf, but she moved closer to him. Asmar looked around, trying to see, unsuccessfully, if there was something he could use to defend himself with, as the wolf reached her snout over to sniff at him then calmly strode away to a large tent set up nearby. When the wolf re-emerged, the old woman that Asmar had thought was part of his dream was with her. The wolf sat nearby in a patch of sun on the ground as the woman approached his bedside.

"Where am I?" he asked her, now sitting fully up. His wounded shoulder was only a dull ache to him now, and his sunburned skin itched.

The woman didn't answer.

"I remember being out in the desert, nearly dead. Then I woke up here—in the middle of an oasis."

"So you *do* know where you are," she said. The wolf sniffed the air and made a little whine. Asmar looked at her, concerned.

"You don't have anything to worry about from the wolf," said the woman.

"She tried to kill me," said Asmar.

"Yes. She was hungry."

"Isn't there the chance she will get hungry again?" Asmar said, eyeing the wolf, who was now busy grooming and licking her fur.

"You are a part of her pack now. She won't harm you."

The wolf looked up from her work cleaning her fur and came over to Asmar. She still limped but seemed to have partially healed already. She approached his bed and then gently placed her head on his lap. Cautiously, Asmar reached out and softly stroked her head.

"Who are you?" he asked the woman, still petting the wolf's head.

"You know who I am," she said. Her eyes glittered where they caught the sun.

"You're the wizard who helped us at the mine!" he said, breathlessly.

"I wouldn't call myself a wizard, actually. But yes, I was the one who helped there."

"Why—who—how?" said Asmar, wanting to ask every question at once.

"That's a bit complicated. We can discuss things when you get a little better."

Asmar *was* feeling tired again, but he felt a sense of urgency.

"We need your help—to stop Malzus. You could do it— you are powerful enough. Why haven't you? Can you?"

The stranger put her hand to her forehead, and then ran her fingers back through her tangled white hair.

"That's even more complicated. For now, you must rest."

Asmar's eyes started to close. "Wait—what's your name?"

She sighed and looked down at him. "I've had many names, none of which I'm particularly fond of," she said, and then paused. "Why don't you pick me a new one?"

As Asmar began to drift off, out of nowhere he remembered the book Remer had discovered in Tuland.

I'll call you the Wanderer, Asmar said, not sure if he said it out loud to her, or in his mind as he drifted off to sleep once again.

When Asmar woke up in the oasis, the Wanderer was sitting next to him, reading a book.

"Ah, good. You're awake." She got up and walked away before Asmar could ask one of his many questions. When she returned, she was carrying a metal pot with steam coming from it in one hand and a wooden cup in the other. She sat down cross-legged in the sand next to Asmar.

"We need to get more of the broth into you."

Asmar sat up as the Wanderer ladled the steaming broth into the familiar cup.

"How long since I got here?" asked Asmar, his voice starting to feel stronger.

The Wanderer looked at the sun and squinted before turning back to Asmar to respond.

"About ten days. Give or take. I wasn't counting that closely."

"Is this where you live?" Asmar indicated the large tent.

The Wanderer shook her head. "I just happened to be in the area. The tent's just something I set up a while ago and I return to from time to time."

"It was lucky for me that you were here."

"Perhaps."

Asmar was going to ask what "perhaps" meant, but his questions were many, and flowing now.

"What's in the tent?"

The Wanderer rose and brushed the sand from her cream-colored talize. "It's hard to explain, but you can see later when you can walk around on your own."

"Why did you help us at the mine?"

"Because I could."

"Then why don't you help us defeat Malzus?"

"Because I can't," she answered, looking Asmar in the eyes.

Asmar tried to rise to his feet, but his knees were too weak. The Wanderer rushed to his side and caught him under his arm.

"I'm glad you are feeling better, but you're much weaker than you think. We have to take this slowly." Her grasp was gentle but firm as she supported Asmar in taking his first tentative steps. After walking a short way, the Wanderer lowered Asmar to the ground and they rested.

"What do you mean you can't defeat Malzus?" he said, trying to catch his breath from the effort of those few steps.

"I have the power to destroy Malzus, but not to defeat him," she replied.

"That doesn't make sense."

The Wanderer smiled. "Forgive me. I'm not used to having to explain these things." She thought a moment, and then continued. "To be as strong and powerful as Malzus, you have to be driven by the same things Malzus is driven by. To destroy him, I would have to want the same things he does... which means I would have to become Malzus... which then would mean I had not really defeated him."

Asmar thought about this in silence for a moment.

"So why did you help us in the mine?"

She didn't answer but reached down. "Give me your arm and let's walk you a bit more. You need to rebuild your strength."

The two walked, one holding up the other, moving patiently along the marshy ground at the pond's edge. The woman nodded to one of the shallows nearby—a section of still water that had separated from the pond. "Look there."

In a murky pool that was not much more than an isolated puddle, Asmar saw a fish trapped, along with several babies.

"Those are fighting fish," the Wanderer explained. "They're small, but they are one of the more aggressive fish in the pond. If food gets scarce, the bigger fish will even eat their own offspring." The mother fish swam to her young and herded them to a small supply of water plants. She let the young feed as she watched over them.

The Wanderer let Asmar slowly sink to the ground and then she picked up a branch from nearby, using it to dig a small channel from the puddle to the pond. The fish eagerly swam to the larger body of water.

"That was a good thing you just did," remarked Asmar. "You saved the lives of those fish."

"Won't do any good, most likely," she shrugged.

"What do you mean?"

"Do you think the other fish in the pond are going to be glad I saved the fighting fish?"

"Why'd you do it then?"

"Because she didn't do what was expected. She broke free of her conditioning. So I decided to help her have another chance."

"Do you often help fighting fish?" Asmar asked.

"Come," she said, once again avoiding the subject. "It is time for another round of broth."

* * *

Days passed like this—phases of walking and eating, bouts of discussion that would never answer all the questions— and slowly, bit by bit, Asmar regained his strength. He had progressed to solid food, although he had developed quite a fondness for the broth. The Wanderer had given him a sand-colored talize that was comfortable during the day and warm at night. In the evenings, the Wanderer would disappear into the tent.

Recently the Wanderer had prescribed swimming in the oasis's water as part of his rehabilitation, and Asmar was just coming back from the morning's swim when he saw her working in a small clearing, sorting some plants. He went to greet her.

"You promised me you'd tell me what was in the tent."

"If you're interested, I'll show you. I'm a little bit proud of what's inside."

Asmar followed her as she moved to the front of the tent and pulled aside the flaps of the doorway.

He stepped inside and immediately was overwhelmed by the scale of it all. He found himself surrounded by the strangest collection of things he had ever seen. In the center, he recognized a table that looked like the ones the wizards had used to operate on Areana. But surrounding them on shelves were endless books and tools and apparatuses and glass bottles that held liquids of varying colors.

"Let me give you a tour. It's not often that I have visitors." She smiled, adding, "And even less often that I'm willing to share any of this." She led Asmar to the operating table. "This is where I sewed you up. It comes in handy once in a while."

"What's that?" Asmar said, pointing to a mechanism consisting of a delicate metal tube suspended over a tiny glass platform that sat on a low table near them.

The Wanderer smiled. "That's a special device I made to help me peek more deeply into the recesses of objects for examination."

Asmar looked confused.

"Look into the eyepiece and tell me what you see," she said. The Wanderer adjusted a small crystal at the bottom to reflect light onto a clear piece of glass that she placed upon the little platform. Asmar put his eye at the top.

"I don't see anything."

"Turn that knob on the side until things become clear."

Asmar turned the knob and a breathtaking new world came into focus. He had no words to describe what he saw—he immediately thought to himself, *Remer would know all about this!* He could discern the tiniest creatures, unlike any that he had ever seen before. They had a shell around them and you could see their insides, spinning and whirring. He looked at the Wanderer, who was smiling.

"That is a drop of water from the pond."

"How's that possible? I can't see any of that in the water."

"There's a lot we can't see with only our eyes, that is nevertheless still there. If you looked at the desert, you can't see the individual grains of sand, but if you get close enough, they become visible. I used the techniques of the Aris, but instead of making swords, I made a curved crystal that makes small objects bigger. What you see there are the tiny denizens that call the water their home."

The Wanderer removed the piece of glass that held the water drop and put another at the bottom of the tube. "Take a look at this."

Asmar bent over to look again, peering into the tube as he adjusted it. "It's like a wall made from bricks, but you can see inside each brick."

"That's a piece of your skin."

"It can't be."

"But it is." The Wanderer moved to a stack of about fifty slender volumes that leaned in a precarious tower against one table and picked one book out at random.

"I've tried to draw what I've seen through that eye-piece," she said, flipping through the thick pages of the book. Over her shoulder, Asmar spied colors and shapes flashing by until he could contain himself no longer and reached out excitedly, taking the volume from her to hold in his own hands. Slowly, he pored through the pages, each with a carefully drawn image, similar to what he had seen via the magnifying tube. A host of illustrations were colored in similar reds and yellows, while others were shaded in greens and blues, with the different parts of the objects meticulously separated and sometimes labeled. On the bottom of each page was text detailing what the image was documenting.

One of the pages had the title "Sand" at the bottom, but it looked like small multicolored pebbles, not the uniform beige of the desert. "This isn't what sand looks like," said Asmar.

"It depends on how you look at it," the Wanderer replied.

Asmar looked around at the stacks of volumes. He reached over and took another book from its perch and flipped through the pages. It also was full of hand-drawn images and meticulous notes.

"There must be thousands of these illustrations."

"I told you I was proud of them. I don't usually get a chance to show off my work like this."

"Why do you do it?" Asmar asked, picking up yet another massive book and scrolling through.

"To learn," she responded, simply. "I don't just draw the images. I look for patterns. All the plants I look at have certain shared characteristics, even when they are very different in other ways, and all the animal samples also have similarities."

"How are they different?"

The Wanderer opened another one of the large books.

"Take this one—this is a plant that I looked at. You see there is a very heavy wall surrounding each brick?" Asmar nodded. The Wanderer went to a different pile and opened a different book. "While this drawing is of is a brick from my own skin. Do you see how there is only a thin wall here?" Asmar had to concentrate, but he did finally see what the Wanderer was pointing to. She went on: "All the plant bricks have that heavy wall and none of the animal ones do. There are also other similarities among plant bricks. They all seem to have special shapes inside of them. You see here? These round objects and here, those more amorphous shapes? Those are only in the plant bricks. I find that very interesting."

"Why?"

The Wanderer laughed. "I don't know. I just do. I am seeing connections in things. But," she added, "there are other uses for that magnifying tube."

The Wanderer now led him over to a shelf that held many small vials containing liquids of different colors. Asmar was curious as to the use of these liquids, and mesmerized at the array of colors.

"These are all medicines. That green one I invented to stop infections. I used it on your shoulder." Reflexively, Asmar reached up to touch what remained of his mostly healed wound. "That yellow one helps reduce inflammation—I put some of that in the liquid that was dripped into your arm. I sometimes use the magnifying tube to determine whether the medicines I have created help or hurt, by pouring a bit of the medicines on the sample and watching carefully what results, and how the sample is affected."

Asmar was intrigued, but all he could think was Remer would be so excited about all of this.

"How do you know if a medicine you create works?" he asked her, becoming more and more curious.

"You'd be surprised how much has already been discovered about medicines. I start with that understanding and then try variations, like making a medicine more concentrated—or combining a few together. I keep detailed notes on everything I observe: what works in repeated tests, and what doesn't."

"Is there more than this?"

"Yes, much more. But not here."

"Do you have tents like this in other places?"

"I think this is the only tent," she said, laughing, "but there are other places I do my work and try things out."

In his training, the wizards had taught Asmar about many medicines and how to treat illnesses, but they didn't have anything like the magnifying tube or the illustrations. Suddenly, the world seemed very different to him; a whole new layer of awareness had opened up. He was fascinated and excited to be with the Wanderer and learning so much from her. In that moment, he felt like he could spend years right there, learning and gaining understanding from her.

"You have to meet with the wizards," Asmar said, his eyes shining with the joy of discovery. "You can help them—help so many—in so many ways."

The Wanderer looked suddenly concerned, and waved her hand dismissively.

"Your wizard friends aren't ready to learn. All they would want is for me to do their bidding, and that I will not do."

Asmar reflexively was about to argue, but then stopped. He realized she was right; so much of what the Wanderer studied was dedicated to healing others, while the wizards had shown him they were most interested in how to control others. Asmar looked around him, trying to absorb all the knowledge that was in this one single tent.

In the back of his mind, though, he remembered his mission. Someone needed to stop Malzus. And there was Remer, whom he needed to look after. Asmar fought back against his yearning to stay there. He knew right then that if he spent too much more time in the oasis, he would never want to leave.

"I have to leave," he said, not able to hide the regret in his voice.

"Why?"

"I am needed to stop Malzus," he responded, though the words sounded false and empty even to him as he said them.

The Wanderer only nodded with understanding. "When do you plan to leave?"

"Soon." Then, with more conviction, "Tomorrow. I will leave in the morning."

"So be it. I think, then, that you'll need these." She went to another table and handed Asmar a folded bundle—his white robe—the bronze staff resting across the top.

Asmar held up the robe and examined it. It had been repaired so expertly that it looked as if it had never been damaged. The Wanderer also handed Asmar a flask filled with water. "Next time, please don't go out into the desert so unprepared."

"*That* was part of the test—" Asmar started to respond, but the Wanderer interrupted him.

"Only *you* should get to test yourself. Don't give that power to anyone else."

Asmar looked at her as he took that advice in and nodded.

"I am in your debt. I wish there were some way I could repay you. I don't have much, but anything I can give you, that you can name, is yours."

She paused for a brief moment and her eyes seemed to flicker in the dust-speckled light of the tent.

"Does that offer include your beautiful golden ring? The one that hides itself beneath the ring of bronze pulcher on your hand?"

Asmar's hand nervously and protectively shifted to the finger where his mother's golden pulcher ring rested in hiding. The bronze pulcher ring, as always, lay over it; its edges curled ever so slightly so as to keep the golden ring concealed beneath it. Asmar slipped the ring off his hand and turned it over to make sure the golden ring still lay inside the hollow groove of bronze. It did.

"It would serve you right if I took your ring and used its power," laughed the Wanderer hoarsely.

Asmar waited to see what the Wanderer would do.

She shook her head, "You should get some rest now," she said, with blunt finality. Asmar nodded and went back out to the tree where his bed waited.

The next day, as the sun rose, Asmar slipped on the white robe and picked up his bronze staff, tucking the water flask in a deep pocket. The Wanderer was there to meet him at the edge of the oasis, the wolf—now fully healed, her fur shining—sitting at her side.

"I suggest you head out that way." The Wanderer pointed into the desert. "It's not the fastest way back to Dolcere, but I think you will find it the best way."

Asmar thumbed the ring on his finger thoughtfully, and then, with a sense of regret, said farewell to the Wanderer and wolf. He was sad to leave them but was grateful for how they had helped him heal and for what he had learned. He began to walk into the desert, thinking how he would explain this meeting to the council. Suddenly he stopped and turned to the oasis.

"Will I ever see you again?" he blurted out—but she, the wolf, and the whole oasis were gone. Asmar blinked in the desert light. He wouldn't have been surprised to find he dreamed the whole encounter. Nothing surprised him anymore.

CHAPTER 18

REMER WAITED ANXIOUSLY FOR ASMAR in front of the wizards' tower in the hope of seeing his cousin and making sure he was okay. In fact, it had been seven days since he had last seen Asmar, and the widening, silent gaps increasingly bothered Remer.

Asmar and Preadus finally emerged from the wizards' tower. Remer looked at his cousin in his white robe and it struck him how different Asmar looked. He was no longer the boy he had been a year ago, when they'd first arrived. Asmar was holding a bronze pulcher staff as he strode, deep in thought, next to Preadus. Asmar was almost as tall now as the Great Wizard, but broader and not nearly as gaunt. Remer had grown as well, but he was still a head shorter than his cousin. Seeing Asmar, Remer felt an emptiness well up inside him. He missed his cousin and the warmth they had shared, which now seemed to be fading. It didn't help that he hadn't seen his mother in over a year, either. In fact, if it wasn't for Shara, he'd be utterly and completely alone. He was so grateful to her, especially as he watched Asmar head away from him; it made him want to run to Shara and tell her how important she was to him. But he tamped those feelings down and held himself back, unsure of what he would do if she didn't feel the same.

He decided to follow behind Asmar and Preadus as they strode away from the wizards' tower. Asmar never looked at him or even in his direction, but Remer felt pretty sure his cousin knew he was there.

Preadus and Asmar continued to the limits of the city and then walked, without hesitation, past the giant crystals and out into the desert.

Remer wanted to follow them, but then hesitated. He remembered what had happened the last time he passed through the crystals: the blinding light, the confusion and panic he suffered. Instead, he decided to wait for Preadus and Asmar to return.

He waited patiently and was just wondering whether he should stay longer or head back to the tower and the library, when Preadus emerged through the crystals—but without Asmar. Remer rose and was about to accost the Great Wizard to find out where his cousin was, but as soon as he started after Preadus, he forgot what he was going to demand. By the time he remembered, the Great Wizard had disappeared. Remer turned back to the edge of the city and sat back down in the cool shade under a tree and waited for his cousin. As he leaned back against the tree, he thought back to the last time he and his cousin had met after school, when Asmar had been the one to wait for him. Asmar, he recalled, had been so upset about being thrown out of class, but he had also been defiant and wouldn't harm the little piece of bronze pulcher. Remer smiled, remembering that, and their walk home that day.

Home. He felt a heaviness at that thought and the much-too-distant memories of the last night they had spent in Tuland, the last night they spent with Lupa. Remer fought off the desire to go home almost every day. He knew if he gave into that desire, there wouldn't be anyone to protect Asmar. And he knew if he left, he would never see Shara again.

While he had been lost in thought under the tree, a half day had already passed and Asmar still hadn't emerged from the crystals. Remer slumped back down under the tree, concerned, and decided to continue waiting. Why was Asmar out in the desert alone, anyway? Remer suddenly pictured Asmar stuck in the soft sands, or being sucked down by a wosake, or lying somewhere in the blistering sun, completely dehydrated and calling out for him.

Remer leapt up from his protective shade and, ignoring his fear of the vastness that was beyond the crystals, ran toward them, heading straight out into the open desert—but as he passed the first of the imposing mounted crystals, a searing flash of light cut across his vision. Momentarily blinded, he stumbled forward and nearly fell face-first into the desert sand. He caught himself, and throwing one arm up over his eyes, he worked to regain his balance on the shifting surface. Once steadied, he resumed walking toward the open desert, but walking slower and more carefully this time. Something wasn't right. As he neared the second crystal, it was a struggle to go forward, the light intensifying painfully in his eyes with every step. He closed his eyes tighter and tried to focus on maintaining his direction, going straight out of the city. But the light became brighter and brighter, and it burned his eyes even through his closed lids. The sand felt like it was melting away under his feet. He cried out for his cousin several times, but no response came.

He felt coolness on his face, and through his eyelids, the light and overwhelming brilliance subsided. Slowly, tentatively, he opened his eyes. As his vision cleared and the world in front of him came into focus, he looked around to see where he was.

He was back in Dolcere. He had failed to get out into the desert. Asmar was still out there—alone.

Remer collapsed onto the packed sands of the city street, thoroughly exhausted, and rose with a sigh, brushing off the sand from his clothes as best he could. He suddenly realized that he was supposed to have met Shara at the library that morning. He didn't want to miss her. He needed to tell her what had happened. He sprinted in the direction of the library.

When he arrived, gasping, trying to catch his breath, Shara was sitting there in the subterranean library room. She wore a bright-yellow dress that almost glowed and was in contrast to the grayness of the room. Remer looked up at her and at the same moment, smelled the faint scent of flowers.

"We were supposed to meet this morning," Shara began, looking a little irritated, but then her gaze traveled over him, and her eyes widened. Then he looked down at his clothes. Even after brushing the worst of the street dust off, he was completely caked in sand, and there was sand embedded in his hair.

"What's happened to you?" she exclaimed, motioning him to sit on one of the hard wooden benches. Remer gratefully collapsed on the seat.

"It's Asmar—I'm worried about him. I saw him and Preadus go off into the desert—and I think Preadus just left him out there." His heart was still racing, and he was still confused and worried, but he began to feel a bit better by confiding to her.

"Is that unusual?" Shara asked. "After all, Asmar's a wizard. Isn't he supposed to be able to survive in the desert, or pretty much anywhere?"

Remer wanted to tell her that Asmar wasn't an ordinary wizard. He wasn't the type of wizard who could survive the desert. Not yet, anyway.

"Give him some time. If he's not back in a day or two, go find Preadus and ask him to tell you where Asmar is." Shara reached out for Remer's arm, and the touch of her warm hand made him feel better.

"Come on. I had planned to take you somewhere— where we can talk." She paused and looked up shyly. "There's something I want to tell you." She reached out and took both his hands in hers.

They left the library and walked into the sun of Dolcere. Shara's dress shifted in the breeze and she put her hand around Remer's waist. Remer pressed his arm around her and breathed in deeply.

He followed, distracted, lost in a whirl of thoughts and emotions, and barely noticing when Shara led him off the main street. Of course, he reasoned, as they wound their way through the smaller side streets and alleys, Shara was right. There was really nothing to be concerned about. The wizards were not going to let their prize disciple and hope for the future come to harm before his mission had even begun. But Remer's worries kept pushing to the surface. He decided that he would wait by the crystals every day until his cousin returned.

Shara stopped in front of a small store, and Remer bumped into her, almost knocking her over. The store was worn with age, the sign advertising its name having long ago fallen away.

Remer raised his head and looked up, noticing where they were for the first time. The smell of fresh baking had come over him in a wave, stirring an instant flood of memories of Tuland and everything he had there, that was now lost: his home, his mother—and now even Asmar. He took a deep breath, inhaling as much as he could of that smell of bread, of home ... and he tightened his grip around Shara's waist.

Through the window, they could see that inside the small, clean shop were neatly aligned glass display cases polished to crystal-clarity, and well-scrubbed counters. There were breads and fancy pastries perfectly arranged on display behind the glass.

Shara stroked Remer's cheek and gently lifted his hand. They pushed open the door to the shop and entered, the scent of baking now fully enveloping them. Shara walked up to the counter where an elderly man stood slightly hunched over the breads and pastries. As he turned and looked to see who had entered, a broad smile spread across his creased features.

"We haven't seen you for a long time, Shara. What's kept you away?" he said, and as he did, his gray eyes turned toward Remer and he gave another warm smile. Remer felt himself blushing.

"I've been very busy in the library and haven't had much time to myself. How is Uxor?"

"She's doing well—out and about buying ingredients for the store at the moment. She'll be sorry she missed you."

"I won't be away as long next time, I promise."

The man put two flaky pastries into a brown cloth bag and handed it to Shara. "You have to promise to come back when Uxor is here."

Shara smiled, nodded, turned, and walked out of the shop—without paying, Remer noted, although the owner didn't seem to mind—as Remer quickly shuffled his feet to turn and follow her.

"Is he a relative of yours?" asked Remer, once they were a few steps from the shop.

Shara just shook her head side to side.

"He didn't ask you to pay anything."

"He's a good friend," Shara said, looking down at her hands.

For most of the last year, Remer and Shara had talked almost every single day. He had told her all about his family: about Lupa, about Asmar, about how his father had been killed by the Sitire. She, in turn, had told him about the wondrous and diverse books she had read, and what ideas they inspired in her. She talked about the wizards, their ways, and the library and Dolcere and a lot of history—but she never mentioned her own family, and Remer now realized he had been so wrapped up in his own and Asmar's affairs, he hadn't thought to ask.

"I want to show you something," Shara said, looking straight ahead, and leading him to a little park tucked away in a back street.

"What is this place?" he asked, as they stepped into the quiet refuge. It was small and deserted, with only a few benches and a tall, swaying tree. There were patches of spiky grass mixed in with the sand, and blue desert wildflowers dotting the ground. Most of the park was unkempt, except for the area around the bench.

"I spent so much of my childhood here—reading," Shara explained. "It's always been kind of a special place to me."

The two sat down on the bench and Shara offered him one of the pastries.

"What is this?" Remer asked.

"It's a scion," she replied. Remer just looked at it, with curiosity. "You've never had one before?"

He shook his head and closed his eyes, breathing in the aroma again.

"This reminds me of my mother," he said. "She used to bake a lot."

He felt comfortable telling this to Shara and found himself needing to tell her more.

"Lupa always had something for Asmar and me when we got home from school." He bit into the sweet flaky pastry and looked around. "I promised Lupa that I would protect him, but I don't know how."

Shara put a hand on his knee. "Just be there, like you are for me. That's enough."

Remer looked into Shara's dark, beautiful eyes.

"Remer," Shara began, with a slight quiver in her voice. She took a deep breath and began again, "Remer, I love you." Remer just stared at her until Shara turned away, her eyes welling with tears. "I shouldn't have said anything."

"No—I mean, of course you should!" Remer stammered, putting down the pastry so that he could take her hand. He could feel a dampness on her palms, and a slight tremble in her fingers.

"I feel the same way about you," he started, nervously. "I just didn't realize how you felt—"

Shara pulled him to her and kissed him before he could stammer another word. He wrapped his arms tightly around her and pulled her close. He could feel her breasts pressed against his chest. Time seemed to stop; all worries temporarily disappeared. For a moment, nothing else existed. Then Shara put her hand gently against his shoulder and softly pushed herself away—or was she pushing him back?

Remer flushed. "What's wrong?" he asked.

Shara brushed her dark hair over her ear and smoothed an imaginary crease from her yellow dress. "Not here," she said, looking around the park.

But the closest people to them were out on the main street, at the other end of the little alley that led to their secluded park, and no one was bothering to look in their direction. Remer was feeling swept away in the power of the moment and didn't see what was wrong with kissing her. He tried to pull her close again.

"No," said Shara harshly. Remer dropped her hand and felt all of his insecurity rush to the surface. Then, more gently, Shara said, "Can we just... talk now, for a bit?"

Remer felt himself flush deeply. He wanted to kiss Shara again, more than anything—but maybe he was going too fast? Or she felt he was? He sat on the bench next to her, trying not to worry. In an effort to calm himself, he tried, nervously, to make conversation.

"You never told me about your family. Do you have any brothers or sisters?"

Shara shook her head.

"What about your parents? You never told me anything about them."

Shara stood suddenly and turned her back to Remer. Remer rose, feeling he had said something terribly wrong.

"What's the matter?" he stammered, worried she was going to leave him.

"Why do you want to know about my parents?" she said, not facing him.

"You—you said we should talk," Remer stammered. He put a hand on her shoulder, but she pulled away. Something must have happened to her parents, something terrible. Remer reached for her hand, but she jerked it back, away from his grasp.

"I was separated from them when I was nine," Shara said, her voice slightly breaking.

"What do you mean, 'separated'?" asked Remer.

Shara breathed in deeply, paused and, Remer could see, worked to maintain her composure before continuing. She looked around furtively, but it was just the two of them. "I know you have told me so much about yourself, but I haven't told you much about myself at all." She stared down at the ground.

"You don't have to if you don't want to," he said, trying to reassure her.

Shara raised her eyes up into the lone tree's canopy and seemed to be considering things, but then she spoke with a measured, unflinching finality.

"No, I need to. I should have told you sooner . . . but the fact is, you may not like what you learn."

"I might not, but I'll still love you," Remer said, his heart beating loudly.

Shara turned to face him.

"I really hope so." There was a long pause. Then: "Remer, I am not what I seem."

Remer was completely still.

"What does that mean?" he asked, staying as calm as he could.

"Where do you think I'm from?" she said, looking him squarely in the eyes.

Remer hadn't thought about that before. The city was divided into sections, each for one of the groups that were allied with the wizards. Shara had taken him to the section of the native born Dolcere. "I assumed you were born here in Dolcere."

"Well, I wasn't. I was born in Sitim."

Remer looked at her and shook his head. "You couldn't have been. That's a Sitire city."

Shara nodded. "My parents were Sitire. I am Sitire."

Remer paused and stared at Shara.

Then he saw it. Most people from Tuland and Dolcere had brown eyes or blue like Areana's; Shara's were far, far darker. You could barely see her pupils at all. He had always thought them so enchanting and beautiful. It had never occurred to him that they were the eyes of a Sitire.

"The Sitire—they killed my father," he said, his voice cracking.

Shara dropped her hands to her sides and looked back at Remer, her eyes wide.

"*It wasn't me.* I haven't been with them since I was nine years old."

Shara reached for Remer's arm but he pulled it away. Shara was now talking quickly, stumbling and stammering as if she knew she needed to tell her full story to him— now, immediately—before he ran away.

"When I was nine, I was with my family in a caravan crossing a stretch of the desert. We had just set camp when the Aris attacked us. My parents hid me under a blanket in the corner of our tent and then disappeared to help the others. There was so much confusion, Remer. People were running in every direction. And there was fighting—I could hear—" She faltered for a moment, a look of anguish on her face. "I was so scared, I couldn't move. When things got quiet, I came out and looked around the camp ... all I saw were dead people." She looked at Remer. He was listening intently. "I wandered through the dead, searching for my parents, until a wizard found me. It was Rogi. He took my hand and helped me look. Eventually, we found them. Even though..."

"What?"

"I don't actually remember seeing their bodies. I just remember that we found them..." Her eyes clenched shut for a moment as she struggled with the memory. "The Aris didn't know what to do with me, so Rogi took me with him to Dolcere."

Remer stayed silent.

"The wizards looked after me, at least a little bit. And they put me to work in the library. I tried going to school for a while, but the other students figured out I was Sitire and made me an outcast; they didn't want me there. So the library became my refuge. Motus, the shopkeeper, and his wife showed concern for me, and I was so thankful to get to spend time with them—with anyone. They even let me stay in a spare room so I could get out of the wizards' tower and experience, even if briefly, a more normal life." Shara paused. "I am very grateful to them."

Remer looked at Shara's tear-streaked face. He wanted to reach out to her, to hold her in his arms to tell her it was alright, but he couldn't.

"The Sitire killed my father," he repeated, tears welling in his eyes.

He looked at Shara one more time, and then saw his father's face in his mind.

He turned and ran from her as fast as he could, leaving her standing alone in that empty park, not stopping or looking back even for a brief moment to see her shocked expression. He fled back to the wizards' tower and ran up the stairs to his small cell where he threw himself onto his simple plank bed. His father was gone, he had left his mother behind, Asmar was gone, and now Shara was gone to him too. He could never forgive her for being Sitire, and for hiding that from him all this time. He had been betrayed and let down by everyone.

For the next few days, Remer rose with the sun and walked by himself to the edge of Dolcere, where he sat, waiting, hoping he would see Asmar return. And each day, Remer would return alone to the wizards' tower again. Sometimes, upon returning in the evening, he would see Shara going out of the library. He wanted to go to her but couldn't let himself.

Remer repeated his vigil, waiting at the edge of Dolcere every day, but still there was no sign of Asmar. He also would search the halls of the tower some evenings, looking for Preadus to demand information on his cousin, but every time he saw the Great Wizard, Preadus would quickly evade Remer by moving ahead into the maze of winding corridors.

After thirty days, Remer felt desperation rising, and he decided to make another attempt to break through the crystals and go into the desert. Changing from his city clothes into his red talize, he worried he wasn't going to have any more success than his previous attempt. As discouragement set in, he suddenly realized what he needed to do. He only had one hope.

Morning came, and Remer set out and headed toward the Aris section of Dolcere. Once there, he did his best to ignore the smells of burning animal flesh and the stalls of weapon vendors. He was looking for someone specific: a soldier that he had been told had returned to Dolcere, but he wasn't sure would still be in the city. In the end, it didn't take long for Remer to track down the one he was searching for, as everyone he passed in the streets knew where she was.

He found her, caped and hooded in her red talize, practicing swordplay with her crystal weapon and a partner in an area reserved for training. She was tall and muscular and stood out from the rest of the Aris practicing their skills. She towered over her opponent, her movements producing a graceful array of greens and yellows that emanated from her crystal sword.

Remer was transfixed. He remembered the time that Areana pulled him from the desert sands, which now seemed so long ago. Remer snapped back to action, realizing the woman he needed to speak to had sheathed her sword and was walking away.

"Wait!" Remer yelled. Areana swiveled around and her hood fell back to reveal her startled expression. But then Areana recognized Remer, and her features softened.

"It's Remer, yes?"

"Yes, commander," he responded and swallowed, struggling to breathe calmly and sound normal. "Asmar's cousin."

"Yes, I know. And you may call me Areana. You're not under my command."

"No—but I wish to be," Remer blurted out, instantly feeling he had stated this poorly.

"You—you want to fight the Sitire?" Areana asked, walking up to him.

Remer looked into her blue eyes. For a moment, he got lost, but then he steadied himself.

"No," he said, carefully, "I need your help to find Asmar. He's been missing in the desert for over thirty days." Remer stood waiting for Areana to react—perhaps show concern or panic—but instead, she just shook her head and made a dismissive gesture.

"I've spent much more time than that in the desert." She turned to walk away.

"You had supplies. He has nothing but his robe and staff."

"Your cousin's a wizard," Areana said. "He'll be fine. He knows what he's doing."

This wasn't the response Remer had hoped for.

"No he doesn't. I know him better than anyone else." Remer ran around and blocked Areana's path, getting more desperate. "Please—I need you. Asmar's in trouble and needs our help and I can't find him without you."

"*Our* help?" Areana repeated, irritated. She put a firm hand on Remer's shoulder and moved him aside. Once she had moved past him, she turned around to look at Remer with a curious expression.

"What do the wizards say?"

"They ignore me," Remer said. He paused for a moment but then blurted out, "I don't trust them!"

Areana regarded him for a moment and then burst out laughing.

"I don't trust them either," she said, slapping him on the back so hard that Remer stumbled forward. "I'll tell you what; I was about to leave Dolcere anyway, to return to my troops. I can get a few of my soldiers and search on our way back."

"No! No one else must know. If the wizards find out, they'd stop us somehow, I know it. It must be only the two of us and we have to leave right away—right now—before anyone suspects anything."

Areana looked unconvinced. "Why should I agree to this?" she asked.

"Because," Remer said simply, "you owe him your life."

Areana looked at the Tulander in silence for what seemed an eternity. If she said no, he would have to venture out into the desert alone, and he knew what had happened the last time he did that.

"Alright, I will help you," she said. Remer breathed an audible sigh of relief. "But you get four days, and that's it."

They agreed to meet back where Asmar had left the city.

Remer rushed back to the tower, grabbed whatever supplies he could, and quickly made it back to the crystals, where he waited anxiously for Areana to meet him. For a moment, he feared she had changed her mind.

Finally, he saw her—appearing like a giant astride a massive sand-colored horse, her red talize flowing behind her in the breeze. She held on to a second set of reins that were leading a smaller dark-brown horse at her side. The horse held his head high with an air of both confidence and gentleness and had a way about him that helped put Remer more at ease.

Areana motioned for Remer to mount the smaller horse, and after two unsuccessful attempts, he managed to hoist himself onto the saddle. Then it was time to head out of the city, Remer bouncing up and down in the saddle, struggling to steady himself.

"What about the lights?" Remer asked, trying to keep the panic out of his unsteady voice.

Areana was unconcerned.

"The horses will help with that. They aren't affected by the crystals. Just close your eyes, hold on tight, trust your mount, and you'll end up in the desert. It's best to go quickly, though."

Remer adjusted himself as his mount quickly followed the lead of Areana's, needing little coaxing to get up to speed. As the horse charged toward the desert, the line of crystals hurled toward them and Remer clenched his eyes shut in anticipation of the blazing, searing light. The sound of hooves pounded in his ears, and the brilliant light overcame them and then disappeared, all in an instant.

As soon as the brightness faded, Remer opened his eyes; his horse was slowing to a canter and then a walk.

Around him, Remer saw the desert stretching out in all directions. He let out a deep sigh of relief and looked back; all he could see was a vague outline of the city.

Remer caught up to Areana, who was peering out into the distance.

"There's nothing out this way—no water, and no shelter. And all he had with him, you say, was his robe and staff?"

"That's all."

"Then your wizard friend may indeed need help."

Areana reached down and took a small bundle from the pack strapped to her horse. Moving her horse closer to his, she handed him the bundle.

"The Sitire have been seen recently raiding in this part of the desert."

Remer unwrapped the package. It was a short metal sword.

"I don't think they'll be any trouble, but we need to be prepared."

Remer, remembering Asmar's warning about carrying a weapon, looked at her apologetically.

"Thank you, but . . . I don't want this. I just want to find Asmar and come right back."

Areana pulled her horse around to face Remer, her eyes burning.

"I didn't ask if you *wanted* the sword, did I? This is my mission, and my command. You don't question what I say. If you question any directive I give, we could die—and I'm not quite ready to do that yet. Do you understand me?"

Remer managed to nod and did his best to stop his hands from shaking as he secured the sword to his side.

"Do you know how to use that?" Areana asked.

"Of course," Remer responded, defensively. "Geiz taught me all about the weapon."

"Geiz is a good man, sure—but a practice field and a combat field are very different."

"I can take care of myself."

Areana laughed. "Sure you can."

They rode onward into the rising heat of the desert. By midday, Remer's backside ached just from the effort of staying upright on his horse. As sunset neared, Areana dismounted and started unpacking the horses.

"Give me a hand," she said, removing a hinged stake from her supply packs and opening it up to extend it to its full length. When planted in the sand, it stood slightly taller than her horse. She looped a tarp over the top by using a hole that had been woven into it near the middle of its longest edge, then staked the corners as Remer held the pole steady, angling it like a lean-to against the direction of the blowing sands. Remer was impressed by the simplicity and efficiency of the design. This would provide protection for them and both of the horses, though it would be a tight fit.

"Now we eat and then get some sleep," instructed Areana.

Settling down near the center pole, she handed Remer two travel cakes and a flask of water. She took one cake for herself. When they'd finished, Areana slid into her sleeping bag lengthwise near the front of the tent. The horses whinnied comfortably above her as the evening winds started to kick up dust.

"Where should I set up the sleeping bag for me?" asked Remer. The space was cramped and it didn't seem like the two of them could fit alongside the horses.

"We don't use two bags when we're set up like this," she said. "There's no room. Besides, we need protection from the falling temperature."

"You mean... we sleep together?"

Areana laughed one of her hearty, but soft, laughs. "That's how it's done, Remer. Believe me, there's nothing romantic about it. Most of the soldiers I've slept with are pretty foul smelling. You'll be a welcome relief."

Remer felt suddenly engulfed in her warmth. He tried his best to remain as still as possible. After a time, he heard a gentle snore come from his sleeping partner. Remer couldn't sleep, so he watched the wisps of sand collect in curling drifts around the edges of the tent until, at last, exhaustion took hold of him and his eyes slowly closed.

Early the next morning, Remer was awakened by a shove, as Areana jostled him and shook the sand off the tarp.

"Do you have any idea where Asmar was going?" she said, busying herself with packing up the tent. Remer shook his head.

"Get yourself moving," she ordered, and tossed him a travel cake.

The next two days went the same as the first. The two traveled during the heat of the day and camped in the evening. The wind seemed less harsh and relentless on the last day than it had been when they started. Remer figured he was getting used to the sound.

He searched the horizon continually, looking for signs of his cousin, as the desert stretched out before them. Remer tried to comfort himself by mentally pulling up passages from books about the vastness of the desert and how objects could blend into the horizon. Remer knew Asmar was out there, but it was frustrating him that he couldn't see him—yet. Remer had to just keep going.

The sun was lowering at the end of the third day out of the four that Areana had said she would give to the search. Remer noted the position of the sun and had studied the stars for hours the night before. At first he had hoped Areana was widening her search for his cousin, but now he realized her real plan: she was turning back. They were heading back to Dolcere!

"Asmar's not in Dolcere," he said. "So if you think you've been fooling me by traveling in a wide circle and heading back, I'm not that stupid. I know which way the sun rises and sets."

"You ungrateful—" Areana caught herself and let her words trail off. "I'm not trying to fool you, idiot."

"We should be traveling further into the desert," Remer said, upset. "That's where he is. You can't turn back now. I have to get to him—he needs me!"

Areana's eyes and demeanor were calm.

"I promised you four days; that's it. So what did you expect me to do? It's two days out, then we circle back. Your cousin saved my life. I owed him as much. But there are others who rely on me also. I can't spare more time for this, especially without the slightest clue that he even came this way."

"You're going to let him die!" Remer yelled over the desert winds.

Areana shot him an icy, angry stare. "How *dare* you!" she shot back. Her voice was still controlled but incredibly forceful and fierce at the same time. Remer recoiled as her anger rose toward him.

"Don't you dare accuse *me* of letting him die. You have no idea how many times I've had to decide who dies and who lives, who was sent into battle and who stayed behind. But your wizard friend *chose* to go out into the desert. *He* chose, not me." She stopped abruptly.

Remer had never seen her as angry as this, and he suddenly was scared at what she might do. Her eyes were fixed on Remer like daggers, and he wanted to turn his horse around and gallop away, but instead he stood his ground and met her gaze. Rather than continuing to lash out at him, Areana looked away. The next words she summoned were calmer.

"Without any proof he's even out there, I'm heading back tomorrow. That is my decision."

Areana started to ride away, then abruptly pulled up her horse.

Remer brought his horse around in front of her.

"Can't you give me just a few more days? I know he's out there."

Areana didn't answer. Silently, she dismounted and stood staring at the sand. Remer followed her gaze, and then he saw them: footprints.

"We must get to those rocks." She indicated the outcropping near them.

"What—what's going on?" Remer implored.

"Sitire," she said, in almost a whisper.

"If we can see these tracks, it means they passed by here recently—earlier today, in fact. You need to be quiet now; sound travels." Her face was grave. "And don't kick up any sand. They can see that from a distance. The rocks will provide some protection. They may not see us if we shelter there."

Remer sat up tall in his saddle, trying to catch a glimpse of any soldiers. He felt a hard sudden tug and found himself pulled off his mount and facedown on the ground.

"Don't be so stupid. You see them, and it means they'll be able to get a good look at you as well. Follow my lead: get up and walk your horse extremely slowly to the rocks."

When they reached the outcropping, they hid themselves and their horses as best they could and watched the far-away moving column of Sitire. As the sun set, the haze surrounding the moving distant soldiers all disappeared.

"That was close," Remer said.

"The danger's not over yet. If they pick up our trail, they'll be after us. From now on, we must do the extra work of covering our tracks."

"Won't the sandstorms take care of that?"

"The winter solstice was five days ago. You know what happens after the solstice?"

"Of course." Remer was embarrassed he had needed to be reminded. He closed his eyes and found the reference he needed, as recited: "*The winds stop for a few days. Then there's a major sandstorm and rain, before everything returns to normal.*"

"Yes, so for the next few days we'll have to cover our tracks because the winds won't do it for us. Tonight, we'll have to make camp here."

The two settled in for the long night the same way, lying back to back. Remer found this comforting, although it made him think of Shara. He still felt the shock and pain. How could she have lied to him for a year? When he had been telling her all about his father, she could have told him the truth then. Remer actually found himself missing the sound of the sands, because it at least distracted him from thinking of her. He fell asleep to the sound of wolves howling in the distance.

The sun was rising as Areana began to break camp. As she was working, she suddenly signaled with urgency for him to come over to where she was, and pointed to a faint red spot on the rock.

"Blood."

Remer's breathing sped up.

"I can't tell if it is human or animal, but something passed this way. Look around to see if you can find anything else."

"Remer!" Areana hissed.

Remer was at her side instantly.

"A piece of cloth... it's definitely from a white robe." There was no emotion in her words.

"That's what Asmar was wearing when he left Dolcere," Remer replied, his heart racing.

"The edges are jagged, as if ripped by wolves. And there's blood on the corners." She held the cloth out to

Remer to examine. He took the fabric in his hand and turned it over. This was definitely Asmar's.

"He's been injured. We have to find him!" said Remer, in a panicked whisper.

"Remer," Areana said, quietly but firmly, "your cousin was attacked by wolves. They travel in packs and don't leave their prey around afterward." Her voice was hard, but Remer saw sadness in her eyes.

"He's not dead! He still lives, I know it!" Remer yelled.

Areana suddenly smacked him hard across the face, knocking him down. Grabbing his shoulders, she whispered into Remer's face, her eyes wild. "Shut up!" she demanded in a hushed but furious, desperate voice. "You probably just told every last Sitire in the desert where we are. Maybe you want us both to end up dead as well? Be quiet, I order you!"

"Nobody's dead," Remer stammered in a panicked whisper. "He's alive, I'm telling you. I know it. I'm sure of it."

"Don't be a fool."

Remer could no longer stand it. He tore away from Areana and ran off into the desert, his eyes filled with tears. He heard Areana calling out, but he didn't care. He was going to find Asmar with or without her or anyone's help.

Again, the calls from Areana, getting closer and closer. Remer turned and saw her riding swiftly toward him with one hand held up high. Colored lights flickered in his eyes. Her sword was unsheathed and ready for action—she was coming for him. He was a soldier who had disobeyed orders and she was going to kill him for desertion.

She was almost upon him and showed no sign of slowing. The crystal blade swung back, then forward in a graceful arc. He heard the blade's deadly strike and heard a dull moan immediately follow.

Remer turned to see a Sitire soldier lying on the ground beside him, a wound from Areana's sword in the man's chest, blood bubbling out and into the sand, saturating the ground around him. He was dead.

Areana, breathing heavily from the effort, brought her horse around to face Remer, her mouth moving, her expression fierce. Through a fog, he finally discerned what she was yelling: "*Sitire!*"

Only then did Remer look up and see the three Sitire soldiers on foot, closing in on him. He realized he should draw his sword immediately, but all his training seemed to evaporate in that moment.

"Draw your sword, you idiot," Areana commanded as she came up beside him. "You said you knew how to use it—now's your chance."

Areana spurred her horse forward. Remer looked at the body on the ground. A man was dead. The game he had played with Geiz was no longer a game.

Remer watched and saw things as if they were happening in slow motion: Areana slashing at two of the foot soldiers. The third dodging her blows and heading straight for him. What could this soldier possibly want with him? Then he looked down at the sword in his own hand and realized the Sitire thought Remer was a soldier. Remer dropped his sword as the Sitire approached. *Now there would be no need to fight*, Remer thought.

But the Sitire didn't stop. Instead, he raised his sword to strike as he charged. Remer's training suddenly returned to him. He dodged the blow and threw himself to the ground in a forward roll, retrieving his sword at the same time. *Geiz would be proud of me*, Remer thought. But there was very little time to think; the Sitire was on him again. This time, the Tulander was prepared and parried his blow. Remer struck back, but his attempt was turned aside. The Sitire swung and Remer parried again. This was like the duels with Geiz: parry, attack, parry, attack. Remer saw his advantage and he pressed it. As he readied his sword, the Sitire rolled to one side and threw a handful of sand at Remer's eyes. Geiz had never done that. Remer tried to shut the sand out, but it was too late. The tiny particles reached him and the world went black. Acting on instinct, Remer jumped to one side and thrust his sword forward. He heard the clang of metal against metal as he partially blocked the attack, then felt a searing pain in his side as a razor-sharp blade ripped into his flesh.

Remer lost his balance and tumbled down to the sand. His side felt warm where he was cut. He struggled to see through tears and saw a form move toward him, then back away. Another shadowy image came into view. Remer rubbed his eyes and cleared his vision, his side burning as he dragged himself out of the way. Areana was exchanging blows with the Sitire. Remer grasped his sword firmly and advanced, one hand on his injured side. The Sitire turned to him, sword raised, but then a whirl of color flashed across Remer's eyes as Areana's rainbow blade descended. The Sitire dropped to the ground.

Areana launched herself out of her saddle, looking to make sure there were no more attackers, and then was at Remer's side in an instant. She pulled his robe aside to do a cursory examination of his wound.

"It's not too bad," she said, as she reached into her saddlebag and pulled out a bandage. She went to work, affixing it tightly to his side, then helped him up onto her horse. "We need to get going. There'll be more coming soon. The desert's crawling with Sitire. We won't be doing Asmar any favors by getting ourselves killed."

Areana remounted and cantered them back to the rocks to retrieve Remer's horse. She held the reins of his horse as he shifted clumsily back into his own saddle, and together they began to ride off in a direction he assumed was toward the invisible city. Remer's side stung as they rode, and every so often he looked down at the wound. Areana hadn't thought it was serious, but the pain was worsening.

"We can't leave Asmar out here—he may just be wounded somewhere. He may need help," he said.

"When we return to Dolcere, I'll put together and lead a company to search for your cousin and destroy the Sitire. Any other course of action right now would be foolish."

"Okay, okay. But once the search party is assembled, I want to go back out with you to search."

"Your 'distaste' for obeying orders and your total inexperience in battle makes you a liability to me." Remer couldn't see her face from where he rode trailing slightly behind, but her tone was ice cold.

He urged his mount to go faster and came up beside her, turning to address her to her face.

"He's my family, my cousin, Areana," he said, using her name for the first time.

For several moments she said nothing, and they rode onward in silence, but after a time, she pulled up on the reins to stop abruptly, Remer coming to a halt alongside her.

"If you cause any more trouble for me—any whatsoever—you'll stay behind in Dolcere." Her look was grave.

"Agreed," said Remer, swallowing hard.

She nodded curtly, then sighed and looked around to survey where they were in the desert, her jaw clenched in thought.

"We can't go directly back to Dolcere," she explained, talking more to herself. "If we do that, we'll run into more Sitire."

Remer felt the pain from his wound more sharply now, and he worked to suppress his rising panic. Was he going to be killed by the Sitire, just like his father? His mind and heart raced, but what scared Remer the most was that even Areana now seemed worried.

"We'll need to draw them out further into the desert... and then cut back at night to move toward Dolcere." She sounded tentative, not entirely confident.

"Are you sure it will work?" Remer asked.

"It all depends on the Sitire commander in charge. If they can be lured away from patrolling the area between here and Dolcere, there's a chance we could circle back and slip past."

"Would *you* fall for that?" Remer asked, feeling doubtful himself.

"Do you have a better plan in mind?" Areana asked, irritated.

Remer looked down and could only shake his head.

The two set out once more, not bothering to cover their tracks, hoping to entice the Sitire to follow. They traveled until sunset and then stopped to make camp. Once they were set up for the night ahead, Areana inspected Remer's wound again. Her rough hands ripped away the old bandage that was stuck to his side with dried blood. Remer didn't intend to yell out as it was torn off, but he couldn't help himself. He yelped. Areana gazed at him with tired disapproval.

"It doesn't look too bad," she said, looking down at the wound and dabbing it clean with water, then adding a salve that would help ward off infection.

"It really isn't bad," Areana repeated, with a slight tone of reassurance.

"That's easy to say when it's not your own side that got cut," Remer shot back.

Areana stared at him a moment and then stood, lifting her talize up past her stomach. Remer was startled at first, not understanding what she was doing, and he instinctively averted his eyes.

"Look up!" Areana commanded. Remer raised his eyes and stared at her bare waist and stomach, to see a web of long-healed scars and even some that seemed more recent and freshly healed. There were at least six just on her front and three more on her back when she turned around. Then she let her talize drop, to be covered up once again.

"Trust me—your wound isn't that bad."

Remer silenced himself, shocked, and sucked in his breath and any complaints he might have been wanting to utter.

They broke camp and this time took pains to cover their trail. There was no wind that night. Areana slept as she rode—seasoned from years of training and experience. Remer, however, was awake most of the night, the wound in his side making it extremely painful to stay in the saddle. At one point, when he did manage to drift slightly into sleep, he ended up falling from his horse and causing his wound to re-open. Areana was jolted awake, and they lost precious time as she had to redress the wound. Remer was worried that the bloodied bandages would attract wolves, but Areana advised that with two people and horses in their group, the wolves would probably look for easier prey.

As the night waned and the sky slowly brightened, Remer—bleary and in pain—brought his horse up right beside Areana.

"I'm not seeing any Sitire. Do you think your plan worked?" he asked, hopeful.

"It is too early to say yet," Areana replied, not taking her eyes away from the scenery they were riding toward. "I hope you're in better shape than you look. We may have to fight today."

"Or... run?" Remer offered.

"Running won't help much," Areana responded, not disguising her irritation.

"Why not?"

"I know you didn't sleep much, but your horse slept even less. If we run into Sitire who have rested horses, we won't have much of a chance of outrunning them."

"But you think we can outfight them?" he asked incredulously.

Areana still didn't take her eyes off the route ahead.

"Let's just hope the plan worked," she answered.

They rode on toward Dolcere, and Areana showed Remer how to ride while directing his horse to lift his hooves high to kick up as little sand as possible. They suddenly paused, and Areana scanned the horizon. She froze for a second, and then pointed off to their left.

"Sitire!" she screamed, and spurred her horse forward. Remer instantly did the same and was following her as closely as he could, trying to keep them together.

Areana saw him struggling to keep up with her and slowed only very slightly. It was enough for Remer to catch up to her, but he could tell he was endangering her, holding her back.

"I thought you said we couldn't outrun the Sitire!" Remer yelled as the two galloped onward.

"We can't, but we have to try. There are ten of them. I don't think we could outfight them."

Areana pulled ahead, hoping to get both of their horses to run faster. Remer twisted in his saddle to count the Sitire. He felt his wound opening and blood ooze out. He closed his eyes and reassured himself the wound wasn't serious.

"They're gaining on us," Remer screamed at Areana. "What do we do?"

"Keep riding!" Areana answered as she urged her horse on.

Areana directed them both toward a large dune that would give them the advantage of height. The exhausted horses dropped their riders at the foot of the dune, and Areana drew her sword and made her way to the top, walking almost sideways up the dune as the sand slipped under her feet. Remer tried to follow, but every time he managed to make it up part way, he started sliding back down. He kept looking over his shoulder at the Sitire closing in on them. He fell to his hands and knees and tried crawling up the dune, but he just slid back down. Sand got into his wound and tears clouded his eyes. Suddenly he felt yanking on his arm, and a moment later he was hoisted up onto Areana's shoulder. He felt like a child needing to be carried, but there was no time to think about it; he couldn't have made it up the dune on his own. He looked back as they clawed their way up, to see the Sitire had dismounted but were now also struggling to climb the dune. Remer thought that they would have been more experienced at making their way up through the sand, but their swords and longer talizes seemed to be hampering them.

"Get ready to fight!" Areana yelled.

Remer struggled to his feet, feeling dizzy. He dropped to his knees and retched. "I'm not sure I can do this." He clutched his side; his bandage was damp with blood.

"You can do it. Just get on your feet *now*, soldier. Draw your sword!" Areana swung her crystal sword through the air in a flash of light and color, readying for the approaching Sitire.

Remer struggled to his feet. Shara's face was looming inside him every time he looked at the Sitire soldiers approaching. Their dark eyes bored into him, as her eyes had. The two Sitire soldiers were now halfway up the dune. He could see their silver blades and the small shields strapped over their arms. They were tall and broad and looked much stronger than Geiz had been. He was struggling to remember his lessons. Geiz had told him how to deal with a larger opponent.

"I'm not sure I can kill someone," he said.

"You better get over that, fast. The Sitire will have no qualms about killing you," Areana said through her teeth, staring down the dune.

Remer's hands were slippery and wet with a mix of sweat and the blood from his wound. He watched the Sitire climb ever closer. The first two attackers split, one going after Areana while the other came toward him. As the Sitire swung his sword, Remer raised his and parried the blow. His hands stung from the power of the Sitire, and his sword's handle slipped in his hand, but he managed to hold on.

He was only able to partially block the next blow as it violently slashed his arm, opening up a cut that went from his shoulder to elbow. He was lucky: the blow was not to his sword arm, and he could still move it. He looked away from the new wound and in the next moment, everything slowed down as Remer raised his blade to protect himself from the Sitire's next blow. But then came a blinding flash of bronze light, and the blow never came.

Remer looked over his shoulder at Areana. He saw another flash of bronze turning Areana's sword aside as it was about to strike the Sitire. Next to her was a figure robed in white, carrying a bronze staff. It moved gracefully, turning aside swords. The staff arced across the cloudless sky as it landed on the arm of a Sitire, the blade falling from his hand. The next blow struck Areana, deflecting a blow meant for the now-unarmed Sitire soldier. Remer tried to get to his feet, but his head was spinning from nausea. Colors were swirling wildly overhead. He again saw Shara's face and then heard his own voice rising up as he cried out.

"Asmar!"

And then the world went black.

* * *

When his head began to clear, he felt a comforting hand laid on his arm and a healing warmth flowed through him. Could it be that he was alive? He didn't know how it was possible, but he had survived. He wanted to cry, to yell, to jump up and run all the way back to Dolcere; to find Shara in the library and take her in his arms—and tell her that he loved her.

His vision slowly began to clear; light filtered in. Leaning over him was a wizard . . .

"Asmar!" Remer cried, the tears rolling down his cheeks.

"Yes, Remer. It's me. Now, stay still while I bandage your arm."

Remer struggled to raise himself up slightly, using his good arm. "Where are they—all the Sitire?"

"Gone," Asmar responded calmly. "They wouldn't attack a wizard."

Remer turned his head to see Areana was staring down at him.

"Asmar wouldn't let them attack. He kept blocking their blows. And mine as well." Remer heard the disapproval in her voice.

"You're safe now and that's all that matters," Asmar said.

Remer fell back to lying down, repeating that precious phrase to himself.

He was safe now. He would see Shara again. These were the last two thoughts he could hold onto, before he drifted calmly and completely out of consciousness.

CHAPTER 19

WAIT!

Asmar heard the command coming from Thurmore, who was still invisible to the others and who communicated directly to Asmar's mind.

Asmar sat down in the warm sand, his bronze staff laid beside him, to wait for Rogi and Thurmore, as he had been instructed.

Remer turned, and seeing Asmar sitting in the sands, rode back.

"What are you doing?" he said, once he was closer to his cousin.

"I need to wait here for a while."

Areana looked around impatiently. "For what? For whom?"

"Wizards," Asmar said, flexing his shoulder casually. It was still stiff from the wolf's bite. He closed his eyes, and the drawings of the Wanderer all came back to him.

"Have you ever seen pictures from a magnifying tube?" Asmar asked Remer.

"I've never even heard of a magnifying tube," Remer said. "What is it?"

"It makes very small objects appear so large that you can actually see inside of them. I saw the small bricks that make up my skin."

Remer shook his head.

"I've seen magnifiers that help you see distant, far-away objects, but if you used them to look at your skin, all that would happen is it would look bigger. There are some books I read in Tuland that talked about something like that. They were very old and I couldn't entirely decipher them. What did the 'bricks' in your skin look like?"

"They had a wall around them, and inside were other shapes that seemed to move."

"What were the other shapes for? Did the Wanderer explain any of that?"

"I didn't ask."

"How could you not ask?" Remer shook his head. "I would have asked that, and probably much more. Asmar, you need to introduce me to her. Maybe I could help her research."

Asmar smiled. "I'm sure you could. I'll remember to ask more questions next time."

"I could write down some questions."

"Why don't we just wait and see what happens. I don't even know if I'll see her again," Asmar said, but he hoped he would.

The sun was setting by the time the wizards arrived. Thurmore, strong and lean, led the way, followed by Rogi. They ignored Areana and Remer and sat next to Asmar, their blue robes caked with sand and their skin darkened by their traveling in the desert.

Thurmore reached out with his mind.

You disappeared from us. We thought you were dead.

Asmar responded, also using his mind.

I was attacked by wolves. I tried to reach out to you. I was dying.

We know, said Thurmore. *It's what happened afterward we don't understand.*

How long have you been looking for me? Asmar asked him. *It must have been more difficult once the Wanderer found me.*

The Wanderer? Thurmore seemed confused.

The other wizard. She took me in and saved my life.

She? Thurmore looked incredulously at Rogi and then back at Asmar. *That can't be, there's never been a woman strong enough to be a wizard.*

Oh, she's strong enough, Asmar replied.

Thurmore paused, trying to process this new information. *Where is this woman now? We were sent to find her.*

Wait, Asmar said, confused. *Weren't you both sent to find me?*

Rogi shook his head.

That would've violated the test, he said simply.

The test? Asmar replied, his voice rising in disbelief.

If you couldn't break through the barriers we set and find your way back to Dolcere, you wouldn't have been much good to us.

And if I were dead, I wouldn't be much good to you, either.

But you're not dead. Thurmore's thought came through dispassionately, which infuriated Asmar.

"I'm alive, no thanks to you!" he said aloud, looking at the shock in the other wizards' faces.

Be that as it may, we came to find you because we thought you could help us locate the woman, Thurmore said, ignoring Asmar's outburst.

And it doesn't concern you that I could have died? Asmar said, pointedly.

It absolutely concerns us, but what concerns us much more is getting the golden staff away from Malzus. That is the mission, and we need strong wizards to be able to do that. You're stronger now than you ever were, Thurmore replied.

Asmar was silent as he tried to understand what Thurmore had said.

We must find her, Rogi interjected, breaking into the conversation.

Thurmore looked at Asmar and spoke in a commanding voice. *We must find her,* he said. *She may be of some help to defeat Malzus.*

Although they were communicating mind to mind, Asmar could sense with some confusion that Thurmore was doing his best to conceal just how upsetting the idea of a female wizard was; Asmar didn't understand why until he thought back at all the teachings in the Talum and realized they were all written by men.

She won't help, Asmar said to him, making no effort to conceal his indifference. He adjusted the bandage on his shoulder slightly.

Thurmore stood and looked down at Asmar. *We need to know if she's our friend or our enemy.*

Asmar stood also. He was as tall as Thurmore and broader.

She's neither, he said.

That's troubling, but we still need to find her.

You won't be able to, Asmar assured him.

Why not? Rogi asked.

Because she doesn't want to be found, Asmar replied. In the very next moment, he felt Thurmore suddenly reach further back into his mind. Before Asmar realized what was happening, Thurmore knew of the oasis. Asmar reacted as quickly as possible, shutting Thurmore out before he could find out anything about the wolf or the magnifying tube.

"How dare you!" shouted Asmar, out loud so that everyone could hear. Remer started to walk over to where the wizards stood, but Asmar put a hand up to stop him.

Asmar reached out again through his mind to Thurmore, barely able to contain his anger: *Don't ever do that to me again.*

Don't make it necessary, Asmar, Thurmore responded. *We're on the same side. Best you not forget that.*

The two wizards turned to leave. Asmar reached out with one more question.

Did you at least help at the dune? The Sitire attack, did you help stop it?

We wanted to, Rogi said, *but couldn't.*

Asmar breathed in deeply, which helped hold back his anger: *Yes, you could have.*

Rogi nodded apologetically. *Yes. We could have, but we didn't.* Rogi sighed and looked at Thurmore. *We need to go,* he said, and the wizards walked away, disappearing into the desert.

Remer came over to Asmar. "What did they want?"

"To meet the one who showed me the magnifying tube."

"That's it?" said Remer. "You've been gone for over thirty days in the desert and all they want to know about is the Wanderer? Did they even care that you were almost killed—or that we were? I know they don't think much of me, but Areana is their most skilled general."

Areana smiled wryly. "I'm accustomed to the wizards' indifference," she said. "If you're going to spend any time in Dolcere, you'd better get used to it as well."

"Dolcere? I'd actually rather go find the Wanderer," Remer answered. "She sounds incredibly interesting. I could assist her—offer her the use of all the books I've ever read. It sounds like the perfect direction to head in."

"I'm sure you'd be an asset to her." Asmar smiled at Remer's enthusiasm. "But if I'm going to stop Malzus, I still need to complete the test—and that means I must find Dolcere."

They made camp as the sun set. The absence of the wind cloaked the landscape with an eerie silence. When later on the sandstorms were to start up again, they would return stronger and more dangerous, but even more concerning would be the torrential rains that always followed.

They'd soak the desert and make the sands soft; wosakes would come out in large numbers, and any travel in the desert would be dangerous.

For now, the sky was clear and Areana had swiftly pitched her tent and laid out the sleeping bags. Asmar sat by himself, staring up at the sky and the little dots of light. He wondered if the Wanderer had looked up at this great expanse as much as she had looked down into the vast depths of things. He longed to be able to head straight back to the oasis and bring Remer with him, but his mission to stop Malzus was too important to allow him to do what he wanted.

Remer, his red talize pulled tightly around him, came over to where Asmar sat. "I can't sleep. I've been thinking a lot about home."

"So have I," said Asmar.

"Are you glad you left?"

"That's complicated. Tuland was safe and I was happy. But Malzus was still out there; we just didn't know about him. And that is a problem we would have had to face in time." Asmar hesitated as he sorted through his feelings. "Now I feel I *have* to do something about Malzus. So, I guess I can say I am glad to have left. What about you?"

"I miss Lupa. But if I hadn't left, I would never have met . . ." Remer let the sentence hang.

"Shara?" Asmar said, completing the thought.

Remer nodded. He started to open his mouth to say something, but stopped himself.

"Do you love her?" Asmar asked.

Remer shook his head. "I can't."

"Why not?"

Remer's eyes welled slightly with tears, but he worked to hold them back. "Shara is not what she seems."

"You mean because she's Sitire?"

Remer looked at Asmar in shock. "You already knew?"

"Of course. She has dark eyes and the features of the Sitire. How could you have not seen that?"

Remer looked down and pulled his talize even tighter around him. "They killed my father."

Asmar stood and put a hand on Remer's shoulder, careful not to touch his injured arm. "How many Sitire did Areana kill while you were looking for me?"

"Four," Remer said, tears trickling down his cheeks. "I didn't want to fight. I dropped my sword, but they kept coming." The anguish in his voice was palpable when he cried, softly, "What else could I have done?"

Asmar tightened his grip on Remer's shoulder. "You love Shara."

"*Someone* has to be held responsible." Remer wept, unable to hold back the tears. "All I have of him are tales. Stories. I'll never know what he was really like. If he would have liked me. What it was like to have him as a father. Shara's people stole that."

Asmar put an arm around his cousin. "She's alone in the world. Maybe Shara needs you as much as you need her."

Remer nodded, exhausted, and dropped back down to the sand, wiping his face on a corner of his talize. "If I had died out there in the desert, she would've been left thinking I hated her. I don't want that."

Asmar sat beside Remer, whose head rested on his cousin's shoulder as his breathing slowed, and who finally, giving way to exhaustion, began to snore softly. Areana came over and together they gently carried Remer to the campfire and laid him on the ground, taking care to avoid his injuries. Areana draped a sleeping bag over him.

"He cares about you very much," she sighed. Asmar nodded. "It's a wonderful thing. I wish I had someone who cared for me like that."

"You have the whole Aris army," Asmar said, with a soft smile.

"There's always a distance between myself and them." Areana turned and crawled into the other sleeping bag. Asmar nodded in understanding. It was the same, being a wizard; nobody would ever again get close to him. He was grateful he had Remer.

The next morning, they set out once again as soon as light touched the sands. "We should be near enough now to find Dolcere." Areana scanned the seemingly empty horizon. "I've never had trouble finding it before."

"It's out there," Asmar said, blinking in the morning light. "The wizards are hiding it from me on purpose. I need to figure out how to find it."

Asmar sat down on the warming sand and closed his eyes. He reached out his mind and felt the presence of Remer and Areana, then he sensed Thurmore and Rogi walking toward the oasis. He even felt the presence of the Sitire that had attacked them, but he couldn't sense Dolcere. He tried to understand how the wizards could hide a city of several thousand people. He searched deeper and started to sense small animals and insects scurrying in the sand. He felt connected to the animals and the desert.

He wasn't exactly sure what he was looking for, but he let his senses expand further and further. Suddenly, he felt an absence, a space where nothing seemed to exist, and he knew that's where Dolcere was. The wizards could hide life, but it still left behind an imprint. A void.

"I know how to find Dolcere!" he announced to Areana and Remer. "When it's dark, we will find it."

"What are we looking for?" Remer asked.

"Nothing. Or rather, we are looking for nothing where something should be." Remer nodded dutifully in agreement, but Asmar knew he didn't understand.

The sun dipped down, the sky dimmed, and the wolves began to howl. Unhindered by any sandstorms, they hunted early. The wolves grew closer and Areana drew her sword. Remer drew his as well, but it slipped to the sand as he tried to hold it. Asmar peered into the night sky looking for patterns until he noticed darkness where there should have been stars. This was the absence he was looking for.

"That is where Dolcere is." He pointed straight ahead.

"I don't see anything," said Remer, leaning forward on his horse.

Asmar concentrated, trying to block out the interference of the wizards. He felt the minds of the wolves and he told them to hunt somewhere else and felt them move away. He turned back to reaching out into the desert and felt where life seemed to disappear. In that moment, the horizon cleared and he saw the lights of Dolcere.

When the sun rose, Asmar, Remer, and Areana found themselves standing at the edge of Dolcere, the city now clearly visible. They'd made it back. As they walked past the crystals, Asmar felt a shooting pain and Remer gasped. Asmar blocked the worst of it from himself and Remer while Areana walked on her own, her hands clenching and unclenching. Behind them, the horses followed, unperturbed. As they passed the last crystal and were fully inside, the pain finally stopped. Preadus was there, waiting.

You have passed your test. The council awaits.

Asmar, exhausted from their long journey back, glared at the Great Wizard.

I reached out to you from the desert. You didn't come.

He then turned to Remer and said, "Go find Shara." As soon as the words were out, Remer was running. Asmar then turned back to Preadus. *I'll be in the council chamber soon.*

Asmar felt Preadus about to object, about to tell Asmar to come now. But instead, the Great Wizard turned and walked back toward the wizards' tower without a word.

As Preadus took his leave, Asmar noticed Areana looking in the other direction, watching Remer's hasty departure. She shook her head and yelled after him, "You're welcome!"

Asmar looked at her and smiled. "Thank you for looking after him."

Areana nodded and put a hand on Asmar's shoulder. "Next time you go wandering in the desert, I suggest you bring water with you," she said. With that, she took the two horses and went off toward the Aris district.

Asmar walked to his rooms alone, his footsteps resonating in the empty hallway once he was back at the tower. He had trusted Preadus, but Preadus would've let him die. All because of their test. His anger welled up. The wizards didn't care about him; he was just a tool. Asmar wondered if he had made a mistake coming to Dolcere. He changed and cleaned himself up, drank some water, and took deep breaths to bring his emotions back under control. He then proceeded to the council chamber.

All the wizards who were in Dolcere were assembled; the others were linked with their minds.

We're glad to have you back with us, Wellum began.

Are you? Asmar stared icily at his fellow wizard. *Then why did you all abandon me?*

Enough! Preadus rose from his seat, his silver staff clutched in his hand. *This is not about you. All of us are expendable if it means returning the golden staff back to the council in Dolcere. When you confront Malzus, you will be alone. We all wanted to go into the desert and bring you back. But if we had done that, your training would have been rendered pointless; you'd always be needing our help, and we won't be able to give it.*

And if I had perished? asked Asmar.

We would have mourned your loss, deeply.

Asmar felt a wave of profound grief coming from Preadus, and it surprised him.

Thurmore said you were with the Renegade, Wellum continued.

Is that what you're calling her? Asmar said, feeling protective.

Preadus ignored Asmar and said, *Thurmore has found the oasis.*

Asmar shot Preadus an icy glare: *Thurmore had no right to steal that memory from me!*

You had no right to withhold it, Preadus replied, calmly. *In any event, all was deserted when they got there.*

Asmar kept his feelings hidden from the others, but inwardly, he was deeply relieved, though he wondered how the Wanderer could have moved everything so quickly—or had the tent been just an illusion?

We'll keep looking for her, but right now we have other things to discuss. Preadus continued to address Asmar directly. *Now that you have succeeded in passing your final test, we need to know if you're still dedicated to the mission of stopping Malzus.*

Asmar wanted to say "No!" He wanted to tell the wizards who had left him for dead that he owed them nothing—but he knew he had to think of others. There was too much at risk for too many.

He stood up from his seat and faced Preadus squarely. *Yes, I am.*

Preadus smiled. *Then you are to be fully recognized as a wizard. The ceremony will be held tomorrow, when Thurmore and Rogi have returned.*

The next morning, Preadus came to escort Asmar to the dining hall for the Meal of Joining. *Get dressed,* the Great Wizard commanded, flinging a fresh white robe at Asmar's feet, *and come with me.*

The dining hall was rarely used by the wizards. Between their travels out of Dolcere and frequent fasts, there was not much need for the hall. But today was different; today, Asmar would become a wizard.

The dining hall was small compared to the council room, but was equally opulent, glowing with the radiance of bronze pulcher. The wood shone, and an Aris-crafted chandelier hanging from the ceiling created tiny swirling rainbows from the refracted morning sunlight. There were again nine blue stone chairs surrounding the table, just as in the council hall, when Preadus led Asmar in.

As they entered, all the wizards rose from their seats. Preadus escorted Asmar to the opposite end of the table, the place of lowest rank.

One by one, the wizards approached Asmar, took his hand in their own and said aloud and ceremonially: "We open our minds to you so that you may share our burden and responsibility." Then each returned to his seat.

All except Preadus had welcomed Asmar, and now he turned to the new wizard and asked, "Will you open your mind to your fellow wizards and agree to share their responsibilities and burdens?"

"I will," came Asmar's soft response.

"Then it is my honor to welcome you, Asmar, to the Council of Wizards—and I also agree to open my mind to you, so that you may share my burdens and responsibilities."

With that, Preadus walked up to where Asmar was standing at the table and embraced him, and then handed him a neatly folded blue robe. The fabric shimmered and felt magical in Asmar's hands. He looked up at the old wizard; he was gaunt and weathered, actually resembling the statue that stood in the center of Tuland, by the fountain. The severe expression of the elder wizard seemed softer in the warmth given off by the bronze pulcher, and he nodded approvingly as Asmar slipped the blue robe over his white one.

Next, Wellum brought over a silver staff. Preadus took it in his hands and silently presented it to Asmar, gesturing afterward for Wellum to take away the bronze staff Asmar had leaned against his chair. The young wizard ran his hands reverentially over the new staff, having had so little chance to work with or feel the special silver wood, and he felt its energy flow through him. Preadus smiled.

"The staff you are holding previously belonged to my dear friend Vetus," he said, and with that, he turned and walked back to the head of the table and sat down.

The first food to be brought to the table, still warm, was a loaf of dark, sweet bread. This was put before Preadus.

"With this bread we bind our fates," he said out loud, as he cut the bread and waited as the attendants distributed it to all seated.

More plates of food followed, one after the other, and as they did, Preadus would recite the appropriate prayer and send the food around to all the wizards at the table.

The final dish was brought out on a beautiful platter made of fine silver mined by the Cautes in the mountains and worked by their craftspeople into delicate and intricate patterns. Covering this silver tray was an equally magnificent silver dome that hid the last course.

The covered tray was placed on the table in front of Preadus, who closed his eyes, lifted his arms and recited.

"To bind our flesh with one another, we share our meal." With that, the cover was lifted to reveal a small, roasted animal—a brare. A red fruit had been placed in its mouth and its eyes stared out of their sockets.

Asmar's stomach instantly roiled, and he instinctively rose up from his chair at the table.

You must complete the ritual, came Preadus's words into Asmar's mind. Asmar felt the Great Wizard holding him gently but firmly in place.

It's time you leave behind your past convictions and embrace the traditions of the wizards. Asmar began to struggle in an attempt to move away from the table, as Preadus began slicing the roasted flesh into thin ovals.

One by one, plates were passed down each side of the table and placed in front of each wizard, while the eyes of the brare pointed straight at Asmar from the elaborate silver platter. As the attendants came closer to serving him— the very last of the wizards to be served—Asmar began to fight back more forcefully against Preadus's restraining grip.

The Great Wizard pressed harder into Asmar's mind. The very smell of the brare made Asmar feel ill and dizzy.

Under the control of the older wizard, Asmar found himself forced to mechanically cut the flesh of the brare on the plate in front of him.

No! Asmar vehemently yelled with his mind to the whole council. Closing his eyes with the exertion, Asmar pushed back as hard as he could one last time. An emptiness suddenly engulfed him, leaving a void where Preadus had been. He felt the hold on him loosen, his breath able to return. Asmar was able to lower the still-untouched forkful of meat away from his lips. He stood up and grabbed his silver staff for support as he began to walk slowly toward the door. He needed to get away, to escape the dining hall.

As Asmar neared the exit, he thought he was free and had broken Preadus's control. He was just at the door, about to turn the heavy handle, when suddenly his knees started to buckle and a searing pain racked his body—pain that he knew would only end if he returned to the table and finished the ritual. Realizing what was happening, Asmar dug down, determined to fight back. He tightened his hold on his silver staff and was able to let his mind drift away from the pain. Preadus sent another surge through Asmar. Asmar tried again this time but couldn't dismiss the pain, so he let the pain embrace him and flow through him. Pressing himself against the door, he managed to turn the handle and go out, toward the hallway and toward freedom.

The pain suddenly ceased; he was free. Preadus had stopped his attack.

For the remainder of the day, Asmar was in shock. He sat on his plank bed, trying only to block out the horror of what had just happened. He was sure of only two things: the wizards had left him to die out in the desert, and now they were trying to control him and make him do things he refused to do. He had to escape Dolcere as soon as possible. He wanted to get back to Lupa and Tuland, the only place he had ever been happy. He would tell Remer tomorrow that they were leaving.

As these thoughts circulated he felt a gentle touch invading his mind. It was Preadus. Asmar could tell the old wizard was being careful not to be controlling. For Asmar, it was too late; he no longer could trust any of the wizards.

After Asmar refused Preadus's communications, the Great Wizard came directly to his cell and let himself in.

"Asmar—I deeply regret what transpired in the dining room. Please understand: it is a tradition that has been observed and followed by many, many generations of wizards."

"It was wrong to do that," Asmar said, refusing to look directly at Preadus.

Preadus sighed. "Yes, I see now that it was wrong."

His words took Asmar by surprise. He had never heard Preadus admit to doing anything wrong, ever.

"You're a wizard," Preadus continued. "The ceremony was just a tradition and a formality. You have the skills. You have completed the training."

"I've decided to leave Dolcere tomorrow and return home," Asmar responded, devoid of any emotion.

Rather than object, Preadus nodded. "I understand, Asmar, and I won't stop you from leaving. But think: what will happen to Lupa and Remer and all that you know and hold dear, when Malzus defeats us and goes on to destroy your beloved Tuland? And what will happen to the Aris and the Cherts if nothing is done to stop Malzus from his destructive path?" Preadus paused, but when Asmar didn't respond, he went on. "Please," Preadus implored, for a moment sounding more like the old storyteller Mendicus than the Great Wizard. "Don't blame them and everyone else for my error."

Asmar took in a breath and finally looked up at Preadus. He examined the wizard's face, for the first time noticing that Preadus looked much, much older. Asmar did not trust him at all. He couldn't, after all that he had experienced. But the threat Malzus posed to everyone was real.

Asmar nodded, exhausted. "I will stay."

Preadus let out an audible sigh and covered his face with his hands. "Your journey will begin in seven days. Others have been summoned to assist you, and the last of them will arrive here in five days' time. Your mission is to find and return the golden staff to the Council of Wizards in Dolcere. Once that is done, the council will deal with Malzus."

"How am I supposed to get Malzus to give me the staff?" Asmar asked, tired from the events of the day.

"You need to get to Malzus in his tower and confront him. The rest will fall into place once that happens.'

"That isn't a plan. He's so much stronger than me."

"But he doesn't know who you are."

"What does that mean?"

Preadus stared at him and then turned abruptly and left the room.

Asmar looked at the closed door and pulled his legs up to sit cross-legged on the bed. What did Preadus mean that Malzus didn't know him? How would that help him defeat Malzus?. Asmar cleared his thoughts and attempted to reach out to the Wanderer for help. Maybe she knew what Preadus meant, but she was nowhere to be found. He wondered if she had been an illusion, but the bandage on his shoulder told him otherwise.

For five days, Asmar remained in his cell, fasting and meditating, trying to understand what had happened.

At the end of the fifth day of his meditations, Asmar was summoned by Preadus to the practice field. When he arrived at the prescribed time, Preadus was there, and so was Remer, Areana, and two others—one Chert and the other Caute, by the look of their clothes.

Preadus stepped forward to greet him. "Welcome. These are your companions." He gestured to make introductions. "This is Bradoc, a general from the Chert army." Bradoc bowed his head in a quick, respectful nod, but his eyes seemed downcast. He certainly looked the part of a general, Asmar thought. The man was broad shouldered and muscular, a bit shorter than Asmar, but his physical build made him appear somehow taller and bigger. At his hip was fastened a blood-red sword made from one finely honed gem. The skill and artistry was more like that of the Caute than the Chert.

"And this—" Preadus indicated a tall lean man with dark skin and soft brown eyes, with a bow slung over his shoulder, "is Prince Wetell of the Cautes." The prince also gave a quick nod of respect.

Preadus cleared his throat and continued.

"Areana will travel with you, as will Remer."

With that, Preadus was gone. Asmar looked at his cousin and then at the others. He sat down on the sandy ground of the practice field, his staff laid across his knees.

"Other than my cousin, none of you seem particularly excited to be here."

"Our desire is not of issue," Bradoc answered. "Preadus made it clear that you are our best hope for defeating Malzus, and that's all of our goal. We're committed to you until we accomplish that goal or die."

"I hope it doesn't come to that," Remer interjected.

"Let's go over your plan for defeating Malzus," requested Bradoc, ignoring Remer's comment.

Asmar stood up and took a few steps away, then turned back to face the group:

"I have no plan."

Bradoc's eyes widened, his hand rested on the hilt of his sword.

"I—don't understand. Is this a joke? You must have forged a plan."

Asmar solemnly shook his head. Bradoc began to pace back and forth in the sand, deep in thought.

"I have no plan for defeating Malzus, but I do have a plan. Although I don't think any of you will want to be part of it."

Wetell stepped forward.

"Then what is your plan?"

Asmar paused and took a deep breath. He thought of his time with the Wanderer and then answered.

"To acquire knowledge and understanding."

Bradoc, who had stopped pacing, glared furiously at Asmar. "You're kidding, right? How is knowledge and understanding going to defeat the Sitire and Malzus?"

Asmar sighed. "It's okay. I can't expect any of you to understand—at least not yet. And I don't need any of you to come with me to carry out this plan."

"I'm coming with you," Remer said immediately. Complete silence followed.

"I'm also with you," said Areana, cutting into the silence after a long pause and stepping forward. "I am not sure I know what you mean by this strategy, but I owe you my life and I've seen you do things that I don't understand. If the wizards think you're the key to defeating Malzus, I'm in."

Wetell shrugged, resigned. "I have no idea what will come of this, but I've seen everyone and everything else fail. I'm willing to give it a try. I'm with you."

Now they all turned to Bradoc, who had ended his pacing.

"I don't believe in any of this, but I've been told to accompany this wizard, and as a soldier that's what I have to do, despite how I may feel. So, I guess I'm with you."

"I will leave Dolcere in two days," Asmar said to the group, and then turned and walked away.

Back at the wizards' tower, Asmar sequestered himself in his room and lost himself in deep contemplation. He thought of the Wanderer and all of the vast knowledge she had acquired. Asmar felt, despite the council's faith in him, that he wasn't strong enough or smart enough to defeat Malzus, at least not yet. But if he could gather more wisdom, learn more and understand more—maybe something might be possible.

* * *

The day of their departure arrived, and Asmar met his companions at the edge of Dolcere. He was surprised but glad to see Shara had accompanied Remer; they must have reconciled. He watched as Shara gave Remer a long, lingering goodbye kiss and handed him a small package after Remer had mounted his horse.

Asmar was also given a mare to ride. He preferred walking into the desert, but they had too much ground to cover and he knew that every day and every moment they delayed would allow Malzus to become more powerful.

They made their way through the crystals at a gallop, Asmar feeling only a brief glow from them. Once they had passed through, Areana took the lead, her rainbow sword fastened at her side. Bradoc was following, his blood-red crystal sword tucked into its sheath. At his side was Wetell with his bow of bronze pulcher, a quiver full of arrows with hardened silver tips, and his own long, graceful sword of the same toughened silver sheathed in a leather scabbard.

Behind this group of experienced soldiers, Remer followed, a small sword hanging uncomfortably at his side. Every few moments, he would adjust his belt to attempt to make the ungainly weapon hang more comfortably, without success.

Asmar brought up the rear. His blue robe shimmered in the desert light, his silver staff glowing in the sun . As they continued onward and were enveloped by the midday heat, Remer let himself fall back to ride side-by-side with his cousin.

"Shara is special, isn't she?" Remer asked.

Asmar let out a small laugh. He'd forgotten what it was like to have a normal conversation, and in that moment, finally away from the intensity of his training and the pressures and expectations of the council, he realized how much he missed his cousin.

"In what way?"

"In every way. The way she looks, the way she talks. I don't know, everything about her is special," Remer said, wistfully.

"What did she give you as we left?" Asmar asked, his curiosity piqued.

"Two scions. One is for you."

"What exactly is a 'scion'?" Asmar asked, raising an eyebrow.

"It's a pastry, only better. Really Asmar, you surprise me sometimes with how much you don't know," Remer said, laughing, and handed one of the pastries to his cousin.

Asmar took a bite of the scion and closed his eyes briefly in appreciation to savor it. Then he responded, his mouth full. "This is delicious." Asmar swallowed, then went on, "Remer, you have many hidden talents. Sometimes I think the wizards may have erred in selecting me."

Remer grinned.

"You know, I often thought so myself. I bet it was really me that was supposed to be a wizard and they just chose you by mistake. You always were the luckier one."

"No, cousin—I think you are the lucky one," Asmar responded. His cousin had changed so much since he'd met Shara.

Remer looked over. "I love you, Asmar."

Asmar smiled. "You also love Shara, don't you?"

Remer blushed.

"I want to ask you something," Remer said, looking around furtively to make sure the others were too far to hear. Asmar waited, sensing Remer's embarrassment.

"When I got back from the desert, something happened."

"Something good?"

"I think so. It was good at the time. I mean yes, it was good. Very good." Remer paused before going on. "I ran immediately to the library and found Shara there. I just ran to her and said I was so sorry and I asked her to forgive me."

"And did she?" asked Asmar.

"Yes . . . in a . . . serious way. She started kissing me, and then I started kissing her back . . . and then . . . things just started to happen," Remer said, in a hushed voice. "She took me to her room in the tower . . . and we made love."

Asmar realized his face had flushed. He was a wizard; he should be able to control his feelings and emotions, but he felt extremely uneasy at his cousin's confession.

"What do you want me to say?" responded Asmar, uncomfortably.

"I don't know . . . what I should do next? Do I treat her differently?"

"Why would you do that?" asked Asmar, a little irritated.

"I don't know. This has never happened to me before. Have you ever made love?"

Asmar looked down past his saddle to the moving sand below.

"No, I haven't."

In that moment, he found himself fighting back a wave of jealousy that suddenly washed over him. Asmar realized right then that Remer had experienced something he would never get to experience, now that he was a wizard and had taken an oath of celibacy. But it was more than that. Asmar realized he would always, from now on, be looked at as a wizard, not as a real, feeling person.

It was starting to grow dark when Areana called out to everyone. "Halt. We'll make camp here for the night."

They all dismounted and set up camp, working together to build a small fire, making sure to bank it to hide the light of the flames and reduce the smoke. Areana cautioned everyone.

"At this time of year, when there's no wind, the wolves travel in larger packs, searching for food. We'll need to post a guard to warn of any danger."

When camp was all set, the five sat around the fire.

"What are we supposed to do to capture the staff?" Bradoc asked. "Just walk into Tellurium and ask Malzus to give it to us?" His frustration with their lack of any real, clear plan was more than evident. An awkward silence hung over the group.

"When we're close to Tellurium and Malzus, I'll determine a strategy," Asmar said. The words of Preadus kept echoing in his mind: *He doesn't know who you are.* That had to be the key, but Asmar had no idea why.

"Surely three commanders and a wizard should be able to devise a strategy," Remer said, staring into the fire.

"If this is the best we can do for now, so be it," Areana concluded. "We should rest and get an early start."

The night was dark and Remer had fallen fast asleep as soon as he lay down. Asmar watched his cousin and listened to the soft rumbling of his snores as he had done in Tuland when they shared a room. Asmar pushed his jealousy far, far down; in truth, he was genuinely happy his cousin had found love with Shara.

Asmar quietly got up and walked to where Areana sat. He reached out to gently touch her shoulder when there was a sudden flash, and a sword sliced the air near his head. He automatically threw himself to the side, the blade barely missing him as he fell to the sand. Areana was already on her feet and standing over him, extremely tense, her sword raised.

"It's only me," breathed Asmar in a loud, clear whisper.

Her fierce gaze softened and her muscles relaxed. "Don't *ever* do that again."

"I didn't want to wake the others."

"There was a time, wizard, when you wouldn't have been able to sneak up on me."

Asmar felt himself cringe inwardly when she called him "wizard."

"Please—call me Asmar."

"As you wish … Asmar. When you first started training, you didn't seem like a wizard, to be honest."

"And now?" he asked.

"Right now—I'm not sure. You still don't really have the—the look of a wizard. But there are times, like just now, when you make me seem like a new recruit. And only a wizard can manage to do that." She smiled and paused, and then asked, softly, "Shouldn't you get some rest?"

"I don't need much sleep," Asmar responded.

"Then I welcome the company."

The two sat looking out over the shifting, cooling sands. Areana shivered a little.

"Sit closer," she said. "We often huddle together on lookout as protection against the cold desert night winds."

As part of his wizard training, he had learned to block out temperatures and not register the cold. But he found himself following her instruction and moving closer.

"This is how we keep warm," she said. She lifted her talize up and wrapped it around both of their shoulders, encasing them together. Her soft, thin shirt let the heat of her body combine with his.

"That's much better," she said.

He could smell the scent of her hair and the warmness of her arm against his. He inched closer and found himself putting his arm around her waist. He had been expecting more warmth and softness, but instead he felt strong muscle through the thin shirt. Areana let out a slight laugh and gently lifted his arm up, placing it back at his own side.

"We're on guard duty. There can't be any distractions," she advised, though she didn't move away. He even thought she inched closer. "Have you ever sat up at night with a girl, watching the stars?"

"No," Asmar replied. "The girls in Tuland never found me particularly interesting."

"They didn't?" Areana said, shaking her head as if surprised. "I think you're one of the most interesting—and confusing—people I've ever met."

Asmar smiled. "Funny . . . I was just thinking the same thing about you."

Areana draped an arm over his shoulder, as she had done for many a fellow soldier. There was warmth and understanding. But no passion. Asmar knew then that he and Areana would never have what Remer and Shara shared. Still, he was grateful. It was in many ways a relief to be sitting next to her, talking freely. It had been a very long time since he had had that experience with anyone other than Remer.

He told Areana of growing up in Tuland, and of his being kicked out of school for his ideas about the pulcher. Areana laughed, and it was a warm laugh that made him relax. She told him of her childhood, huddled around a campfire with her father, being held close to him after her mother had been killed in battle. She worked to describe the special warmth and compassion she felt being with her father and the other soldiers as she grew up. She recounted to Asmar the story of her very first battle, and the first man she had ever killed. Her eyes looked far away but impassive as she spoke.

"I still remember his face," she said. "His eyes were dark, even for a Sitire—almost black. He was young, about the same age I was at the time. It may have been his first battle as well. He wasn't very experienced, and I quickly won the advantage." Areana's voice grew somber. "It was much like the practice field where I had sparred with many of my friends; I usually won there too. The difference was in the practice field we would laugh and go at it again and again. Somehow, in this first battle, I felt the same way. I felt like saying to that poor frightened boy, 'Let's go at it again.' I even lifted my sword from his throat as I had done so many times on the practice field. And you know what he did?"

"What?"

"He stabbed me—right between the ribs. That's when I killed him, and then I collapsed. I almost died. My father said it served me right, that I had gotten lucky."

"But the boy wasn't," Asmar said, flatly.

"No, he wasn't," Areana responded, her head lowering. "I still see his face sometimes in my dreams. I don't enjoy battle, as some soldiers do. There are moments before a battle that are so beautiful, so transcendent, despite what is about to happen. But the fighting itself? No." She shuddered. "I don't enjoy it. Not at all." She cast a protective glance back at their companions, sleeping around the campfire.

"Then why do it?"

"It's necessary," she said, without any emotion. "It's imperative that we protect and defend ourselves." Silence hung in the moonlit air for a moment.

"Is there really no other way?" Asmar asked, directing the question as much to the open, vast night sky as to her.

"I remember the time on the practice field when you asked me this same question," Areana said softly, looking straight at him. "The answer is still no."

They sat in silence, comfortable in sharing each other's warmth.

"How still the night is," Areana said.

The minute she uttered these words, it was as if it awoke something in both of them.

"Yes—a bit too still," Asmar said, starting to unravel himself from their cozy envelope. He stood and stared out into the blackened desert, some low clouds obscuring the normally starry and bright sky. He closed his eyes and felt his way out across the dark expanse with his mind.

"What is it?" Areana asked, now alerted.

"You'd best wake the others—now," Asmar commanded in an urgent, whispered instruction.

Areana raced to the tents to summon the others. The first to appear was Bradoc, his blood-red sword drawn and ready. Close behind was Wetell, bow in one hand, arrow in the other, standing ready. Areana stood with them, her rainbow sword clutched firmly in her right hand and a crystal dagger in her left. Last, Remer emerged, still clumsily strapping on his sheathed weapon.

Asmar addressed them together. "Something's headed this way. I don't know what—or who." As he spoke, he felt a shiver run down his back, but he maintained his focus. "We must leave here at once."

"What's the danger?" Wetell asked.

"I can't say exactly," said Asmar.

"It's usually best to stand and fight," Bradoc said, with a slight smile crossing his face.

Asmar shook his head. "I don't think that will be possible in this case."

"Is it—wolves?" Areana asked.

"Yes, but—" Asmar stopped himself. He knew these weren't ordinary wolves heading toward them; he sensed an unusual strength and power. "We must hurry," Asmar pleaded.

From their place near the dim light cast by the fire, they could suddenly see the faint outline of a giant wolf. Another, and then another, passed and circled; then even more still. Asmar could now sense at least twenty of these beings waiting restlessly at the edge of the darkness.

"This is very strange," Areana said, doing her best to sound in control. "There haven't been any howls. How can that be? And what do they want?" Her voice was struggling to be steady.

Asmar turned and looked at her. "They want me," he said.

He couldn't tell her how he knew; he couldn't even tell himself.

"They want me. I have to leave, and right away."

A frightened but determined voice interrupted their frantic whisperings.

"I'll be coming with you, then." It was Remer.

"No," Asmar snapped back, "and there's no time to—"

"No one goes anywhere alone," Areana commanded, reasserting her authority.

THE SILVER FOREST – Book One

"Then we must go *right now*," Asmar said, starting to feel deep foreboding.

The group hastily grabbed whatever supplies they could and hurried in the opposite direction of the wolves, who had entered the camp. Asmar wanted to let the horses free, but the wolves had cut off their access.

"They just want me. You have a chance to escape now, if you run. Once they find me, they won't go after you."

"We're not abandoning you," said Areana, looking frantically around them. "Over there, everyone," Areana directed, pointing to a rocky outcrop. "We can hold them off from there."

The group hurriedly followed Areana in the direction of the high ground, but Asmar didn't race with them, sensing something else out in the darkness. He stood, stoically waiting for the wolves. There was something odd about the energy he was feeling... something he had to face—alone. He could now see the wolves coming toward him. Asmar waited, fighting his urge to run as he drew a deep breath in. The beasts were massive, each one-and-a-half times the size of an ordinary wolf, and they were all pure black, almost invisible in the night.

Asmar gripped his silver staff, opened his mind, and walked right toward the terrifying creatures. He could sense the usual energy and reactions of wild animals: hunger, fear, desperation. Yet there was something more: a greater purpose for this pack, and that energy was clearly coming from the largest of the wolves, the leader.

Asmar focused his mind on this wolf, whose coat was so black as to seem like it absorbed all light. He was twice the size of the next-largest wolf in the pack. Asmar faced him and opened his mind to him, to tell him that they needn't fight. But as he did, a blinding flash ripped through his head. He yelled in pain, and the wolf leapt forward toward him. Asmar threw himself down, rolled to the side and was back on his feet just in time to avoid the attack.

The other wolves by now had circled and cut him off from his group. He was trapped.

From the new stronghold on the higher rocks, Wetell let an arrow fly. It zipped through the air and Asmar heard a wolf howl in pain and fall with a thud stiffly to the sand.

"No!" Asmar screamed, as forcefully as he could. "Stop. Let them be."

Wetell, confused, lowered his bow, and Asmar heard Areana swearing.

The winds around them started to pick up and grow stronger. Nothing about this wind felt right. The wolf lunged again; Asmar barely anticipated the attack as the wolf's claws glanced off Asmar's arm. The wind blew harder and sand was whipping against Asmar's face. The wolf crouched and leapt again, just as a small gray figure shot out from behind Asmar; it was the Wanderer's wolf. Asmar recognized her and watched helplessly as the smaller gray wolf rolled in the whipping sands with the black wolf, three times her size.

Asmar instinctively jumped forward to separate them, but sharp teeth ripped at his hand. He fought through the pain and pushed it back and, placing his staff between them, was able to uncouple the wolves. The larger black wolf lay on the ground, panting hard but unable to get up.

The small gray had surprised her larger opponent. She stood protectively in front of Asmar, snarling at any other wolf that tried to approach.

"Go!" Asmar cried out to the gray wolf, through the wind that was now blowing so powerfully Asmar could barely see directly in front of him. "Go find the Wanderer!"

The wolf paused for a moment, then disappeared out into the swirling, relentless sands. Asmar's assailant lay collapsed and exhausted, unable to rise. The other wolves started to run as their leader lay helpless and the winds grew in strength.

The winter sandstorm descended upon their entire area now, in full force.

Asmar was completely blinded as he tried to pull the cowl of his robe over his head and face. He was grateful that his wizard's robe offered some measure of protection from the sand, but he knew it couldn't protect him from whatever presence had controlled the black wolf. He suddenly realized that presence he had felt—the presence that had controlled the wolf—was Malzus.

He knew Malzus would continue looking for him, and Asmar couldn't risk endangering his friends. He had no choice: this was his mission, not anyone else's. He felt Remer reach out to him, wanting him to join them, but he couldn't. Instead he walked off into the desert, away from Remer and the others.

— ✦ — CHAPTER 20 — ✦ —

MALZUS FUMBLED WITH HIS ROBE, looking blankly at the stone wall. His hands grew sweaty as he thought about physically leaving the security of his bare solitary rooms, but his supply of drugs was dwindling; making more Saeren had required him to step up his usage. More olera plants had to be collected, and this was the best season to refresh his supply, as the edenda bugs would have just laid their larva. His fingertips grazed a stone on the wall and effortlessly, the rocks pivoted, revealing the hidden staircase that led down to the open fields that surrounded the tower.

Squinting as he emerged into the early morning light, he shut his eyes at the freshness of the air and the smell of the wind. Experiencing the outside world physically and directly—as opposed to being inside the Saeren—was much more intense than he had remembered: birds with their high-pitched voices calling to each other felt ear-shattering; the smell of dirt and grass as the wind swept over them was like a vast, overwhelming wave. He propped himself up against the door closing behind him; the outline of the threshold disappeared.

Malzus pulled his black robe tighter around him to shut out the cold air, but then he let it go. He was a wizard! He should be able to shield his mind and body from reacting to the temperature. He started north, toward the rocky plains. It was the bitterness of the weather and the harshness of the terrain that had forced the olera plants over generations of adaptations to develop such a strong poison.

The terrain became rockier. A light snow was falling, dusting the dark stones with its powder. The council had spent years looking for the tree here but had never found so much as a trace.

As he approached a rocky outcropping to begin a steep climb, Malzus slipped on a broad, flat patch of ice and fell hard. As he lifted himself up on his hands and knees, he saw his fall had wiped away the remnants of snow from the smooth frozen ice and he came face to face with his own reflection. At first he thought he was looking into the worn and broken face of a Saeren . . . but no, it was him: his gray face, his gaunt eyes. He remembered himself differently, as a young and powerful wizard. But when he looked again, he still saw a wraithlike creature.

It had to be the drugs that were aging him, but he couldn't stop; he needed them.

The sky was darkening as Malzus combed the rocky heights for the plants he needed. They were usually found in the most inaccessible corners and crevices, so he over-turned small boulders and clambered over rocks, peering into high clefts and jagged niches. He reassured himself that, however gaunt and skeletal, he was still strong in both body and mind, and that was more important than how he appeared.

At the top of a plateau, under the shadow of a boulder that stood alone in the rubble of what had been a land-slide, Malzus found what he had come for. The bright-red flowers were glowing in the twilight as he pushed the small stones gently aside. He smiled at the bounty; there were at least ten plants there, poking through the gravel, the underside of each leaf covered with the larval sacs of the tiny green bugs. This would be enough to last Malzus for at least a year.

He had brought his gloves for handling the plants, but he decided not to use them. He wanted the poison from the leaves to enter his body through the tips of his fingers. He carefully and gently dug up the plants, including the roots. After extracting each one, carefully wrapping them in cloth, and placing them in his pack, he fell back against the boulder to rest and looked up into the still-darkening sky. Points of light started to flicker into existence.

He reached out his mind deep into the desert, wanting to be free of his loneliness; he was looking for his pack of wolves. After searching over sands and dunes, he finally found them lazing in the shadow of a stony ridge, noses to the air, anticipating the coming hunt with the onset of twilight. Malzus hovered over them until he spied their leader, and then gently closed in to merge with the enormous wolf's body. As their minds joined, Malzus delighted in the distinctive smell of the sand and stone through his newly sharpened senses. The others in the pack understood the change and came up to him to nuzzle him; they prized him for his ability to find prey, particularly at this time of year—the lull between the windstorms. The evening winds would start again soon enough, but until then, hunting was always more difficult. But Malzus could sense their prey and was an expert tracker. And with every successful hunt undertaken, he felt a vital surge of power flow into him as the life flowed out of his victims.

The wolves were still shaking off their daylight sleep. They were hungry, but there was no scent of prey on the still air. Malzus methodically began his search, casting about the bleak landscape with all his senses until he pinpointed the anxious tremble of a brare, gnawing furtively on a root.

Malzus howled and leapt to his feet, signaling the pack to follow him. The brare, however, was sensitive as well and quick to detect their approach and bolted frantically across the desert sands toward a hiding place. Malzus closed in on the brare and was ready to lunge when the brare disappeared almost instantaneously down an escape hole it had dug for protection. Frustrated, Malzus howled and pawed at the ground. He tried to enter the mind of the brare, but the brare had burrowed too far down; their primal instinct for survival was simply too strong.

After clawing at the ground until his paws started to bleed, Malzus knew he had to give up. He licked his wounded paws and sniffed the air once again. This time, he caught the musky scent of horses and the sweat of humans. All the wolves picked up the scent and, in unison, headed in the direction of this new prey.

But for Malzus something different was detected. A strange presence. He couldn't place it, but he felt his senses fully awaken. He picked up the pace and ran faster now, as he began to fully understand there was a wizard among the prey.

For a brief moment, Malzus thought perhaps his father had come out into the desert to find him and call him back to the council. Or maybe one of the wizards had decided to break with the others and join him. Maybe enough time had passed and his era of loneliness would be broken.

His wolf's heart raced as he pushed himself even faster; his mind also raced. He didn't recognize this presence. It had to be someone new, but... a new wizard? Malzus tried to understand what was happening, but the mind of the wolf was too small for all that he was thinking.

He needed to stay calm, but it was obvious the wizard wasn't looking for him; no one even knew he would be with the wolves. Malzus bared his teeth. The council must have replaced him with this new wizard. That could only mean one thing: the council, and his father, wanted him dead.

He howled into the darkening sky, releasing his rage into the night air. *How could they do this?* He would teach them; he would destroy this wizard and anyone else they sent after him.

With Malzus now in the lead, his wolf's eyes glowing fiercely in the dark, the pack descended on the camp, swarming through the tents and tearing into anything left behind.

With his nose lifted high in the air, Malzus knew the wizard was no longer in the camp. He howled in frustration and feverishly sniffed the cooling sand for traces. Finding a faint scent, he ran off toward it and then stopped suddenly; there were five people standing atop a rocky outcropping, their weapons poised and ready. Malzus stopped just out of range of their weapons and skulked in the dark.

He could make out an Aris by the reflection of her crystal sword bending the twilight. There was also a Caute, who held a bow with an arrow aimed straight at Malzus's heart. A Chert man stood next to him, a red crystal sword pulled from its scabbard and raised for attack.

Of the two remaining, he knew one was of no consequence; that one fumbled with a small sword and smelled of fear. But the final person Malzus homed in on wore the unmistakable pale-blue robe of a wizard.

The rest of his pack closed in near him, holding their ground and growling at the intruders. Malzus attempted to reach out, to get into the wizard's mind and find out who he was—but this wizard was strong, and the wolf's mind was not able to break through.

Malzus pushed harder and a searing pain shot through his skull. At the very same moment, he heard the wizard scream out in anguish. Malzus fought through the pain and concentrated. He smelled fear from the other four in the group, but the wizard gave no sense of any emotion. The two locked eyes.

He lunged straight at the throat of the wizard—his jaws opening wide.

But also in the same instant, the wizard spun aside faster than Malzus thought possible, and Malzus missed, his jaws closing on air as he plunged to the ground, sprawling with a mouthful of sand.

An arrow shot by with a rush of air, barely missing Malzus. Behind him there was a thud and a yelp; one of his wolves had fallen.

Malzus hurled himself forward again; this time his claws tore into the flesh of the wizard's arm. He fell onto the sand and licked the blood from his paw. He needed to finish off the wizard, so he sunk low and, using all the power in his hind legs, propelled himself forward toward the wizard's thin, vulnerable neck. The wind was pelting his thick fur with sand as his teeth parted for the final attack. All his senses were focused on the prey.

Suddenly there was a hurtling gray blur in his peripheral vision, and he felt an excruciating strike to his side that threw him off his course and left him gasping for air as needle-like claws ripped into his left eye. He howled in pain and, half blind, managed to make out a small gray wolf on top of him, attacking and slashing at his face. Another swipe from the needle-like claws and his nose was ripped, flooding his nostrils with the metallic scent of his own wolf's blood, which dripped back down its throat.

For the first time in years, Malzus was afraid. Trapped in the wolf's body, the unknown wizard had managed to lure him out and corner him, and had succeeded in partially blinding him and leaving him completely exposed.

And it was at that very moment that sharp teeth dug fiercely into his leg, hitting the bone underneath. Malzus collapsed, writhing in pain. He lashed out, but his jaws caught only the desert wind. He could no longer pick up any scent of the wizard or the gray wolf. Sand was seeping into his wounds. He tried rising, but his legs couldn't support his body. Malzus released himself from the mind of the black wolf and fell back against a pile of cold stones, looking up into the clear night sky.

He was too weak to move. Looking down at his arm, he could see no puncture wounds, and as he blinked, he was grateful to find he had sight in both eyes. He stayed there, leaning back against the rocks until the next morning. His tears were flowing freely, now that he understood that his father wanted him dead. He watched each star die as the sun emerged to eclipse them. As his tears died away, he was certain the only way to save his life was to find the tree before the wizards could carry out their own pathetic plan of killing him.

With the drugs wearing off, he felt small and insignificant—the way his father had made him feel when he was a wizard of the council. He reached his hand up and touched his shoulder again. He could still feel the pain from the bite of the lone gray wolf, and the needle-like claws scraping into his eye socket. His hands shook as he grabbed his water flask and gulped until it was dry. That calmed him enough that he could gather the bag with his collection of plants and, using the golden staff for support, begin to make his way back to Tellurium.

CHAPTER 21

"TIE YOURSELVES TOGETHER!" AREANA SHOUTED over the howling, rising winds; the swirling sand now blocked all light, so she was just a shadow to Remer.

"We must find shelter, quickly." Her voice strained with the effort of competing with the wind. She wrapped a rope around Remer's waist, tugging to keep it taut.

"Where's Asmar?" yelled Remer, trying to shield his face while pulling himself toward her, until he was directly at her side.

There was a brief pause.

"He's on his own," said Areana, who was now almost invisible in the blowing sand.

Remer planted his feet as firmly as he could in the shifting desert. "No! We can't leave him!" he cried out.

"What choice do we have?" yelled Prince Wetell. "And in this storm, he could be standing right next to us and we wouldn't see or hear him."

"He can't survive out there by himself. No one could!" implored Remer, and he started pulling away from them, but all he could see was a golden wall of sand. If he was going to search for Asmar, he didn't know which direction to go in.

"We'll look for him when the storm dies down," Wetell screamed into the wind, his hand up, trying to block his face from the needle-like granules that were pelting him.

"But that won't be for three days! It will be too late!" Remer screamed, but no one heard him at all now in the blasting wind. The line grew taut and Remer had no choice but to follow them. As he trudged forward, the sand cut his face and entered his mouth, nose, and eyes. He pulled the hood of his talize over his head tighter, but the sand was relentless. He pointed his face downward, hoping to shield himself and be able to catch a breath, cupping his hands over his nose and mouth when he inhaled. When he lowered his hands, he saw blood on his fingers from where the sand had scraped his cheeks raw. Closing his eyes in the hopes of a moment of relief, he stumbled and fell down.

He struggled back up and continued trudging along with no sense of time or place until, slowly, he felt the ground becoming firmer under his feet, and the wind's relentlessness weakening. As the wind lessened, he became more and more aware of the countless painful small wounds covering his face and hands.

"This will do, everyone," he heard Areana say. Remer suddenly realized the winds had stopped. He instinctively took a much-needed deep breath, immediately gagging as the sand that was clogging his mouth trickled into his throat. He reached up without thinking to rub his eyes as he coughed, and screamed; it was like pushing in shards of glass.

"Bring water—hurry!" ordered Areana, her voice filled with urgency. Cool water poured over his eyes, and more was carefully used to rinse his mouth. Slowly the burning pain subsided.

"That'll do for now," Remer heard Areana saying. When Remer looked in her direction, all he saw was a blur.

"I can't see!" he yelled, panic rising. A firm hand was placed on his shoulder; he didn't know whose.

"How'd his face get so cut up?" Bradoc asked. A wet cloth was gently placed over Remer's eyes, but he flinched violently on contact. His whole face felt like an open wound.

"He didn't pull out the face and hand screens from his talize," Areana replied. "It's my fault. I thought he knew."

Remer shut his eyes and slipped into unconsciousness. When he woke later, he still couldn't see. He tried to yell out but was only able to manage a gravelly, harsh cough that made his lungs and throat feel like fire. He could make out Areana's voice but it sounded far away, as if in a dream.

"It's not ideal in here, but it's better than being in the open desert."

"How'd you know the cave was here?" asked Bradoc.

"I knew a series of caves lay just north of where we were. The winter storm always comes from the north, so that meant if we walked directly into the wind, we had a chance of finding something. We were incredibly lucky."

And with that, Remer fell back into a fevered sleep.

When he next awoke, he sat up quickly, opening his inflamed eyelids. Everything was red and blended together.

"I'm blind!" he blurted out—the first words grating out from his parched, inflamed throat.

"You've got a bad fever," he heard Areana say, as she helped lift him to a seated position. "This will help."

She raised something up to his mouth. Remer reached out a shaky hand and felt a cup in front of his face, pressed gently up to his lips. A vile-smelling liquid was held beneath his nose, causing Remer to cough and gag.

"What is that?" Remer croaked, groping the air, trying to push the cup far away from him.

Remer sensed a large shadow blocking out the light. "We made a broth from the dried meats we had, and what was left of our water." It was Bradoc.

Remer shook his head violently, "No! I can't!" He turned his face to the side, his lips shut tight.

"You *must* eat something, Remer."

It was Wetell's voice now, but everything faded into the background as Remer drifted back into a fevered, fitful sleep.

When he next woke, all he saw was blackness. He shot up and a heavy cloth fell away from his face; thankfully, his breathing became easier.

A cool hand gently touched his forehead.

"The fever has broken." It was Wetell speaking to him.

"Where am I?" Remer asked. He had been dreaming he was back in Tuland, with Lupa gently rubbing his forehead with a cool cloth.

"You're in a cave. We all are. We've been here for two days."

Remer was weak but he managed to sit up, although it made him extremely dizzy.

"You need to eat something to regain your strength."

Remer nodded, as Wetell helped him hold a metal cup. He lifted the cup to his lips but as the smell reached his nose again, he just could not get himself to take a sip.

"I just—I just can't."

"This is absolutely mad!" Bradoc bellowed at him. "Listen to me. We have to get out of here, and you're too weak to travel. You have to drink this. We need you to regain some strength."

Remer worked to get himself standing upright but immediately regretted trying. Everything started to spin.

"I—I can't see anything." Remer managed to utter, his spinning head throbbing.

"It's usually temporary," he heard Areana say. "You had a lot of sand in your eyes. When the scars heal, you should be able to see better."

"Will I be able to really see again?" Remer paused. "Will I be able to read?" He started to sweat.

A hand—Areana's—gently fell onto Remer's shoulder. "Don't panic yet. Give it more time." Remer nodded and pushed back at his anxiety.

"If we're going to get out of here, we have to find him something—anything—he can eat," the prince could be heard saying.

"He has to eat the dried meat!" Bradoc commanded.

Remer groaned.

"He's a Tulander. He can no more eat that than you can eat the waste of a mountain sheep," Wetell countered.

"Whether Remer should or shouldn't eat what we have isn't the issue: the fact is, he isn't and he can't." It was Areana's voice. "So I'm going out to look for provisions. Anything I can find. The storm is at least dying down and I have to find us more water for the journey, anyway."

Remer managed to raise himself and sit back up. Someone—Wetell, he could tell just by the sounds of his footsteps—came over to him.

"This is just water. Sip it slowly—we're almost all out."

"What happened to my pack? My provisions?" Remer said, before taking a small sip.

"We all grabbed what we could when the storm began. If you didn't secure your pack and provisions, they're gone."

"You shouldn't even be with us." Bradoc came and stood over Remer. "You know nothing about survival or fighting; you're a total liability to us. When we get out of here you should be sent back to Tuland, and leave us to take care of things."

"Maybe if you weren't so sure of yourself, and had just told me about the screens in the talize, this wouldn't have happened," Remer shot back. "I'm not leaving my cousin in the hands of people like you!"

"And what exactly are 'people like me?'" asked Bradoc.

"It's getting dark," Wetell interrupted; his voice was farther away. Remer guessed he had gone to the cave mouth and was looking out into the desert. "We should set a fire for Areana so she can find her way back."

Remer could sense changes in the light around them, once Wetell had a fire going, and he was grateful for the warmth. Without his vision, Remer found himself focusing on all the sounds of the desert.

As he listened to the desert, his mind relaxed. He thought he heard small animals scurrying through the sand.

"I hear someone coming," Remer said, sitting up and calling out to Wetell and Bradoc.

"It's her. Areana is returning," Wetell replied, stepping out of the cave and bringing her straight over to the fire.

"This is all I could find," Remer heard her saying to the others, followed by the sound of a sack being opened. "A couple of sagu plants from not too far away. It isn't much, but it has enough water for us to replenish our supplies, and the flesh of the plant should help our young Tulander recover."

The sagu was cut and stewed in their new water over the fire, and Remer gratefully drank the broth. It felt healing as it trickled down his throat, soothing him and clearing away what was left of the sand trapped there. He felt better. Even a bit stronger.

The next day, the final traces of the winds had stopped. Areana stood at the entrance of their enclosure, blocking the light so that Remer could make out her form.

"It is time for us to leave. We will make our way to Arane."

"Wait," Remer said, guiding himself with a hand on the cold stone cave wall as he made his way toward her. "You said we'd look for Asmar after the wind storm."

"We need to go see my father first and get more soldiers to search the desert. We'll never find him on our own."

Remer was about to argue, but he realized Areana was right. He was blind and would only slow them down. They needed others to help in the search.

"I will guide you." She gently touched Remer's face. "The cuts are healing well and shouldn't leave any permanent marks. Can you see any better today?"

Remer reached a hand up and touched his face: he felt raised lumps and bumps all over. He wondered if Shara would still love him if his face didn't heal and he ended up being permanently disfigured. He blinked a few times, trying to clear his sight.

"I can make out my hand more clearly if I hold it up right in front of my face," he replied.

"That's a very good sign," Areana responded and patted Remer's cheek. "When we get to Arane, we'll get you fixed up even more. I have to say, it's rather a good sign you're back on your feet this quickly."

Remer smiled, hearing Areana's praise. He *would* get through this and show them a Tulander was tough.

* * *

The four traveled all day, straight into and through the desert heat. Remer, despite his partial recovery, was still very weak but followed along, keeping up as well as he could with Areana. He was exhausted every night when they made camp but, Areana told him, they made good time. Each evening, once they were settled, Areana rinsed out his eyes and tended to his healing.

After seven days of traveling through the desert and the evening treatments he received from Areana, Remer could make out his hand clearly and see things within close range. He no longer tripped and fell as much and, Areana decided, he no longer needed to be tethered to her.

After two more days they could see Arane—at least that's what Areana told him, as Remer could only see things at an arm's length distance. Anything further was still blurry.

"Something is not right," said Areana, who began to move more quickly.

"What's going on, Areana? I can't see—what is happening?" he said, starting to panic, not sensing Areana around.

"There's been a battle." Remer heard Wetell's voice quaver. "Areana and Bradoc have gone ahead to help."

"We must hurry, then, too!" Remer said, beginning to pick up his pace.

As they got closer, Remer could make out shadowy figures running back and forth. There was a familiar smell in the air—he remembered it from the first time he met Areana, when she saved him from the soft sands. It was the smell of blood.

"Stay here," Wetell ordered. "I need to help."

Remer heard Wetell run off, leaving him alone among the sounds of people running everywhere.

The smell of death was so strong, it made Remer retch into the sand. He stood up slowly and squinted. He needed to be able to see. As he concentrated, his sight got better, but he almost wished it hadn't. Bodies were strewn like garbage on the sand.

Remer now could see well enough and was looking for anything he could do to help.

"Don't stand there!" came a booming voice from behind him. Remer turned. There was an Aris soldier in a red talize, with darker red spots from blood.

"What can I do?" Remer asked.

The soldier pointed, without hesitation. "Over there."

Remer carefully made his way through the bodies lying everywhere to a group of soldiers at the fringe edge of the camp.

"I'm here to help," he told them.

"Aren't we lucky." An older soldier that had been hunched over one of the bodies came and stared at him. "What can you offer? Any particular skills?"

"I—I—" Remer stammered.

"We need someone who can write. Can you write?"

"Yes," Remer exclaimed. "Yes, I can do that."

"Good—take this and follow me."

The soldier handed Remer paper attached to a board. Remer was also given a crude pencil. He squinted at the paper and could make out lines and columns with headings like "Name," "Rank," and "Possessions."

The soldier led Remer to where bodies were laid in neat rows. Remer's excitement at being able to see the page was gone, and a feeling of dread replaced it.

"Lork," came another voice that seemed far away. Remer stood still, not knowing what "Lork" meant.

"I said—*Lork!*" the voice directed with insistence. "What are you waiting for? Write it down, boy. I don't have all day."

The soldier was kneeling next to a body with half its face cut away. Remer's knees started to buckle. A shadow passed in front of his face and then he felt the sharp pain across his left cheek. It brought everything immediately back into focus.

"You've never been on grave detail before, have you?" The question came from the soldier who was overseeing the dead.

Remer shook his head.

"Apologies about the slap, but that was the quickest way to get you to focus."

Remer's hand went to his cheek; that was why it hurt.

"This soldier's name is Lork. L-O-R-K. You write the name here." The soldier pointed to the appropriate spot on the paper.

Remer nodded dutifully, as he put L-O-R-K in the column labeled "NAME." Remer followed the soldier closely and wrote what he was told, column by column, body by body. He became numb to all that was happening, now that he had a duty and a task, and he was able to focus on the work, even after seeing each mutilated body.

As the sun was setting and Remer was at the point of exhaustion, Areana appeared where he was working.

"We've done all we can. We need to leave now and go into the city to meet with my father."

Remer sighed. He noticed Wetell and Bradoc were already with Areana. As he followed her, the faces of the dead kept reappearing before his eyes. Remer was lost in his thoughts and only vaguely aware they were now walking through the city. They must have passed homes, but he didn't take note of them. It seemed as if out of nowhere, the voice of a man was addressing him.

"What's the matter with him?" he heard the man bark.

"He was put on grave duty," followed Areana's response.

Remer attempted to return his focus to where he was. The man who had spoken was sitting on a glistening crystal throne. The light passing through it created a rainbow that enveloped the entire room. Remer was in a large tent with intricately woven rugs in warm, opulent reds and purples covering the sandy floor. Soldiers stood in obvious deference to the seated man who, Remer realized, had to be Olmar, ruler of the Aris—and Areana's father.

"We must retaliate," Areana was insisting.

"Of course," Olmar agreed, "but you cannot lead the army."

Areana looked as if she wanted to argue, but stopped herself.

"Of course," she replied looking down.

And then all of a sudden, another figure emerged from behind the throne and walked toward him. Remer's whole body froze when the person came into focus; it was Preadus, cloaked in his blue robe and carrying his silver staff.

"You've lost the wizard Asmar?" Preadus's booming voice questioned.

Prince Wetell responded, "It—seemed to be his choice."

"You were supposed to stay with him," the cloaked wizard said, accusingly.

"How could we do that when he didn't want to be followed?" Bradoc responded, sounding defensive.

"The time is extremely critical. Asmar must go north and challenge Malzus now or it will be too late."

CHAPTER 22

WHEN MALZUS ARRIVED AT THE base of the tower in Tellurium with his pouch full of the olera plants, he paused; he realized he didn't have the strength—or the desire—to climb all the way back up to his cold, isolated rooms. Looking up, he felt the emptiness of the world he had created, awaiting him in the tower. He missed the comfort of the wolves and found himself wanting that again. He wondered if it was possible to return to Dolcere, to the other wizards, and to his father. It had always been his plan to come back to Dolcere in triumph after finding the Silver Forest, or at least proving his way of interpreting the Koan was right. Now, after so much had passed— so much fighting, so much death—he doubted that was possible, but he still felt lonely and found himself longing for companionship.

He sat down on the ground, leaning back against the tower wall, and stared up at the clouds as they drifted overhead. With them, a memory drifted in . . . of the very first time he had come to the town of Adular, accompanying his father. He remembered the crowded streets lined with shops and, in that moment, wanted to be there, among people who were laughing and happy. He even remembered an especially beautiful shop whose windows were filled with an assortment of bright pink sweets. This memory overtook him, and he smiled.

He stood up and touched the one special stone in the tower wall that opened the secret door, and he placed his bag of plants and the golden staff inside the doorway so they would be safe. But no sooner had the staff left his grasp when a vast emptiness engulfed him. Panicked, he grabbed it back into his hands and felt a wave of calm return.

He needed to leave the staff where it was safe so that he could go explore, but it was not possible; he couldn't be separated from the touch and energy of the golden pulcher.

He reached into the folds of his robe and, from an inner pocket close to his heart, took out the golden ring he had fashioned with his own hands years ago for his wedding. He held it up to the light, inspecting it and stroking its smooth surface.

His wedding. For many years he had refused to reach out to his bride. Remembering what he had done to her was too painful, and when he finally decided to search for her, to find out what had happened, he encountered only emptiness. After that, he hadn't looked again.

Malzus thought of all he had given up—his father, the other wizards, his wife—and was beginning to doubt if his sacrifices had been worth it. Staring up at the spire of the great tower looming over him—contemplating the civilization that could build such a marvel—he had to believe he made the right choice. Rediscovering the lost secrets and using them to create even greater cities was, without question, more important than any one person's life. This sacrifice he had made willingly, despite the sobering realization that his father wanted him dead.

He again placed the staff inside the doorway and quickly slipped on the ring. He still felt an emptiness like a shroud over him, but the ring brought him enough energy to make it bearable.

Malzus couldn't walk into the city in his black robe. Even without the golden staff, he would be recognized. Although he could control the minds of the Adularians so they wouldn't know him, he had found himself hoping Adular would be a place where he could go for refuge. To be accepted.

As he got closer to the city, small homes made from the same rock as the castle began to dot the landscape and gradually became more numerous, lining the main road. Passing one of these, he helped himself to a dark-crimson shirt and forest-green pants (favorite colors of the Adularians) that had been hung out to dry. As he hid his robe under a stone, two children came running out of their house: a boy around seven and his younger sister, around five. Malzus still had his shirt off, revealing his thin, gray torso. He expected the two children to run in fear and tell whomever was inside, but instead they stood there, curious but not afraid in the slightest. He thought to reach into their minds and make them instantly forget seeing him. But he realized that he wanted them to see him. He waved in their direction, and they smiled back and ran off to play.

Malzus pulled the shirt over his head. It was like a tent over his emaciated body, and the pants were too short. He felt ridiculous.

The first thing Malzus noticed when he entered the town was the absence of the noise and activity he had been craving. The stone buildings looked gray and tired, many with broken windows and doors missing or hanging askew from their hinges.

Malzus closed his eyes, trying to recall the people walking through the streets many years ago; he felt fear permeating the city now. He walked slowly down each street, looking for someone to connect with. There seemed to be activity within a few of the shops on streets that were otherwise abandoned: one small store selling implements for farming, another selling clothes.

Malzus approached the clothing store and noticed that the clothes they were selling seemed out of place. There were no reds or greens, but blues, yellows and pinks. The fabrics were also much finer than what he had stolen on his way into town; they seemed more appropriate for a party.

As he turned to walk away, he caught the eye of the shopkeeper, a thin gray-haired woman. She smiled at him, beckoned him to come inside. Malzus tried to manage a smile back at her, but it came out more like a grimace, and he hurriedly walked away.

Near the end of the street, he recognized a smell that was familiar to him and instantly brought back memories of his home in Insula: the scent of freshly baked bread.

He was now standing outside the small bakery, its windows crystal clear, the view inside of a neat, tidy space in contrast to the decrepit buildings on either side. The smell was intoxicating. He breathed it in deeply.

The door opened and a boy of about fourteen stepped out in front of him.

"Come on in," the boy chirped. "We have freshly baked breads, just out of the oven.. You'd be my first customer."

Malzus stepped inside the shop and took another deep inhalation. He walked to the glass counter and surveyed its shelves: there were a dozen loaves of bread cooling on a wire rack.

"You're new here," said the boy.

Malzus didn't trust his voice and nodded.

"Where'd you travel from? Is there still fighting going on? We never get strangers here, so we don't know what's happening. It would be nice if the fighting stopped. Then we'd get more travelers and maybe some of the shops would open again." The boy looked around furtively. "It's been terrible since that wizard took over the castle in Tellurium."

Malzus gave a start, his heart thumped. Did the boy recognize him? If so, Malzus could not risk him telling any others. Malzus was about to reach into the mind of the boy to wipe his thoughts and convert him into a Saeren, but paused; the boy was too young and wouldn't make the best Saeren. Before he could act to enter the child's mind, the boy ran behind the counter and beamed at him.

"So, what about some bread for you, sir?"

Malzus froze, realizing the boy hadn't recognized him.

"Maybe a whole loaf is too much for one person," the boy went on, very matter-of-factly. "Maybe you'd prefer a scion instead?"

Malzus looked to where the boy pointed and saw a delicate flaky pastry with pale pink cream oozing out. "They're not the traditional style. My mother puts flavored creams in the middle. Some customers complain, but I like them so much better."

Suddenly, with the sight of that pastry, it all made sense: that's why all this was familiar. He had a distant memory of his mother before he had left Insula. He had been taken away from her when he was very young, to begin his training, and his mother would visit him and bring him pastries... that is, until his father had put a stop to it.

"I'll take the scion," Malzus said, his voice dry and raspy after so many years of disuse. The boy stared at him until he pointed to the pastry, repeating, "The scion. I'll take that."

The boy smiled and removed the pastry from the case, wrapping it in pure-white paper and tying a bow around it with red string. Malzus had to control his impatience as he watched, wanting to tear into it and devour it.

The neatly wrapped package was handed to him, and Malzus was about to walk out when he heard the boy say, "That's five pecun, please."

Malzus turned around, not understanding what the boy meant.

"The scion..." said the boy. "It costs five pecun."

It had been so long since Malzus had bought anything. Because he was a wizard, everyone gave him what he needed. He had no pecun and wasn't about to return the scion.

He and the boy stared at each other. The boy looked more closely at him, in his voluminous shirt and too-short, comical pants, and nodded.

"Just take it, sir. I understand. Many of us have fallen on hard times. Just... don't tell my mother." The boy winked at him and turned his back.

Malzus stared at the boy for a moment, and then collected himself and walked out. He waited until he was all the way down the block, where the aroma from the shop began to fade. He looked around guiltily as he tore open the package and touched the flaky pastry. He thought of the crimson plants he had touched where the poison flowed in through his fingertips. He looked at the scion and thought how the desire it brought was poisoning his mind. This was not allowed. He wasn't to have these temptations.

He threw the scion to the ground without having taken a single bite, and watched as the dust enveloped the pink cream, turning it powdery gray. He didn't need sweets. He needed to be where people were gathering, talking, living.

He looked down another empty street. Reaching out, he sensed a presence from one of the buildings off the main street. He followed his senses until he found where the feeling was coming from. He had to stoop a little as he entered through the front door.

Inside, there were about a dozen Adularians sitting at tables, eating and drinking and laughing. This was what he needed.

A silence fell over the whole room as they all looked at him. A man, about a head shorter than Malzus, came up to him and stuck out a hand.

"We don't get many strangers these days. I apologize for the rudeness of my friends. Can I get you something? A drink?"

"No," Malzus answered. He didn't trust his voice to say more.

"Where'd you travel from?" the man asked.

"I'm from the south," Malzus replied, his voice low but growing less raspy. It felt good to be using it again.

"How's the fighting down there?"

"It's going well," Malzus replied. "It shouldn't be much longer until the Cautes and Aris are defeated."

"That's great news." The man slapped Malzus on the back and instinctively Malzus grabbed the man's arm and twisted it hard in self-defense. He instantly realized what he had done, and he let go. The room went quiet and one man stood and pointed at him. "It's—him—it's the monster! He killed my wife!" Two others tried to hold the man back, but he broke through their grasp. Malzus slashed at the man's mind, ripping out his consciousness. The man fell to the floor, motionless.

There was complete silence, not even the sound of breathing, as everyone in the room looked at him, frozen.

Though not a single one of them spoke, their feelings were as easy to sense as those of his attacker.

They all wanted him dead—just like his father did.

Rage boiled up inside of him and, one by one, he ripped out their thoughts, reaching into their minds and savagely tearing away their consciousnesses.

Finally his rage subsided and Malzus sank to the floor. He was alone with the dead.

They didn't understand. It had been foolish to pretend any would care for him or understand him until he found the tree. He got to his feet but collapsed. He breathed deeply, stood up again and steadied himself. Slowly he walked from the room and out into the streets, making his way one wobbly step at a time until he felt his strength return. Then he ran through the town as fast as he could and back to his fortress. Flinging open the hidden door, he gripped the golden staff tightly and felt a surge of power rush into him. Slowly, he climbed the stairs, and when he got to his cell, he collapsed again. Tearing off the red and green garments from Adular, he threw them onto the stone floor and pulled on a new black robe. As his hands emerged from each sleeve, he stared at the veins running along his arms, visible through his pale gray skin. There was no one left for him. Everyone wanted him dead.

* * *

THE SILVER FOREST

BOOK TWO

J.D. RASCH

Summer 2024

ABOUT THE AUTHOR

J.D. RASCH is a writer, artist, social activist and author. His debut fantasy series, The Wanderer, explores social, political and religious themes. His writing, like his painting explores the mysteries of the world and our place in the greater scheme of the universe. For many years he worked in international finance, both in developed and emerging economies. Even in his work in finance he was interested in social justice, developing ways to assess the social behavior of companies. He also serves on a number of not-for-profit boards in an attempt to make the world a better place.

Connect with J.D. Rasch at
www.jdrasch.com and **www.raschart.com.**

Printed in the USA
CPSIA information can be obtained
at www.ICGtesting.com
JSHW022253290324
60085JS00008B/6